Amerika:
The Missing Person

Cover of the first edition of *Der Heizer* (The Stoker),
which later became the first chapter of *Der Verschollene*
(The Missing Person). Subtitled "A Fragment," the story
was published in Germany in 1913 by Kurt Wolff Verlag
as part of a series of works by promising new writers
called *Der Jüngste Tag* (The Last Judgment).

FRANZ KAFKA

Amerika:
The Missing Person

A NEW TRANSLATION,
BASED ON THE RESTORED TEXT

Translated and with a preface by
MARK HARMAN

SCHOCKEN BOOKS, NEW YORK

Preface and translation copyright © 2008 by Mark Harman

Publisher's note copyright © 2008 by Schocken Books,
a division of Random House, Inc.

All rights reserved. Published in the United States by Schocken Books,
a division of Random House, Inc., New York, and in Canada
by Random House of Canada Limited, Toronto.

Schocken Books and colophon are registered trademarks
of Random House, Inc.

This translation is based on the German language text *Der Verschollene:
Kritische Ausgabe,* edited by Jost Schillemeit, published by S. Fischer Verlag,
Frankfurt am Main, in 1983. Copyright © 1983 by Schocken Books, a
division of Random House, Inc. *Amerika* was originally published in German
in different form by Kurt Wolff Verlag A.G., Munich, in 1927.

Portions have previously appeared in
Gettysburg Review and *New England Review.*

Library of Congress Cataloging-in-Publication Data

Kafka, Franz, 1883–1924.
[Amerika. English]
Amerika : the missing person : a new translation, based on the restored text /
Franz Kafka ; translated and with a preface by Mark Harman.
p.   cm.
Includes bibliographical references.
ISBN 978-0-8052-4211-9
I. Harman, Mark. II. Title.
PT2621.A26A2313 2008   833'.912—dc22   2008013393

www.schocken.com

Printed in the United States of America

First Edition

2   4   6   8   9   7   5   3   1

CONTENTS

Publisher's Note   vii
Translator's Preface   xv

  I   The Stoker   3
 II   The Uncle   35
III   A Country House Outside New York   50
 IV   The March to Ramses   85
  V   At the Occidental Hotel   114
 VI   The Robinson Affair   141

       The suburban street in which the automobile . . .   184
       "Get up! Up!" cried Robinson . . .   242

       FRAGMENTS

       Brunelda's Departure   259
       At a street corner Karl saw . . .   267
       They traveled for two days . . .   288

       Acknowledgments   289
       Chronology   291
       Bibliography   295

PUBLISHER'S NOTE

Dearest Max, my last request: Everything I leave behind me . . . in the way of diaries, manuscripts, letters (my own and others'), sketches, and so on, [is] to be burned unread. . . .
    Yours, Franz Kafka

These famous words written to Kafka's friend Max Brod have puzzled Kafka's readers ever since they appeared in the postscript to the first edition of *The Trial*, published in 1925, a year after Kafka's death. We will never know if Kafka really meant for Brod to do what he asked; Brod believed that it was Kafka's high artistic standards and merciless self-criticism that lay behind the request, but he also believed that Kafka had deliberately asked the one person he knew would not honor his wishes (because Brod had explicitly told him so). We do know, however, that Brod disregarded his friend's request and devoted great energy to making sure that all of Kafka's works—his three unfinished novels, his unpublished stories, diaries, and letters—would appear in print. Brod explained his reasoning thus:

My decision [rests] simply and solely on the fact that Kafka's unpublished work contains the most wonderful treasures, and,

Schocken Books would like to acknowledge the scholarly assistance given by Professor Mark Anderson and Dr. Anthony David Skinner in the preparation of this note.

measured against his own work, the best things he has written. In all honesty I must confess that this one fact of the literary and ethical value of what I am publishing would have been enough to make me decide to do so, definitely, finally, and irresistibly, even if I had had no single objection to raise against the validity of Kafka's last wishes. (From the postscript to the first edition of *The Trial*)

In 1925, Max Brod convinced the small avant-garde Berlin publisher Verlag Die Schmiede to publish *The Trial,* which Brod prepared for publication from Kafka's unfinished manuscript. Next he persuaded the Munich publisher Kurt Wolff to publish his edited manuscript of *The Castle,* also left unfinished by Kafka, in 1926, and in 1927 to bring out Kafka's first novel, which Kafka had meant to entitle *Der Verschollene* (The Missing Person), but which Brod named *Amerika.* The first English translation of *The Trial,* by Edwin and Willa Muir (who had already translated *The Castle* in 1930), appeared in 1937 simultaneously in England and the United States, the latter edition published by Knopf with illustrations by Georg Salter. Neither the German nor the English-language editions sold well, although they were critically well received. Edwin and Willa Muir's translation of *Amerika* was first published in the United States in 1940 by New Directions.

Undeterred, Max Brod enlisted the support of Martin Buber, André Gide, Hermann Hesse, Heinrich Mann, Thomas Mann, and Franz Werfel for a public statement urging the publication of Kafka's collected works as "a spiritual act of unusual dimensions, especially now, during times of chaos." Since Kafka's previous publishers had closed during Germany's economic depression, he appealed to Gustav Kiepenheuer to undertake the project. Kiepenheuer agreed, but on condition that the first volume be financially successful. But the Nazi rise to power in

1933 forced Kiepenheuer to abandon his plans. Between 1933 and 1938 German Jews were barred from teaching or studying in "German" schools, from publishing or being published in "German" newspapers or publishing houses, or from speaking and performing in front of "German" audiences. Publishers that had been owned or managed by Jews, such as S. Fischer Verlag, were quickly "Aryanized" and ceased to publish books by Jews. Kafka's works were not well enough known to be banned by the government or burned by nationalist students, but they were "Jewish" enough to be off limits to "Aryan" publishers.

When the Nazis introduced their racial laws they exempted Schocken Verlag, a Jewish publisher, from the ban against publishing Jewish authors on condition that its books would be sold only to Jews. Founded in 1931 by the department store magnate Salman Schocken, this small publishing company had already published the works of Martin Buber and Franz Rosenzweig as well as those of the Hebrew writer S. Y. Agnon as part of its owner's interest in fostering a secular Jewish literary culture.

Max Brod offered Schocken the world publishing rights to all of Kafka's works. This offer was initially rejected by Lambert Schneider, Schocken Verlag's editor in chief, who regarded Kafka's works as outside his mandate to publish books that could reacquaint German Jewry with its distinguished heritage. He also doubted its public appeal. His employer also had his doubts about the marketability of six volumes of Kafka's novels, stories, diaries, and letters, although he recognized their universal literary quality as well as their potential to undermine the official campaign to denigrate German Jewish culture. But he was urged by one of his editors, Moritz Spitzer, to see in Kafka a quintessentially "Jewish" voice that could give meaning to the new reality that had befallen German Jewry and would demonstrate the central role of Jews in German culture.

Accordingly, *Before the Law,* an anthology drawn from Kafka's diaries and short stories, appeared in 1934 in Schocken Verlag's Bücherei series, a collection of books aimed to appeal to a popular audience, and was followed a year later—the year of the infamous Nuremberg Laws—by Kafka's three novels. The Schocken editions were the first to give Kafka widespread distribution in Germany. Martin Buber, in a letter to Brod, praised these volumes as "a great possession" that could "show how one can live marginally with complete integrity and without loss of background" (from *The Letters of Martin Buber* [New York: Schocken Books, 1991], p. 431).

Inevitably, many of the books Schocken sold ended up in non-Jewish hands, giving German readers—at home and in exile—their only access to one of the century's greatest writers. Klaus Mann wrote in the exile journal *Sammlung* that "the collected works of Kafka, offered by the Schocken Verlag in Berlin, are the noblest and most significant publications that have come out of Germany." Praising Kafka's books as "the epoch's purest and most singular works of literature," he noted with astonishment that "this spiritual event has occurred within a splendid isolation, in a ghetto far from the German cultural ministry." Quite probably in response to Mann's article, on 22 July 1935, a functionary of the German cultural ministry wrote to Schocken complaining that the publisher was "still selling the complete works of Franz Kafka, edited by Max Brod," although the work of both Kafka and Brod had been placed by the Nazis on the "list of harmful and undesirable writings" three months earlier. Schocken moved his production to Prague, where he published Kafka's diaries and letters. Interestingly, despite the Nazi protest against the collected works, he was able to continue printing and distributing his earlier volume of Kafka's short stories in Germany itself until the government closed down Schocken Verlag in 1939. The German occupation of Prague that same year put an end to Schocken's operations in Europe.

In 1939, he reestablished Schocken Books in Palestine, where he had lived intermittently since 1934, and editions of Kafka's works in the renewed Hebrew language were among its first publications. In 1940, he moved to New York, where five years later he opened Schocken Books with Hannah Arendt and Nahum Glatzer as his chief editors. While continuing to publish Kafka in German, Schocken reissued the existing Muir translations of the novels in 1946 and commissioned translations of the letters and diaries in the 1950s, thus placing Kafka again at the center of his publishing program. Despite a dissenting opinion from Edmund Wilson in *The New Yorker* (where he nonetheless compared Kafka to Nikolai Gogol and Edgar Allan Poe), a postwar Kafka craze began in the United States; translations of all of Kafka's works began to appear in many other languages; and in 1951 the German Jewish publisher S. Fischer of Frankfurt (also in exile during the Nazi period) obtained the rights to publish Kafka in Germany. As Hannah Arendt wrote to Salman Schocken, Kafka had come to share Marx's fate: "Though during his lifetime he could not make a decent living, he will now keep generations of intellectuals both gainfully employed and well-fed" (letter, 9 August 1946, Schocken Books Archive, New York).

Along with the growing international recognition of Franz Kafka as one of the great modern writers, scholars began to raise doubts about the editorial decisions made by Max Brod. Although the manuscript of *Der Verschollene* (The Missing Person) lacks chapter headings and often even chapter breaks, Kafka did jot down on a sheet of paper headings for the first six chapters (complete with page numbers). He left no such instructions for the remainder of the text. After Kafka's premature death in 1924 of tuberculosis, Brod did everything he could to achieve for his friend the recognition that had largely eluded him during his lifetime. As a result, in editing the manuscript of this novel for its original German publication in 1927, Brod was, as he explained in his afterword, "primarily concerned with the broad line of the story, not with philological work." While he followed Kafka's stated intentions for those first six chapters, he divided the remainder of the text into two additional chapters, for which he devised the headings "A Refuge" and "The Nature Theater of Oklahoma." In the case of the latter, Brod also rounded off the chapter—and indeed the novel—by adding two final passages that were clearly fragments from a subsequent never-completed chapter. Finally, he relegated to an appendix two passages concerning Karl's service at Brunelda's, since they did not, he felt, greatly advance the story.

Salman Schocken was among the most eager for new critical editions of Kafka's works. "The Schocken editions are bad," he wrote in an internal memo. "Without any question, new editions that include the incomplete novels would require a completely different approach" (29 September 1940, Schocken Archives, Jerusalem). However, Max Brod's refusal to give up the Kafka archive in his Tel Aviv apartment or to allow scholars access to it made such new editions impossible until 1956, when the threat of war in the Middle East prompted him to deposit the bulk of the archives, including the manuscript of *The Castle,* in a Swiss vault. When the young Oxford Germanist Malcolm Pasley learned of the archives' whereabouts, he received permission from Kafka's heirs in 1961 to deposit them in Oxford's Bodleian Library, where they were subsequently made available for scholarly inspection. The manuscript of *The Trial,* which Kafka had given to Brod in 1920, remained in Brod's personal possession, passing to his companion and heiress Ilse Ester Hoffe when he died in 1968. It was not until the late 1980s that Ms. Hoffe agreed to sell the manuscript, which was auctioned for a record sum by Sotheby's in November 1988 to the German national literary archives in Marbach, where it is now kept.

Since 1978 an international team of Kafka experts has been working on German critical editions of all of Kafka's writings, which are being published by S. Fischer Verlag with financial support from the German government. The first of these editions, *Das Schloss* (The Castle), edited by Malcolm Pasley, appeared in 1982 in two volumes, the first containing the restored text of the novel drawn from Kafka's handwritten manuscript, the second containing textual variants and editorial notes. Mark Harman's translation of the restored text was published by Schocken in 1998. The critical edition of *Der Verschollene* (The Missing Person), edited by Jost Schillemeit, appeared in 1983, also in two volumes. Harman's translation is based on the restored text in the first volume, which corrected numerous transcription errors in the earlier editions and removed Brod's editorial and stylistic interventions. In the restored text, for example, Schillemeit employs only the chapter headings mentioned by Kafka and inserts chapter or section breaks based on evidence gleaned from the manuscript.

This translation generally follows the example set by the editors of the critical editions, although, as Harman explains in his preface, a few inconsistencies have been silently rectified (for example, Kafka's erratic spelling of New York as Newyork or New-York and the odd use of capitals in "Hotel occidental"). As in the case of our new translations of *The Trial* and *The Castle,* we have not included the variants and deleted passages that appeared in the second volume of the critical editions of these books. The chief objective of these new translations, intended for the general public, is to provide readers with versions that reflect as closely as possible the state in which Kafka left the manuscripts.

TRANSLATOR'S PREFACE

There is little doubt that Karl Rossmann, the young hero of *The Missing Person,* who is banished to America by his parents, was Kafka's favorite alter ego. On sending his future fiancée, Felice Bauer, the first chapter, he urged her to receive the "little youth kindly, set him down beside you and praise him, as he so longs to be praised."[1] Readers will, I hope, not only come to share Kafka's affection for Karl, as I did while working on this translation, but also gain a new appreciation for this novel, which has for too long been overshadowed by *The Trial* and *The Castle.* If approached afresh, this book could bear out the early claim by Kafka's friend Max Brod that "precisely this novel . . . will reveal a new way of understanding Kafka."[2]

The Missing Person is a poetically coherent work that can be read on a number of levels, as an episodic picaresque tale, a bildungsroman or coming-of-age novel, a story of emigration or exile, a dark vision of urban civilization, a self-reflective modernist novel, and finally an at times dryly humorous send-up of the American dream. In creating his vision of America, Kafka was inspired by sources ranging from newspaper accounts of America, writings by European travelers, silent movies, and possibly the autobiography of Benjamin Franklin—which he pointedly gave to his own father to read[3]—as well as an established tradition of German-language writing about America, in which the New World was portrayed either as an idyllic refuge or as a dystopia.[4]

As his diaries and letters suggest, Kafka's fascination with America grew out of a sense of imprisonment or inner exile. His native city Prague, which he once famously called a "little mother with claws," could never be his *Heimat* (home or homeland). In a diary entry of 20 August 1911 he writes of wanting to spread himself out "in all earthly directions," as he may be said to have done vicariously in his first novel.[5] This desire to break away from Prague, even if only in his imagination, never left him. Toward the end of his life, on seeing a group of refugees packed into the banqueting room of the Jewish Town Hall in Prague, he writes to his lover Milena Jesenská: "If I'd been given the choice to be what I wanted, then I'd have chosen to be a small Eastern Jewish boy in the corner of the room, without a trace of worry, the father in the centre discussing with other men, the mother, heavily wrapped, is rummaging in the traveling bundles . . . and in a few weeks one will be in America."[6]

When this novel first appeared in London in 1938 in Edwin and Willa Muir's beautiful English translation, there was little awareness of what Kafka knew about America, and, since he himself had never set foot on these shores, it was easy to dismiss what he liked to call his "American novel" as sheer fantasy. However, thanks to meticulous scholarly reconstructions of the annihilated world of the German-speaking Prague Jews and of the debates about literature, religion, philosophy, Jewish identity, and Zionism in which Kafka participated, *The Missing Person* no longer seems quite so ahistorical, nor so apolitical, as it once did.

Although Kafka never crossed the Atlantic, he had specific ideas about the kind of America he wanted to portray. For instance, when, on the suggestion of the poet Franz Werfel, his German publisher Kurt Wolff used an old-fashioned print of a sailing boat approaching New York Harbor as a frontispiece for "The Stoker"—the first chapter of the novel, which was initially published in 1913 as a separate story—Kafka protested on the grounds that he had portrayed "the most modern New York."[7]

Together with "The Judgment" and "The Metamorphosis," "The Stoker" forms a trilogy of what Kafka dubbed his domestic tragedies. All three stories feature sons who are punished by their parents, and the manuscripts attest to the close relationship between these three characters: on several occasions in "Metamorphosis" Kafka wrote "Karl" rather than "Gregor" (the main protagonist in "Metamorphosis"), and similarly five times in the manuscript of "The Stoker" he mistakenly wrote "Georg" (the hero of "The Judgment") instead of "Karl."[8] Three days after achieving what he considered his literary breakthrough, in writing "The Judgment" during the night of 22–23 September 1912, he began to compose his "American novel."

Unlike "The Judgment," *The Missing Person* had a lengthy gestation—Kafka wrote at least three versions—and its roots extend far back in his imaginative life. We know from a diary entry of 19 January 1911 that as a child or adolescent he wrote a story with a related theme, in which America serves as a refuge. Then, after beginning a draft in winter 1911 (which has not survived), he wrote the first seven chapters of the novel between September 1912 and January 1913. He subsequently turned his attention to other projects, and it was not until October 1914—after he had started work on *The Trial*—that he wrote the last completed chapter of *The Missing Person*.

The title *Amerika,* which emphasizes the setting and by which the novel has become widely known, is not Kafka's but rather was used by Max Brod in the first German edition in 1927—three years after Kafka's premature death of tuberculosis at the age of forty-one. Kafka himself clearly entitled the novel *Der Verschollene* (The Missing Person) in a letter to

Felice Bauer in November 1912, thereby underscoring the fate of the young hero.[9]

In the diary entry of 1911 about the juvenile "American" story Kafka recollects sitting with members of his family (unfortunately he does not specify his age at the time) writing a story featuring two brothers. One brother ends up in a prison in Europe, whereas the other—the "bad" one—escapes to America. An uncle grabbed a page from him, glanced at it, and declared to the rest of the family, dismissively, "The usual stuff." The twenty-eight-year-old diarist describes how this verdict gave him a "glimpse of the cold space of our world" and made him feel "banished." Those metaphors anticipate the predicament of the young hero in the opening lines of *The Missing Person:*

> As he entered New York harbor on the now-slow-moving ship, Karl Rossmann, a seventeen-year-old youth who had been sent to America by his poor parents because a servant girl had seduced him and borne a child by him, glimpsed the Statue of Liberty, which he had been observing for some time, as if in a sudden burst of sunlight. The arm with the sword now reached aloft, and about her figure blew the free winds.

Much ink has been spilled over these introductory sentences and, especially, the surreal description of the Statue of Liberty. In famously endowing the statue with a sword rather than a torch, Kafka defied conventional expectations. Although one reviewer noted this seeming slip, on the first appearance of "The Stoker" in May 1913,[10] Kafka declined to alter it in a second printing of the story in 1916, in which he made some minor changes. There can be no doubt that the choice of the sword was quite deliberate.

Some critics argue that Kafka transformed the American emblem of freedom into an icon of justice and that the sword is drawn not against "the social injustices bred by America's cap-

italism . . . [but] against Karl's conscience."[11] Others see the
sword as a symbol of violence, anticipating the struggles that
Karl will face against an inhumane technological civilization.
Still others point to traditional representations of Justitia in
European paintings. Moreover, the sword in the hand of Kafka's alienated version of the Statue of Liberty may recall the
cherubim and the fiery revolving sword that guard the gates of
the Garden of Eden after the expulsion of Adam and Eve, at
least in the influential old Greek translation of Genesis.[12]

While some readers might be inclined to approach this novel
as a dream narrative, in the manuscript Kafka sought to diminish this possibility and the psychological interpretations that it
would invite. In the opening lines of the novel, just after Karl
has glimpsed the Statue of Liberty, Kafka first wrote the following sentence and then immediately crossed it out: "He looked
up at her and dismissed what he had learned about her." *(Er
sah zu ihr auf und verwarf das über sie gelernte.)* That crossed-
out sentence, which almost sounds postmodern, might imply
that the young hero is imposing his preoccupations on the
statue—precisely the kind of easy psychological explanation
that Kafka sought to exclude.[13] Just as it is impossible to dismiss as a nightmare the perception of Gregor Samsa in "Metamorphosis" that his body has been mysteriously transformed
overnight into that of a bug (the text states quite unambigu-
ously that "it was no dream"), we cannot simply explain away
this surreal Statue of Liberty as a subjective perception of Karl
Rossmann. Moreover, the placement of this altered monument
at the beginning of the novel may be Kafka's way of warning us
not to take the tale that follows as a realistic account of a
young man's experiences in America.[14]

There has been much debate about whether Karl Rossmann
develops in the course of the novel, as one would expect of the
hero of a bildungsroman. Kafka himself acknowledged a debt

to one of the great English novels of development, Dickens's *David Copperfield,* specifically mentioning motifs shared by the two novels, such as "the story of the trunk, the boy who delights and charms everyone, the menial laborer, his sweetheart in the country house, the dirty houses etc." However, he was critical of Dickens's "coarse characterizations" of his figures, which, having learned a great deal about narrative art from Flaubert, Kleist, and, despite often-shoddy productions in Prague, the Yiddish theater, Kafka had been able to avoid. *The Missing Person* bears only a parodistic resemblance to the classic European bildungsroman, Goethe's *Wilhelm Meister,* and is much closer to *Jakob von Gunten,* an anti-bildungsroman by the quirky Swiss modernist Robert Walser, about a character who sets out to become a nobody.[15]

How can we explain the sudden ability of Karl Rossmann, who has few literary or artistic interests aside from a rudimentary ability to play the piano, to suddenly imagine himself changing his American "circumstances" through the sheer power of his playing? Kafka's diaries can shed some insight here, especially a series of seminal entries in June 1910 in which Kafka (or rather his partly biographical, partly fictional alter ego) explores how his education and upbringing have made it impossible for him to develop naturally and left him instead with a "dead bride"—a metaphorical term for his full potential. Could Karl have a comparable potential locked inside him? Be that as it may, his dreams of artistic success anticipate the last completed chapter of the novel, which features a giant theater and a character named Fanny who tells him that he is indeed an artist.[16]

The element of social criticism in *The Missing Person* is more pronounced than it is anywhere else in Kafka's oeuvre. For instance, at one point Karl Rossmann remarks that America is a country where "one could not hope for pity" and where only those who are fortunate seem to "enjoy their good fortune amid the indifferent faces on all sides."[17] At such moments Kafka's critical perspective on American society in the robber-baron era can seem remarkably congruent with that of American novelists such as Theodore Dreiser in *Sister Carrie* (1900) and Edith Wharton in *The House of Mirth* (1905).[18]

Far more characteristic of Kafka's first novel than such explicit social criticism, however, are passages in which he transforms abstract critiques of modern urban civilization into vivid tableaux, thereby anticipating such early movie classics as Fritz Lang's *Metropolis* and Charlie Chaplin's *Modern Times*.[19] Take, for instance, the depiction of the busy telegraph room in the enterprise of Karl's American uncle, where an employee's right arm lies almost inert, "as if it were a heavy burden," and "only the fingers twitched away at a rapid and inhumanly uniform pace"; or the scene at the gigantic Occidental Hotel, in which the heads of the information-dispensing underporters become so hot they need to be doused with water.[20] Through such unexpected details Kafka suggests analogies between the business world and the factories of America, which he never describes from the inside. Kafka, who as an accident insurance lawyer by day visited factories throughout Bohemia, could easily imagine the working conditions in similar enterprises in America.[21] On one occasion he expressed surprise that the workers injured in factory accidents did not come and break down the doors at his insurance company.

In creating his vision of America, Kafka drew on reportage by a Hungarian Jewish socialist called Arthur Holitscher, which he first read in installments in the journal *Neue Rundschau*. He bought a copy of Holitscher's subsequent book *Amerika Heute und Morgen* (America Today and Tomorrow) for his personal library and also attended an illustrated lecture by a Czech Socialist called František Soukup about his travels in America,

which then also appeared in book form. Holitscher and Soukup both attribute the cruelly hectic pace of life in America to
the predominance of the profit motive: "This murderous tempo,
this fearful rush which only ceases at the grave."[22]

While Kafka does draw on such material, he reveals himself
to be a creative borrower. Take, for instance, the odd depiction
of the Statue of Liberty in the opening paragraph of the novel.
Although Kafka does not describe Ellis Island, he may be graft-
ing onto his description of the statue an image that Holitscher
used in portraying the island: "No Blake could have drawn or
sung of the avenging angel who reigns over this island in a
cloud of fear, whimpering, torture and blasphemy every single
day that we spend in this free country."[23] It would be entirely
characteristic of Kafka's magpielike ways if he had borrowed
that Blakean angel from Holitscher, placing her instead on the
pedestal of the Statue of Liberty and using the word "free,"
which Holitscher imbues with heavy sarcasm, in a characteristically wry manner.

Kafka playfully acknowledges his own prior readings about
America when he has Karl compare his impressions of an
ostensible Irishman called Robinson with a warning he read
somewhere that newcomers should be wary of the Irish in
America: Holitscher asserts that the Irish produced the most
successful type of "political padrone, boss, slave-holder, and
vote catcher" and even records a passenger in steerage asking
hopefully: "How long do you have to live in America before
becoming an Irishman?"

Kafka himself had a number of American relatives, such as
his uncle Otto Kafka, who may have been a partial model for
Karl Rossmann's American uncle, and a namesake cousin,
Franz or Frank Kafka, who left for America at the same age as
Karl.[24] Like the uncle in the novel, Otto Kafka was a self-made
man who, after a series of colorful adventures in South Africa

and South America, emigrated to the United States, where he eventually accumulated sufficient wealth to buy a home near the Rockefeller mansion at Tarrytown, New York. Yet we need to approach these tantalizing biographical items warily, since it is difficult to distinguish between biographical sources, Kafka's readings about America, and his own inventions. And while the tone of a letter from Otto Kafka to the U.S. assistant attorney general (cited by Anthony Northey in his thoroughly researched 1991 study *Kafka's Relatives*) is indeed comparable to the voice Kafka attributes to the fictional uncle, there is also something almost generic about such rags-to-riches stories.[25]

As the great Argentinean writer Jorge Luis Borges suggested[26]—and as critics such as Robert Alter have specifically shown in the case of *The Missing Person*[27]—Kafka wove numerous religious, and in particular Old Testament, motifs into his portrayal of Karl's American adventures, raising questions for us as readers. To what extent is a metropolis such as New York, with the hundred thousand "eyes" of its many Babel-like skyscrapers, at the mercy of those winds and of the "restlessness" wafting in from the sea? What, for instance, are we to make of the mysterious gales blowing through the vast mansion that Karl visits outside New York, especially near the chapel? How should we read images such as that of "a glass roof stretched over the street . . . being violently smashed into fragments at every moment"?

However dark the plight of his heroes, Kafka himself never loses his sense of humor. In *The Missing Person* that humor is often hidden between the interstices of his sentences. The discrepancy between Karl's relentlessly sober perceptions and the often-ludicrous events in which he is caught up make it difficult for us not to chuckle in spite of our increasing empathy with the hapless young hero. Take, for example, his exchanges with the ostensible Irishman Robinson, which are punctuated by precise descriptions of the latter's messy eating habits, or the description of the bathing rituals of Brunelda, a grotesque character whose Wagnerian-sounding name turns out to be quite apt. Moreover, Karl's lack of a strong sense of identity gives rise to a number of comic scenes, especially those featuring his dubious companions Delamarche and Robinson. Worth mentioning in passing—since the names of Kafka's characters can be telling—is the meaning of the surname of the servant who seduces Karl: Brummer (Buzzer), or "noisy fly," an appropriate, if unsettling, name for her, especially since the *Ross* in Karl's surname *Rossmann* means "steed" or "horse."[28]

Readers may well be puzzled by the fascinating but enigmatic last completed chapter. Heightening the enigma is the gap in the novel just before this chapter: after a brief account of Karl's entrance into a brothel-like institution with an industrial-sounding name, Enterprise Nr. 25, the narrative breaks off, and then without any transition we find ourselves reading a poster in which a mysterious theater advertises its openings. When Kafka finally sat down in 1914 to write this chapter (which Max Brod entitled "The Nature Theater of Oklahoma," even though it had no title in the manuscript), he may have been attempting to do with *The Missing Person* what he had already done with *The Trial,* namely, first write a final chapter and then try to fill in the missing parts. However, as in the case of *The Trial,* he never did fill in the gaps. So inevitably readers will come away from this chapter, and indeed from the novel as a whole, with divergent interpretations, depending on which level of meaning they choose to emphasize: the social, the metaphysical, the psychological, the apotheosis or parody of the American dream, and so on.[29]

There are two alternative versions of how Kafka wanted to end this never-completed novel. According to Brod, he intended to conclude it in a conciliatory fashion, and he used to hint

smilingly that within "this 'almost limitless' theatre his young
hero was going to find again a profession, some backing, his
freedom, even his old home and his parents, as if by some para-
disiacal magic."[30] Perhaps. But on the other hand, in a diary
entry of 30 September 1915 Kafka explicitly compared the
fates of the heroes in *The Missing Person* and *The Trial*: "Rossmann and K., the innocent and the guilty, both executed without distinction in the end, the innocent one with a gentler hand,
more pushed aside than struck down."[31] Characteristically am-
bivalent about the kind of ending he wanted, and having worked
on the novel on and off for three years, he may at some point
have changed his mind about Karl's fate.

In the chapter featuring the Theater of Oklahama (Kafka
consistently misspelled the name of the state), the "biggest theater in the world" claims that it can take on all who apply. But
how credible is the organization? Will it finally allow Karl
to reach a degree of fulfillment? Some critics claim that the
theater represents a model of religious redemption; others, a
social utopia; others still, a surreal version of the American
dream. Finally, what are we to make of the decision by Karl,
who has lost his identification papers, to identify himself as
"Negro," the nickname he claims was given him in previous
positions (which Kafka never got around to describing)?[32] The
insertion of the word *negro* into the text was a deliberate act on
Kafka's part, for he had originally written "Leo"—perhaps an
allusion to an alter ego, Leopold S., who engages in a transpar-
ently autobiographical, if enigmatically fragmentary, dialogue
with a character named Felice S. in a diary entry of 15 August
1913—then went back and changed the name nine times to
"Negro."[33] Certain signs indicate a turn for the better—for
example, Karl has a couple of promising encounters with figures from his past—that might seem to bear out Kafka's purported plans for a positive ending. However, a grim image in

Holitscher's travelogue—a photograph depicting a lynching with a group of grinning white bystanders, which Holitscher sarcastically entitled "Idyll aus Oklahama" (Idyll from Okla-hama), with the same misspelling as in Kafka—might make one lean toward a darker interpretation of this chapter and of Karl's final journey.

The multilingual Kafka was acutely aware of the challenges facing translators and of the need to negotiate between some-times conflicting linguistic and literary claims. Though he praised his first Czech translator, Milena Jesenská, for her faithfulness to his German, he also asked "whether Czechs won't hold its very faithfulness against you." His comments on her Czech rendering of the first two sentences in the novel are particularly revealing, since this is one of the trickier passages in the book. What, for instance, are we to make of the ambiguous statement that Karl has been sent to America by his *"arme Eltern"* (poor parents)? Kafka was not happy with Milena's decision to elimi-nate the ambiguity of "poor" by inserting the adjectival phrase "financially needy," suggesting that Karl's parents are impover-ished. He emphasized that *arme* (poor) "here also has the sec-ondary meaning: pitiable, but without any special emphasis of feeling."[34] Could this reference to Karl's "poor parents" be an ironic, or even sarcastic, comment by the narrator? Perhaps. But Kafka disclosed another interpretative possibility when he revealed to Milena that the expression mirrors Karl's feelings toward his parents: "an uncomprehending sympathy that Karl, too, has with his parents."[35]

Kafka also commented on the *"freie Lüfte"* (literally, "free airs") blowing about the Statue of Liberty. He noted that the German phrase is "a little more grand" than Milena's Czech rendition as "free air"—like English, Czech cannot easily use the word *air* in the plural. But then he added, with his characteristic awareness of the inherent limits of translation, that "there's probably no alternative." I ended up choosing the phrase "free winds," which like Milena's Czech term is less elevated than the original German, partly because I wanted to retain that simple but resonant word *free*.

In general I have sought to keep the interpretative options open and to follow Kafka whenever he chooses to be ambiguous and whenever he flouts conventions. For instance, in describing the mysterious Theater of Oklahoma, he avoids straightforward German verbs such as *einstellen* (to hire), and I have sought to make the English text comparably elusive.[36] The same goes for the punctuation, which some readers may find a little unsettling. Kafka employs it rather erratically—for example, some questions are followed by question marks, others not. Here we must keep in mind that, with the exception of the "Stoker" chapter, he never revised the manuscript for publication and that we cannot know precisely what he would have changed had he done so. For stylistic reasons, he preferred to use punctuation sparingly, and I have tried to be comparably thrifty. After all, at least in the original German, the very lightness of the punctuation helped to create prose that is often full of sharply observed detail—as in the first chapter—yet still flows with seemingly miraculous ease.

Max Brod corrected obvious slips, such as a bridge stretching from New York to Boston, a sudden shift in the U.S. currency from dollars to pounds, and conflicting indications as to whether Karl Rossmann is sixteen or seventeen; these editorial corrections were adopted by Edwin and Willa Muir, who used Brod's edition as the basis for the first English translation (1938). The more recent German-language editors of Kafka's novels have refrained from making such changes, on the grounds that it is preferable to offer readers as close an approximation as possible of the state in which Kafka left his texts. Although I have usually followed the editors of the German critical edition in retaining idiosyncratic features of the original manuscript, I have silently rectified several minor inconsistencies, such as Kafka's somewhat erratic spelling of *New York* (sometimes as one word, sometimes as two, sometimes linked by a hyphen) and *Occidental Hotel* (in the original the spelling of the former word is generally lowercase), while retaining the names of a tycoon's son, who is called Mak and subsequently becomes Mack.

The greatest challenge for me as a translator lay in endeavoring to re-create in English a style that would mimic such seemingly disparate traits of Kafka's prose as its "provocatively 'classic' German,"[37] its meticulous attention to detail, its "flowing vivacity,"[38] and its modernist adherence to the restricted perspective of the main character. Although some critics who are native speakers of German have found Kafka's style in *The Missing Person* jarring,[39] such criticism fails to acknowledge the startling modernity that is often hidden under its surface conservatism. There certainly is something very modern about the way he tells the story, switching back and forth between indirect interior monologue and an unobtrusive narrator, who occasionally winks to the reader over the hero's head, thereby alerting us to the irony and humor beyond the awareness of the all-too-earnest young hero.[40]

Although Brod's once widely accepted portrayal of Kafka's works as religious allegories has not aged well, he may not have been too far off in claiming that this novel can yield a new interpretation of Kafka, and also—I would add—a new appreciation of neglected qualities in his writing.

— MARK HARMAN
Elizabethtown College

NOTES

1. Kafka, *Letters to Felice* (New York, 1973), p. 267. Here, as elsewhere, the cited translations have been modified whenever appropriate. Early versions of this preface were presented at the Kentucky Foreign Language Conference and at Duke University.

2. Brod sought to make the purported salvation of the young hero the centerpiece of his argument that Kafka was a writer with an ultimately positive faith in man and in the possibility of divine grace. Many subsequent readers have rejected Brod's sunny insistence that the hero's "misfortune is kept in check by his child-like innocence and touchingly naïve purity." See Max Brod, "Nachwort" in Kafka, *Die Romane* (Frankfurt, 1969), p. 254.

3. In a passage in his famous letter to his father (1919), Kafka explains that he gave Franklin's autobiography to Hermann Kafka partly "because of the relationship between the author and his father" (p. 218), and elsewhere in the same letter he connects his own largely imaginary travels to his need to avoid spaces that his father already occupies: "Sometimes I imagine the map of the world spread out and you stretched diagonally across it. And I feel as if I could consider living in only those regions that either are not covered by you or are not within your reach" (p. 231). *The Basic Kafka* (New York, 1979). See also John Zilcosky, *Kafka's Travels: Exoticism, Colonialism, and the Traffic of Writing* (New York, 2003).

4. See *Amerika in der deutschen Literatur,* ed. Sigrid Bauschinger et al. (Stuttgart, 1975). The volume includes a characteristically insightful essay by Walter Sokel on *The Missing Person.* See also *Das Amerika der Autoren,* ed. Jochen Vogt and Alexander Stephan (Munich, 2005).

5. See Heinz Hillmann, who also examines the relationship between *The Missing Person* and Holitscher's book, in "*Amerika:* Literature as a Problem-solving Game," in *The Kafka Debate,* ed. Angel Flores (New York, 1977), pp. 279–97. Mark Harman, "Biography and Autobiography: Necessary Antagonists?" in *Journal of the Kafka Society* 10, nos. 1–2 (1986), pp. 56–62; and Mark Harman, "Life into Art: Kafka's Self-Stylization in the Diaries," in *Franz Kafka (1883–1983): His Craft and Thought,* ed. R. Struc (Waterloo, Ont., 1986), pp. 101–16.

6. Kafka, *Letters to Milena,* ed. Willi Haas (New York, 1962), p. 196.

7. Kafka, *Letters to Friends, Family, and Editors* (New York, 1977), p. 98.

8. See Wolfgang Jahn, "Kafkas Handschrift zum *Verschollenen,*" in *Jahrbuch der deutschen Schillergesellschaft* (Stuttgart, 1957), p. 549.

9. The German title, *Der Verschollene,* presents a challenge for translators, since it is impossible to do justice in English to all nuances of the original. *Der Verschollene* is both characteristically succinct—consisting solely of a noun derived from the past participle of a verb and the masculine definite article indicating the gender of the missing person—and paradoxical, for it raises a metafictional question about the provenance of this story about a youth who has gone missing without trace, especially since the infinitive of the verb in question, namely, *verschallen,* means "to cease making a sound" or "to fade away." See *Wahrig Deutsches Wörterbuch* (Gütersloh, 1972).

10. See Camill Hoffmann's early review of "The Stoker" in *Franz Kafka: Kritik und Rezeption 1912–1924* (Frankfurt, 1979), pp. 47–49.

11. Heinz Politzer, *Franz Kafka: Parable and Paradox* (Ithaca, N.Y., 1966), p. 123.

12. For a discussion of the critical reception of *Der Verschollene*, see *Kafka-Hardbuch*, vol. 2, ed. Hartmut Binder (Stuttgart, 1979), pp. 407–20.

13. See Mark Harman, "Making Everything a 'little uncanny': Kafka's Deletions in the Manuscript of *Das Schloß*," in *Companion to the Works of Franz Kafka*, ed. James Rolleston (Rochester, N.Y., 2002), pp. 325–46.

14. See Mark Anderson, "Kafka and New York: Notes on a Traveling Narrative," in *Modernity and the Text: Revisions of German Modernism*, ed. Andreas Huyssen and David Bathrick (New York, 1989), p. 149.

15. Kafka's pun on the double meaning of the word *Laufbahn*—"career" or "racetrack"—in a letter about Robert Walser anticipates a comparable conceit in the theater chapter of *The Missing Person*. See *Robert Walser Rediscovered*, ed. Mark Harman (Hanover, N.H., 1985), pp. 139–40.

16. The theater chapter at the end of the novel is prefigured by a brief fragment—probably written in early February 1912—in which Karl corrects the words of a servant who has introduced him as an actor by saying that he merely wants to become one. See *Der Verschollene: Apparatband* (Frankfurt, 1983), pp. 49, 71–73.

17. Karl adds that this negative verdict confirms what he has already read about the United States. If Kafka is referring obliquely here to Holitscher or Soukup, he—or at least his hero Karl—is endorsing stinging critiques of the American system. Some early critics detected a strong element of social criticism in the novel. For instance, the philosopher Adorno argued that Kafka's insight "into economic tendencies was not so alien . . . as the hermetic method of his narrative techniques would lead us to assume." See Theodor W. Adorno, *Prisms* (Boston, 1977), p. 260. One German scholar even asserted that the novel "mercilessly" uncovers "the hidden economic and psychological mechanism of this society and its satanic consequences." See Wilhelm Emrich, *Franz Kafka*, trans. S. Z. Buehne (New York, 1968), p. 276. Others rejected the idea that the novel represents a critique of American—or capitalist—society on the grounds that its true theme is "not the reality, present or future, of a civilization far away from Kafka's Prague, but the growth, both personal and intellectual, of Karl Rossmann." See Politzer, *Parable*, p. 124.

18. While *The Missing Person* challenges notions of realism in a way those two more conventional portrayals of the robber-baron era do not, its dissection of the American dream can be as caustic as those of Dreiser and Wharton. If Karl Rossmann were a first-person narrator and more given to introspection, he might sound like Wharton's Lily Bart toward the end: "I have tried hard—but life is difficult, and I am a very useless person. I can hardly be said to have an independent existence. I was just a screw or a cog in the great machine I called life, and when I dropped out of it I found I was of no use anywhere else." Of course, while there is some ambiguity in Wharton's treatment of Lily Bart's death, Kafka leaves

the ultimate fate of Karl Rossmann entirely unsettled. See Edith Wharton, *The House of Mirth,* ed. ·Elizabeth Ammons (New York, 1990), p. 240.

19. For an exploration of Kafka's interest in film, see Hanns Zischler, *Kafka Goes to the Movies,* trans. Susan H. Gillespie (Chicago, 2002).

20. Similarly if, as some critics have suggested, the fictional Occidental Hotel owes something to Holitscher's description of the Atheneum Hotel at Chautauqua, New York, Kafka darkens Holitscher's uncharacteristically euphoric account of an American grand hotel, where lowly elevator boys converse freely in the lobby with affluent guests. For instance, a graduate of Columbia University and medical student, who was working temporarily as a porter at the Atheneum and was described by Holitscher, may have metamorphosed into the overworked medical student known as "Black Coffee," from whom Karl Rossmann learns a lesson about the pitfalls of such extreme absorption. Moreover, if there is an echo of Soukup's caustic description of the ships transporting immigrants across the Atlantic ("a storehouse in which human beings are exported as wares to America") in the description of the stoker's quarters in the novel ("a bed, a closet, a chair, and the man were packed together, as if in storage"), Kafka can be said to introduce his own touch—a hint of humor—without thereby eliminating all traces of the social criticism that is far more emphatic in Holitscher and Soukup.

21. Kafka had read about the Taylor system of work measurement in Holitscher's travelogue. See Holitscher, *Amerika Heute und Morgen,* 12th ed. (Berlin, 1923), pp. 292ff.

22. Ibid., p. 367.

23. Ibid., p. 338.

24. As we know from his diaries, Kafka also had conversations in Prague with another American cousin, Emil Kafka (1881–1963), and listened attentively to his description of the Chicago mail-order firm Sears, Roebuck and Co., where he worked. Since he had a relative working at Sears, Kafka must have read with interest Holitscher's description of the "metallic din" emitted by the Sears, Roebuck building, "which hovers above the coal dust and the Illinois fog like some uncanny music of the spheres, desolate and cold like the whole of the modern world and its civilization" (ibid., p. 308). It's worth juxtaposing a photograph of the vast Sears typing pool in Holitscher's travelogue with the description of the busy telegraph room in Uncle Jakob's business in *The Missing Person.*

25. In late fall 1911, when Franz Kafka was working on a draft of his American novel, Otto Kafka took his new American wife, Alice Stickney (daughter of a then-prominent American family and a possible model for the fictional Klara Pollunder), to visit his relatives in Kolin, Bohemia. It's likely that Kafka heard reports of his relatives' impressions of these two American visitors. Otto Kafka was evidently fond of a saying one could easily imagine on the lips of Karl Rossmann's American uncle: "One must learn to obey before one commands." A nononsense, self-confident individual, he never allowed himself to be cowed, even by powerful and well-connected opponents; he sued his business partner, General Coleman T. Du Pont (a former postmaster general and member of the well-known Du Pont industrialist family)—a headline in the *New York World,* 29 Jan-

uary 1918, read: "Kafka Threatens Du Pont with Suit." Several years later he sued the Mexican foreign minister, Adolfo de la Huerta—"Names de la Huerta in $2,500,000 Suit" ran a headline in the *New York Times,* 13 June 1922, p. 21. In a letter dated September 1918 to the assistant U.S. attorney general petitioning for his release from prison, where he was held unjustly on suspicion of being an enemy spy, Otto Kafka mentions that he began life in America "as a porter with a corset concern at $5 a week"; although Karl's American uncle does not mention having worked as a porter, he does take great pride in the fact that he employs a large number of porters. See Anthony Northey, *Kafka's Relatives: Their Lives and His Writing* (New Haven, Conn., 1991), pp. 52–56.

26. Borges suggested that Kafka is "closer to the Book of Job than to what has been called 'modern literature,' " and that his work is "based on a religious, and particularly Jewish, consciousness." See Jorge Luis Borges, *Selected Non-Fictions,* ed. Eliot Weinberger (New York, 1999), p. 501.

27. See, for instance, Robert Alter, "Franz Kafka: Wrenching Scripture," *New England Review* 21, no. 3 (2000), pp. 7–19.

28. Rossmann's hybrid name links him with a large number of hybrid half-human, half-animal or half-insect creatures in Kafka's fiction, ranging from the bug-man Gregor Samsa to Bucephalus in "The New Advocate," a lawyer and steed, who in a previous incarnation was the battle horse of Alexander the Great, and also with the narrator of the sketch "The Wish to Be a Red Indian," who imagines himself riding on the American prairie on a horse that is gradually vanishing underneath him.

29. As several critics have suggested, that odd theater, with its religious trappings, conjures up Holitscher's sketch of the charismatic sects in Chicago, where "on Sundays the dear Lord has a different face and a different name at every five paces" (pp. 285–89), and his description of how land is handed out to settlers in Winnipeg, Manitoba (pp. 131–37).

30. Max Brod, "Afterword," in *Amerika* (New York, 1954), p. 299.

31. Karl's American uncle uses a similar image to describe the way Karl's parents have treated him: in banishing him to America, they pushed him outside like a cat that has made a nuisance of itself.

32. Kafka asserts to Milena Jesenská, a Gentile, in a letter of August 1920, that he and Milena's Jewish husband "both have the same Negro face." Kafka, *Letters to Milena,* trans. Philip Boehm (New York, 1990), p. 136. For a discussion of Kafka's self-image as a Jew, see Sander L. Gilman, *Franz Kafka: The Jewish Patient* (New York, 1995).

33. See *Der Verschollene: Apparatband,* p. 85.

34. Kafka is scarcely implying that Karl's parents are without means, especially since we subsequently learn that Karl's father has a business that is sufficiently prosperous to employ a considerable number of people. See *Letters to Milena,* p. 13.

35. Here Kafka seems to imply that he harbors a comparable feeling toward his own parents; indeed, as Hartmut Binder has pointed out, he used the phrase "poor parents" similarly in a letter to Felice Bauer of 13–14 January 1913, con-

cerning his sister Valli's marriage: "My parents (here I cannot resist the temptation to call them 'my poor parents') were delighted with the festivities." See Hartmut Binder, *Kafka-Kommentar* (Munich, 1982), p. 85.

36. Although Karl Rossmann is interviewed at what seems like a hiring fair, Kafka never once uses the word *einstellen* (to hire). Instead, in the course of this short chapter he uses the word *aufnehmen* or variants thereof—i.e., "to be admitted or received"—some thirty times.

37. Kafka's German biographer Reiner Stach adds that Kafka's prose in *The Missing Person* "makes both things and people emerge in exaggeratedly sharp contours, as though seen under neon light." This seems just about right. See Stach, *Kafka: The Decisive Years*, trans. Shelley Frisch (New York, 2005), pp. 117–18.

38. Nicholas Murray, *Kafka: A Biography* (New Haven, Conn., 2004), p. 224.

39. For instance, the Prague-born critic Heinz Politzer praised the first sentence in the original German for its controlled and "intricately patterned periods" but censured the second as "artless, not quite coherent, and inconclusive." Politzer, *Parable,* p. 123. However, indicting Kafka for being inconclusive surely amounts to condemning Kafka for being Kafka. Besides, modern writers such as Joyce and Beckett have taught us to appreciate the way Kafka can slip into the consciousness of Karl Rossmann without inserting the kind of transitions one would expect in a nineteenth-century novel.

40. To the novelist Robert Musil, who linked Kafka and the Swiss writer Robert Walser in an early review of "The Stoker" and *Meditation (Betrachtung),* Karl Rossmann evokes a "feeling of excited children's prayers and something of the uneasy zeal of carefully-done school exercises and much which one can only describe with the phrase moral delicacy." See *Kafka: Kritik und Rezeption,* p. 35.

Amerika:
The Missing Person

I

THE STOKER

As he entered New York Harbor on the now slow-moving ship, Karl Rossmann, a seventeen-year-old youth who had been sent to America by his poor parents because a servant girl had seduced him and borne a child by him, saw the Statue of Liberty, which he had been observing for some time, as if in a sudden burst of sunlight. The arm with the sword now reached aloft, and about her figure blew the free winds.

"So high," he said to himself, and although he still had no thoughts of leaving, he found himself being pushed gradually toward the rail by an ever-swelling throng of porters.

In passing a young man whom he knew from the voyage said: "So you don't feel like getting off yet?" "Oh, I'm ready all right," said Karl with a laugh, and in his exuberance, sturdy lad that he was, he lifted his trunk up on his shoulders. But looking out over his acquaintance, who swung his walking stick several times as he set off with the other passengers, he realized that he had forgotten his umbrella below deck. Quickly he asked his acquaintance, who seemed not at all pleased, whether he would be so kind as to wait there for a moment with his trunk, surveyed the scene quickly so he could find his bearings on his return, and hurried off. Downstairs he was disappointed to find a passageway that would have certainly shortened his path blocked off for the first time, probably on account of all those disembarking passengers, and was obliged to make his way laboriously through numerous small rooms, corridors that constantly turned off, many short stairs in rapid succession and an empty room with an abandoned desk, until at last, having gone that way only once or twice and always in company, he had quite lost his way. In his uncertainty, not encountering a soul and hearing only the constant scraping of a thousand human feet above him, and from a distance like a last gasp the final workings of the engine being shut down, he began without further reflection to knock at random on a little door before which he had halted. "It's open," cried a voice from within and, sighing with genuine relief, Karl stepped into the cabin. "Why do you have to bang on the door like a madman?" a huge man asked, almost without looking at Karl. Through a skylight somewhere a dull light, already expended on the upper decks, fell into the miserable cabin, where a bed, a closet, a chair, and the man were packed side by side, as if in storage. "I've lost my way," said Karl, "on the voyage over I never really noticed what a terribly big ship this is." "Yes, you're right," the man said with a certain pride as he tinkered with the lock on a small suitcase, which he opened and closed continually with both hands, listening for the bolt to snap into place. "But do come in," the man continued, "you're hardly going to stand there like that." "Am I not disturbing you?" Karl asked. "How could you disturb me?" "Are you a German?" Karl sought to assure himself, for he had heard a great deal about the dangers facing newcomers in America, especially from Irishmen. "Yes, yes," said the man. Karl continued to hesitate. Suddenly the man seized the door handle and pulled Karl into the cabin along with the door, which he promptly shut. "I simply can't stand having people stare in at me from the corridor," the man said, toying with his trunk again. "Everyone who walks by looks in; who could possibly stand that?" "But the corridor is completely empty," said Karl, who was pressed uncomfortably against the bedpost. "It is now," said the man. When else but now? thought Karl. It's not easy talking to this man. "Lie down on the bed, that'll give you a bit more room," said the man. Karl crawled in as best he could, laughing loudly at his initially futile attempt to swing himself onto the bed. No sooner was he lying down than he cried: "Oh, my goodness, I forgot all about my trunk." "Well, where is it?" "Up on deck, an acquaintance of mine is keeping an eye on it. Let me see, his name is . . . ?" From the secret pocket his mother had attached to the lining of his coat, Karl drew a visiting card: "Butterbaum, Franz Butterbaum." "Do you really need the trunk?" "Of course I do." "Then why did you give it to a stranger?" "I had forgotten my umbrella below deck, so I ran to get it, but didn't want to drag along my trunk. And then I got lost." "You're alone? Unaccompanied?" "Yes, I'm alone." Perhaps I should stick with this man—thought Karl—for where else could I find a better friend just now? "And you've lost your trunk too. Not to mention your umbrella," and the man sat down on the chair as though he had begun to take an interest in Karl's affair. "But I don't believe that my trunk is lost." "Blessed are those who believe," said the man, giving his thick short dark hair a vigorous scratching. "People's conduct on board ship varies from one port to the next; in Hamburg your friend Butterbaum might have looked after your trunk, but here both will probably disappear without a trace." "Well, in that case I'll have to check up on deck at once," said Karl, looking around for a way out. "Stay," the man said and, putting his hand on Karl's chest, pushed him roughly back onto the bed. "But why?" asked Karl, who had become annoyed. "It makes no sense," said the man. "I'll be leaving in a moment, and we can go together. Either the trunk has been stolen, in which case it's hopeless and you can moan about it till the end of your days, or that person is still looking after it, in which case he's an idiot and should keep on looking after it, or else he's just an honest man who has left the trunk there, and it'll be easier to find if we wait till the ship has emptied out completely. The same goes for your umbrella." "Do you know your way around the ship?" Karl asked suspiciously, for he believed there must be some hidden flaw in the otherwise convincing notion that his belongings could be more easily found when the ship was empty. "But I'm a stoker," said the man. "You are a stoker," Karl cried with delight, as if this announcement surpassed all his expectations, and propping up on his elbows, he took a closer look at the man. "One could see into the engine room through a hatch next to the cabin in which I slept in with the Slovaks." "Yes, that's where I worked," said the stoker. "I've always been very interested in technology," said Karl, following his own train of thought, "and would no doubt have eventually become an engineer if I hadn't had to go away to America." "But why did you have to go away?" "Ah well!" said Karl, dismissing the entire affair with a wave of his hand. At the same time he smiled at the stoker as though seeking indulgence concerning matters that he had not disclosed. "But there must have been a reason," said the stoker, and one could not tell whether he was requesting an explanation or attempting to forestall one. "I too could become a stoker," said Karl, "my parents no longer care what I do." "There'll be an opening for my job," said the stoker, and basking in this knowledge, he put his hands in his trouser pockets and stretched out by swinging his legs, which were clad in creased leatherlike iron-gray trousers, onto the bed. Karl had to move closer to the wall. "You're leaving ship?" "Oh yes, we're marching off today." "But why? Don't you like it here?" "Well, that's just how it is; one's own preferences aren't always taken into account. Besides, you're right, I don't like it here. In any case, you're probably not completely set on becoming a stoker, though that's actually when it's most

likely to happen. So I strongly advise against it. If you wanted
to study in Europe, why wouldn't you want to study here? The
American universities are, of course, incomparably better."
"That may well be so," said Karl, "but I've barely any money
to pay for my studies. I once read about someone who worked
for a business by day and studied at night till he became a
doctor and then, I believe, a mayor. But that takes great perse-
verance, doesn't it? And that's something I'm afraid I lack.
Besides, I wasn't an especially good student, and it wasn't that
hard for me to leave school. And the schools over here may be
even stricter. I know hardly any English. In any case people
here are often very prejudiced against foreigners." "So you've
already run into this too? In that case everything is fine. Then
you're my man. You see, we're on a German ship, it belongs to
the Hamburg Amerika Line, so why aren't all of us here Germans? Why is the chief machinist a Romanian? His name is
Schubal. It's really incredible. And that scoundrel mistreats us
Germans on a German ship. Now I don't want you to get the
idea"—he was out of breath now and fanned himself with his
hand—"that I'm complaining for the sake of complaining. I
know you've no influence and are only a poor little fellow. But
this is too awful." And he pounded several times on the table,
keeping his eyes on his fist as he did so. "I've served on so many
ships"—he reeled off twenty names as if they were a single word;
Karl became very confused—"made my mark, got praised, all
of the captains greatly appreciated my work, and even spent
several years serving on the same merchant vessel." He stood
up as if this were the high point in his life—"and here on this
tub, where everything is kept on such a tight leash, where one
may not even joke around—I'm useless, always get in Schubal's
way, am simply a lazybones who deserves to be thrown out,
and am paid only out of pity. Can you understand that? I certainly can't." "You shouldn't stand for it," Karl said in an agi-

tated voice. So at home did he feel on the stoker's bed that he had almost lost the feeling that he stood on the uncertain ground of a ship moored off the coast of an unfamiliar continent. "Have you been to the captain? Have you sought to obtain your rights from him?" "Oh go away, just go away. I don't want you here. You don't listen to what I have to say and then try to give me advice. How could I possibly go to the captain?" And the stoker sat down wearily, burying his face in both hands. "I couldn't have given him any better advice," Karl said to himself. And it occurred to him that he should have fetched his trunk rather than remain here and make suggestions only to hear them dismissed as stupid. On entrusting him with the trunk, his father had asked him in jest: How long will you hang on to it? And now that expensive trunk was perhaps lost. The only consolation was that his father would not discover anything about his present circumstances, even if he were to make inquiries. All the shipping company could say was that he had reached New York. Karl did regret, though, that he had barely made use of the belongings in the suitcase, especially since he should have changed his shirt sometime ago. So he had been economizing in the wrong places; now, at the outset of his new career, precisely when he needed to appear in clean clothes, he would have to turn up in a dirty shirt. What wonderful prospects! Otherwise the loss of the trunk wouldn't have been so bad, since the suit he wore was better than the one in the trunk, which was meant only for emergencies and had been patched by his mother shortly before he left. He remembered now that there was still a piece of Veronese salami in the trunk, which his mother had packed in as an extra present, but of which he had eaten only the tiniest portion, for he had not had much of an appetite during the voyage and the soup handed out in steerage had more than sufficed. He would have liked to get his hands on the sausage so that he could bequeath it to the stoker. For one could gain the confidence of such people quite easily, merely by slipping them a little something; Karl knew this from his father, who had gained the confidence of all the lower-ranking employees he dealt with by handing out cigars. All that remained for Karl to give away was a little money, but now that he had perhaps lost his trunk, he did not want to touch that for the moment. His thoughts returned to the trunk, and he could no longer understand why he had even bothered to keep such close watch over his trunk that he had barely slept, only to let somebody relieve him of it so easily. He recalled the five nights he had lain in bed always suspecting that a little Slovak two beds away had his eyes on the trunk. That Slovak had awaited the moment when Karl would at last succumb to weakness and doze off so that he would then be able to take the long stick, with which he had played or possibly practiced all day, and pull the trunk over to his bed. By day the Slovak looked fairly innocent, but when darkness fell he would rise occasionally from his bed and look over at Karl's trunk with a mournful expression on his face. Karl could observe this very clearly, for there was always someone prey to an emigrant's unease who would turn on a little light—even though the ship's regulations expressly forbade this—and attempt to decipher the incomprehensible brochures put out by the emigration agencies. If there was such a light nearby, Karl could doze off for a while, but if it was some distance away or the room was dark, he had to keep his eyes open. These exertions had left him quite exhausted. And had perhaps been in vain. Woe betide that Butterbaum, should he ever run into him again!

Just then, interrupting the perfect silence, came the sound of short little taps, as of children's feet approaching from afar; as they came closer, the sound grew louder and was now that of steadily marching men. They seemed to advance in single file, as was only natural in this narrow passageway; one could hear a clashing as of weapons. About to stretch out in bed and fall asleep, freed at last from all concerns about trunks and Slovaks, Karl gave a start and nudged the stoker so as to alert him, since the head of the procession appeared to have reached the door. "It's the ship's band," said the stoker. "They've played up on deck and are going inside to pack. Everything's ready, so we can leave. Come on." Taking Karl by the hand, he at the last moment seized a picture of the Madonna from the wall above his bed, stuffed it into his breast pocket, grabbed his trunk, and left the cabin quickly with Karl.

"I'm going to the office to give these gentlemen a piece of my mind. There's nobody around anymore, so it's no longer necessary to watch what one says," the stoker said repeatedly, using a variety of formulations, and without breaking stride gave a few side kicks to flatten a rat that had crossed his path, but he merely succeeded in driving it even more quickly into its hole, which it reached just in time. Besides, his movements were slow, for though he had very long legs, they nonetheless weighed him down.

They passed through a section of the kitchen where some girls in dirty aprons—which they wet deliberately—were washing dishes in great tubs. The stoker called over a certain Line, put his arm around her hips, and as she pressed coquettishly against his arm, swept her along for a moment. "It's payday, you want to come along?" he asked. "Why should I bother, you can bring me my money," she replied, and, slipping out from under his arm, ran off. "So where did you pick up that pretty boy," she cried out again, without expecting a reply. One could hear laughter from all of the girls, who had interrupted their work.

Nevertheless they continued on their way and soon reached a door capped with a little pediment supported by small gilded caryatids. As a fixture on a ship, it looked fairly extravagant.

Karl realized that he had never entered this area, which was probably reserved during the voyage for first- and second-class passengers, but just before the great ship cleaning, the partition doors had been taken down. Indeed, they had already encountered several men carrying brooms on their shoulders, who had greeted the stoker. Karl marveled at the bustle; in steerage he had for sure witnessed little of this. Also, there were electrical cords strung along both sides of the corridor, and one could hear a little bell ringing continuously.

The stoker knocked on the door respectfully, and when a voice cried "Come in," he motioned to Karl that he should enter without trepidation. He complied but did not advance far beyond the door. Through the room's three windows Karl could see the ocean waves, and as he watched their cheerful movements, his heart began to beat more rapidly as though he had not spent five long days gazing uninterruptedly at the sea. Large ships crossed one another's paths, yielding to the rolling waves only insofar as their weight permitted. If one narrowed one's eyes, the ships seemed to rock under the pressure of their weight. Upon their masts were narrow but elongated flags that, though tautened by the ships' motion, still flapped to and fro. The sound of gun salutes could be heard, probably from warships; as reflected on a glistening coat of steel the cannon barrels of one such passing ship seemed almost coddled by its smooth, steady, yet not-quite-straightforward progress through the waves. At least from one's position by the door one could catch but a distant glimpse of the huge number of small ships and boats constantly slipping through the gaps between the large ships. Behind all this, however, stood New York, gazing at Karl with the hundred thousand windows of its skyscrapers. In this room one knew where one was.

Sitting at a round table were three gentlemen, one an officer in the blue uniform of the ship, the other two harbor authority officials in black American uniforms. Piled high on the table were various documents, which the ship's officer first skimmed, pen in hand, before passing them to the other two, who now read them, now copied out passages, now put them in their briefcases, unless the official who made almost continuous little grinding noises with his teeth happened to be dictating a transcript to his colleague.

By a desk at the window, with his back to the door, sat a smallish gentleman who was occupied with great folio ledgers, which were lined up before him on a sturdy bookshelf at head level. Beside him stood an open cash box, which—at least at first glance—was empty.

The second window, which was vacant, afforded the best view. At the third, however, stood two gentlemen, speaking in undertones. One, leaning against the window and dressed in the ship's uniform, toyed with the handle of his sword. His interlocutor, who stood facing the window, moved a little now and then, exposing the row of decorations on the other man's chest. The latter wore civilian clothes and carried a small thin bamboo stick that, owing to the way both hands rested on his hips, stood out like a sword.

Karl had little time to gaze at everything, for before long an attendant approached them, looked at the stoker as though he did not belong there, and asked him what he wanted. Responding as softly as he had been asked, the stoker said that he wished to speak to the chief bursar. The attendant dismissed this request with a wave of his hand, but nonetheless, tiptoeing in a wide arc around the circular table, he approached the gentleman beside the folios. At last that gentleman, who, as one could see quite clearly, almost froze on hearing the attendant's words, looked around at the man who wished to speak to him, dismissed the stoker with a vehement gesture and, just to be sure, the attendant likewise. The latter returned to the stoker and, as if imparting a confidence, said: "Get out at once!"

Upon hearing these words, the stoker gazed down at Karl, as though Karl were a sweetheart to whom he was silently pouring out his woes. Without further reflection Karl broke free, ran straight across the room, and even brushed up against the officer's chair; the servant ran after him, bent low, arms ready to make a catch, as though chasing vermin, but Karl reached the chief bursar's table first and clung to it in case the servant should try to pull him away.

All of a sudden the entire room became animated. The ship's officer jumped up from the table; the gentlemen from the port authority watched, calmly but alertly; the two gentlemen at the window now stood side by side; the attendant, believing his presence was no longer required since even the distinguished gentlemen were now taking an interest in the matter, stepped aside. By the door the stoker waited intently for the moment when his help should be needed again. And finally the chief bursar in his armchair swiveled sharply to the right.

Karl rummaged through his secret pocket, which he had no hesitation in showing to these people, took out his passport, and rather than saying a few words by way of introduction, simply laid it down open on the table. The chief bursar seemed to attach little significance to the passport, for he flicked it aside with two fingers, whereupon Karl put it away, as though the formality had been satisfactorily resolved. "If I may say so," he began, "I believe that the stoker has been treated unjustly. There's a certain Schubal on board, who's been giving him trouble. He's served in a most satisfactory manner on many ships—he can give you their names—is diligent, does his work in good faith, and so it's rather difficult to understand how he could possibly be ill suited for a job on this particular ship, where the work is not so exceedingly difficult as, say, on merchant vessels. So those slanderous allegations are all that stands between him and the advancement and recognition that would otherwise be his due. I've addressed this matter only in the most general terms, he himself will inform you about his specific complaints." Karl had directed his remarks at all of the gentlemen, since everybody was indeed listening, and it seemed much more likely that there should be a fair-minded person in their midst than that the fair-minded one should happen to be the chief bursar. Karl had, to be sure, neglected to mention that he had not known the stoker long. Also, he would have come up with an even better speech had he not been distracted by the red face of that gentleman with the little bamboo stick, and indeed it was only now from this new vantage point that he had first noticed him.

"It's all true, word for word," said the stoker, before anyone had asked him a question, let alone glanced in his direction. The impulsiveness of the stoker would have been a grave mistake if the gentleman with the decorations—who, as Karl now realized, was indeed the captain—had not already decided to hear out the stoker. The captain reached out his hand and called to the stoker: "Come here!" in a voice so firm that one could have almost hit it with a hammer. And now everything depended on how the stoker conducted himself, for Karl had no doubt about the justice of his case.

Fortunately, it soon became clear that the stoker was a man who had seen a great deal of the world. With exemplary composure he reached into his little suitcase and on his first attempt pulled out a little bundle of papers and a notebook, and then, as if this were the most obvious course of action, completely ignoring the chief bursar, he went over to the captain and spread out his evidence on the windowsill. The chief bursar had no alternative but to join them. "That fellow is a notorious crank," he said by way of explanation, "he spends more time in the bursar's office than in the machine room and has driven even Schubal, who's such a calm man, to despair. Now listen to me once and for all!" he said, addressing the stoker, "you've been far too intrusive. How often have you been justifiably thrown out of the disbursement rooms for continually making such demands, which always turn out to be completely unreasonable! How often have you run over from those rooms to the main cash office! How often were you politely informed that Schubal is your immediate superior and that you, as his subordinate, must learn to live with him! And you even come in here when the captain is present; you're not ashamed to disturb him and dare to bring along this little fellow, whom you've taught to reel off your fatuous accusations and whom I'm now seeing for the first time on board."

Karl had to restrain himself from intervening. However, the captain had already approached them and said: "But let's listen to what the man has to say. In any case I think Schubal has become much too independent of late, though this doesn't necessarily speak in your favor." Those last words were directed at the stoker; of course, it was only natural that the captain could not take his side right away, but otherwise everything seemed to be going well. The stoker launched into his explanations, and, overcoming his reluctance, began by addressing Schubal as "Mister." This greatly pleased Karl, who stood by the chief bursar's deserted desk, pressing the letter scales repeatedly in sheer delight: Mr. Schubal is unfair. Mr. Schubal gives preferential treatment to foreigners. Mr. Schubal banished the stoker from the engine room and made him clean toilets, which was certainly not his responsibility. At one point the stoker even questioned the competence of Mr. Schubal, which was, he claimed, more apparent than real. Whereupon Karl directed a most intent look at the captain, assuming an engagingly collegial expression merely so as to prevent such an awkward manner of speaking from disposing the captain unfavorably toward the stoker. There was indeed little enough to be gleaned from the latter's many speeches, and although the captain continued to stare into space with eyes that showed his determination to hear out the stoker, the other gentlemen were becoming impatient, and ominously enough, the stoker's voice no longer held sway in the room. The gentleman in civilian clothes was the first to move, stirring his little bamboo stick and tapping the parquet floor with it, if ever so lightly. Every now and then the other gentlemen glanced over; clearly in a hurry, the gentlemen from the harbor authority returned to their files and began to peruse them, if still rather absently; the ship's officer returned to his position beside his table, and believing that he had carried the day, the chief bursar heaved a great ironic sigh. The only person who was evidently immune from this general distraction was the attendant, who could at least partially sympathize with the sorrows of a poor man who had suddenly been set down amid the mighty, and who nodded gravely at Karl, as though wishing to explain something.

Meanwhile, beyond the windows, the life of the harbor went on: a flat cargo ship transporting a huge pile of barrels, which must have been marvelously well stacked to prevent their rolling about, passed by, plunging the room into almost complete darkness; little motorboats, which Karl could have observed more closely if only he had had the time, rushed straight ahead, guided by the jerking hand of a man who stood erect at the steering wheel; now and then peculiar floating objects bobbed up from the choppy waters of their own accord, only to be quickly covered and to sink before one's startled eyes; perspiring sailors rowed away from ocean steamers in boats filled with passengers who remained seated expectantly, mostly in silence, in the same seats into which they had been pressed, although some could not refrain from turning their heads to gaze at the changing scenery. There was endless motion, and unrest borne from the restless element to helpless men and their works.

But although everything cried out for haste, clarity, and the

most precise description, what did the stoker do? He had certainly talked himself into a sweat and was no longer able to
hold the papers on the windowsill in his trembling hands; he
kept thinking of new complaints about Schubal from every
conceivable angle, each of which would, he believed, have sufficed to demolish Schubal, although he had managed to give
the captain only a pathetic mishmash of all that. For some
time now the gentleman with the little bamboo stick had been
whistling softly at the ceiling; the gentlemen from the harbor
authority had detained the officer at their table and gave no
sign that they were about to release him; only the composure
shown by the captain made the chief bursar refrain from bursting in, as he longed to do. The attendant, who stood at attention, awaited an imminent order from his captain with regard
to the stoker.

Karl could no longer remain idle. So he walked slowly toward
the group, considering all the more quickly as he approached
how best to tackle the matter. It was truly high time—any
moment both could be sent flying from the office. The captain
might indeed be a good man and might especially now, Karl
thought, have a particular reason for wishing to show himself a
just superior, but in the end he was not merely an instrument
one could go on playing until it fell apart—and that was precisely how the stoker was treating him, though of course only
out of the boundless indignation of his heart.

So Karl said to the stoker: "You must speak more simply,
and more clearly too; the captain cannot understand your story
because of the way you're telling it. Can he really be so utterly
familiar with all of the family names, let alone the first names,
of the machinists and the messengers that you need only give
somebody's name and he will know at once whom you mean?
Organize your complaints, start off with the most important
followed by the rest, and then you may never have to mention

the greater part of them. After all, you've always given me such clear explanations of everything." If one can steal trunks in America, one can also tell a lie every now and then, he thought to himself by way of excuse.

If only it had helped! Might it be too late? On hearing that familiar voice, the stoker broke off in spite of the fact that he could hardly even recognize Karl, for his eyes were filled with tears, tears of wounded male honor, of dreadful memories, and of his extreme current distress. But how—the thought occurred to Karl, who had fallen silent, as he stood facing the now equally silent stoker—but how was he all of a sudden supposed to change the way he spoke, especially since he believed he had already brought up everything that needed to be said without obtaining even the slightest acknowledgment, and as if on the other hand he had still not said anything and could hardly expect the gentlemen to listen to everything all over again? And at that very moment along comes Karl.

"If only I had come sooner instead of gazing out that window," Karl said to himself, and, lowering his head in front of the stoker, he slapped the seams of his trousers to signal the end of all hope.

However, possibly sensing that Karl harbored furtive reproaches against him, the stoker misunderstood the gesture and, with the praiseworthy intention of getting Karl to change his mind, crowned his deeds by picking a fight. And did so just now, when the gentlemen at the round table had become annoyed at the useless noise distracting them from their important work, when the chief bursar had finally found the captain's patience incomprehensible and was tempted to erupt there and then, when the servant, now back in his masters' sphere, was sizing up the stoker with wild looks, and finally, when the gentleman holding the little bamboo stick—even the captain cast friendly glances at him every now and then—

having become completely deadened to the stoker and even
disgusted by him, took out a small notebook, and, evidently
preoccupied with entirely different matters, let his eyes wander
back and forth between his notebook and Karl.

"Yes, I know, I know," said Karl, who had difficulty warding off the torrent of words that the stoker now directed at
him; yet amid all the strife he still managed to spare a smile for
him. "You're right, quite right, I never had the slightest doubt
about it." Anxious about blows, Karl would have liked to
catch the stoker's flailing hands or, better still, push him into a
corner so as to whisper in his ear a few soft, soothing words,
which no one else needed to hear. But the stoker had already
gone berserk. Karl even began to draw a certain comfort from
the thought that the stoker could in a pinch overpower all
seven men in this room through the sheer force of his despair.
In any case, as a quick glance at the desk showed, it had a panel
for the electric current with far too many buttons on it, and a
single hand pressing down on them could make the entire ship,
and all its passageways filled with hostile people, rise up in
rebellion.

The seemingly indifferent gentleman with the little bamboo
stick then approached Karl, and asked quite softly, though
loudly enough to be clearly overheard over the shouting from
the stoker: "So what's your name?" At that moment, as if someone had waited behind the door until the gentleman uttered
those words, there was a knock. In response the servant looked
at the captain; the latter nodded. Whereupon the servant went
to the door and opened it. In an old imperial frock coat stood a
man of medium build, who judging by his appearance was not
especially cut out for working with machines, yet it was indeed
Schubal. Had Karl not been able to gather as much from the
hint of satisfaction in everyone's eyes, to which not even the
captain was immune, he would inevitably, and much to his dis-

may, have recognized it in the posture of the stoker, who had clenched his fists at the end of his stiffened arms, as if this clenching were paramount, and as if he were prepared to sacrifice his entire life for its sake. All of his strength was concentrated there, even that which held him erect.

And so there stood the enemy, looking sovereign and fresh in his fancy suit, with an account book under his arm, probably the stoker's pay dockets and work records, and—without making the slightest effort to conceal that his foremost desire was to gauge everyone's mood—he looked each person in the eye, one by one. All seven were his friends, for even if the captain had had reservations about him earlier or had perhaps merely feigned to have had, after all the trouble the stoker had caused him, he would surely no longer have the slightest objection to Schubal. One could not be sufficiently severe with a man such as the stoker, and if Schubal could be reproached in any way it was for not having succeeded over time in reining in the stoker's obstinacy well enough to ensure that he would not have the audacity to appear before the captain as he had just done.

Well, perhaps one could still assume that the effect that this juxtaposition of the stoker and Schubal would have on a higher forum would not be lost on human beings, for even if Schubal managed to put on a sham, he could not necessarily keep it up indefinitely. His vileness need only peek through for a moment, and the gentlemen would notice it; Karl would make sure that would happen. After all, he had more than a passing acquaintance with the shrewdness, weaknesses, and moods of the various gentlemen, and so at least from that point of view, the time he had spent here had not been wasted. If the stoker had only stood his ground, but he seemed absolutely unable to fight. Had they dangled Schubal before him, he might have taken his fist and split that hated skull, like a thin-shelled nut. But even those few steps toward Schubal would probably be beyond him.

Why had Karl not foreseen something so easily foreseen, namely, that Schubal would finally be obliged to come, if not on his own initiative then on a summons from the captain? Why hadn't he devised a precise battle plan as he walked over with the stoker instead of entering mercilessly unprepared simply because there was a door there? Could the stoker still speak, say yes and no, as he would be required to do in the cross-examination that would take place only if everything turned out for the best. The stoker stood there, legs apart, knees slightly bowed, head raised slightly, and the air went in and out of his open mouth as if he had no lungs left inside to handle his breathing.

Still, Karl felt stronger and more alert than he had perhaps ever felt at home. If only his parents could have seen him defending a good cause before respected figures in a foreign land, and even if he had still not achieved victory, he was fully prepared to embark on the final conquest. Would they change their mind about him? Set him down between them and praise him? And then once, only once, take a look into these eyes, eyes that were so devoted to them? What uncertain questions, and what an inappropriate moment to be asking them!

"I've come because I think the stoker is accusing me of some kind of dishonesty. A girl from the kitchen told me she had seen him heading this way. Captain, all you gentlemen, I'm ready to refute each such accusation by drawing on my papers and, if necessary, on statements from independent and impartial witnesses, who are standing outside." Those were Schubal's words. He had certainly given a clear, manly speech, and one might have assumed from the changed expressions on his audience's faces that it had been quite some time since they had last heard a human voice. So of course they failed to notice that this fine speech had a few holes in it. Why was "dishonesty" the first pertinent word he came up with? Wouldn't it have been better to start off with that accusation rather than with his nationalistic prejudices? A girl from the kitchen had seen the stoker going toward the office, and Schubal had immediately understood what was going on? Mustn't his wits have been sharpened by guilt? And hadn't he brought along witnesses and even called them unprejudiced and impartial. It was a scam, nothing but a scam, and weren't the gentlemen not only tolerating it but even recognizing it as proper conduct? Why had he let so much time slip by after being told by the kitchen girl, if not simply to let the stoker wear down the gentlemen and thereby ensure that they would slowly lose their ability to make clear judgments, from which Schubal had most to fear? After standing outside the door, no doubt for some time, had he not waited to knock until after the gentleman had asked that trivial question and he could with good reason hope that the stoker had already been dispatched?

All this was very clear and indeed that is how Schubal had presented it, quite against his will, but one had to tell the story to the gentlemen in a different way, even more explicitly. They had to be given a jolt. So get moving, Karl, and at least take advantage of the time before the witnesses enter and inundate everything.

Just then, however, the captain waved away Schubal, who stepped aside at once—for his affair seemed to have been put off for a while—and, turning to the servant, who had just joined him, he began a muttered conversation, underscored by the most emphatic gestures and frequent sidelong glances at the stoker and at Karl. Schubal seemed to be preparing in this way for his next great speech.

"Mr. Jakob, wasn't there something you wanted to ask this young man?" the captain said to the gentleman with the bamboo stick amid general silence.

"Certainly," said the latter, thanking the captain for his attentiveness with a little bow. And he reiterated the question that he had asked Karl: "So what's your name?"

Karl, who believed that the important matter at stake could be best served by getting rid of this stubborn questioner as quickly as possible, answered briefly, without, as was his custom, introducing himself by producing his passport, which he would in any case have first needed to find: "Karl Rossmann."

"But," said the man who had been addressed as Jakob, smiling almost incredulously, and he withdrew a few steps. On hearing Karl's name, the captain, the chief bursar, the ship's officer, and even the servant clearly showed excessive astonishment. Only the gentlemen from the harbor authority and Schubal responded with indifference.

"But," repeated Mr. Jakob, approaching Karl with a rather stiff gait, "but then I am indeed your uncle Jakob, and you are my beloved nephew. Just as I suspected all along," he said to the captain before embracing and kissing Karl, who endured this display of affection in silence.

Sensing that he had been released, Karl asked very politely yet also quite unmoved: "What's your name?" At the same time he sought to predict the repercussions that this latest occurrence might have for the stoker. There was no sign just now that Schubal could profit from this affair.

"Try, young man, try to understand your good fortune," said the captain, who believed that the question that Karl had asked had offended the dignity of Mr. Jakob, who had gone to the window, evidently to avoid having to show his agitated face, which he even dabbed with a handkerchief. "The man who identified himself as your uncle is none other than State Counselor Edward Jakob. Probably very much in contrast to your previous expectations, you can now look forward to a dazzling career. Try to understand this as well as you can right now, and make an effort to pull yourself together."

"I do have an uncle Jakob in America," said Karl, turning to the captain, "but if I understood you correctly, Jakob is just the state counselor's family name."

"Yes, that's quite true," said the captain expectantly.

"Well, Jakob, my mother's brother, has Jakob as a baptismal name whereas his family name would have to be identical to my mother's, and her maiden name is Bendelmayer."

"Gentlemen!" cried the state counselor, responding to Karl's statement as he returned in good spirits from his refuge by the window. Everyone, aside from the harbor officials, burst out laughing, some as if moved, others rather inscrutably.

What I said wasn't all that ridiculous, Karl thought.

"Gentlemen," the state counselor repeated, "you're taking part in a little family scene, and I owe you an explanation, since I believe that only the captain"—this remark led to an exchange of bows—"has been fully informed about this."

"Now I'll really have to pay attention to every word they say," Karl said to himself, and he was pleased to see from a side glance that the stoker was beginning to show signs of life again.

"Throughout all the long years of my American sojourn— but the word *sojourn* hardly suits the American citizen that I certainly am with all my soul—throughout all those long years I have lived completely cut off from my European relatives for reasons that are, first, beside the point and, second, too painful to disclose. I even fear the moment when I shall be compelled to disclose them to my dear nephew, for there's unfortunately no way I can avoid saying a few frank words about his parents and their kin."

"He is my uncle, there's no doubt about it," Karl said to himself, and he listened carefully. "He probably had his name changed."

"My dear nephew was simply—let's not shy away from the word that really describes what happened—was simply cast aside by his parents, the way one throws out a cat when it becomes annoying. I certainly don't want to gloss over what my nephew did to merit that kind of punishment—one doesn't gloss over things in America—but his guilt is such that merely identifying it is excuse enough."

That's not bad at all, Karl thought. But I don't want him telling everyone. Besides, how can he know? Who could have told him? But we'll see, maybe he does know everything.

"He was, you see"—Karl's uncle continued, and as he spoke he kept tilting forward a little on his small bamboo stick, which he had propped up before him, thereby managing to relieve the affair of a certain solemnity it would otherwise have assumed— "he was, you see, seduced by Johanna Brummer, a servant girl, who's about thirty-five years old. In using the word *seduced,* I certainly don't wish to hurt my nephew, but it's hard to come up with a term that's just as apt."

Karl, who had moved close to his uncle, turned around to gauge the impact of the story from the expressions of all present. Nobody laughed, everyone listened patiently and in earnest. Well, one doesn't laugh at the nephew of the state counselor the first time one gets a chance to do so. But the stoker seemed to be smiling at Karl, even if only faintly, which was, first, a welcome new sign of life and, second, excusable, for this matter which now was being discussed so openly was one that earlier in the cabin Karl had sought to keep a special secret.

"Well, this Brummer woman," his uncle continued, "had a child by my nephew, a healthy boy, who was given the name Jakob at baptism, no doubt in honor of my humble self, and even though any references to me could only have been very casual they must nonetheless have left a big impression on the girl. And I'd say that was quite fortunate. For to avoid paying child support or whatever part of the scandal touched them directly—and here I should emphasize that I have no knowledge of the laws there nor of his parents' circumstances in other respects, and that everything I know comes from two begging letters I received from his parents a number of years ago, which

I kept but never answered, and this was the only, and naturally one-sided, correspondence I've had with them the entire time— well, to avoid those child support payments and the whole scandal, his parents shipped off their son, my dear nephew, to America and, as one can see, made such inadequate and indeed irresponsible provision for him that if the boy had been left to fend for himself in this manner—leaving aside the omens and wonders one can still encounter, especially here in America—he would no doubt have gone to seed quickly in some alleyway or other in New York Harbor if the servant girl hadn't given me a complete account along with a description of my nephew and also, very cleverly, the ship's name in a letter that after various lengthy detours reached me only the day before yesterday. If my main intention was to entertain you, gentlemen, there are several passages in this letter"—from his pocket he drew two enormous sheets of paper filled with cramped writing and waved them about—"that I could certainly read aloud. It would definitely leave an impression on you, for it is written with a rather artless, if always well-meant, cunning and with much love for the father of her child. But I don't wish to entertain you more than is necessary for the sake of clarification; nor do I wish to hurt any feelings my nephew may still have for the girl, especially just as he's being made welcome here; if he wishes, he may for his edification read this letter in the quiet of his room, which is now ready to receive him."

Karl, however, had no feelings for that girl. Amid the crush of a past that he had pushed back ever further, she sat in the kitchen beside the cabinet, with her elbows resting on the countertop. She would look at him when he went to the kitchen to fetch a glass of water for his father or to run an errand for his mother. Sometimes she would be sitting beside the cabinet in that same awkward position, writing a letter and drawing inspiration from Karl's face. Sometimes she would hide her eyes with her hand, and then no greeting could reach her. Sometimes she would be kneeling in her narrow little room next to the kitchen, praying to a wooden cross, and at such moments when he walked past, Karl would merely watch her timidly through the slightly open door. Sometimes she would race around the kitchen, and whenever Karl happened to get in her way, she would shrink back, breaking out in witchlike laughter. Sometimes she would close the kitchen door after Karl had entered and keep her hand on the knob until he asked for permission to leave. Sometimes she would fetch things that he did not even want and press them into his hands without saying a word. On one occasion, however, she said "Karl!" and then, grimacing and moaning, led Karl, who was still astonished at being addressed by his first name, into her little room, which she locked behind her. She put her arms around his neck and seized it in a stranglehold, and though she had asked him to undress her, it was she who undressed him and put him in her bed, as if she would never surrender him to anyone else and wanted to go on stroking him and caring for him until the end of the world. "Karl, oh my Karl," she cried, as if she could see him and was confirming that she now had possession of him, whereas he could see nothing and felt uncomfortable under the many warm bedclothes that she had evidently heaped up especially for him. Then she lay down beside him and wanted him to tell her secrets, but he had none to tell, and she became annoyed, whether jokingly or in earnest, shook him, listened to his heart, offered him her breast so that he too could listen but could not induce Karl to do so, pressed her naked belly against his body, searched between his legs with her hand—in such a revolting manner that Karl shook his head and throat out from under the quilts—then pushed her belly up against him several times; it felt as if she were part of him; hence perhaps the terrible helplessness that overcame him. In tears, after listening to repeated wishes that they should meet again, he reached his bed. There was no more to it than that, but his uncle still managed to make a big thing of it. So the cook had actually thought about him and had let his uncle know he was coming. That was good of her, and at some point he might well repay her.

"And now," cried the senator, "I want you to tell me frankly whether I'm your uncle or not."

"You are my uncle," said Karl, kissing his uncle's hand and in turn receiving kisses on the forehead. "I'm very pleased to have met you, but you're mistaken if you think my parents said nothing but bad things about you. But even aside from that, your speech did have a couple of mistakes in it; for instance, I don't really think that's how everything happened. Also, you can't gauge things that well from over here; besides, it'll be no great harm if the gentlemen were slightly misinformed about an affair that surely means little to them."

"Well put," said the senator, and leading Karl toward the visibly sympathetic captain, he said: "Don't I have a splendid nephew?"

"Mr. Senator," said the captain, bowing in a manner only people with military training can carry off, "I'm happy to have become acquainted with your nephew. It was a great honor for my ship to have been chosen as the setting for such an encounter. But your voyage in steerage must have been quite dreadful; well, one can never tell who's being transported in there. Even, for instance, the firstborn son of the top Hungarian magnate—I've already forgotten his name and the reason for his voyage—who made a crossing once in steerage. I only found out about it much later. We do everything we can to make the voyage easier for those in steerage, a lot more than, say, the American lines, but we still haven't succeeded in making such voyages pleasurable."

"It did me no harm," said Karl.

"It did him no harm!" the senator repeated, laughing very loudly.

"But as for my trunk, I'm afraid I've lost . . ." And just then it all came back to him, everything that had happened and everything that still needed to be done, and looking about him, he saw that every person in the room still stood in the same position, silent in astonishment and respect, with their eyes fixed on him. Only in the harbor officials could one see—insofar as their severe, complacent faces revealed anything whatsoever—that they regretted having come at such an inconvenient moment and indeed they showed greater interest in the watch lying in front of them than in anything going on in that room and in anything that might still go on there.

Oddly enough, the first person after the captain to express his good wishes was the stoker. "My heartfelt congratulations," and he shook Karl's hand, thereby seeking to convey something akin to appreciation also. Yet when he subsequently attempted to address the same words to the senator, the latter withdrew as if the stoker had overstepped his bounds; the stoker immediately desisted.

The others, however, saw what was needed, and quickly gathered about Karl and the senator in a clamoring mass. In this way Karl even received Schubal's congratulations, which he accepted and for which he in turn thanked Schubal. Finally, the harbor officials joined them, and amid the renewed silence, said two words in English, which left a ridiculous impression.

Intent on savoring the occasion to the full, the senator reminded himself and the others of the more incidental details, which everybody not only tolerated but listened to raptly. He observed that he had jotted down in his notebook a list of Karl's most distinctive traits, as described in the cook's letter, so that he could, if necessary, refer to it quickly. Then, while the stoker kept up his intolerable chatter, he had pulled out his notebook, simply as a little diversion, and playfully tried to connect the cook's observations, the accuracy of which would scarcely satisfy a detective's standards, with Karl's actual appearance. "So this is how one finds one's nephew," he concluded, sounding as if he wished to be congratulated all over again.

"What will happen to the stoker?" asked Karl, ignoring his uncle's last remark. In his new position he could, he believed, say anything that crossed his mind.

"The stoker will get what he deserves," said the senator, "and what the captain considers appropriate. Besides, I think we've had enough of the stoker, more than enough, as I'm sure all the other gentlemen will agree."

"But that's beside the point when it's a matter of justice," said Karl. Karl stood between his uncle and the captain, and, perhaps swayed by his vantage point, he believed that the decision now lay in his hands.

The stoker, however, seemed to have abandoned all hope. His hands were half tucked into his trousers belt, which his agitated movements had exposed along with the stripes of a patterned shirt. This did not in the least bother him, for he had finished complaining about his sorrows, and they should get to see the pair of rags hanging from his body before they carried him off. He imagined that the two lowest-ranking people in the cabin, the servant and Schubal, would be the ones who were supposed to do this last good deed for him. Then Schubal would have some peace and wouldn't be driven to despair, as the chief treasurer had put it. The captain could sign up an all-Romanian crew, Romanian would be spoken throughout the ship and everything might actually run more smoothly. There would no longer be a stoker chattering away in the main bursar's office, though they would remember his last bit of chatter quite fondly, for, as the senator had specifically noted, it had indirectly led to the moment when he had recognized his nephew. Besides, the nephew had thanked him adequately long before that wonderful moment of recognition; the stoker wouldn't even think of asking Karl for anything else. In any case, even if he was the captain's nephew, he certainly wasn't the captain himself, and in the end the harsh words would come from the captain's lips.—In keeping with such views the stoker tried not to look at Karl, but unfortunately in this room full of enemies there was nowhere else to rest his eyes.

"Don't misunderstand the situation," the senator said to Karl, "it is perhaps a matter of justice, but it is at the same time a matter of discipline. And on board ship it is the captain who determines both, and especially the latter."

"That is so," muttered the stoker. Whoever noticed his muttering and understood it smiled disconcertedly.

"But we've already so hindered the captain in his official duties—which must surely mount incredibly once the ship reaches New York—that it's high time for us to leave instead of intervening quite unnecessarily and thereby turning a trivial squabble between two machinists into a full-blown incident. My dear nephew, I can understand your behavior completely, and that's precisely what gives me the right to whisk you away."

"I'll have a boat lowered at once," said the captain, but much to Karl's astonishment, he did not seek to raise the slightest objection to his uncle's remarks, even though they could undoubtedly be considered self-demeaning. The chief bursar hurried over to the desk and telephoned the captain's order to the boatswain.

"Time is running out," Karl said to himself, "but I cannot do anything without insulting almost everyone. After all, I can't leave my uncle, who has only just found me. The captain is polite, but that's about it. Once this becomes a disciplinary matter, he will cease being polite, and Uncle must have been expressing the captain's sentiments also. I don't want to talk to Schubal and even regret that I shook hands with him. And the rest of the people here are nothing but chaff."

Absorbed in such thoughts he approached the stoker slowly, pulled the latter's right hand from his belt, took it in his own, and began to toy with it. "So why don't you speak out?" he asked. "Why do you put up with everything?"

The stoker merely furrowed his brow as if he were seeking the right words with which to convey his thoughts. He glanced down at Karl's hands and at his own.

"You've suffered greater injustice than anybody else on this ship, I'm quite sure of that." And Karl drew his fingers back and forth between the stoker's fingers; with a sparkle in his eyes, the latter looked around on every side, as though overcome by a great joy, but one that nobody ought to hold against him.

"But you must defend yourself, say yes and no, otherwise people won't have any idea about the truth. You must promise me you'll do as I say, for I fear that for various reasons I'll no longer be able to help you." And Karl wept as he kissed the stoker's hand and took that chapped, almost lifeless hand and pressed it to his cheeks, like a treasure one must relinquish. However, his uncle, the senator, was already by his side and pulled him away, if only with the slightest pressure. "The stoker seems to have bewitched you," he said, casting a knowing look at the captain over Karl's head. "You felt abandoned, then found the stoker and now you're grateful to him, which certainly speaks in your favor. But don't carry this too far, if only for my sake, and do try to understand your position."

A commotion began outside the door; one could hear shouts, and it even seemed as if someone was being thrust violently against the door. A sailor entered looking rather disheveled, with a maid's apron tied around his waist. "There are a few people outside," he cried, thrusting out his elbows as though he were still surrounded by a crowd. Finally he regained his composure and was about to salute the captain when he noticed the servant's apron, tore it off, threw it on the ground, and shouted: "That's revolting, they've tied a maid's apron around me." Then he clicked his heels, however, and saluted. Someone made an attempt to laugh, but the captain said severely: "Somebody appears to be in a good mood! So who's outside?" "They're my witnesses," said Schubal, stepping forward. "I most humbly beseech you to excuse their unseemly conduct. Once the men have the voyage behind them they sometimes start acting like madmen." "Call them in," the captain commanded, and turning immediately to the senator, he said quickly but courteously: "Mr. Senator, could you be so kind as to follow this sailor, who'll escort you to the boat? And it goes without saying, Mr. Senator, that it was a great pleasure and an honor for me to make your acquaintance. I can only hope that I shall soon get another chance to resume our interrupted conversation about the state of the American fleet, and maybe we can ensure that next time too it'll be interrupted in an equally pleasant manner." "Well, one nephew seems quite enough for now," said Karl's uncle, laughing. "Please accept my most heartfelt thanks for the kindness you've shown, and now I should like to bid you farewell. By the way, it's not inconceivable"—he pressed Karl to his chest affectionately—"that we could spend more time together on our next voyage to Europe." "I should be only too delighted," said the captain. The two gentlemen shook hands; Karl had to be satisfied with holding out his hand briefly for the captain without being able to say a word, since the latter was already preoccupied with the roughly fifteen people led by Schubal, who entered somewhat diffidently yet also very noisily. After asking the senator for permission to go ahead, the sailor divided the crowd for the senator and Karl, who made their way easily through the bowing crowd. These otherwise good-natured people seemed to regard Schubal's fight with the stoker as nothing more than a joke, which lost none of its hilarity even in the presence of the captain. Among them Karl noticed the kitchen maid Line, who winked at him cheerfully as she tied on the apron that had been cast aside by the sailor, for it was indeed hers.

Continuing to follow the sailor, they left the office and turned into a little passageway that led them after only a few paces to a little door, from which a short stairway led down into the boat, which was already prepared for them. With one great bound their guide leaped into the boat, whereupon the sailors immediately rose and saluted. While the senator was urging Karl to take care climbing down, Karl, still on the top step, burst into vehement tears. The senator put his right hand under Karl's chin, and with his left hand pressed him firmly against his chest and caressed him. Thus did they descend the ladder, one step at a time, and closely entwined, they stepped onto the boat, and the senator found a good spot where Karl could sit right opposite him. At a signal from the senator, the sailors pushed the boat away from the ship and immediately set to work. They had rowed only a few meters from the ship when Karl noticed with surprise that they were on the same side as the windows of the main pay office. All three windows were occupied by Schubal's witnesses, who greeted them cordially and waved at them; even his uncle thanked them, and a sailor performed the feat of blowing a kiss up to them without interrupting the even rhythm of his rowing. It was as if the stoker had ceased to exist. Karl took a closer look at his uncle, whose knees were almost touching his own, and he began to doubt whether this man could ever take the place of the stoker. His uncle also avoided his glance and looked out at the waves heaving about their boat.

II

THE UNCLE

In his uncle's house Karl soon became accustomed to his new circumstances. His uncle always obliged him even in trifling matters, and Karl therefore did not have to wait to learn from those bad experiences that so often embitter the early days of one's life abroad.

Karl's room was on the sixth floor of a building, whose five lower floors and three additional ones deep underground were occupied by his uncle's business. Each morning on entering his room from his little sleeping alcove, he always marveled at the light coming through two windows and a balcony door. Where might he have been obliged to live had he come ashore as a poor little emigrant? And perhaps he wouldn't even have been admitted to the United States, which was very likely according to his uncle, who was familiar with the immigration laws, and the authorities would have sent him home, completely ignoring the fact that he no longer had a home country. For one could not hope for pity here in this country, and the things that Karl had read about America in that regard were quite true; here it was only those who were fortunate who truly seemed to enjoy their good fortune amid the indifferent faces on all sides.

A narrow balcony ran along the full length of his room. In his native city it would surely have been the highest lookout, yet here it offered little more than the view of a single street that ran in a straight line between two rows of veritably truncated buildings and therefore seemed to flee into the distance, where the outlines of a cathedral loomed monstrously out of a great haze. In the morning and in the evening and at night in his dreams, this street was filled with constantly bustling traffic, which seen from above seemed like a continually self-replenishing mixture of distorted human figures and of the roofs of all sorts of vehicles, constantly scattered by new arrivals, out of which there arose a new, stronger, wilder mixture of noise, dust, and smells, and, catching and penetrating it all, a powerful light that was continually dispersed, carried away, and avidly refracted by the mass of objects that made such a physical impression on one's dazzled eye that it seemed as if a glass pane, hanging over the street and covering everything, were being smashed again and again with the utmost force.

Cautious as he was in all matters, Karl's uncle advised him that he should not become seriously engaged in anything for the time being. While he should take a look at everything and always examine matters carefully, he should not let anything beguile him. Indeed, the first days of a European in America could certainly be likened to a birth, he said, and then he added—so Karl would not have any unnecessary fear—that even though one adapted more quickly here than if one were entering the world of man from the hereafter, one should also keep in mind that one's first judgment was always quite shaky and that maybe one should not allow it to upset all the future judgments that one would need to make if one wanted to go on living in this country. He had known recent arrivals who, instead of following these sound principles, had, say, stood about on their balconies for days on end gazing down at the street like lost sheep. It could lead only to confusion! All that solitary idleness, that wasteful staring out on a bustling New York day, was permissible for people who were traveling for pleasure, though not unreservedly so, but for anyone who wanted to remain in this country, it was a calamity—a word one could certainly use at this point even if it was an exaggeration. And indeed his uncle always grimaced in irritation whenever he encountered Karl on the balcony during one of his visits, which occurred only once daily and, moreover, always at a different time. Karl soon noticed this grimace and consequently, insofar as possible, denied himself the pleasure of standing on the balcony.

However, that was by no means his sole pleasure. In his room stood an American desk of the finest kind, such as his father had wanted for years and had sought to buy at a reasonable price at all kinds of auctions, though owing to his limited means, without success. Of course, there was no comparison between this desk here and those supposedly American desks that made the rounds at European auctions. For instance, it had in its base a hundred drawers of all sizes, in which even the President of the Union could have found a suitable place for each of his files, and what's more it even had a regulator on the side, so that simply by turning the handle one could move about and rearrange the drawers in all sorts of combinations to suit one's every need and whim. Thin little side panels would descend slowly, forming the bottoms of new drawers or the tops of others that rose from below; even after only a single winding, the entire base looked completely different, and depending on the speed at which one turned the handle, everything moved slowly or at a crazy pace. Though it was a most recent invention, it vividly reminded Karl of the nativity scenes at home that were shown to gaping children at the Christmas market, and Karl too had often stood before it, bundled up in his winter clothes, continually comparing the revolutions of the crank, which was being turned by an old man, with the unfolding nativity scene, the faltering progress of the three holy kings, the sudden illumination of the star, and the cramped life in the holy manger. And it always seemed as if his mother, who stood behind him, was not paying sufficient heed to all of the movements; after drawing her over until he could feel her body pressing against his back, he had spoken in a loud voice, continually pointing out the less conspicuous figures, such as a small hare lying on the grass in the foreground, which sat up and begged and then got ready to start running again, until his mother put her hand over his mouth and presumably relapsed into her prior inattentiveness. True, the desk had not been manufactured for the purpose of stirring such memories, yet throughout the history of inventions people had made associations that were just as indistinct as those in Karl's recollections. Unlike Karl, his uncle was by no means in favor of this desk; he had merely wanted to buy Karl a regular desk, and all such desks now came equipped with this new mechanism, which possessed the further advantage that it could be attached to older desks at no great cost. Nevertheless Karl's uncle did not refrain from advising him that he should not use the regulator at all if possible; in an effort to reinforce this advice, his uncle claimed that the mechanism was very sensitive, could be easily ruined, and was expensive to repair. It wasn't hard to see that such comments were merely excuses, especially since one would have needed to add that the regulator could be easily fixed, which his uncle, however, neglected to do.

In the first few days, when naturally there were frequent exchanges between Karl and his uncle, he had said that he had played on the piano at home, only a little but with considerable pleasure, though he had had to make do with the beginner's skills his mother had taught him. Karl was well aware that in telling this story he was in effect requesting a piano, but he had taken a sufficiently good look around to know that his uncle had no need to economize. Still, his request was not granted at once, but about eight days later his uncle announced, almost reluctantly, that the piano had just arrived and that, if Karl wished, he could supervise the move. That was certainly easy work, though scarcely any easier than the actual move, since the building had a special furniture elevator that could easily accommodate an entire furniture vehicle, and it was in this elevator that the piano glided up to Karl's room. Karl could have taken the same goods elevator as the piano and the workers, but since the passenger elevator right beside it happened to be free, he chose that one instead, keeping himself at the same height as the other elevator with the help of a lever and constantly looking through the glass panels of the elevator at the beautiful instrument that now belonged to him. When it stood in his room and he struck the first keys, he felt such wild joy that, rather than continuing to play, he jumped up, preferring to stand some distance away, hands on his hips, gazing at the piano. Besides, the acoustics in the room were splendid, and that helped him overcome the slight discomfort he had initially felt on discovering that he was living in a building made of steel. In reality, though, no matter how steel-like the building seemed from the outside, in the actual room there was no sign of the steel components employed in its construction, and no one could have pointed out the tiniest item in the interior design that would have in any way spoiled the overall effect of complete comfort and ease. In his first days there Karl had hoped to accomplish a great deal through his piano playing and was not ashamed—at least just before falling asleep—to imagine that his playing might directly affect his situation in America. It certainly sounded strange whenever he stood in front of windows opening out onto the noisy street, playing an old soldier's song from his homeland, which the soldiers, who used to lie by the barrack windows at night looking down at the dark square, would sing from one window to the next— but then when he looked down on the street he could see that it had not changed at all and merely formed one small part of a great cycle that one could not actually bring to a halt unless one were aware of all of the forces operating in the circle. His uncle tolerated his playing, did not even say anything about it, especially since, even without being admonished, Karl only rarely granted himself the pleasure of playing; he even brought Karl the scores of American marches and naturally also of the national anthem, but his love of music was surely not the only reason why one day he asked Karl, by no means in jest, whether he might not also wish to learn the violin or the French horn.

Learning English was, of course, Karl's first and most important task. When the young teacher from a business school appeared in Karl's room at seven o'clock each morning, he would find him already seated at his desk, poring over his notebooks or walking up and down, committing phrases to memory. Karl realized that when it came to learning English, there could be no such thing as excessive haste, and that the best way to give his uncle great joy was to make rapid progress. And although the only English words in his initial conversations with his uncle were hello and goodbye, they soon managed to shift more and more of the conversation into English, which led to their broaching topics of a more intimate nature. Such was his uncle's satisfaction over the first American poem that Karl was able to recite one evening—a description of a great fire—that he became deadly serious. At that moment both stood by a window in Karl's room; his uncle was looking out at the sky, from which all trace of daylight had disappeared, clapping his hands slowly and regularly in accord with the verses while Karl stood erect and glassy-eyed beside him, wrestling with the words of the difficult poem.

The greater the improvement in his English, the more eager was his uncle to have him meet his acquaintances, and he arranged that during these encounters the English teacher should for the time being always remain near Karl, simply in case of need. The very first acquaintance to whom Karl was introduced one morning was a young, thin, and incredibly supple young man, whom his uncle led into Karl's room amid a shower of compliments. He was obviously one of those many millionaires' sons whose parents consider them misfits and who lead their lives in such a way that no ordinary person could observe any day in the life of this young man without feeling sad. And as if he were aware of this or at least suspected as much and were trying to counteract it, at least insofar as lay within his power, a happy smile played constantly on his lips and around his eyes, which seemed to be directed at himself, his interlocutor, and the world at large.

With his uncle's unconditional approval Karl spoke with this young man, a Mr. Mak, about riding together at half past five in the morning, either at the riding school or out in open country. However, Karl was initially reluctant to give his consent, for he had never sat on a horse before and first wanted to learn how to ride, but since his uncle and Mak tried to talk him into it by presenting riding as a source of pleasure and a means of healthy exercise rather than as an artistic performance, he finally consented. Now he had to rise as early as half past four, which he often found painful, for probably on account of having to stay alert all day, he suffered from real lethargy: but once in his bathroom he instantly shed all such regrets. The shower head extended over the entire length and breadth of the tub— at home, which of his fellow students, no matter how rich, had anything the like of this and, what's more, all to himself?—and now Karl lay sprawled out there; in this tub he could spread out his arms and let the now lukewarm, now hot, now lukewarm again, and finally icy spurts of water pour down on him, over part of his body or all over, as he chose. As if still experiencing the bliss of the last few moments of sleep, he continued to lie there, taking special pleasure in catching with his closed eyelids the last separate drops, which then opened and streamed over his face.

On being dropped off by his uncle's towering automobile at the riding school, the English teacher would already be waiting for him, whereas Mak always came late. But he didn't have to worry about getting there late, for the lively riding began only after he arrived. When he entered, didn't the horses rear up from their half-sleep; didn't the whip crack more loudly through the hall; and didn't a number of individuals, spectators, grooms, riding students, or whoever they might be suddenly appear on the surrounding gallery? Karl, however, used the time before Mak's arrival to practice at least a few riding exercises, elementary though they were. A tall man, who could almost reach the withers of the biggest horses without raising his arm, gave Karl riding lessons that always only lasted barely a quarter of an hour. Karl met with only modest success and was able to learn English cries of distress, which he shouted out breathlessly to his English teacher, who always leaned against the same doorpost, often greatly in need of sleep. But once Mak arrived, almost all of his dissatisfaction with riding disappeared. The tall man was dismissed, and soon all one could hear in the still half-dark hall were the galloping horses' hooves, and all one could see was the raised arm with which Mak gave orders to Karl. After engaging in such pleasure for half an hour, which passed by as if in one's sleep, they stopped; in a great rush Mak said goodbye, tapped Karl on the cheek if he was especially satisfied with his riding, and in his haste disappeared without even waiting to accompany Karl through the door. Karl then took the teacher along in the automobile, and they drove to their English lesson, mostly via detours, since they would have lost too much time going through the bustle of the main street, which led directly from Uncle's house to the riding school. In any case the English teacher soon ceased to accompany him, since Karl, who reproached himself for unnecessarily dragging that weary man out to the riding school, asked his uncle to relieve the teacher of this duty, especially since it was so easy to communicate with Mak in English. After some reflection his uncle also granted this request.

It took a relatively long time for his uncle to decide to permit Karl even a quick look at his business, even though Karl had often requested one. It was a kind of consignment and shipping business, the likes of which—so far as Karl could recall—could perhaps not be found in Europe. The business involved intermediary trading, which rather than, say, conveying goods from producers to consumers or perhaps to merchants, handled the distribution of all goods and components and their transport to and fro between the large manufacturing cartels. So it was a business that not only encompassed the purchase, storage, transport and sale of goods on a massive scale but also had to maintain the most precise and uninterrupted telephone and telegraph connections with its clients. The telegraph hall was no smaller, in fact even larger, than the telegraph office in his native city, which Karl had once walked through arm in arm with a fellow pupil who was known there. Wherever one looked in the telephone room, the doors of the telephone cells were constantly opening and closing, and the ringing was stupefying. His uncle opened the nearest door, and in the sparkling electric light one could see an employee, oblivious to all the noise coming from the door, with his head tucked into a steel band that pressed the earpieces up against his ears. His right arm lay on a small table as if it were a heavy burden, and only the fingers holding a pencil twitched at a rapid and inhumanly regular pace. He spoke into the mouthpiece sparingly, and often one could even see that he wanted to object to something the speaker had said, but before he could do so, he heard further utterances that compelled him to lower his eyes and write. Besides, there was no need for him to speak, as Karl's uncle explained in a low voice, for the same reports transcribed by this man were also transcribed by two other employees, then compared with one another, so that all errors could be eliminated insofar as possible. Just as the uncle and Karl were stepping out of the doorway, a trainee slipped in and emerged again holding a sheet of paper that already had writing on it. There was constant movement; people ran back and forth in the hall. No one said hello, such greetings having been dispensed with; each person followed in the steps of the person before him, either looking at the floor, which he wanted to cross as quickly as possible, or glancing at the papers in his hands and probably managing to catch only isolated words or numbers from the papers fluttering in his hand, as he ran along.

"You've really accomplished a great deal," said Karl to his uncle during one of these tours through the business, which would take several days in their entirety even if one merely wanted to have a quick look at each department.

"And I set all of this up thirty years ago by myself, I'd like you to know. Back then I had a small concern in the harbor district, and if five cases were unloaded on any given day, that was a lot, and I went home feeling all puffed up. Today I have the third-largest warehouse in the harbor, and the old shop serves as the dining room and tool shed for my sixty-fifth company of porters."

"Well, that's almost miraculous," said Karl.

"Everything happens that quickly here," his uncle said, breaking off the conversation.

One day his uncle arrived just before dinner, which Karl had expected to eat alone as usual, and asked that he put on a black suit right away and accompany him to dinner, at which two business friends would join them. As Karl was changing next door, his uncle sat down at his desk, leafed through an English lesson that Karl had just finished, slapped his hand down on the table, and cried: "Truly excellent!" Though Karl undoubtedly did a better job dressing after hearing this praise, he was already quite confident about his English.

In his uncle's dining room, which he remembered from his first evening, two tall stout gentlemen rose to greet him, one called Green, the other Pollunder, as became evident over dinner. His uncle hardly ever said anything about any of his acquaintances, leaving it up to Karl to discover through his own observations whatever might be considered important or intriguing. After the dinner—in the course of which the conversation was restricted to confidential business matters, which meant that Karl received a good lesson in how to use business terms, they had let him focus quietly on his meal, as if he were a child whose most important task was to eat his fill—Mr. Green leaned over to Karl and, making an unmistakable effort to speak the clearest possible English, asked a few general questions about Karl's first impressions of America. Occasionally glancing at his uncle, and amid dead silence on all sides, Karl answered at length and, by way of thanking them, sought to make a pleasant impression by using turns of phrase with a certain New York flavor. Upon hearing one such expression, all three gentlemen burst out laughing, and Karl began to fear that he had made a vulgar mistake, but not at all, for as Mr. Pollunder explained to him, he had said something that was actually quite felicitous. Moreover, this Mr. Pollunder seemed to have taken a special liking to Karl, and as his uncle and Mr. Green resumed their business conversation, Mr. Pollunder made Karl pull his chair up close and asked him many different questions, first about his name, his background, and the voyage, until finally, so as to let Karl take another rest, he began to talk rapidly, amid considerable laughter and coughing, about himself and his daughter, with whom he lived on a small country estate near New York, though he could only spend his nights there, for he was a banker whose profession kept him in New York all day. And Karl was most cordially invited to visit his country estate; a freshly minted American like Karl would surely feel the need now and then to recuperate from New York. Karl immediately asked his uncle for permission to accept the invitation, and his uncle granted it with seeming pleasure, although he failed to mention a specific date or even to consider one, as Karl and Mr. Pollunder had expected.

The following day, however, Karl was summoned to one of his uncle's offices—in this building alone his uncle had ten different offices—where he found his uncle and Mr. Pollunder sunk in their armchairs, scarcely exchanging a word. "Mr. Pollunder," said his uncle, whom one could scarcely discern in the twilight of the room. "As agreed yesterday, Mr. Pollunder has come to take you to his country estate." "I didn't know it was supposed to be today," Karl answered, "otherwise I would be ready to leave." "If you're not ready to leave, it might be better if we postpone the visit for a while," said his uncle. "Why would he need to get ready!" cried Mr. Pollunder. "A young man is always ready." "It's not for his sake," said his uncle, turning to his guest, "he would have to go up to his room, though, and that would keep you waiting." "I've plenty of time," said Mr. Pollunder, "I predicted a certain delay and closed up early today." "Well," said his uncle, "don't you see what trouble your visit is causing?" "I'm sorry," said Karl, "but I shall be back in a moment," and he began to run off. "Don't rush," said Mr. Pollunder, "you're not causing me any trouble; on the contrary, I'm extremely pleased you're coming." "You'll miss your riding lesson tomorrow, have you canceled it yet?" "No," said Karl; that visit, which he had eagerly anticipated, was becoming a burden. "Well, I didn't know—" "But you still want to go?" insisted his uncle. Friendly old Mr. Pollunder came to his aid. "On our way there we shall stop by the riding school and sort this out." "Well, that's all fine and good," said his uncle. "But Mak will be expecting you." "He won't be expecting me," said Karl, "but he'll go out there all right." "So," said his uncle, as though Karl's answer had not provided the slightest justification. Again it was Mr. Pollunder who made the decisive comment: "But Klara"—she was the daughter of Mr. Pollunder—"expects him this evening, and surely she has priority over Mak?" "Of course," said his uncle, "so run along to your room," and as if involuntarily, he slapped the armrest of his chair several times. Karl had already reached the door when his uncle brought him to a standstill with another question: "But you'll be back tomorrow morning for your English lesson?" "What!" cried Mr. Pollunder from his armchair, turning around in astonishment so far as his girth permitted. "Couldn't he at least stay all day tomorrow? And then I'd bring him back the following day, early in the morning." "That's absolutely impossible," retorted his uncle. "I cannot allow his studies to be disrupted in that fashion. Later, once he has settled into a reasonably stable career, I shall happily allow him to accept your kind invitation, even for a longer stay, for it truly is an honor." The way he contradicts himself! Karl thought. Mr. Pollunder had become dejected. "But for only one evening and one night, it's hardly worthwhile." "That's also what I think," said his uncle. "One simply has to accept what one can get," said Mr. Pollunder, who now laughed again. "Then I shall wait," he called out to Karl, who hurried off since his uncle remained silent. On returning to the office a few minutes later, now ready for the journey, he encountered only Mr. Pollunder; his uncle had already gone off. Mr. Pollunder gladly shook both of Karl's hands as if seeking the strongest possible reassurance that Karl would indeed come. Quite hot from rushing about, Karl in turn even shook Mr. Pollunder's hand; he was pleased that he could go on the excursion. "Wasn't my uncle annoyed that I'm going?" "Oh no! He didn't really mean it that seriously. It's just that he cares deeply about your education." "Did he himself say he wasn't serious about those previous comments?" "Oh yes," said Mr. Pollunder, dragging out the words and thereby proving that he could not lie. "It's rather odd that he was so reluctant to let me visit you even though you are his friend." Mr. Pollunder could not explain this either, although he failed to admit as much, and as they drove through the warm evening in Mr. Pollunder's automobile, both reflected on this matter at length although they immediately began talking about other matters.

They sat close together, and Mr. Pollunder held Karl's hand while he spoke. Karl wanted to hear a great deal about Miss Klara, as if he were impatient with the long drive and could with the help of those stories get there earlier than in reality. Although Karl had never driven through the streets of New York in the evening and one could hear a great din racing across the sidewalk and the roadway, constantly changing directions as in a tornado, as if the noise were not caused by human beings but were a foreign element, Karl, seeking to catch everything that Mr. Pollunder said, had eyes only for Mr. Pollunder's dark waistcoat and the gold chain slung diagonally across it. Leaving behind the streets, where in a great and unconcealed fear of arriving late theatergoers rushed toward the theaters on foot and in vehicles driven at the greatest possible speed, they passed through transitional neighborhoods into suburbs, where mounted policemen repeatedly diverted their automobile into narrow side streets, for the wide thoroughfares were occupied by demonstrations of striking steelworkers, and only the most essential traffic was allowed to drive through the intersections.

Whenever the automobile emerged from the dark, hollowly echoing side streets and crossed one of these main streets, which resembled entire city squares and stretched out on both sides in endless vistas, the pavements seemed inundated with a mass of people moving forward only one tiny step at a time and singing songs that sounded even more uniform than if only one person were singing. But here and there on the cleared roadway, one could see a policeman on a motionless horse, or people with flags, or inscribed banners strung across the street, or a labor leader surrounded by co-workers and assistants, or an electric streetcar wagon that had not hurried away quickly enough and now stood dark and empty, with its driver and conductor still sitting on the platform. Small bands of curious bystanders stood at some remove from the actual demonstrators and remained there despite their evident confusion as to what was happening. But Karl leaned happily on the arm that Mr. Pollunder had put around him; he found great solace in assuming that he would be soon taken in as a welcome guest at a brightly lit country house surrounded by walls and guarded by dogs, and even if he was becoming drowsy and could not quite understand what Mr. Pollunder said anymore, or at least could do so only intermittently, he pulled himself together now and then and wiped his eyes so as to assure himself again that Mr. Pollunder had not noticed his drowsiness, for that is something he wanted to avoid at all costs.

III

A COUNTRY HOUSE OUTSIDE NEW YORK

"We've arrived," said Mr. Pollunder, precisely during one of Karl's absent moments. The automobile stood before a country house that was built in the style of country houses favored by rich people in the vicinity of New York and therefore taller and more substantial than strictly necessary in a country house designed for a single family. Since only the lower part was illuminated, it was impossible to gauge the height of the house. In front were rustling chestnut trees through which—the gate was already open—a short path led to the front steps. Karl thought he could tell from his weariness, as he descended from the automobile, that the journey had indeed taken quite a while. In the darkness under the row of chestnut trees he could hear a girl's voice nearby say: "Mr. Jakob has come at last." "The name is Rossmann," said Karl, taking a hand extended by a girl whose silhouette he could now distinguish. "It's only Jakob's nephew," Mr. Pollunder explained, "and his name is Karl Rossmann." "We're just as pleased to have him here," said the girl, who set little store by names. Nevertheless, as he walked toward the house flanked by Mr. Pollunder and the girl, Karl asked: "You're Miss Klara?" "Yes," she said; weak light from the house fell on her face, which she had inclined toward him, "only I didn't want to introduce myself out in the dark." Was she waiting at the gate for us? thought Karl, awakening slowly as he walked ahead. "By the way, we've another guest

tonight," said Klara. "Why, that's impossible!" cried Mr. Pollunder irritably. "Mr. Green," said Klara. "When did he come?"
asked Karl, as if overcome by a sudden premonition. "A moment ago. Didn't you hear his automobile ahead of yours?"
Karl looked up at Pollunder so as to discern how he was assess-
ing the matter, but the latter had his hands in his trouser pockets and merely stamped his feet more vigorously as he walked
on. "It makes no sense to live so close to New York—we're
always getting disturbed. We shall have to move out even farther. Even if it should take me half the night to drive home."
They halted on the steps. "But it's been so long since Mr. Green
last came to visit," said Klara, who, though obviously in complete agreement with her father, sought to distract his attention
and calm him down. "But why must he come today," said Pollunder, whose words now rolled furiously over his bulging
lower lip, a loose heavy wad of flesh that could easily be set
in motion. "Good question!" said Klara. "Perhaps he'll leave
soon," observed Karl, marveling at his rapport with these people, who had seemed such complete strangers only the day
before. "Unfortunately not," said Klara, "there's some important business he needs to discuss with Papa, and it'll probably
go on quite a while, for he has jokingly warned me that if I
really want to be a good hostess, I'll have to stay up listening to
them till dawn." "That too, on top of everything else. So he's
even going to spend the night here," exclaimed Pollunder, as if
this were the worst thing that could have happened. "What I'd
really like," he said, becoming more amiable as a new idea
took hold, "what I'd really like to do, Mr. Rossmann, is put
you in my automobile and take you back to your uncle. This
evening got off to a bad start, and who knows when your uncle
will let us have you again? But if I take you back to him today,
then he cannot refuse next time." And he was already reaching
for Karl's hand in order to carry out his intentions. However,

Karl did not move, and Klara asked that he be allowed to stay, for then at least she and Karl would not be disturbed by Mr. Green, and finally Pollunder too realized that even his own resolve was not unshakable. Besides—and this was perhaps most decisive—one could suddenly hear Mr. Green call down from the top steps to the garden: "What's keeping you?" "Come," said Pollunder, turning toward the steps. In his wake came Karl and Klara, who now examined each other in the light. "Her lips are so red," Karl said to himself, thinking of Mr. Pollunder's lips and of the beautiful change they had undergone in his daughter. "After supper," she said, "if it's all right with you, we shall go straight to my rooms so at least the two of us will be rid of Mr. Green, even if Papa must still deal with him. And then could you be so kind as to play the piano for me, since Papa told me how you excel at that; unfortunately I'm quite incapable of playing a thing and, for all my great love of music, never even touch my piano." Karl greatly approved of Klara's proposal even though he would have gladly drawn Mr. Pollunder along with them. But watching Green's enormous form unfold little by little as they climbed the stairs—he had already become accustomed to Mr. Pollunder's bulk—he lost all hope that he would somehow succeed that evening in enticing Mr. Pollunder away from this man.

Mr. Green greeted them hastily, as if they had much to catch up on, took Mr. Pollunder's arm, and pushed Karl and Klara ahead into the dining room, which looked very festive, especially with the flowers almost peering out of the strips of fresh foliage, which only made Mr. Green's disturbing presence all the more regrettable. Karl, who stood by the table, waiting for the others to be seated, had just begun to hope that the large glass door to the garden would be left open, for a strong fragrant draft wafted in, as if into a garden house, when Mr. Green began to close the glass door, panting as he bent down for the bottom bolts, and reaching up for the top ones, all at such a brisk youthful pace that the servant who came rushing in found that there was nothing left for him to do. In his initial remarks over dinner Mr. Green expressed astonishment that Karl's uncle should have given him permission for the visit. Raising one full soup spoon after another to his mouth, he explained to Klara on his left and Mr. Pollunder on his right why he was so astonished, and how Uncle Jakob always watched over Karl and how his uncle's love for him was so great that it was more than the love of an uncle. Not content with such meddling, he has to go meddling with me and my uncle, Karl thought, and he was unable to swallow a single drop of the honey-colored soup. At the same time he did not want anyone to see how annoyed he was and silently began to pour the soup down his throat. The meal passed by slowly, like a plague. Only Mr. Green, and sometimes even Klara, were animated and now and then they were able to have a little laugh. Mr. Pollunder allowed himself to be drawn into the conversation only on those few occasions when Mr. Green began to discuss business matters. Yet before long he withdrew even from those discussions, and then, after some time had elapsed, Mr. Green needed to catch him by surprise. He emphasized the fact—at this point in the conversation Karl, who pricked up his ears as if there were danger lurking, had to be reminded by Klara that he had not touched the roast on his plate and that he was an invited guest at a dinner party—that he had had no desire at the outset to come out on this unexpected visit. For even if this business they still needed to discuss was particularly urgent, they could have resolved the most important items in the city that day and left the details for tomorrow or even later. And in fact long before closing time he had gone to Mr. Pollunder's office and, failing to find him there, had had to telephone home to say that he would be away for the night, and then had had to drive all the way out. "Then I owe you an apology," said Karl quite loudly, and before anybody could respond, he went on, "since it's my fault that Mr. Pollunder had to leave his business early today, and I am sorry." Mr. Pollunder covered the greater portion of his face with his napkin while Klara smiled at Karl, though not sympathetically but rather with the intention of influencing him in some way. "There's no need to apologize," said Mr. Green, carving up a pigeon with a few sharp jabs, "on the contrary, I'm glad I can spend the evening in such pleasant company rather than having to eat my supper alone at home, where there's only one old housekeeper to serve me, and she's so old that she even found it hard to make her way from the door to my table; I can spend quite a while leaning back in my chair as I watch her making her way over. It was only recently that I finally managed to persuade her to let the servant carry the dishes as far as the dining room door, whereas she owns the path from the door to my table, so far as I can make out." "My God," exclaimed Klara, "what loyalty!" "Yes, there is some loyalty left in this world," said Mr. Green, guiding a bite of food into his mouth, where, as Karl happened to notice, his tongue seized it with a single flick. He felt almost ill and stood up. Just then Pollunder and Klara both reached for his hand. "You must stay seated," said Klara. And when he sat down, she whispered to him: "We'll soon disappear together. Just be patient." Meanwhile Mr. Green had occupied himself quietly with his food, as if Mr. Pollunder and Klara were naturally obliged to calm Karl, should Green make him feel indisposed.

The meal dragged on, especially because of the meticulous way in which Mr. Green dealt with each course, even though he was always indefatigably prepared to take on each new course when it arrived, and it truly began to seem as if he merely wanted to take a good break from his old housekeeper. Every now and then he praised Miss Klara's skill in running the household, but whereas she was visibly flattered, Karl wanted to fight him off, as though he were attacking her. But even that wasn't sufficient for Mr. Green, who frequently, without looking up from his plate, deplored Karl's conspicuous lack of appetite. Mr. Pollunder defended Karl's appetite although, as host, he ought to have encouraged Karl to eat. The strain of sitting through that dinner had made Karl so sensitive that, even against his better judgment, he construed Mr. Pollunder's words as unfriendly. And such was his state that he first ate at an inappropriately fast pace and then for a long time let his knife and fork drop wearily on his plate and was the most immobile of the guests and the one whom the attendant serving the dishes simply did not know how to handle.

"Tomorrow I shall inform the senator how you have insulted Miss Klara by refusing to eat anything," Mr. Green said, indicating he was joking only through the way he toyed with the cutlery. "Just look how sad that girl is," he added, chucking Klara under the chin. She did not resist, and closed her eyes. "You cute little thing," he cried, leaning back and laughing with a bright red face and the vigor of someone who has eaten his fill. Karl vainly sought to explain the behavior of Mr. Pollunder. The latter simply sat there, looking at his plate, as if that were where the significant action was occurring. He did not pull Karl's chair closer, and when he spoke, he spoke to everyone and had nothing special to say to Karl. Still, he suffered that wily old New York bachelor Green to touch Klara in a manner that clearly revealed his intentions; to insult Karl, Pollunder's guest, or at least to treat him like a child; and to gather his strength in preparation for goodness knew what.

After the meal had ended—on noticing the overall mood, Green was the first to get up and, as it were, raise everyone with him—Karl went alone to one of the large windows, which were divided by thin white mullions and gave out onto the terrace and were, as he noticed on approaching, really doors. What had become of the dislike that Mr. Pollunder and his daughter had initially felt for Green and that Karl had at the time found somewhat incomprehensible? They now stood beside Green, nodding at him. The smoke from Mr. Green's cigar—a present from Pollunder that was as thick as the cigars that Father would mention at home as a known fact, even though he had probably never set eyes on one—spread through the dining room, carrying Green's influence even into those nooks and crannies in which he himself would never set foot. No matter how far away Karl stood, he could still feel a tickling sensation from the smoke in his throat, and it seemed to him that the behavior of Mr. Green, whom he had only once turned to glance at quickly, was disgraceful. He no longer considered it inconceivable that the only reason his uncle had withheld permission for this visit for so long was that he knew of Mr. Pollunder's character weakness, and as a result, even if he could not have exactly foreseen how Karl's feelings would be hurt, he must have known that this was a distinct possibility. Besides, Karl did not care for the American girl, even though he certainly hadn't imagined her to be much more beautiful than this. Ever since Mr. Green had begun to flirt with her, he had been surprised by how beautiful her face could become and, especially, by the sparkle in her quick lively eyes. He had never seen a skirt wrapped so tightly around a body as it was around hers; little creases in the delicate firm yellowish fabric showed just how tightly it was wound. And yet Karl had no interest in her and would have gladly relinquished the opportunity to be led into her rooms had he been permitted to open the door—and just in case, his hand was already on the doorknob—and to get into the automobile or, if the driver were already asleep, to walk to New York alone. After all, the clear night with the full moon was free to all, and Karl believed there was no sense in being afraid of the outdoors. Beginning to feel at ease in the room for the first time, he imagined how, early in the morning—probably the earliest he could reach home on foot— he would surprise his uncle. Though he had never been in his uncle's bedroom and even had no idea where it was, he would certainly ask and find out. Then he would knock, and on hearing the formal "Come in!" he would run into the room and surprise his dear uncle—whom he had always seen fully dressed and buttoned—sitting up in bed, dressed only in his nightshirt, and staring in amazement at the door. This in itself might not seem like much, but one need only imagine where it might lead! Perhaps he would have his first breakfast with his uncle; his uncle would still be in bed and he would sit on a chair, with the breakfast set out between them on a little table, and then their first breakfast together might become a regular event, and such breakfasts could lead to their getting together more often than once a day as they were accustomed to doing—indeed this was only inevitable—and then they could naturally talk more frankly. If he had treated his uncle in a disobedient or, let's say, headstrong, fashion, it was solely due to their never having had such frank exchanges. And even if he had to spend the night there—as, unfortunately, seemed very likely, although they made him stand by the window and left him to his own devices—this unhappy visit would perhaps become the turning point in his relationship with his uncle, and in his bedroom this evening his uncle was perhaps having similar thoughts.

Having consoled himself a little, he turned around. Klara, who now stood before him, said: "So you don't like it here? You don't even want to feel a little bit at home? Come, I'll give it one last try." She led him right across the room to the door. The two gentlemen sat at a side table over tall glasses filled with lightly foaming drinks that Karl had never seen before and would have gladly sampled. Mr. Green, who sat with his elbow propped up on the table, swung his head around so as to be as close as possible to Mr. Pollunder; anyone who had not known Mr. Pollunder might have readily assumed that the affairs they were discussing were of a criminal rather than a business nature. Whereas Mr. Pollunder kept a friendly eye on Karl as he headed toward the door, Green did not even turn to look at Karl—even though one does instinctively tend to meet the eyes of the person opposite—and Karl thought that this behavior reflected Green's belief that each of them should try to get by on the strength of his own abilities—Karl for himself, Green for himself—and that it would take the victory or the annihilation of one or the other before the inevitable social relationship could be established. "If that's what he thinks," said Karl to himself, "then he's a fool. I certainly don't want to have anything more to do with him, and he too should leave me in peace." No sooner had he stepped into the corridor than it struck him that he had probably been impolite, for in keeping his eyes fixed on Green, he had practically let Klara drag him out of that room. So now he was all the more willing to walk beside her. At first he could not believe his eyes as they passed through the corridors, for every twenty paces or so stood a servant in ornate livery, holding the thick stem of a candelabra in both hands. "The new electric wiring has only been installed in the dining room," explained Klara. "We've only recently bought this house and have had it completely renovated, at least as much as one can with such an old house." "So there are old houses in America," said Karl. "Why, of course," said Klara, laughing and pulling him along. "You do have some odd ideas about America." "You shouldn't make fun of me," he said irritably. After all, he was acquainted with Europe and America, she only with America.

Barely reaching out her hand in passing, Klara pushed open a door and without stopping said: "You'll be sleeping here." Karl naturally wanted to take a look at the room right away, but Klara declared impatiently, almost shouting, that there would be sufficient time for that later and that for now he should go with her. For a while they pulled each other back and forth in the corridor, until at last Karl said to himself that he needn't always follow Klara's wishes and, tearing himself free, entered the room. It was surprisingly dark outside by the window, probably on account of a treetop swaying to and fro in its full expanse. One could hear birds singing. But in the actual room, which the moonlight had not yet penetrated, one could scarcely distinguish anything; Karl regretted not having taken along the electric flashlight that his uncle had given him as a present. Here in this house a flashlight was quite indispensable; if one had a few such lamps, one could simply send the servants to bed. He sat down on the windowsill, looked out, and listened. A startled bird appeared to break through the foliage of the old tree. Somewhere in the countryside the whistle of a New York suburban train rang out. Otherwise all was quiet.

But not for long, since Klara came hurrying in. Visibly annoyed, she cried: "What's this?" and slapped her skirt. Before answering, Karl wanted to wait until she became more polite. But she approached him, taking large steps, and cried: "Well, are you coming or not?"; then, whether by design or simply out of excitement, she pushed his chest so forcefully that he would have fallen out the window had he not slipped from the windowsill and had his feet not at the last minute touched the floor. "I was about to fall out," he said reproachfully. "It's a pity you didn't. Why are you so bad? I'll push you back down." With a body steeled by athletics, she seized Karl, who was so bewildered that for a moment he forgot to go limp, and carried him to the window. But on approaching the window he came to his senses, freed himself by swiveling his hips around quickly, and then in turn seized her. "Oh, you're hurting me," she said at once. Karl, however, thought that he should not release her now. He gave her sufficient freedom to move at will but kept following her about and did not release her. Besides, it was so easy to get an arm around her in that tight dress. "Let me go," she whispered; her flushed face was now beside his, indeed so close that he had to strain his eyes to look at her. "Let me go, I'll give you something wonderful." Why does she have to sob like that, Karl thought, it can't be hurting her, I'm certainly not squeezing her, and he did not release her. But then all of a sudden he felt her steadily increasing strength press against his body, and after quickly extricating herself, she caught him in a skillful tackle, warded off his legs with footwork from some unfamiliar wrestling technique, and drove him toward the wall while still taking splendidly even breaths. By the wall, however, was a settee, where she deposited Karl; then, bending down only slightly toward him, she said: "Now see if you can move." "You cat, you wild cat," Karl could barely cry out amid the muddle of anger and shame besetting him. "You're truly insane, you wild cat." "Watch what you say," she said, and slid one hand over his throat, then began to squeeze it so tightly that Karl could only gasp for air; she drew the other hand across his cheek, first touching it, and then withdrew her hand and raised it ever higher in the air, ready to let it fall at any moment with a great slap. "What would you say," she asked, "if as punishment for treating a lady like this, you got a good slap in the face to take home with you? While it might be useful to you as you go through life, it wouldn't exactly leave you with fond memories. I do feel sorry for you—you're a tolerably handsome youth, and if you'd learned some jujitsu, you'd probably have beaten me up. But still—just seeing you lying there like that makes me hugely tempted to slap you in the face. I shall probably regret it; but if I do go ahead, mark my words, I'll be doing so almost against my will. And then of course I won't stop at one slap but shall go on hitting you left and right until your cheeks start swelling. And perhaps you are indeed a man of honor—I should almost like to think so—and after being slapped you simply won't want to go on living and will do away with yourself. But why were you so hostile toward me? Perhaps you don't like me? You think it's not worth your while to come to my room? Watch out! All of a sudden I almost let you have it. If you get off scot-free today, though, make sure you behave more decently next time around. After all, I'm not your uncle, whom you can evidently treat very brazenly. Besides, I'd like you to know that even if I let you off without a single slap, you shouldn't imagine that so far as your honor is concerned, this is quite the same thing as actually getting slapped; if that is what you really thought, I should prefer to give you an actual slapping. Goodness knows what Mack will say when I describe all this to him." Remembering Mack, she released Karl, in whose indistinct thoughts Mack appeared as a rescuer. Still feeling the pressure of Klara's hand on his throat, he wriggled about a little, then lay still.

She demanded that he get up; he did not respond, nor did he move. Somewhere she lit a candle; the room lit up, a pattern of blue zigzag appeared on the ceiling, but Karl lay there quite motionless, his head leaning on the sofa cushion exactly where Klara had set it down, and he did not move it an inch. Klara walked about in the room, her skirt rustling around her legs, and then stood a long while, presumably by the window. "Had a good sulk?" one could hear her ask. Karl found it difficult to accept that he could find no peace in this room that Mr. Pollunder had after all set aside for him. That girl wandered about, then stopped and talked, and he was so indescribably sick of her. His only desire was to take a quick nap and get away. He no longer even wanted to go to bed, just to stay there on the settee. He was merely waiting for her to leave so that he could get up when she left, jump over to the door, bolt it, and then throw himself back down on the settee. He had such a strong urge to stretch out and yawn, though not in Klara's presence.

And thus he lay, staring up into the air and sensing his face become increasingly motionless; a fly circling about him swam before his eyes, although he could not quite tell what it was.

Klara approached him again and bent down to catch his eye, and if he had not restrained himself, he would have had to look at her. "I'm leaving now," she said. "You may feel like coming over later. My room is the fourth on this side of the corridor, beginning with this door here. So you pass three more doors, and then it's the next. I'm not going back down to the dining room and shall stay in my room. You've really tired me out. I cannot promise I'll wait up for you, but if you want to come, then do so. Remember that you promised to play something on the piano for me. But perhaps I have so unnerved you that you cannot move; then stay here and have a good sleep. I won't tell Father about our scuffle for now; I'm just saying this in case you're worried." And in spite of her ostensible weariness she rushed out of the room in two bounds.

Karl immediately sat up straight; all that lying around had become quite intolerable. In order to move about a little, he went to the door and looked into the corridor. How dark it was out there! He was glad when he had shut and locked the door and could be at his table in the candlelight again. He resolved not to stay in this house any longer and to go downstairs to Mr. Pollunder and tell him openly how Klara had treated him—having to confess his defeat did not in the least disturb him—and, armed with this surely adequate explanation, ask for permission to drive or walk home. If Mr. Pollunder raised some objection to his going back at once, Karl would request that the servant at least take him to the nearest hotel. Although one did not generally treat amiable hosts as Karl intended to do, it was even rarer to treat a guest as Klara had done. She had even thought she was being kind in promising not to mention their scuffle to Mr. Pollunder for the time being, but that in

itself was truly outrageous. Had Karl been asked to enter a
wrestling contest in which it was shameful to be thrown about
by a girl who had probably been learning wrestling tricks for
most of her life? And besides, she had even been instructed by
Mack. Well, she could go and tell him everything; he was certainly quite understanding, as Karl knew, although he had never
really had a chance to experience this in person. Karl knew too
that if Mack were to instruct him, he would make better progress than Klara; one day he would come back, probably without actually being invited, and after checking the layout first, of
course, so as to acquire the precise knowledge that had given
Klara such an advantage, use her to dust off the settee onto
which she had just thrown him.

Now it was simply a matter of finding one's way back to the
dining room, where in the initial confusion he had probably
misplaced his hat. Of course, he intended to take along the candle, but even with a little light it was not easy to find one's way
about. For instance, he could not tell whether this room was on
the same floor as the dining room. On the way over Klara had
dragged him, so that he hadn't been able to look around; Mr.
Green and the servants carrying the candelabras had also kept
him busy, and indeed he wasn't even able to say how many
staircases they had passed, one, two, or perhaps even none. If
the view from here was any indication, the room was fairly
high up, and so he tried to imagine them taking the stairs, but
even at the entrance they had had to go up several stairs; so
why couldn't this side of the house be elevated also? If only
there had been a glimmer of light from a door somewhere
along the corridor or one could have heard a voice from afar,
however faintly!

His pocket watch, a present from his uncle, indicated eleven;
he took the candle and went into the corridor. In case the
search should prove futile he left his door open, for he could

then find his room again and also, in case of dire emergency, the door to Klara's room. For safety's sake, he blocked the door with a chair to prevent its blowing shut. In the corridor there was a most unfortunate draft blowing against him—he turned left, of course, away from Klara's door—and although it was actually a very weak draft, it could easily have blown out the candle, so Karl had to shield the flame with his hand and often halt for a moment to let the battered flame recover. Progress was slow, so the route seemed twice as long. Karl had already passed lengthy stretches of walls without any doors; one couldn't even picture what lay behind them. Then came one door after the other; he tried to open several, but they were locked, the rooms evidently uninhabited. This was an unbelievable waste of space, and Karl recalled the eastern neighborhoods of New York that his uncle had promised to show him, where several families apparently lived together in one little room, and a family home amounted to no more than one corner, where children flocked about their parents. And so many of these rooms stood empty, their only purpose being to make a hollow sound whenever anyone knocked. Mr. Pollunder seemed to Karl to be misled by his false friends, infatuated with his daughter, and thereby corrupted. Uncle Jakob's judgment about Pollunder had no doubt been correct, and it was merely his principle of not influencing Karl's judgments of other people that was responsible for this visit and all this wandering about through the corridors. Karl wanted to say so to his uncle first thing the following day, for in accordance with his own principle his uncle would be happy to listen patiently to his nephew's judgment of him. Besides, his uncle's principle was perhaps the only thing Karl disliked in him and even then not absolutely.

Suddenly the wall on one side of the corridor ended and gave way to an ice-cold marble balustrade. Karl put down the candle and leaned over cautiously. A dark void wafted toward him. If this was the main hall in the house—in the glimmer from the candle one could now distinguish part of the vaultlike ceiling—why hadn't they entered through this hall? What purpose could be served by this large, deep space? One stood as if in the gallery of a church. Karl almost regretted not being able to stay until the following day; he would have liked to be led around by Pollunder and have him explain everything to him in the daylight.

Besides, the balustrade did not go on for long, and Karl soon found himself enveloped by the enclosed corridor again. At a sudden bend in the corridor Karl banged into the wall with his full weight, and only by clutching the candle with unflagging concentration did he fortunately prevent it from falling and becoming extinguished. Since this corridor would not end, and there was no window anywhere through which he could take a look, nor any sign of life above or below, Karl was beginning to think he had been going in a circle the entire time, and he even hoped he might come upon the open door to his room, but neither it nor the balustrade came around again. Hitherto Karl had refrained from shouting out loud, for at such a late hour he did not want to make any noise in this unfamiliar house, but he now realized that the noise wouldn't do any harm in this unlit house and he was about to send a loud hello echoing up and down the corridor when he noticed a small light approaching, actually from the direction he had come from himself. But now he could at last gauge the length of this straight corridor; the house was not so much a villa as a fortress. Such was Karl's joy on noticing this saving light that he abandoned all caution and ran toward it; after a few strides his candle went out. He ignored this, for he no longer needed the candle, and the old servant who was approaching with the lantern would, of course, show him the right way.

"Who are you?" asked the servant, raising the lantern to

Karl's face and thereby illuminating his own. His face seemed rather stiff on account of his large white full beard, which reached down to his chest, where it tapered off in silky ringlets. He must be a faithful servant if he's allowed to wear a beard like that, thought Karl, continually gazing up and down the length of the beard without feeling hampered by the scrutiny that he himself was undergoing. Besides, he responded at once, saying he was a guest of Mr. Pollunder's and simply wanted to go from his room to the dining room but had not succeeded in finding it. "I see," said the servant, "we still haven't installed electric lighting." "I know," said Karl. "Don't you want to use my lamp to light your candle," the servant asked. "Yes, please," said Karl, and did so. "It's so drafty out here in the corridors," said the servant, "the candle can easily get blown out, and that's why I have a lantern." "Yes, a lantern is much more practical," said Karl. "You're covered in candle drippings," said the servant, illuminating Karl's suit with the candle. "I hadn't even noticed," cried Karl, much to his regret, for it was a black outfit that, according to his uncle, suited him best. The scuffle with Klara could scarcely have done the suit any good, it occurred to him. The servant was kind enough to clean off the suit as best he could in his haste; Karl turned around in front of him to show him scattered stains, which the servant obediently removed. "Why is there such a draft," asked Karl once they had started moving again. "There's still a great deal of construction left to be done," said the servant, "they've started work on the renovations, but it's going very slowly. And besides all that, the construction workers have now gone on strike, as you may know. There's always trouble with that kind of construction. There are several large gaps that haven't been walled up, and the draft blows right through the house. I couldn't survive it here if I didn't have my ears stuffed with cotton." "Then I should probably raise my voice?" asked Karl. "Your voice is perfectly clear," said the servant. "But to return to the construction, the draft out here is quite intolerable, especially near the chapel, which will eventually have to be closed off from the rest of the house." "So the balustrade along this corridor opens out into a chapel?" "Yes." "Just as I thought," said Karl. "It's well worth seeing," said the servant, "if it weren't for the chapel, Mr. Mack probably wouldn't have bought the house." "Mr. Mack?" asked Karl, "I thought the house belonged to Mr. Pollunder." "Yes, of course," said the servant, "but Mr. Mack played the decisive role in purchasing it. You don't know Mr. Mack?" "Oh yes," said Karl. "But what's the connection between him and Mr. Pollunder?" "He's Miss Klara's fiancé," said the servant. "That I didn't know," said Karl, and he stopped. "Is that so surprising to you?" "I just want to let it sink in. One can make the greatest mistakes if one isn't aware of such relationships," replied Karl. "I'm just surprised they didn't let you know," said the servant. "Well, yes," said Karl, sounding embarrassed. "They probably thought you already knew," said the servant, "after all, it's not exactly news. Besides, here we are," and he opened a door, exposing stairs that led directly up to the back door of the dining room, which was as brightly illuminated as it had been upon Karl's arrival. Before entering the dining room, from which the voices of Mr. Pollunder and Mr. Green still emanated just as they had some two hours previously, the servant said: "If you like, I shall wait for you here, and then I shall take you to your room. On one's first evening here, it's always difficult to find one's way about." "I shall not be going back to my room," said Karl, without quite knowing why it made him sad to say so. "It won't be that bad," said the servant, patting him on the arm and smiling somewhat condescendingly. He had probably thought that Karl meant he wanted to spend all night in the dining room, talking and drinking with these gentlemen. Karl had no desire to make any confession just now; besides, he thought that this servant, whom he preferred to the other servants here, could show him how to get to New York, and he therefore said: "If you're willing to wait, that would be most kind of you, and I gratefully accept your offer. I certainly shall come out again in a little while and tell you what I intend to do. I'm quite sure I'll still need your help." "Fine," said the servant, placing the lantern on the floor and seating himself on a low pedestal, which was empty probably on account of the renovations, "so I'll wait here. By the way, you may leave the candle with me," added the servant as Karl was about to enter the room with the lighted candle. "I'm so distracted," said Karl, handing the candle to the servant, who merely nodded to him, though one could not tell whether this was deliberate or whether it came from the way he shook his head.

Karl opened the door, which rattled loudly, though not through any fault of his own, for it consisted of a single glass pane that almost bent when it was pushed open with the door handle. Startled, Karl released the door, for he had wanted to enter especially quietly. Although he did not turn around again, he clearly sensed that the servant behind him must have climbed down from his pedestal and shut the door carefully, without making the slightest sound. "Pardon me for disturbing you," he said to the two gentlemen, whose large, astonished faces turned toward him. Meanwhile he surveyed the room with a quick glance to see whether he might not be able to find his hat somewhere. But there was no sign of it; the dining room table had been cleared; how unpleasant it would be if someone had carried his hat into the kitchen. "But where did you leave Klara?" asked Mr. Pollunder, who incidentally did not seem to mind being disturbed, for he had turned around in his armchair and now sat squarely facing Karl. Feigning indifference, Mr. Green pulled out a briefcase the size and thickness of which made it a monster of its kind, and he appeared to search through its many pockets for a certain piece of paper while also reading others that he came across. "I do have a request to make, and it's important you don't misunderstand it," said Karl, and hurrying over to Mr. Pollunder, he put his hand on the armrest of his chair so as to get very close to him. "What kind of request?" asked Mr. Pollunder, gazing at Karl with a completely open expression. "It is, of course, already granted." And he put his arm around Karl and drew him between his legs. Karl endured this gladly, although he did in general feel too grown-up for such treatment. But, of course, it now became even more difficult to come out with the request. "So how do you like it here?" asked Mr. Pollunder. "Isn't it liberating to leave the city and be out here in the county? Most evenings"—and at this point he gave Mr. Green an unmistakable side glance, which was partly blocked by Karl—"most evenings this is how I feel." He talks, Karl thought, as if he were unaware of the size of this house, of the endless corridors, the chapel, the empty rooms, and the darkness everywhere. "Well!" said Mr. Pollunder, "now let's hear your request!" and he gave Karl, who stood there silently, a friendly shake. "Please," said Karl, but no matter how hard he tried to lower his voice, it was impossible to prevent Green, who sat nearby, from overhearing everything, and Karl would have been happy to forgo that request, which could be regarded as an insult to Pollunder— "Please let me go home right away, tonight." And now that the worst had been said, everything else tumbled out all the more quickly; without even resorting to the tiniest lie, he said things that he had never even thought of before. "What I'd most like to do is go home. I'll be delighted to come back, for I like being wherever you are, Mr. Pollunder. Only I cannot stay today. As you know, my uncle only reluctantly gave me permission to visit you. No doubt he had his own good reasons for that, as he certainly has for everything he does, and I chose to force him to give me permission against his own better judgment. I simply abused his love for me. Whatever doubts he may have had about this visit are certainly beside the point now. I'm absolutely certain, Mr. Pollunder, that those doubts contain nothing that could possibly hurt your feelings, those of a man who's my uncle's best, his very best, friend. Nobody else even comes close to your friendship with my uncle. That is really the only excuse I have for being disobedient, and it's not good enough. You may not have a precise understanding of my relationship with my uncle, so I shall touch only on what is most essential. Until I complete my English studies and have become reasonably well acquainted with local business practices, I shall have to depend entirely on my uncle's goodness, of which as a blood relative I can of course avail myself freely. You mustn't think that I could already manage to make a decent living—and God preserve me from the other sort. Unfortunately, my education has been too impractical for that. I spent four years as an average student in a European Latin high school, and in terms of earning a living that means less than nothing, since the curriculum in our Latin high schools is rather backward. You would laugh if I told you what I was learning there. If you continue your studies, finish high school, and go on to university, all this probably sorts itself out, and you end up with a decent education that allows you to do something and gives you the resolve to go out and earn money. Unfortunately, I got pulled out of that integrated program of study; sometimes I think I don't know anything; besides, even with everything I would have learned, it still wouldn't be sufficient for America. In my home country they're now setting up a number of reformed high schools, where you can also study modern languages and possibly even commerce; when I left primary school, there were no such schools yet. My father wanted me to take English lessons, but first of all, I couldn't possibly have imagined the misfortune that would befall me and the great need I would have for English, and besides I had to study a lot in high school, so there was not much time left for other things. I'm saying all this to show you how much I depend on my uncle and thus the extent of my obligation to him. You'll surely agree that under these circumstances I cannot allow myself to do anything against even his merely presumed will. And so as to make at least partial amends for the mistake I made in his regard I must go home at once." During Karl's long speech Mr. Pollunder had listened attentively, often pressing him against his body, quite inconspicuously, especially whenever mention was made of Karl's uncle, and several times he glanced earnestly, and as if expectantly, at Green, who was still occupied with his briefcase. Yet as he spoke, Karl became clearly conscious of his position in relation to his uncle; he became increasingly uneasy and unwittingly tried to extricate himself from Pollunder's arm, for everything here was hemming him in, whereas the path to his uncle, through the glass door, across the steps, down the drive, along the roads, and through the suburbs to the main thoroughfare, finally turning in at his uncle's house, seemed to him a coherent whole lying before him, empty, smooth, prepared just for him, and beckoning him with a strong voice. Mr. Pollunder's kindness and Mr. Green's awfulness merged, and all he wanted to procure from this smoky room was permission to leave. Although feeling closed off from Mr. Pollunder and ready to battle Mr. Green, he was filled from all sides with a fear which was indistinct but nonetheless gave him jolts that dulled his eyes.

He stepped back and was now equidistant from Mr. Pollunder and Mr. Green. "Didn't you want to tell him something?" Mr. Pollunder asked Mr. Green, seizing his hand as if beseeching him. "I wouldn't know what to tell him," said Mr. Green, who had finally drawn a letter from his briefcase and put it down on the table before him. "It's very praiseworthy that he should want to go back to his uncle, and one might quite reasonably assume that he will thereby give his uncle great pleasure. Unless he has through his disobedience already made his uncle exceedingly mad, which is certainly possible. In that case it would be better if he stayed. But it's hard to say anything more definitive than that; although we're both friends of his uncle's and it would be hard to detect any difference in degree between my friendship with his uncle and that of Mr. Pollunder, we cannot peer into his uncle's mind, especially not across the many miles that separate us from New York." "Please, Mr. Green," said Karl, and overcoming his reluctance, he approached Mr. Green, "I gather from what you've said that you too think it best that I should return at once." "I said nothing of the sort," declared Mr. Green, who, burying himself in the letter, ran his fingers back and forth along the margins. Evidently he wished to signal in this way that he had been asked by Mr. Pollunder and had answered him but that he really had nothing further to say to Karl.

Meanwhile Mr. Pollunder had approached Karl and gently drawn him away from Mr. Green toward one of the large windows. "My dear Mr. Rossmann," he said, bending down to Karl's ear; and then, as if readying himself, he wiped his face with a handkerchief, stopped at his nose, and blew it. "Surely you don't think I want to keep you here against your will. That's absolutely not the case. But I cannot place the automobile at your disposal, since it's parked far away in a public garage, and I have not yet had the time to set up my own garage, everything still being in flux here. In any case the chauffeur doesn't sleep in the house but somewhere near the garage; I don't quite know where. Besides, he is under no obligation to be at home just now—he must simply arrive here with the automobile on time each morning. But none of this would be an obstacle to your returning home this instant, and if you insist, I shall accompany you at once to the next station on the suburban line, which is so far away that you'd probably not reach home much earlier—we're leaving at seven—than if you went by automobile." "Well, Mr. Pollunder, in that case I should prefer to take the suburban train," said Karl. "I hadn't even thought of the train. You said if I took the train I'd get back earlier in the morning than if I went by automobile." "But it doesn't make much difference." "Still and all, Mr. Pollunder, still and all," said Karl, "I shall always be happy to return, for I have such fond memories of your kindness, assuming, of course, that you still want to invite me after the way I've behaved today, and perhaps next time I shall be able to give you a better idea why I so value each minute that brings me closer to seeing my uncle again." And as though he had already received permission to leave, he added: "But on no account should you accompany me. Besides, it's quite unnecessary. There's a servant outside, who will gladly accompany me to the station. Now I need only look for my hat." And as he said those last words, he was already striding across the room to make one last hasty attempt to see whether he could find his hat. "Couldn't I help you out with this cap," said Mr. Green, pulling a cap from his briefcase, "it may happen to fit you." Astonished, Karl halted and said: "But I'm not going to take your cap away from you. I can perfectly well go bareheaded. I don't need anything." "It is not my cap. Just take it!" "Well, thank you," said Karl, and to avoid any further delay he took the cap. He put it on, laughed since it fit perfectly, then took it off and gazed at it, but could not find the distinctive mark he sought; the cap was brand-new. "It fits so well!" he said. "So it does fit!" exclaimed Mr. Green, hitting the table.

Karl was already on his way to the door to call the servant when Mr. Green rose, stretched out after his ample meal and lengthy rest, slapped himself vigorously on the chest, and sounding as if he was giving advice and at the same time issuing an order, he said: "Before you leave, you must bid farewell to Miss Klara." "Yes, you must," said Mr. Pollunder, who had risen also. One could hear from the way he spoke that his words were not heartfelt; letting his hands fall slackly against the seam of his trousers, he kept buttoning and unbuttoning his coat, which, being tailored in the prevailing fashion, was short, barely reached his hips, and ill became a person of Mr. Pollunder's girth. Besides, seeing him standing beside Mr. Green, one had the distinct impression that Mr. Pollunder's fatness was not at all healthy, for his massive back was rather hunched, his stomach soft and impossibly flabby, a true burden, and his face looked pale and troubled. Beside him stood Mr. Green, who was perhaps even fatter than Mr. Pollunder, but his was a cohesive, self-supporting fatness; he had his feet locked in military fashion and held his head erect, letting it swing back and forth; he was evidently a great gymnast, a star athlete.

"Well then," Mr. Green continued, "you may go to Miss Klara for the time being. That will surely give you pleasure and also fits in nicely with my schedule. For before you leave I have something interesting to tell you that might indeed affect your return. Unfortunately, I cannot disclose anything to you before midnight, on orders from above. As you can imagine, I too find this most regrettable since it's disrupting my night's sleep, but I will carry out my task. It's now a quarter past eleven, so I still have time to finish my business with Mr. Pollunder, and since your presence would be disruptive, you can go and have a nice time with Miss Klara. Show up here at twelve o'clock sharp, and you'll find out what you need to know."

Could Karl turn down this demand, which really required only that he accord Mr. Pollunder the minimum of politeness and gratitude and which was made by an individual who was

usually quite crude and standoffish, whereas Mr. Pollunder—
in other words, the person directly concerned—scarcely inter-
vened with a word or a glance? And what was the interesting
news he wasn't permitted to discover until midnight? If it did
not hasten his return by at least the three-quarters of an hour
by which it was delaying it, then he had little interest in the
matter. But his greatest uncertainty was whether he could go to
Klara, who was, after all, his enemy. If only he had at least
brought along the iron bar his uncle had given him as a paper-
weight. Klara's room might well be a dangerous lair. But now it
was of course completely impossible to say the slightest thing
against Klara, for she was not only Pollunder's daughter but
also, as he had just heard, Mack's fiancée. If she had just treated
him a little differently, he would have admired her openly
because of her connections. While still engaged in such thoughts,
he quickly realized that nobody was about to ask him what he
thought, for Green opened the door and said to the servant,
who jumped up from the pedestal: "Take this young man to
Miss Klara."

That's the way to carry out orders, Karl thought as the
servant, almost running and groaning from old age and infir-
mity, drew him along an especially quick path to Klara's room.
When Karl reached his room, the door to which was still open,
he wanted to step inside for a moment, perhaps so as to calm
down. However, the servant refused to let him do so. "No," he
said, "you must go to Miss Klara. You heard so yourself." "I
would only stay for a moment," said Karl, and he thought of
throwing himself down on the settee for a while to divert himself and thereby ensure that the time from now until midnight
would seem to pass more quickly. "Don't make my task any
more difficult than it already is," said the servant. He seems to
believe that my having to go to Miss Klara is some form of
punishment, Karl thought, and he advanced several steps, only

to halt again in defiance. "But now come along, young man," said the servant, "seeing as you are still here. I realize you wanted to leave at night, but everything doesn't always work out the way one wants; I certainly did tell you right away that this would scarcely be possible." "Yes, I do want to leave and I will leave," said Karl, "I just want to say goodbye to Miss Klara." "Is that so," said the servant, and Karl could see that he didn't believe a word of what he had said, "then why are you reluctant to say goodbye, just come."

"Who's in the corridor," Klara's voice rang out, and one could see her leaning from a nearby door, holding a large table lamp covered with a red shade. The servant rushed over to her and reported the news; Karl followed him slowly. "You're late," said Klara. Refraining from answering just now, Karl said to the servant in a tone of voice that was soft but also, given his character, commanding: "You shall wait for me right by this door!" "I was about to go to sleep," said Klara, putting the lamp on the table. Just as he had done in the dining room, the servant closed the door carefully from the outside. "It's already after eleven-thirty." "After eleven-thirty," Karl repeated quizzically, as if shocked by these figures.

"Then I shall have to leave at once," said Karl, "since I must be downstairs in the dining room at twelve sharp." "My, you must have some urgent business," said Klara, absently straightening the folds in her loose nightgown; her face glowed, and she smiled constantly. Karl thought he could tell that there was no danger of another fight with Klara. "But couldn't you play a little on the piano, as Papa promised yesterday and you promised today." "But isn't it too late now?" asked Karl. He would have been happy to oblige her, for she was very different than earlier, as if she had somehow risen to Pollunder's circle and then on to Mack's. "Yes, it is indeed late," she said, having evidently lost the desire to hear music. "So each note will resound through the entire house; if you play, I'm sure even the servants in the attic rooms will be awakened." "Then I won't play. I'm certainly hoping to return; by the way, if this isn't too great an imposition, do pay a visit to my uncle and, while you're there, take a look at my room. I have a splendid piano. My uncle gave it to me as a present. And then if you'd like, I'll play all of my little pieces for you; unfortunately, there aren't that many, and they aren't suitable for such a large instrument, which should be reserved for performances by virtuosos. But even that pleasure can be yours if you give me advance warning of your arrival, since my uncle is about to engage a famous teacher for me—you can imagine how much I'm looking forward to this— and he plays so well it would be a good idea if you visited during a lesson. Quite frankly, I'm glad it's too late for me to play, for I'm still incapable of playing anything; you'd be surprised how little I can play. And now permit me to take my leave; in any case it's already bedtime." And since Klara gave him a benevolent look and did not seem to bear the slightest grudge over their scuffle, he held out his hand, adding with a smile: "As people say in my homeland, 'Sleep well and sweet dreams.' "

"Wait," she said, without taking his hand, "but perhaps you should after all play." And she disappeared through a little side door, beside which stood a piano. What's the matter? thought Karl, I cannot wait for long, no matter how pleasant she happens to be. There was a knock on the door to the corridor, and the servant, who did not dare to pull it open, whispered through a little crack in the door: "Excuse me, I've just been summoned and cannot wait anymore." "Off you go then," said Karl, confident he could find his way to the dining room on his own, "just leave the lamp outside the door. By the way, how late is it?" "It's almost a quarter to twelve," said the servant. "How slowly time passes," said Karl. The servant was about to shut the door when Karl, recalling that he had not yet given him a tip, took a shilling from his trousers pocket—in American fashion he now carried his change jingling loosely in his trousers pocket and kept his banknotes in his waistcoat pocket—and handed it to the servant, saying: "For all your good work."

Klara had already returned, holding her trim hair with both hands, when Karl realized that he should not have dismissed the servant, for who would now take him to the train station? Well, surely Mr. Pollunder could still get hold of a servant; besides, that same servant might already have been summoned to the dining room and would therefore be available. "So I'm asking you to play a little something for me. We so rarely hear music here that one doesn't want to miss any such opportunity." "Then it's certainly high time," said Karl, and without any further reflection, he sat down quickly at the piano. "Do you want some sheet music," Klara asked. "No thanks, I cannot even read music properly," answered Karl, and began to play. It was only a little song that, as Karl knew only too well, needed to be played very slowly if others, especially foreigners, were to understand it, but nevertheless he raced through it in the tempo of an extremely fast marching song. When it was over, the disturbed stillness returned, as if in a rush, to occupy the old house again. They sat without moving, as if in a daze. "Very nice," said Klara, but after such a performance no polite phrase could have flattered Karl. "How late is it?" he asked. "A quarter to twelve." "I still have a little more time," he said, and then he thought: So it'll have to be one or the other. While I'm certainly not obliged to play all ten songs I know, there's one I could conceivably play well. And he began to perform his beloved soldier's song, so slowly that the listener's roused desire continually reached for the next note, which Karl held on to for some time and then at last released. As with every song, he first had to glance at the keys he needed, but rising within he could sense a sadness that already searched beyond the ending of the song for another ending that, however, it failed to find. "I'm simply no good," Karl said on finishing the song, and looked at Klara with tears in his eyes.

Just then loud clapping rang out from the adjacent room. "There's someone listening!" cried Karl, startled. "Mack," said Klara, softly. And one could already hear Mack calling: "Karl Rossmann, Karl Rossmann!"

Using both legs simultaneously, Karl swung himself over the piano bench and opened the door. He saw Mack seated, half reclining, on a large four-poster bed, the quilt loosely thrown over his legs. The sole, and rather schoolgirlish, adornment on the otherwise very simple bed, which was roughly hewn from heavy timber, consisted of a canopy made of blue silk. There was only one candle burning, but the bedclothes and Mack's nightshirt were so white that the reflected candlelight falling on them was almost blinding; even the canopy, with its slightly billowing and not quite taut silk drapery, shone, at least at the edges. But behind Mack the bed and all else sank into complete darkness. Klara, leaning against the bedpost, now had eyes only for Mack.

"Hello," said Mack, extending his hand toward Karl. "You do play very well, I was only aware of your riding skills." "I'm no good at either," said Karl. "Had I known you were listening, I wouldn't have played. But your lady friend—" he broke off; he was reluctant to say *fiancée* since it was clear that Mack and Klara were already sleeping together. "I thought so," said Mack, "and Klara had to entice you out from New York for that reason, otherwise I wouldn't have heard you play. It's highly amateurish all right, and you made several mistakes even in those songs with the very primitive arrangement that you had practiced beforehand, but still I was very pleased, and not just because I never look down on anybody else's playing.

But wouldn't you like to sit down and stay a little longer? Do give him a chair, Klara." "Thank you," said Karl, hesitating. "Much as I'd like to stay, I cannot. I'm discovering too late that there are such cozy rooms in this house." "I'm renovating everything in the same style," said Mack.

Just then a bell rang out twelve times in rapid succession, with each chime breaking into the previous one; Karl could feel a breeze on his cheeks from the great movement of the bells. "What was this village that had such bells!

"It's high time," said Karl, and merely extending his hands to Mack and Klara without shaking theirs, he ran into the corridor. He could not find the lantern and regretted having tipped the servant prematurely. He tried to grope along the wall toward the open door to his room but had scarcely gone halfway when he saw Mr. Green, candle in hand, tottering hastily toward him. In the same hand as the candle he held a letter.

"Rossmann, what took you so long? Why have you kept me waiting? And what were you up to at Miss Klara's?" He's asking so many questions! thought Karl. And now he's even pushing me up against the wall, for he now stood right before Karl, who leaned his back against the wall. In this corridor Green took on ridiculously large proportions, and Karl jokingly asked himself whether Green might not have gobbled up good old Mr. Pollunder.

"You're really not a man who's true to his word. You promise to come down at twelve but instead you lurk about Miss Klara's door. Whereas I promised you something interesting for midnight, and here I am with it already."

Whereupon he handed Karl the letter. The envelope was addressed thus: "For Karl Rossmann. To be handed to him personally, at midnight, wherever he may be found." "Besides," Mr. Green said as Karl opened the letter, "it should be noted that I drove here from New York for your sake, so you shouldn't make me run down these corridors after you."

"From my uncle!" said Karl, after merely glancing at the letter. "I was expecting it," he said, turning to Mr. Green.

"I couldn't care less whether you were expecting it or not. Just read it," he said, holding out the candle for Karl.

By its light Karl read:

My beloved nephew! As you will have realized during our unfortunately all too brief time living together, I am very much a man of principle. This is very unpleasant and sad not only for those around me but also for myself, yet it is to my principles that I owe everything that I am and no one can ask that I should forsake the ground on which I stand, no one, not even you, my dear nephew, even if you were the first to show up, should I ever consider allowing such a general attack against me to proceed. Then I would much rather catch you in these two hands, with which I'm holding this paper and writing these lines, and lift you up in the air. But since there is at present no sign that this could ever happen, after the incident today I am absolutely obliged to send you away and urgently entreat you not to call on me in person nor to contact me either by letter or through intermediaries. Contrary to my will you decided to leave me this evening, and so you should now abide by that decision throughout your life, for only then will it have been a manly one. As bearer of this message I have chosen my best friend Mr. Green, who will certainly come up with enough lenient words for you, which I don't presently have at my disposal. He is a man of influence and, even if only for my sake, he will support you by word and deed as you take your first independent steps. In trying to understand our separation, which in concluding this letter I again find incomprehensible, I must tell myself over and over again: Karl, nothing good ever comes from your family. Should Mr. Green forget to hand over your trunk and your umbrella, remind him to do so. With best wishes for your continuing well-being,

Your faithful Uncle Jakob.

"Are you finished?" asked Green. "Yes," said Karl. "Have you brought my trunk and my umbrella?" asked Karl. "Here it is," said Green, and he took Karl's old trunk, which he had hidden with his left hand behind his back, and put it on the floor beside Karl. "And the umbrella?" Karl insisted. "It's all here," said Green, and he pulled out the umbrella, which he had hung from one of his trousers pockets. "A certain Schubal, a chief machinist of the Hamburg Amerika Line, brought your belongings, claiming to have found them on the ship. You can thank him at some point." "At least I now have my old belongings again," said Karl, laying his umbrella on the trunk. "But the senator would like to inform you that you should treat them more carefully in the future," declared Mr. Green, and then, evidently out of sheer curiosity, he asked: "But what's that odd-looking trunk?" "It's the trunk that the soldiers in my homeland have to carry when they report for duty," answered Karl. "It's my father's old army trunk. It's extremely practical in other ways too." He added with a smile: "Unless one happens to leave it lying about." "You've learned a lesson at last," said Mr. Green, "and you probably don't have a second uncle in America. I'm also giving you a third-class ticket to San Francisco. I decided that you should go there, first because you'll have better employment prospects in the East, and second because your uncle has his hand in everything you could be considered for here, and we must absolutely avoid the possibility of your meeting again. In 'Frisco you can work away undisturbed, just start off quietly at the very bottom and try to work your way up bit by bit."

Karl could hear no malice in these words; the bad news that had lain within Green all evening had been delivered, and from now on Green would seem a harmless man, one with whom one could perhaps speak more frankly than with anyone else. Even the best person, chosen through no fault of his own as the bearer of such a secret and tormenting decision, would seem suspect—at least so long as he had to keep it to himself. "Well," said Karl, who was waiting for confirmation from this experienced man, "I will leave this house at once, for I was accepted here as the nephew of my uncle, whereas, as a stranger, I have no business here. Could you be so kind as to show me the way out and lead me to a path that will take me to the closest inn?" "But quickly now," said Green, "you're causing me quite a bit of trouble." On seeing the great step forward Green took, Karl hesitated; there was surely something suspect about such haste, and he grabbed Green by the bottom of his jacket; then, realizing all of a sudden what was actually happening, he said: "You've got to explain one more thing. On the envelope it merely says I should receive the letter at midnight, wherever I may be found. So why did you try to keep me here by referring to that letter when I wanted to leave at a quarter past? You went beyond your instructions." Prefacing his answer with an exaggerated gesture that indicated the futility of Karl's remark, Green said: "Now does it really say on the envelope that I should run myself into the ground for your sake, and does the body of the letter really indicate that this is how those words on the cover should be interpreted? And if I hadn't kept you here, I would have had to hand you the letter at midnight on some country road." "No," said Karl, refusing to be deterred, "that isn't quite so. On the envelope it says: 'To be delivered after midnight.' If you were too tired, you couldn't have followed me at all, or I would have reached my uncle's at midnight, which even Mr. Pollunder said was impossible, and finally, it would have been your duty to take your automobile—which there was suddenly no further mention of—and return me to my uncle's, since I was pleading to go back. Doesn't the inscription clearly mean that midnight is still supposed to be my deadline? And you're to blame for my missing it."

Karl looked sharply at Green and thought that he could discern in Green a struggle between his shame at being thus exposed and his joy on having successfully accomplished his purpose. Finally, Green pulled himself together and, as if interrupting Karl, who had, however, been silent for some time, said brusquely: "I don't want to hear another word from you!" and swinging open a small door, he pushed Karl, who had picked up his trunk and umbrella, out into the garden.

Karl was astonished to find himself standing outside. Abutting the house was a staircase without a banister that opened out before him. He had only to go down the steps and turn right a little into the driveway leading to the country road. In this bright moonlight one could not get lost. From the garden below he could hear the constant barking of dogs running about loose in the shadow of the trees. Otherwise it was so quiet that one could hear quite distinctly the sound of the dogs who after their great leaps slammed into the grass.

Karl made his way safely out of the garden, without being bothered by the dogs. He could not determine with any certainty in which direction New York lay; on the way over he had not paid sufficient attention to such details, which would have served him well now. In any case, he said to himself, it was not absolutely necessary that he should go to New York, where nobody expected him and one person most certainly did not. He therefore chose a direction at random and went on his way.

IV

THE MARCH TO RAMSES

—————————

After a brief march Karl reached a small inn, which was in fact only one final little station in the New York railway network and consequently rarely used for overnight lodgings, and asked for the cheapest bed on offer, for he thought he must start saving at once. Upon his request the innkeeper merely motioned to him, as if he were an employee, signaling that he should ascend the stairs, where he was received by a disheveled old woman, who, annoyed at being roused from her sleep, scarcely listened to him and, amid repeated admonishments that he tread softly, led him to a room where, after first hissing "Shush!" she shut the door.

It was so dark that Karl could not tell at first whether the curtains were merely drawn or the room was perhaps windowless; finally he noticed a little attic window and pulled back the cloth, letting in some light. The room had two beds, though both were already occupied. Karl saw two young people, who were fast asleep and seemed less than trustworthy, especially since for no apparent reason they slept fully dressed and one even had his boots on.

Just as Karl uncovered the attic window, one of the sleepers lifted his arms and legs up a little into the air, presenting such a spectacle that Karl, despite his worries, laughed inwardly.

He soon realized that, aside from the fact that there was no other place to sleep, neither a settee nor a sofa, he would get no sleep, for he ought not to jeopardize his trunk, which he had only just recovered, as well as the money he was carrying. Nor did he want to go away, for he dared not go past the chambermaid and the landlord and leave the inn so soon. Finally, it was perhaps no less unsafe here than out on the country road. But it was remarkable that there was no sign of a single piece of luggage in the entire room, at least so far as one could make out in the twilight. But perhaps, and this was most likely, the two young people were house servants, who would soon have to rise to prepare for the guests and therefore slept fully clothed. So while there was no special honor in sleeping with them, there was no danger in it either. Still, he should certainly not lie down to sleep until all such doubts had been resolved.

On the floor near one of the beds was a candle with some matches, and Karl crept over to fetch them. He had no qualms about lighting the candle, for according to the innkeeper's instructions, the room belonged to him as much as to the other two, who had moreover already benefited from half a night's sleep, had possession of the two beds, and were therefore much better off than he. In any case, in bustling about he made every possible effort to avoid waking them up.

First he wanted to check his trunk so as to survey his belongings, which he could barely recall, and in any case the most valuable items would certainly be gone. For if anything got into Schubal's hands, there was little hope of getting it back in one piece. Schubal could certainly have counted on receiving a big tip from his uncle, and if any items had been missing he could always have pointed a finger at the person who was supposed to have watched over the trunk, namely Mr. Butterbaum.

On first opening the trunk, Karl was horrified. All those hours during the voyage he had spent arranging and rearranging the trunk, whereas now everything had been stuffed in so wildly that the lid sprang open as he released the lock. Yet to his delight Karl soon realized that the disorder was merely due to his having during the voyage worn the suit, which was not meant to be packed in the trunk and had been added in with the other things. There was absolutely nothing missing. In the secret pocket of his coat Karl found not only his passport but the money from home, so that when he added in the sum he was carrying, he was well provided for, at least for now. Even the underwear he wore on arrival was there too and had been washed and ironed. He immediately put his watch and money away in his trusty secret pocket. But it was unfortunate that the Veronese salami, which had not disappeared either, had communicated its smell to all of his belongings. Unless it could somehow be eliminated, Karl faced the prospect of going about for months enveloped in this smell.

As he searched through a few objects at the very bottom—a pocket Bible, letter-writing paper, and the photographs of his parents—his cap slipped off his head and fell into the trunk. He recognized it instantly in its old setting; it was his cap, the cap his mother had sent along to be used as a travel cap. However, out of caution he had not worn that cap on the ship, for he knew that people in America generally wore caps rather than hats and therefore wanted to avoid wearing it out before he arrived. And so Mr. Green had amused himself with it at Karl's expense. Perhaps his uncle had given him this task? And in one furious involuntary motion he reached out and seized the lid of the trunk, which slammed shut.

Now there was no going back—he had awakened the two sleepers. First one stretched and yawned; then the other immediately followed suit. Almost the entire contents of the trunk had spilled across the table; if they were thieves, then all they had to do was come over and take their pick. Seeking not only to forestall that possibility but also to clarify the situation at once, Karl approached the beds, candle in hand, and explained why he had the right to be there. They did not appear to have expected an explanation for, still far too drowsy to be able to speak, they simply gazed at him without showing the least astonishment. Although both were still youths, their facial bones had begun to protrude prematurely—whether owing to heavy labor or to some other such ordeal—their unkempt beards hung from their chins, their hair had not been cut in a long time and was very unkempt, and they rubbed their deep-set eyes and even pressed their knuckles into them drowsily.

Determined to take advantage of their temporary weakness, Karl said: "My name is Karl Rossmann, and I am a German. Since we're sharing a room, could you please tell me your names and nationality? I just want to say at once that I'm not claiming a bed, since I arrived so late and have absolutely no intention of sleeping. Besides, you shouldn't take offense at my fine clothes. I am utterly poor and without prospects."

The smaller of the two—the one still wearing his boots— indicated through his arms, legs, and facial expressions that he was not in the least bit interested and that this was not the right time for such chatter, and then he lay down and fell asleep at once; the other, a dark-skinned man, also lay down again, but before falling asleep, he held out his hand casually and said: "That fellow there is Robinson, and he's an Irishman; my name is Delamarche, I am a Frenchman and am asking for some quiet." No sooner had he said those words than he blew out the candle with a great expenditure of breath and fell back on the pillow.

"So the danger has been averted for now," Karl said to himself, and returned to the table. If their sleepiness was not merely a pretense, everything would be fine. The only unpleasant thing about all this was that one was an Irishman. Karl could no longer quite recall in what book he had once read that one should be wary of Irishmen in America. Of course, that time

at his uncle's would have afforded him the best opportunity
to resolve this question about the danger posed by the Irishmen, but he had utterly failed to seize it, believing that he
would always be well situated. Now he at least wanted to take
a closer look at the Irishman in the light of the candle, which he
had relit, and in doing so he discovered that this man actually
looked more tolerable than the Frenchman. There was still a
trace of roundness in his cheeks, and he had a friendly smile
on his face as he slept, insofar as Karl, standing on his tiptoes
some distance away, could make out.

Nevertheless, still firmly determined not to sleep, Karl sat
down on the only chair in the room, put off packing his trunk,
for he had the whole night to do so, and leafed about for a
while in the Bible, without reading anything. Then he picked
up the photograph of his parents in which his diminutive father
stood erect whereas his mother sat a little shrunken in the armchair in front. Father had one hand resting on the back of the
armchair; the other was clenched into a fist on an illustrated
book lying open beside him on a flimsy little jewelry cabinet.
There was also another photograph depicting Karl with his
parents; his father and mother gave him sharp looks, whereas
he had to follow the photographer's instructions and keep his
eyes on the camera. That photograph, though, he did not get to
take along on the voyage.

He therefore scrutinized the one before him all the more
carefully, trying to catch his father's eye from various angles.
But no matter how hard he tried to change his father's appearance by moving the candle around, he refused to become more
animated; besides, there was nothing even remotely true to life
about his firm horizontal mustache; it was simply not a good
picture. But his mother had been better captured; her mouth
was twisted as if she had endured some injury and were forcing
herself to smile. To Karl it seemed that everyone who saw the

picture would be so struck by this that the next moment it seemed as if the very clarity of this impression was too strong and almost nonsensical. How could a picture make one so unshakably convinced of a hidden emotion in the sitter? And for a moment he averted his eyes. When he looked back, he noticed that his mother's hand was hanging over the front of the armrest in the foreground, close enough to be kissed. He wondered whether it wouldn't actually be a good idea to write to his parents, as both of them had indeed requested, and his father very sternly so that last time in Hamburg. True enough, during that terrible evening when his mother had broken the news about the journey to America, he had sworn that he would never write, but in these very different circumstances over here, how much weight should be attached to the oath of an inexperienced youth? He could just as easily have sworn that within a mere two months of his arrival he would be a general in the American militia, whereas in reality he was sitting in the attic room of an inn outside New York with two tramps, and what was more, he had to admit that he was not out of place here. Smiling, he examined the faces of his parents, as though seeking to determine whether they still wanted to receive news from their son.

While gazing thus, he soon noticed that he was indeed very tired and could scarcely remain awake all night. The picture fell from his hands; he put his face on the cool picture, which felt good on his cheek, and fell asleep with a pleasant sensation.

Early in the morning he was awakened by a tickling under his arm. It was the Frenchman who had dared to take such liberties. The Irishman also stood by Karl's table, observing him no less attentively than Karl had observed them at night. Karl was not surprised that he had not been awakened by the noise they made as they got up; in walking about so quietly they had not necessarily acted out of malice, for he had been fast asleep, and besides, they had put little effort into dressing and evidently also into washing themselves.

They now introduced themselves properly, even with a certain formality; Karl discovered that the two youths were locksmiths, who had been long unable to find work in New York and were consequently rather down-at-heels. To prove this was so, Robinson opened his coat, and one could see that he was not wearing a shirt, as was also indicated by the loose-fitting collar attached to the back of his coat. They intended to march to the town of Butterford, a two-day trek from New York, where there were said to be job openings. They had no objection to Karl's accompanying them and promised him, first, that they would carry his trunk every now and then and, second, that if they found work, they would obtain an apprenticeship for him, something that would be easy to arrange if there were jobs available. Karl had no sooner agreed than they gave him the friendly advice that he should take off his beautiful suit, for it would be a hindrance in applying for jobs. Actually at this very inn there was a great opportunity for disposing of the suit, since the chambermaid dealt in used clothing. They helped Karl, who had not yet reached a final decision about the suit, remove it and took it away. Thus abandoned and still rather drowsy, Karl changed slowly into his old traveling clothes, chiding himself for having sold the other suit, which might hurt his chances in applying for a position as an apprentice but could only help with better jobs, and he opened the door to recall them, only to run into them right away; although they put a half dollar on the table by way of proceeds, their faces were so cheerful that one could scarcely persuade oneself that they had not made a profit and indeed an irritatingly large one.

In any case there was no time to talk about it, since the chambermaid came in, just as sleepy as she had been at night, and drove the three of them out into the corridor, explaining that the room had to be prepared for new guests. Of course there was no way that could be true; she said so out of sheer malice. Karl, who was about to tidy up his trunk, had to watch the woman grab his belongings with both hands and throw them into the trunk with full force, as if they were animals that had to be tamed. The two locksmiths tried to intervene by tugging at her dress and slapping her on the back, but if they were indeed trying to help Karl, their efforts were futile. Once the woman had shut the trunk, she pressed the handle into Karl's hand, shook off the two locksmiths, and chased the three of them from the room by threatening that if they failed to obey, she would not serve them any coffee. The woman must obviously have completely forgotten that Karl had not been with the locksmiths from the outset, since she was treating them as if they were one gang. Of course, the locksmiths had sold her Karl's clothes and thereby shown that there was a certain connection.

In the corridor they had to go back and forth for some time, and especially the Frenchman, who had taken Karl's arm, complained continually, threatening to knock down the innkeeper should he dare appear and, as if preparing to do so, he started to rub his clenched fists furiously. At last an innocent little boy came along and had to stretch up tall in order to hand the Frenchman the coffeepot. Unfortunately, there seemed to be only one coffeepot available, and it was impossible to get the boy to understand that they would like some glasses too. So only one person at a time could drink while the others stood beside him, each awaiting his turn. Although Karl had no desire to drink, he did not wish to hurt the feelings of the other two, and so, when his turn came, he simply stood motionless, holding the coffeepot to his lips.

By way of farewell, the Irishman threw the coffeepot onto the stone tiles; they left the building unobserved and stepped

out into the thick yellowish morning fog. They marched along
the side of the road, mostly in silence; Karl had to carry his
trunk, as the others would probably take a turn only if he
asked; every now and then an automobile shot out of the fog,
and the three of them turned their heads to look at the mostly
gigantic cars, so eye-catching in design and passing by so quickly
that one didn't even have time to notice whether they were carrying any passengers. Then, stretched out in five uninterrupted
lines, came columns of vehicles, transporting provisions to New
York, that took up the entire width of the street and were so
tightly packed that no one could cross the street. Now and then
the street broadened out into a square, in the center of which
a policeman strode up and down on a towerlike platform in
order to keep an eye on everything and to use his small baton
to direct the traffic on the main street as well as that flowing in
from the side streets, which then moved toward the next square
and the next policeman without any supervision but kept in
reasonably good order voluntarily by the silent and alert coach-
men and chauffeurs. Most remarkable, Karl found, was the
general calm. Had the unsuspecting animals bound for the
slaughterhouse not bellowed so loudly, one could surely have
heard only the clip-clop of the animals' hooves and the whiz-
zing of the tires. Of course, the traffic did not always move at
the same speed. Whenever traffic had to be redirected along
certain squares because of the great crush from the sides, all
lines were held up and could only proceed step by step, but
then for a while the traffic would rush past at lightning speed
before suddenly calming down again, as if everything were controlled by a single brake. Yet there was no sign of dust rising
from the street—everything moved in the clearest air. There were
no pedestrians about, or any sign of solitary market women
rambling toward the city, as in Karl's homeland, but every
now and then great open vehicles appeared with some twenty

women standing on top, baskets slung over their backs—and so maybe they were actually market women—craning their necks to look out over the traffic so as to find out whether there was any hope of moving along faster. One could then see similar vehicles, with several men sauntering on them, hands stuck in their trouser pockets. Among the numerous signs attached to one of these automobiles Karl noticed the following inscription and gave a little cry as he read: "Hiring dockworkers for Jakob Trucking Company." Just then the car was moving quite slowly, and a small animated hunched-up man, standing on the steps of the car, invited the three wanderers to climb aboard. Karl hid behind the locksmiths, as though his uncle might be aboard the car and could see him. He was glad that the other two also rejected the invitation, although he was somewhat hurt by the arrogant expression with which they did so. They should certainly not think they were too good to enter his uncle's service. He let them know this at once, though of course not in so many words. Whereupon Delamarche requested that he kindly cease meddling in matters of which he had no understanding: this was a fraudulent way of hiring people, it was utterly disgraceful, and the Jakob corporation was notorious all over the United States. Karl did not reply and from then on directed his remarks more to the Irishman; he even asked him to carry his trunk for a moment, which after repeated requests from Karl, the former finally did. He kept on complaining about the weight of the trunk, though, until it became quite clear that his sole aim was to lighten the trunk by removing the Veronese salami, which he had probably first noticed with delight at the hotel. Karl had to unpack it; then the Frenchman took it to cut it up with his daggerlike knife and ate almost all of it himself. Robinson received a slice only every now and then, whereas Karl, who was obliged to carry his trunk again so that it would not get left on the country road, received nothing, as though he had already helped himself to his share. Begging for a little piece would be too petty, he thought; but his blood was boiling.

All of the fog had disappeared; shimmering in the distance was a tall mountain range whose wavy ridges led to an even more distant sunny haze. By the roadside lay poorly cultivated fields that stretched out past factories that stood smoke-blackened in the open countryside. In individual tenements set down at random, the windows trembled; moving to and fro and caught in various shades of light, and on all of the flimsy little balconies, women and children attended to various tasks, while all about them, covering and obscuring them, hung cloths and articles of linen, which fluttered in the morning wind and billowed vigorously. If one's gaze slid from the houses, one could see larks high above in the sky and below them swallows flying not far over the heads of the three travelers.

Many of these sights reminded Karl of his homeland, and he was not sure whether it would make sense for him to leave New York and head inland. In New York there was the sea and always the possibility of returning to his homeland. So he halted and told his two companions that he did after all wish to remain in New York. And when Delamarche simply attempted to drive him on, he refused to let himself be driven and said he still had a right to make decisions for himself. The Irishman first had to intervene and declare that Butterford was much more beautiful than New York, and then both had to plead with him repeatedly before he would set off again. And even then he would not have gone on had he not told himself that he might be better off in a place where he had only a slight possibility of returning to his homeland. Certainly he would work better and get ahead there, for he would no longer find himself held back by useless thoughts.

And now he was pulling the other two, who were so pleased with his eagerness that, without waiting to be asked, they took turns carrying the trunk; Karl could not quite understand precisely how he gave them such great pleasure. They arrived in a region that sloped upward, and each time they halted and looked back, they could see the panorama of New York, with its harbor, stretching out ever farther. The bridge connecting New York to Boston hung delicately over the Hudson and trembled if one narrowed one's eyes. It appeared to bear no traffic, and a long, smooth, lifeless strip of water stretched out underneath. In both of these giant cities everything appeared empty and erected to no avail. And there was scarcely any difference between large and small buildings. Down in the invisible depths of the streets life probably went on as usual, but all they could see above them was a light haze that was motionless yet seemed easy to chase away. Peace had even descended on the harbor, the largest in the world, and only here and there— perhaps influenced by the memory of vessels seen from close up—could one see a ship dragging itself forward a little. Yet one could not follow it for long; it escaped one's gaze and disappeared.

But Delamarche and Robinson could obviously see a great deal more; they pointed right and left, arching their outstretched arms over squares and gardens, which they identified by name. They found it impossible to understand how Karl could have spent over two months in New York and seen little more of the city than a single street. And they promised him that once they had made enough money in Butterford, they would go with him to New York and show him all the worthwhile sights, paying special attention to those districts where one could amuse oneself royally. And then Robinson began to sing a song at the top of his voice, with Delamarche clapping his hands in accompaniment; Karl recognized it as a melody from an operetta in his homeland, and on hearing the English libretto, he found that he now liked it much better than he had at home. Then there was a little outdoor concert, in which everybody took part except for the city below, which supposedly enjoyed the melody yet seemed oblivious to it.

Karl asked once where the Jakob Trucking Company was and immediately saw the extended index fingers of Delamarche and Robinson pointing either to the same spot or possibly to different ones that were miles apart. When they set off again, Karl asked when was the earliest they would have earned sufficient money to be able to return to New York. Delamarche said that might well take only a month, for there was a shortage of labor in Butterford, so the wages were quite high. Since they were such good comrades, they would naturally pool their money and in this way even out any incidental differences in their earnings. Karl disliked the notion of pooling their wages, although the two of them would of course earn more as skilled workers than he would as an apprentice. Besides, Robinson noted, if there was no work to be found in Butterford, they must certainly keep going and either find jobs as farm workers somewhere or possibly go to California and find work at the gold-panning sites out there, which was the plan Robinson himself favored, judging by his elaborate stories. "But why did you become a locksmith only to decide now that you want to go to those gold-panning sites," asked Karl, who was less than pleased to discover that it would be necessary to undertake further uncertain journeys of that nature. "Why did I become a locksmith?" said Robinson. "Well, certainly not because I wanted this mother's son to end up starving. Those gold-washing outfits pay very well." "Once did," said Delamarche. "Still do," said Robinson, and he spoke of many acquaintances who had grown rich from working there and were still there but no longer had to lift a finger and who, for friendship's sake, would help him—and of course his comrades also—to make a fortune. "Once we get to Butterford we'll force them to give us jobs," added Delamarche, and although he was giving voice to Karl's own innermost thoughts, his choice of words was not exactly confidence-inspiring.

All day they halted only once, at an inn where they sat outdoors at what Karl believed was a cast-iron table, and ate almost raw meat that could not be cut with a knife and fork and had to be torn apart. The bread was shaped like a cylinder, and each loaf had a long knife sticking out of it. The black beverage that was passed around with the food left a burning sensation in one's throat. But Delamarche and Robinson liked it and frequently raised their glasses to celebrate the fulfillment of various wishes, holding their glasses in the air for a moment before clinking them. Seated at the adjacent tables was a group of workers in lime-spattered overalls, all drinking the same beverage. Numerous passing automobiles blew clouds of dust across the tables. Large newspaper sheets were handed around; people talked excitedly about the construction workers' strike, the name Mack was often mentioned; Karl asked about him and discovered that he was not only the father of the man he knew but also the biggest building contractor in New York. The strike was costing him millions and possibly also jeopardizing his business. Karl could not believe a word of this gossip, coming as it did from such ill-informed and malicious people.

For Karl the meal was further spoiled by the thought that they would scarcely be able to pay the bill. The obvious thing to do would have been for each to pay for himself, but on several occasions Delamarche, and indeed Robinson too, had mentioned that they had spent the last of their money on the previous night's lodgings. There was no sign of a watch, ring, or other disposable item on either of them. Besides, Karl could hardly scold them for having profited a little from the sale of his clothes, for that would be insulting and would lead to a

parting of ways. Rather astonishingly, however, neither Delamarche nor Robinson was at all concerned about the bill; indeed, they were in such good spirits that they kept trying to
strike up conversations with the waitress, who walked proudly
up and down between the tables, with a heavy gait. Her hair was
loosened at the sides and hung over her forehead and cheeks;
she pulled it back continually by running her hands through it.
Finally, just when one might at last have expected her to say a
few friendly words to them, she approached their table, put
both hands on it, and asked: "Who's paying?" No hands ever
shot up faster than those of Delamarche and Robinson, who
pointed at Karl. Karl was not startled, for he had certainly foreseen this and could not really blame his comrades for making
him pay for a few trifles—after all, he himself had expected to
receive certain benefits through them—though it would have
been more decent to talk things over before matters came to
a head. Only he found it embarrassing that he first had to
retrieve the money from his secret pocket. He had originally
intended to save the money for an extreme emergency and at
least for the time being put himself, so to speak, on the same
level as his colleagues. Outweighing the advantage he had
through that money and, above all, through not disclosing it
to his companions was the fact that they had been in America
since early childhood, that they had sufficient knowledge and
experience to be able to earn money, and finally that they were
not accustomed to a better standard of living than their current
one. This payment need not necessarily upset Karl's previous
intentions concerning his money, for he could easily part with a
quarter pound, simply put a quarter pound on the table and
announce that this was all he had and that he was willing to
sacrifice it for their journey to Butterford together. It should be
perfectly adequate for going on foot. But he was not sure
whether he had enough small change, and besides, those coins

and the banknotes that he had put away with them were now somewhere in his secret pocket, and the best way of finding anything in there was to empty the entire contents onto the table. Moreover, there was absolutely no need for his companions to find out about this secret pocket. Fortunately, his companions still seemed more interested in the waitress than in Karl's efforts to come up with the money for the payment. Delamarche enticed the waitress to approach them by requesting that she put the check down on the table between Robinson and himself, and she succeeded in warding off their insistent advances only by putting her entire hand on the face of one or the other and pushing him away. Sweating from the exertion, Karl hunted about in his secret pocket for the coins with one hand and took them out one by one while gathering them under the table in the other. Although he was not yet entirely familiar with the American currency, he finally managed to gauge from the pile of coins that he had a sufficiently large sum, and laid it on the table. The clinking of the coins immediately disrupted their joking. To Karl's annoyance and to the astonishment of everybody else, there was nearly a full pound lying there. Although no one asked Karl why he had never said a word about the money, which would have sufficed for a comfortable rail journey to Butterford, he was still highly embarrassed. After paying for the meal, he put the money away slowly, although not before Delamarche had taken from his hand a coin that he needed as a tip for the waitress, whom he embraced and pressed against his body, handing her the money from the other side.

Karl was also grateful to them for not commenting about the money as they marched on and for a moment even thought of divulging all his wealth, but he could not find an appropriate moment to do so. Toward evening they arrived in a more fertile rural district. All around they could see open fields, in their first burst of green, laying themselves over gentle hills, opulent country houses lining the road on each side; for hours they walked between the gilded railings of the gardens, crossing the same slow-flowing stream again and again and often hearing trains thundering by on the soaring viaducts.

Just as the sun was setting on the straight edge of the distant woods, they threw themselves down on a grass mound amid a little clump of trees in order to rest from their exertions. Delamarche and Robinson lay on the ground, stretching out as best they could; Karl sat up, gazing at the street a few meters below, where, as they had done all day, the automobiles continually rushed by in rapid succession, as if a precise number were being repeatedly dispatched from afar and an equal number lay in wait in another far-off place. All day, since early morning, Karl had not seen a single automobile stop nor a single passenger alight.

Robinson suggested spending the night there, since everyone was quite tired and this would enable them to march off that much earlier, and after all, between now and the onset of complete darkness they could scarcely find anything that was cheaper or better situated than this spot. Delamarche agreed, but Karl nonetheless felt obliged to add that he had sufficient money to pay for a night in a hotel for everyone. Delamarche said that they would need the money later and that Karl should keep it in a safe place. Delamarche did not make the slightest effort to conceal the fact that they were already counting on having Karl's money at their disposal. Now that his first suggestion had been accepted, Robinson announced that they would need a decent meal before going to bed so as to fortify themselves for the day ahead and that one of them should fetch everyone some food from the hotel, which was on the country road nearby and bore an illuminated sign with the words "Occidental Hotel." Being the youngest, and since no one else had volunteered, Karl did not hesitate to offer his services and, after receiving orders for bacon, bread, and beer, went over into the hotel.

There must have been a big city close by, for the very first hall in the hotel that Karl entered was filled with a noisy crowd, and at the buffet, which ran down the length of one wall and across two side walls, numerous waiters constantly ran about with white aprons slung across their chests without quite succeeding in satisfying their impatient guests, for everywhere one could hear cursing and fists hitting the table. No one paid any attention to Karl; there was no table service in the hall itself; sitting in groups of three at tables so tiny as to be almost invisible, the guests fetched themselves everything they needed from the buffet. Standing on each little table was a large bottle of oil, vinegar, or the like, which they first poured over all the food that they had carried over from the buffet. If Karl attempted to reach the buffet—where, especially with such a large order, the real difficulties would probably begin—he would have to force his way between many tables, and even if he were as careful as possible, he could not do so without rudely disturbing the guests, who however endured everything with apparent indifference, even when a guest bumped Karl against a little table, which nearly got knocked over. Although he apologized, they evidently did not understand him; nor could he understand a single word they called out to him.

At the buffet he finally succeeded in finding a spot, where his view was momentarily blocked by the elbows that his neighbors kept propped up. Here it seemed customary to sit with your elbows propped up and your fists pressed against your temples; Karl could not help thinking of his Latin teacher Dr. Krumpal, who had hated that particular posture and who would always approach by stealth and in one painful sweeping motion, by means of a ruler that suddenly appeared out of nowhere, brush one's elbows off the table.

Karl stood tightly pressed against the buffet, for no sooner had he stood in line than a table was set up behind him, and whenever the guest seated there leaned back as he spoke, he brushed against Karl's back with his large hat. And yet there was so little hope of obtaining anything from the waiter, even after Karl's two plump neighbors had gone away happily. On several occasions Karl had reached across the table and seized a waiter by the apron, but each time the waiter had torn himself away with a grimace. Not a single one could be stopped—they simply ran and ran. If only there had been something suitable to eat and drink in Karl's vicinity, he would have taken it, asked the price, paid up, and left feeling very pleased. But all he saw were dishes full of herringlike fish with black scales, the edges of which shone like gold. Those could be very expensive and would surely not satisfy anybody. Besides, there were a few small bottles of rum within reach, but he did not want to take any rum back to his comrades, for already at every opportunity they went only for the most concentrated alcohol, and he did not wish to encourage them any further.

Karl therefore had no alternative but to seek another spot and to exert himself anew. But it was now very late. The clock at the other end of the hall, whose hands one could barely discern through the smoke, indicated that it was already after nine. But elsewhere at the buffet the crush was even greater than at his previous spot, which was a little out of the way. Besides, the later it got, the more crowded the hall became. New guests were continually entering through the main door, shouting hello. Several guests imperiously cleared off the buffet, sat down at the counter, raised their glasses, and drank to one another; those were the best places, for one could see out over the entire hall.

Although Karl continued to press ahead, all hope of achieving anything was gone. He even chided himself for volunteering for this errand, since he had no idea how things worked here. His companions would quite rightly give him a scolding and might even believe that he had returned empty-handed only so as to save money. He now found himself in an area where hot meat dishes garnished with beautiful yellow carrots were being eaten at the little tables, and he could not understand how those people had managed to procure this.

Then a few steps in front of him he saw an older woman, who clearly belonged to the hotel staff, talking and laughing with a guest. She fiddled about in her hair continually with a clip. Karl immediately decided to place his order with this woman, first because she was the only woman in the hall and seemed to him to stand apart from all the noise and commotion, and then for the simple reason that she was the only hotel employee within reach, assuming of course that she would not run off on some errand at the first word he said. But exactly the opposite happened. Karl, who had been eavesdropping, had not yet addressed her when she looked up at him and, interrupting what she was saying and using English that was as clear as a grammar book's, asked in a friendly voice if he was looking for something. "Yes indeed," said Karl. "I can't get anything here." "Then come along with me, little fellow," she said; then she said goodbye to her acquaintance, who raised his hat, which seemed like an unbelievably polite gesture in these surroundings, and, taking Karl by the hand, went to the buffet, pushed aside a guest, opened a hinged door in the counter, and with Karl in tow, crossed the corridor behind the counter, where one had to watch out for the tirelessly circulating waiters, and opened a double door that had been covered with wallpaper, and now they found themselves in large cool pantries. "You simply have to know the mechanism," Karl said to himself.

"So what do you want?" she asked, and in her eagerness to help she bent down toward him. She was very fat, with a body that was seesawing, but her face, at least in contrast, had almost delicate features. Seeing all the different kinds of food stacked so carefully on the shelves and tables, Karl was tempted to come up with an order for a more elegant dinner, especially since he could expect that this influential woman would serve him at no great expense, but in the end he could not think of anything suitable and merely asked for bacon, bread, and eggs. "Nothing else?" the woman asked. "No thanks," said Karl, "but it's for three." When the woman asked about the other two, Karl said a few words about his companions; being asked a few questions like this gave him pleasure.

"But that meal is fit only for convicts," said the woman, clearly awaiting Karl's further wishes. But the latter, fearing she would give him everything as a present and would not want to accept any money, did not respond. "We'll put that together right away," said the woman, and then, with astonishing agility given her girth, she approached a table, cut off a large piece of thick streaky bacon, picked up three bottles of beer from the floor, took a loaf of bread from a shelf, and put everything in a light straw basket, which she then handed to Karl. Meanwhile she told Karl that she had brought him into the pantries because, though the food items on the buffet were always consumed quickly, they always lost their freshness in the smoke and all the odors. But for these people out there anything would suffice. Karl now fell silent, for he had no idea what he had done to deserve such special treatment. He thought of his companions, who, however well they knew America, might not have penetrated to these pantries and would therefore have had to make do with the spoiled food on the buffet. One could not hear a sound from the hall; the walls must have been very thick to keep these vaults sufficiently cool. Karl had been holding the straw basket in his hand for a while, without thinking of paying and remaining quite still. Only when the woman tried to pick up another bottle, similar to those on the tables, and put it in the basket did he thank her. "Do you still have a long march ahead of you?" asked the woman. "To Butterford," Karl answered. "That's still quite far," the woman said. "Another day's worth," said Karl. "That's all?" the woman asked. "Oh, no," said Karl.

The woman straightened out several items on the table; a waiter entered, looked about for something, was directed toward a large dish covered with a heap of sardines sprinkled with parsley, and then carried the dish in his upraised hands out into the hall.

"But why do you want to sleep out in the open?" asked the woman. "We've enough room here. Sleep here with us in the hotel." For Karl this was quite enticing, especially since he had just had such a bad night. "My luggage is still outside," he said hesitantly and not without a certain vanity. "You need only bring it in," said the woman, "that's no obstacle." "But what about my companions!" said Karl, who quickly realized that they certainly were an obstacle. "They too may stay the night," said the woman. "Come along! Don't make me beg." "All in all my companions are decent fellows," said Karl, "but they're not clean." "Haven't you noticed the dirt in the hall?" the woman asked, screwing up her face. "Even the worst people can come to us. I shall therefore ask to have three beds made up at once. But it will only be in the attic, since the hotel is fully occupied; I myself have moved to the attic, but it's certainly better than being outdoors." "I cannot bring my companions," said Karl. He was imagining how much noise those two would make in the corridors of this elegant hotel, how Robinson would soil everything and how Delamarche would inevitably start pestering this woman. "I don't understand why it's so impossible," the woman said, "but if that's what you wish, just leave your companions outdoors and come alone." "It's impossible, quite impossible," said Karl, "they're my companions, and I must stay with them." "You're being so pig-headed," the woman said, looking away, "one means well, wants to help you, and yet you resist with all your might." Karl saw the truth in all of this but could not think of a solution and merely said: "I should like to thank you for your kindness," but then, remembering that he had not yet paid, he asked how much he owed. "You needn't pay until you return my straw basket," said the woman. "I need it by tomorrow morning at the latest." "Thanks," said Karl. She opened a door, which led directly outside, and as he bowed on his way out, she added: "Good night. You're not doing the right thing, though." He had already gone a few paces when she called out: "See you tomorrow!"

He was barely outside when he heard the noise from the hall again, still as strong as ever but now interspersed with the sounds of a wind ensemble. He was glad he hadn't had to go through the hall on his way out. All five floors of the hotel were now lit up, brightening the full expanse of the street in front. There were still automobiles driving past, though no longer in a continuous line; looming up out of the distance faster than in the daytime, they probed the pavement with the white beams of their headlights, crossed the illuminated area around the hotel with paling headlights, and then, lighting up, rushed into the darkness beyond.

Karl found his companions already fast asleep; he had, however, stayed away too long. He was just about to spread out the items he had brought in an inviting fashion on some papers he had found in the basket, when to his consternation he saw that his trunk, which he had locked before leaving and the key to which was in his pocket, was open and half his belongings strewn on the grass. "Get up," he cried. "You're still sleeping though thieves have been here." "Well, is there anything missing?" asked Delamarche. Although Robinson was not yet fully awake, he was already reaching for his beer. "That I don't know," cried Karl, "but the trunk is open. Now that's really careless of you, to go to sleep and leave the trunk lying about like that." Delamarche and Robinson both laughed, and the former said: "So next time maybe you shouldn't stay away so long. The hotel is only ten paces from here, yet it takes you three hours to get there and back. We were hungry, thought you might have something to eat in your trunk, and kept fiddling with the lock until it sprang open. In any case there was nothing inside, and you can calmly pack everything away again." "Well," said Karl, staring at the rapidly dwindling contents of the basket and listening to the odd sound Robinson produced as he drank, for the liquid first went far into his throat, shot back with a whistling sound, and only then in one great gush rolled down into the depths. "Had your fill," he asked, as the two took a moment's break. "But haven't you eaten already at the hotel?" asked Delamarche, who believed that Karl was demanding his share. "Hurry up if you still want to eat," said Karl, and walked over to his trunk. "Is he ever moody," said Delamarche to Robinson. "I'm not moody," said Karl, "but was it right to force open my trunk while I was away and to throw my belongings on the ground like that? I realize that there are some things one must simply tolerate among comrades, and I was prepared for that, but this is really going too far. I'll spend the night at the hotel and will not go to Butterford. Now eat up quickly—I must return the basket." "You see, Robinson, that's how one should speak," said Delamarche, "it's such a refined way of speaking. Of course, he is, after all, a German. You warned me about him a while back, but I was quite a fool and took him along. We placed our trust in him, dragged him along for an entire day, and as a result we lost at least half a day, and now—simply because someone at the hotel enticed him over there—he takes off, simply takes off." "But being a two-faced German, rather than doing so openly, he comes up with that excuse about the trunk, and being a coarse German too, he cannot leave without calling us thieves and insulting our honor, simply because we played a little prank on him with his trunk." Without turning around, Karl, who was packing his belongings, said: "If you go on talking like that, you'll simply make it easier for me to leave. I know what true companionship is. I had friends in Europe too, and none of them could reproach me for behaving in a false or nasty manner. We're no longer in touch, naturally enough, but if I ever go back to Europe, they'll receive me with open arms and recognize me right away as their friend. As for you, Delamarche, and you, Robinson, how could I possibly have betrayed you, since you were so kind as to take me on and hold out the prospect of an apprentice position in Butterford. But this is really about something else. You have nothing to your name, and though that doesn't in the least diminish you in my eyes, you begrudge me my few belongings and for this reason try to humiliate me; I cannot stand it. And now after having broken open my trunk, you don't offer me a word of apology, you even swear at me, then swear at my compatriots—which makes it impossible for me to stay with you. By the way, Robinson, this isn't about you. The only criticism I have of your character is that you're too dependent on Delamarche." "Of course, we can now see," said Delamarche, and approaching Karl, he gave him a little push, as if to make him pay attention, "of course, we can now see you showing your true colors. All day you ran around after me, held on to my coat, imitated my every movement, and for the rest were quiet as a little mouse. But now that you sense you have some backing at the hotel, you start holding forth in a big way. You're just a little smart aleck, and I'm still not sure whether we'll grin and bear this. Or whether we won't demand fees for the knowledge you've gained from watching us all day.

Listen, Robinson, can you hear what he's saying, he's saying we envy him his possessions. In one day's work in Butterford—never mind California—we would earn ten times more than the sum you've shown us, in addition to whatever else you may have concealed in the lining of your coat. So watch your trap!" Having risen from the trunk, Karl caught sight of Robinson, who was still drowsy, though the beer had revived him a little. "If I were to stay much longer," he said, "I might well experience further surprises. You seem to feel like beating me up." "My patience is not unlimited," said Robinson. "It would be better if you held your tongue, Robinson," said Karl, without letting Delamarche out of his sight, "deep down you think I'm right but you have to act as if you were siding with Delamarche." "Could you be trying to bribe him?" asked Delamarche. "Not at all," said Karl, "I'm happy to be going away and don't want to have anything more to do with either of you. There's just one other thing I want to tell you; you chided me for having money and for hiding it from you. Assuming that is true, wasn't it the right way to deal with people whom I had known only for a couple of hours, and aren't you yourself confirming through your present conduct that I acted wisely." "Don't move," said Delamarche to Robinson, although the latter had not stirred. He then asked Karl: "Since you are so outrageously honest and since we're having such a cozy time together, why don't you be even more honest and own up to the real reason why you wanted to go to the hotel." Karl had to step over the trunk since Delamarche was now so close. But refusing to be deterred, Delamarche pushed aside the trunk, advanced a pace, stepping on a white undershirt lying on the grass, and repeated his question.

As if in response a man with a bright flashlight came climbing up toward the group from the street. It was a waiter from the hotel. No sooner had he spotted Karl than he said: "I've spent almost half an hour looking for you. I've already searched through all the bushes on both sides of the road. The head cook says to let you know she urgently needs the straw basket she loaned you." "Here it is," said Karl, sounding uncertain in his excitement. Delamarche and Robinson had stepped aside in a seemingly unassuming manner, as they always did before well-off strangers. The waiter took the basket and said: "Well, the head cook wants to know whether you haven't had second thoughts and wouldn't perhaps want to spend the night at the hotel. Besides, the other two gentlemen would be welcome if you'd like to take them along. The beds are already prepared. It's a warm night, but here on this slope it's not entirely safe sleeping outdoors, for one can encounter snakes." "Since the head cook is so kind, I shall indeed accept your invitation," said Karl, and then he waited for his companions to respond. However, Robinson simply stood there impassively; Delamarche gazed up at the stars, with his hands in his pockets. Both evidently took it for granted that Karl would take them along. "Well," said the waiter, "in that case I have been instructed to take you to the hotel and to carry your bags." "Then could you please wait a minute," said Karl, who bent down in order to pick up a few items that still lay about, and put them in the trunk.

Suddenly he straightened up. The photograph was missing; it had been at the very top of the trunk, and now there was no sign of it. Everything else was still there—only the photograph was missing. "I cannot find the photograph," he said to Delamarche. "What kind of photograph," asked the latter. "The photograph of my parents," said Karl. "We didn't see a photograph," said Delamarche. "There was no photograph in there, Mr. Rossmann," said Robinson in confirmation. "But that's impossible," said Karl, whose imploring glances drew the waiter closer. "It was right on top, and now it's gone. If only you hadn't played that prank with the trunk." "We can't possibly be mistaken," said Delamarche, "there was no photograph in the trunk." "It meant more to me than anything else in that trunk," said Karl to the waiter, who walked about, searching in the grass. "You see, it's quite irreplaceable, I can't get another copy." And once the waiter abandoned his futile search, Karl added: "It was the only picture I had of my parents." Whereupon the waiter said, in a loud voice and without mincing words: "Perhaps we could also search through the pockets of these gentlemen." "Yes," Karl said at once, "I have to find that photograph. But before I start searching through your pockets, I want to say that the person who voluntarily gives me the photograph will receive the entire trunk together with all of the contents." After a moment of general silence, Karl said to the waiter: "So my companions clearly wish to have their pockets searched. But I'm still willing to promise the entire trunk to the person in whose pocket the photograph is found. That's the best I can do." The servant set about searching Delamarche at once, since he considered him more difficult to handle than Robinson, whom he left for Karl. He informed Karl that both had to be searched at the same time, since one of them could discard the photograph without being seen. On his first try Karl found one of his ties in Robinson's pocket, but he did not take it and called out to the waiter: "No matter what you find on Delamarche, please let him keep everything. I only want the photograph, nothing except for the photograph." As Karl searched through Robinson's chest pockets, his hand brushed against his hot fat chest, and all of a sudden he realized that he was perhaps doing his companions a great injustice. He now hurried as much as he could. In any case all was in vain; the photograph was simply not to be found, neither on Delamarche nor on Robinson.

"It's no use," said the waiter. "They've probably torn up

the photograph and thrown away the pieces," said Karl, "I thought they were my friends, but in secret they sought only to do me harm. Well, not Robinson, he would never have hit on the idea that I'm very attached to the photograph, but Delamarche most certainly would." In front Karl could see only the waiter, whose lantern lit up a small circle, whereas everything else, including Delamarche and Robinson, was completely in the dark.

And now of course the idea of taking those two to the hotel was completely out of the question. The waiter swung the trunk up on his shoulders, Karl took the straw basket, and they left. Karl was already out on the road when he interrupted his thoughts, stood still, and shouted into the dark: "Listen here! If one of you still has the photograph and wants to bring it to me at the hotel—he will still get the trunk and won't—I swear—won't be reported." There was no real answer from above, only a few muffled sounds, the first words of a call from Robinson, whom Delamarche evidently shut up at once. Karl waited quite a while to see whether the two above might not change their minds. He shouted twice, at intervals: "I'm still here." But there was no answering cry, only a stone that rolled down the slope, perhaps by accident, perhaps from a poorly aimed throw.

V

AT THE OCCIDENTAL HOTEL

At the hotel Karl was led at once into some kind of office, where the head cook stood, notebook in hand, dictating a letter to a young typist. Her extremely precise dictation and the controlled and elastic pounding of the keys raced past the only intermittently audible ticking of the clock, which indicated that it was already twelve o'clock. "Well!" said the head cook; she closed her notebook, and the typist jumped up and pulled the wooden case over the machine without taking her eyes off Karl as she went about this routine task. She still looked like a schoolgirl; her apron had been very carefully ironed and, for instance, even had ruffles at the shoulders; her hairdo went up very high, and after noting these details, one was slightly surprised to see her serious face. After first bowing to the head cook, then to Karl, she went off, and Karl involuntarily gave the head cook a searching glance.

"It's nice that you did come," said the head cook. "What about your companions?" "I didn't bring them," said Karl. "They'll surely be marching off early tomorrow morning," said the head cook, as if seeking to explain the matter to herself. Mustn't she think that I too am marching off? Karl asked himself, and so as to exclude all doubt, he said: "Our parting was less than amicable." The head cook seemed to regard this as welcome news. "So you're free?" she asked. "Yes, I'm free," said Karl, to whom nothing seemed more worthless than this freedom. "Now then, wouldn't you like to take a job at the hotel?" the head cook asked. "Very much so," said Karl. "I've dreadfully few skills. For instance, I cannot even write on a typewriter." "That's not so important," said the head cook. "Well, you would for the time being receive only a very minor position, and then it would be up to you to get ahead by applying yourself diligently and staying alert. In any case I think it would be better, and more fitting, if you were to settle down somewhere instead of strolling about the world like that. You really don't seem the type." "Uncle would agree with all of that," Karl said to himself, nodding in assent. Just then it occurred to him that the person toward whom she showed such concern still hadn't introduced himself. "Excuse me," he said, "I haven't introduced myself, my name is Karl Rossmann." "You are a German, aren't you?" "Yes," said Karl, "I haven't been in America very long." "So where are you from?" "From Prague, in Bohemia," said Karl. "Well, I never!" cried the head cook, in German but with a strong English accent, almost raising her arms, "then we're compatriots. My name is Grete Mitzelbach, and I come from Vienna. And I certainly know Prague extremely well; I worked for six months at the Golden Goose on Wenceslas Square. Just imagine!" "When were you there?" asked Karl. "That was many years ago." "The old Golden Goose was torn down two years ago," said Karl. "Ah yes," said the head cook, who had become lost in thoughts of bygone days.

Suddenly becoming animated again, she took Karl's hands and cried: "Now that you've turned out to be my compatriot, you absolutely mustn't go away. You simply cannot do that to me. Would you like, say, to be a lift boy? Just indicate 'yes,' and the post is yours. Once you've seen a bit more, you'll realize that it isn't especially easy to find such jobs, since it's impossible to imagine a better place in which to start out. You'll get to

meet all of the guests, you'll always be visible and will be
entrusted with little tasks; in short, every single day you'll get a
chance to better your lot. And I'll take care of everything else!"
"I should very much like to be a lift boy," said Karl, after a
brief pause. It would be pointless to have reservations about
the lift boy position simply because of his five years in secondary school. Here in America there would be sufficient reason
to feel ashamed of those five years in secondary school. Besides, Karl had always liked lift boys; he had always considered
them the jewels of a hotel. "Isn't a knowledge of foreign languages required?" he insisted. "You speak German, and beautiful English too. That's quite sufficient." "I first began to learn
English on coming to America two and a half months ago,"
said Karl; he thought he should not hide the only advantage he
possessed. "That's already enough of a recommendation," said
the head cook, "when I think of the difficulties I myself had
with English. But that was some thirty years ago. I was talking about this only yesterday. You see, yesterday was my fifti-
eth birthday." And with a smile she sought to determine from
Karl's countenance the impression her dignified age had left.
"Then I wish you good luck," said Karl. "One can always use
that," she said; she shook Karl's hand and was half-saddened
again by this old expression from her homeland, which had
occurred to her while she was speaking German.

  "But I'm detaining you here," she cried. "You must be very
tired, and besides, we can discuss everything much better in the
daytime. One's joy at meeting a fellow countryman can make
one quite heedless. Come, I shall take you to your room." "I do
have one other request, Madame Head Cook," said Karl, espy-
ing a telephone stand on a nearby table. "It's possible that
tomorrow, perhaps even at a very early hour, my former companions will bring me a photograph that I urgently need. Could
you kindly telephone the porter and ask that he either send

those people to me or have someone get me?" "Certainly," said the head cook, "but wouldn't it suffice if he took the photograph from them? Besides, what kind of photograph is it, if you don't mind my asking?" "It's a photograph of my parents," said Karl, "no, I must speak to those people in person." The head cook, who did not answer, relayed the appropriate order over the telephone to the porter's lodge, referring to Karl's room as number 536.

They passed through a door directly opposite the entrance and entered a short corridor, where a small lift boy was sound asleep, leaning on the balustrade of an elevator. "Well, we can help ourselves," said the head cook softly, motioning to Karl that he should enter the elevator. "A ten- to twelve-hour workday is just a little too much for such a boy," she said as they ascended in the elevator. "But it's peculiar in America. Take that little boy, for instance; he too only came half a year ago, with his parents; he's an Italian. Right now it seems as if he could not possibly endure the work, there's no flesh left on his face, he falls asleep while he's on duty though he is by nature very willing—but he has only another six months to serve, either here or somewhere else in America, and will have no difficulty enduring everything, and in five years time he'll be a strong man. I could go on for hours, giving you more such examples. And it's not you I have in mind, since you're such a sturdy youth. You're seventeen years old, aren't you?" "Next month I shall be sixteen," replied Karl. "You're still only sixteen!" said the head cook. "Well, don't lose heart!"

Once upstairs she led Karl into a room, an attic room with a sloping wall, though otherwise very snug-looking in the light from two glow lamps. "Don't be startled by the decor," said the head cook. "You see, it's not a hotel room but a room in my apartment, which has three rooms, so you won't disturb me in any way. I shall lock the connecting door so you can feel completely at ease. As a new hotel employee, you will of course receive your own room tomorrow. If you had come with your companions, I should have given you a bed in the servants' dormitory, but since you came alone, I think this will suit you better, even if you have only a sofa to sleep on. And now sleep well so you can fortify yourself for the work ahead. He'll probably not yet be too strict tomorrow." "Thank you very much for your kindness." "Wait," she said, halting at the door, "you'd have been awakened before long." And she went to a side door in the room, knocked, and cried: "Therese!" "Yes, head cook," the voice of the little typist replied. "When you come to wake me in the morning, you must go through the corridor, there's a guest sleeping in this room. He's dead tired." She smiled at Karl as she said so. "You got that?" "Yes, head cook." "Well then, good night!" "I wish you good night."

"You see," the head cook said by way of explanation, "I've been sleeping very badly these past few years. At present I can certainly be satisfied with my position and really don't need to worry at all. But those earlier worries must be causing my insomnia. I can count myself lucky if I manage to fall asleep at three in the morning. But since I have to be back on duty as early as five, or at the latest at five-thirty, I need to have someone awaken me gently, so I don't become even more nervous than I already am. And so it's Therese who wakes me. But you really know everything now and I haven't gone yet. Good night!" And despite her heaviness she almost glided from the room.

Karl was looking forward to his sleep, for the day had greatly fatigued him. And he could not have wished for more comfortable surroundings for a long, undisturbed sleep. True, the room was not set up as a bedroom—it was more like a living room or rather one of the head cook's reception rooms, and a wash table had been brought in just for him for the night, but instead of feeling like an intruder, Karl felt all the better cared for. His trunk had been put back in order again and was now probably more secure than it had been in a long time. On a low cabinet with drawers and covered with a large coarsely woven woolen blanket were various photographs, some framed, others under glass; while looking around the room, Karl stopped to gaze at them. They were mostly old photographs; the majority depicted girls dressed in outmoded, uncomfortable clothes with loosely fitting but elongated little hats, their right hands propped on their umbrellas, facing the viewer but keeping their eyes averted. Among the portraits of the gentlemen, Karl was especially struck by the picture of a young soldier with a shock of wild black hair who had laid his military cap on a little table and stood completely erect, filled with proud yet suppressed laughter. The buttons on his uniform had been gilded after the shot was taken. All of these photographs were no doubt still from Europe, as one could probably have read on the reverse, but Karl did not want to handle them. Just the way these photographs here were arranged, that's how he would like to set up the photograph of his parents in the room that would soon be his.

Stretching out after a thorough washing of his entire body, which he had sought to carry out as quietly as possible on account of his neighbor, and eagerly anticipating how pleasant it would be to sleep on his settee, Karl thought he could hear a faint knock on one of the doors. It was impossible to determine on which door—perhaps it had simply been some incidental noise. Besides, the sound did not repeat itself at once, and Karl was almost asleep when it came again. But now there was no longer any doubt that it was indeed a knock and that it came from the typist's door. On his tiptoes Karl ran to the door and asked so softly that even if, despite everything, someone were still asleep next door, his voice couldn't have awakened anyone: "You'd like something?" The reply came at once: "Would you care to open the door? The key is on your side." "Please," said Karl, "I must get dressed first." For a moment there was silence, followed by the words: "It's not necessary. Just open the door and get in bed. I shall wait a moment." "Fine," said Karl, who did as he was told, and he also turned up the electric light. "I'm in bed now," he said in a louder voice. And then, from her dark room, dressed exactly as she had been in the office downstairs, the little typist emerged; during all that time she had probably not thought of going to sleep.

"Many apologies," she said, standing slightly stooped before Karl's settee, "and please don't give me away. I don't wish to disturb you for long, I know you're dead tired." "It's not that bad," said Karl, "but perhaps it would have been better if I had put on my clothes." He had to lie down flat so that he could be covered up to his neck, for he did not own a nightshirt. "Well, I shall only stay for a moment," she said, reaching for a chair. "May I sit beside the settee?" Karl nodded. She seated herself so close to the settee that Karl had to move toward the wall so that he could look up at her. She had a round regular face— only her forehead was unusually high, but perhaps solely on account of her hairstyle, which didn't entirely suit her. Her outfit was very clean and meticulous. In her left hand she was squeezing a handkerchief.

"Are you staying long?" she asked. "That still isn't entirely certain," Karl answered, "but I think I shall stay." "That would be really great," she said, wiping her face with her handkerchief. "I'm really very lonely here." "I find that surprising," said Karl, "after all, the head cook is very friendly toward you. She certainly doesn't treat you like an employee. I was beginning to think you were related." "Oh no," she said. "My name is Therese Berchtold, I'm from Pomerania." Karl introduced himself also. Whereupon she looked squarely at him for the first time, as if he had through the exchanging of names become a little more alien to her. For a moment they were silent. Then she said: "I don't want you to think I'm ungrateful. If it weren't for the head cook, I would be far worse off. I used to be a kitchen maid at the hotel and was in great danger of being dismissed, for I couldn't keep up with the heavy work. They do demand a lot of us here. Last month a kitchen maid fainted from sheer overexertion and spent fourteen days in the hospital. And I'm not very strong, I had to endure a great deal of suffering early on and as a result developed more slowly; you probably couldn't tell I'm already eighteen. But I'm getting stronger." "The service here must really be very strenuous," said Karl. "Downstairs I just saw a young lift boy asleep on his feet." "But those lift boys actually have it best," she said, "they earn great money in tips; besides, they don't have to struggle nearly so much as those in the kitchen. But then I had a real stroke of luck; the head cook happened to need a girl to arrange the dinner napkins for a banquet and sent down for a kitchen maid—there are some fifty such girls—I happened to be at hand and was able to please her with my work, since I've always known how to arrange dinner napkins. And so from that moment on she kept me beside her and trained me little by little to become her secretary. I've learned a lot from doing that." "Is there so much writing to be done?" asked Karl. "Oh, a great deal," she answered, "you probably cannot even imagine how much. You saw that I worked until half past eleven today, and today is just an ordinary day. But I don't spend all the time writing, I run many errands in the city too." "Well, what's the city called?" Karl asked. "You don't know?" she said. "It's Ramses." "A big city?" Karl asked. "Very big," she answered, "I don't like going there. But you really don't want to sleep?" "No, no," said Karl, "I still don't know why you came." "Because there's nobody I can talk to. I'm not whiny, but when one doesn't really have anybody, one is naturally happy when someone finally listens. I saw you in the hall earlier on, I came to get the head cook just as she was taking you into the pantries." "It's a dreadful hall," said Karl. "I don't notice it anymore," she answered. "I was about to say that the head cook has been as kind to me as my late mother. But the difference between our positions is too great for me to be able to talk openly with her. I used to have good friends among the kitchen maids, but they left a long time ago and I barely know the new girls. Besides, it sometimes seems to me that my present position is more exhausting than the previous one, though I don't even do so good a job, and that the only reason the head cook keeps me on in this post is out of pity. After all, if you want to become a secretary, you do of course need to have had better schooling. Though it's sinful to say so, often, often I fear I'm going mad. For God's sake," she said, suddenly speaking much faster and groping about to find Karl's shoulders, for he had kept his hands under the blanket, "but you mustn't mention any of this to the head cook, for otherwise I'm truly lost. It would be really dreadful if, besides the trouble I'm already giving her with my work, I should hurt her feelings too." "Of course I won't tell her anything about it," replied Karl. "Very good," she said, "and do stay. I should be happy if you stayed, and, if it's all right with you, we could stick together. I've trusted you from the moment I first saw you. And yet—see, that's how bad I am—I feared that the head cook could give the secretarial post to you and dismiss me. It was only after spending quite a while sitting here alone—while you were down in the office—that I realized how wonderful it would be if you took over my tasks, since you'd have a better understanding of them. If you didn't want to do those errands in the city, I could hang on to that job. In any case I would certainly be much more useful in the kitchen, especially since I've become a little stronger." "It's already all set," said Karl, "I'll be a lift boy, and you'll stay on as secretary. If you give the head cook even the slightest hint of your plans, I shall disclose everything else you've told me today, however much I'd regret having to do so." Therese was so upset by Karl's tone that she threw herself down by the bed and began to whimper, pressing her face against the bedclothes. "I certainly won't disclose anything," said Karl, "but you mustn't say anything either." Now he could no longer stay entirely hidden under the blanket; he stroked her arm a little and, finding it impossible to come up with anything appropriate to say, simply reflected that life here was bitter. At last she calmed down, at least enough to be ashamed of her weeping, looked gratefully at Karl, and after encouraging him to sleep late the following morning, promised that if she could find the time, she would come up shortly before eight o'clock and wake him. "You're so good at waking people," said Karl. "Yes, some things I can do," she said, and letting her hand slide softly over his blanket in farewell, she ran into her room.

Next day Karl insisted on taking up his duties at once, even though the head cook had wanted to let him take the day off to visit Ramses. But Karl responded frankly that there would be more such opportunities, and that his most important task now was to start work, for at a younger age in Europe he had fruitlessly broken off work that was directed toward a different goal, and now here he was starting off as a lift boy at an age when in the natural sequence of events the more assiduous youths at least were about to take on higher-level positions. It was, he said, very fitting that he should start as a lift boy but equally fitting that he should do so with special haste. Under these circumstances a visit to the city would give him no pleasure whatsoever. He could not even decide to take a short route suggested by Therese. And he kept thinking that if he was not diligent, he might end up like Delamarche and Robinson.

At the hotel tailor's he was fitted out in the uniform of a lift boy, which was very splendidly adorned with gold buttons and gold ribbons but made Karl shiver a little as he put it on, for the coat was cold, especially in the armpits, and so drenched with the sweat of the lift boys who had previously worn it that it could not be dried. The uniform had to be especially loosened for Karl, particularly above the chest, since none of the ten ready-made uniforms on hand would fit him. Despite these necessary alterations, and although the master tailor seemed quite meticulous—the uniform that had been duly delivered was on two occasions flung back into the workshop—in barely five minutes everything was finished, and Karl left the studio looking like a lift boy, in close-fitting trousers and a little jacket that was, in spite of the master tailor's categorical assurances to the contrary, very constricting and continually tempted one to do breathing exercises to see whether it was still possible to breathe.

Then he reported to the head waiter, under whose command he was supposed to serve, a thin handsome man with a large nose who was probably already in his forties. He had no time to engage in even the briefest conversation and simply rang for a lift boy, who happened to be the very one that Karl had seen the previous day. The head waiter addressed him only by his first name, Giacomo, as Karl discovered only later, for the way his name was pronounced in English made it unrecognizable. This youth was now instructed to show Karl what he needed to know about the lift service, yet he was so timid and hasty that Karl couldn't even grasp the little that needed to be shown. Besides, Giacomo was probably annoyed, for he had had to leave the lift service on account of Karl and had been given the task of assisting the chambermaids, which, after certain experiences that he would not divulge, he considered dishonorable. Karl was especially disappointed to learn that the only contact a lift boy had with the elevator machinery was when he pushed a button to set it in motion, and that the hotel's machinists were always called whenever the engine needed to be repaired; for instance, although Giacomo had served at the lift for six months, he had never set eyes on the engine in the cellar, or on the machinery inside the elevator, even though, as he explicitly said, he would have greatly enjoyed doing so. Besides, the work itself was monotonous and, because of the twelve-hour shift and the alternating day and night shifts, so exhausting that, from what Giacomo said, it would have been intolerable if it had not been possible to catch a few minutes' sleep as one stood there. Though Karl said nothing, he was well aware that this very trick had cost Giacomo his job.

Karl was very pleased that the elevator he had to look after was reserved solely for the top floors and that he would therefore not have to deal with the extremely demanding rich guests. Still, it would not be possible to learn as much there as one could elsewhere, so it was useful only at the beginning.

Already after his first week Karl realized that he was very much a match for the service. The brass on his elevator was always exceedingly well polished; none of the thirty other elevators came close, and it would have glistened even more brightly had the youth serving alongside in the same elevator been even half so diligent as Karl and not felt that he could be all the more nonchalant thanks to Karl's diligence. He was a native-born American called Rennel, a vain youth with dark eyes and smooth, if rather sunken, cheeks. He had an elegant personal suit and on his free evenings would rush off into the city lightly perfumed; now and then he would ask Karl to substitute for him in the evenings, for family reasons, he said, and was not in the least concerned that his elegant appearance belied all such excuses. Still, Karl was very fond of him and was pleased whenever Rennel stopped by at his elevator downstairs, dressed in his own suit, offered a few more excuses while pulling his gloves over his fingers, and then went off down the corridor. In filling in for him Karl simply wanted to do him a favor, as at first seemed only natural with an older colleague, but this ought not to become a lasting arrangement. For this everlasting riding up and down in the lift was certainly tiring enough, especially in the evening hours, when there were almost no lulls.

Karl soon learned how to give the short low bows expected of lift boys and always caught the tip in midair. Then it disappeared into the pocket of his waistcoat, and from the expression on his face one could not tell if it was a big or a small tip. For the ladies he opened the door with a touch of gallantry, easing himself slowly into the elevator in their wake, for they usually entered more hesitantly than the men on account of their skirts, hats, and accessories. While the elevator was in operation, he stood by the door as inconspicuously as possible, with his back to the passengers, and held the handle of the elevator door so that he could quickly push it aside on arrival without startling anyone. Only rarely during the ride would a person tap him on the shoulder with a request for information, and then he would spin around, as though he had expected such a question, and answer in a loud voice. In spite of the number of elevators available, there was often such a bustle, especially after the theaters had closed or a certain express train had arrived, that no sooner had he deposited the guests upstairs than he was obliged to race back down to collect those still waiting below. He also had the option of increasing the usual speed by pulling on a cable that ran through the elevator; but the elevator regulations stated that this was prohibited and even dangerous. Karl never did so while riding with passengers, yet whenever he dropped them off upstairs and there were others waiting below, he became reckless and worked on the cable

with strong rhythmical tugs, like a sailor. Besides, he knew that
the other lift boys were doing likewise and did not wish to lose
his passengers to those other youths. Some guests who lived
at the hotel for longer periods, which was incidentally fairly
common, would occasionally indicate with a smile that they
recognized Karl as their lift boy; Karl gladly acknowledged
their friendliness, though he did so with a serious face. Every
now and then, when the traffic had eased off a little, he could
take on special little errands, such as fetching some small item
forgotten by a hotel guest who wished to avoid having to go up
to his room, and then he would race up alone in the elevator,
which at such moments felt especially familiar to him, enter
the stranger's room, where there were usually curious objects
that he had never previously encountered lying about or hanging on the clothes racks, sense the characteristic aroma of a
stranger's soap, perfume, or mouthwash, and without even
halting for a moment, rush back with the item that—for all the
vague instructions he had been given—he mostly succeeded in
finding. He often regretted not being able to take on bigger
errands, for those were the preserve of special servants and
messengers who went about on bicycles and even motor bicycles, whereas Karl was at best used only to carry messages
between the guest rooms and the dining or gaming rooms.

When he returned from his twelve-hour shift, for three days
at six o'clock in the evening and for the next three at six
o'clock in the morning, he was so weary that he ignored everybody else and went straight to his bed. It was in the lift boys'
shared dormitory; the head cook, who may not have had so
much influence as he had imagined that first evening, had tried
to procure him a little room of his own and would no doubt
have succeeded in doing so; Karl, however, on seeing the difficulties to which this gave rise and the number of calls the head
cook had to make to his boss, that ever-so-busy head waiter,

turned down the offer and persuaded the head cook he was serious by explaining that he did not want to be envied by the other youths for an advantage he had not actually earned.

One certainly couldn't call this dormitory a quiet bedroom. For since each of them divided his twelve hours of free time differently between eating, sleeping, diversions, and side jobs, there was always a great commotion in the dormitory. Some boys slept with the blankets pulled up over their ears so that they would not hear anything; whenever one of them was awakened, he would yell so furiously over the yelling of the others that even the sound sleepers could no longer hold out against the noise. Nearly every youth had a pipe; they were considered a luxury; Karl had acquired one too and soon took pleasure in it. But smoking was not allowed on duty, and as a result everyone in the dormitory smoked, unless one happened to be fast asleep. Consequently, each bed was enveloped in its own cloud of smoke, and all was lost in a general haze. Although approved by the majority, the suggestion that only one light should be left burning at the far end of the dormitory proved impossible to implement. Had it been possible to adopt that suggestion, those who wished to sleep could easily have done so in the dark half of the dormitory—it was a large room with forty beds—whereas the others in the illuminated part of the room could have played dice or cards and carried out any other activities for which light was required. If anyone whose bed lay in the illuminated section had wanted to sleep, he could have lain down in the dark on one of the empty beds, for there were always sufficient empty beds and nobody objected to someone else making such short-term use of his bed. But this arrangement was never put into effect, not even for one night. Again and again there were some, let's say two, who, after taking advantage of the dark to catch some sleep, felt like playing cards on a board they had spread out between them and switched on an electric lamp, and its piercing light would startle the boys opposite. You could certainly go on tossing and turning for another little while, but in the end your only recourse was to start a game with your neighbor, who had also been awakened in the glow of yet another lamp. By then, of course, all of their pipes were glowing again. But there were certainly others— Karl was usually among them—who, determined to sleep at all costs, rather than put the pillow underneath their head, covered their head with it or wrapped it around their head, but how could you go on sleeping when the occupant of the adjacent bed rose in the middle of the night so that he could enjoy a little diversion in the city before reporting for duty, washed himself noisily, splashed water in the basin affixed to the head of his bed, pulled on his boots noisily, stamping his feet on the floor to force them up higher—they were mostly too tight even though they were American-style boots—and then finally, on discovering that some little item in his clothing was missing, lifted up the pillow, where you lay in wait, long since roused from your sleep, eager to let fly at him. They were all athletic and young, mostly sturdy fellows who did not want to pass up any opportunity for sports. And whenever you were awakened in the middle of the night by some great noise and jumped up, you inevitably encountered two boxers on the floor by your bed and, under glaring lights, numerous experts standing on all of the surrounding beds in their shirts and underpants. Once, during one such nighttime boxing match, one of the combatants fell upon the sleeping Karl, and the first thing he saw on opening his eyes was the blood running from the youth's nose, and before he could do a thing, the blood poured down all over his bedclothes. Frequently Karl spent almost all of his twelve hours off duty trying to get a few hours' sleep, although he too was greatly tempted to take part in the other boys' pastimes; but again and again he was struck by the thought that all of the others had an advantage over him in life, for which he would have to compensate by working more diligently and by making certain sacrifices. Although he was very determined to get his sleep, mostly for the sake of his work, he never complained to the head cook or to Therese about the conditions in the dormitory since, first of all, every youth in there had a hard time as well and never seriously complained about it, and secondly, all that bother in the dormitory was inevitably part of his task as a lift boy, which he had after all gratefully accepted from the hands of the head cook.

Once a week, on changing shift, he had twenty-four hours off, which he used partly to pay a visit or two to the head cook and to have a few brief exchanges with Therese—usually in some corridor and only rarely in her room—during one of the miserably infrequent moments when she was off duty. Sometimes he accompanied her on her errands to the city, which needed to be carried out most expeditiously. Then they would almost run to the closest subway station, with Karl carrying her bag; the journey passed by in a flash, as if the train were being pulled along without meeting the slightest resistance; now they had already descended from it, and instead of waiting for the elevator, which they found too slow, they clattered up the steps; there then appeared great squares, with streets that radiated out like a star, causing turmoil in the traffic, which came streaming in straight lines from every direction; yet staying close together, Karl and Therese rushed into various offices, laundries, warehouses, and stores in which they had to convey some orders and complaints, which by the way were not so weighty that they could not have been easily dealt with by telephone. Therese soon noticed that Karl's help was not insignificant, for it certainly helped expedite matters. Whenever he went along, she never had to wait as she usually did until the exceedingly busy merchants stopped to listen to her. He went to the counter and rapped on it with his knuckles until he received an answer; he shouted through walls of people in an English that still sounded too emphatic and could easily be distinguished even amid a hundred voices, and he approached those people unhesitatingly, even if they had withdrawn disdainfully into the recesses of the deepest business chambers. He did so not out of exuberance, for he could understand their resistance, but because he believed he had a secure position, one that afforded him certain rights since the Occidental Hotel was a customer that could not exactly be scoffed at, and also since Therese, for all her business experience, needed some help. "You should always come," she would say at times, laughing happily, as they returned from an especially well-executed enterprise.

Only on three occasions during Karl's one-and-a-half-month stay in Ramses had he spent more than a few hours in Therese's room. It was of course smaller than any of the head cook's rooms; her few possessions were piled up around the window; but from his experiences in the dormitory Karl knew just how important it was to have a relatively quiet room of one's own, and although he never said so explicitly, Therese nevertheless noticed that he did like her room. She kept no secrets from him, and after her visit that first evening, it was hardly conceivable that she had any left to keep. She was an illegitimate child; her father was a foreman on a construction crew and had brought the mother and child over from Pomerania, but as if he had thereby done his duty, or as if he had expected to find someone other than the worn-out woman with the weak child whom he met on the landing dock soon after their arrival, he had emigrated to Canada without ever giving any real explanation, and the wife and child he left behind never received a letter or any other news from him, but this was scarcely surprising, for somewhere in the teeming districts on New York's East Side they were irretrievably lost.

On one occasion Therese—Karl stood beside her, looking

down at the street—spoke of her mother's death. She described how on a winter's evening—she must have been about five years old at the time—her mother and she had hurried through the streets looking for a place to sleep, each with her own bundle. And how at first her mother had led her by the hand, for a snowstorm was blowing and it wasn't easy to move forward, until her hand grew limp and then, without even glancing behind her, she let go of Therese, who then had to struggle to hold on to her mother's dress. Therese often stumbled and even fell down, but her mother seemed as if in a craze and did not stop. And then those snowstorms blowing across the long, straight New York streets! Karl had not yet experienced a New York winter. When you walk into the wind and it turns in a circle, you cannot open your eyes; the wind continually rubs the snow into your face, you walk on without getting any farther, the situation becomes very desperate. Of course, a child does have an advantage over adults; it can run under the wind and take pleasure in everything. And so even then Therese could not understand her mother and was absolutely convinced that if she had responded more sensibly to her mother that evening—she was still such a small child at the time—her mother wouldn't have had to endure such a miserable death. She had been out of work for two days; there wasn't even the smallest coin left in their pockets, they had spent all day outdoors without a bite and carried only useless rags in their bundles, which they dared not throw away, maybe out of superstition. Her mother had been promised work on a construction site, starting the following morning, but as she had sought to explain to Therese all day, she feared she couldn't seize the opportunity, for she felt dead tired; to the consternation of passersby, she had coughed up a great deal of blood along the way and merely wanted to get into the warmth somewhere and have a good rest. But on that particular evening it was impossible to find

such a place. Even in those places where the custodian did not
turn them away from the entrance, where one could at least have
recuperated from the weather a little, they hurried on through
the narrow icy corridors, climbed through the upper stories,
went in a circle around the narrow terraces of the courtyards,
knocked randomly on doors, at times not daring to approach
anyone, at others asking everyone who came along, and once
or twice her mother crouched breathlessly on the steps of a
quiet staircase, drew over Therese, who almost fought with her,
and kissed her, pressing painfully against her lips. On finding
out afterward that those were her last kisses, one cannot quite
understand how—even if one was only a little mite—one could
have been so blind as not to grasp this. In some rooms that they
passed the doors had been pushed open to let out the suffocat-
ing air, and amid the smoky haze filling the rooms, as though
from a fire, one saw entering through the doorway a single isolated figure who indicated, either through his silence or through
a few words, that they could not possibly be accommodated
in that particular room. In hindsight Therese believed that
it was only for the first couple of hours that her mother had
made a serious effort to find a place, for she had probably not
approached anyone else after midnight, even though she rushed
on until dawn, taking only a few breaks and even though there
is always life stirring in those buildings where the gates and the
apartment doors are never shut and you run into people every
step you take. Of course they made rapid progress, not by running but by exerting themselves to the utmost, and in reality
they may have been only crawling along. Therese did not know
how many buildings they had entered between midnight and
five o'clock in the morning, whether it was twenty, or two, or
perhaps only a single one. While the corridors of these buildings are cleverly designed to optimize the use of space, they also
make it hard to find one's way; how often must they have

passed through those same corridors! Therese did have a dim
memory of their going out through the front gate of a building
that they had endlessly searched; she also believed that on
reaching the street, they turned around at once and rushed back
into the same building. For a child this was a source of incomprehensible torment; being dragged along, sometimes with her
mother holding her, sometimes holding on to her herself, without ever hearing a consoling word, and the only explanation
she could come up with—due to her limited reasoning powers
at the time—was that her mother wanted to run away and
abandon her. So even when her mother took her by one hand,
with her other she still clasped her mother's skirt for safety's
sake, howling at intervals. She wanted to avoid being left
behind among the people stomping up the stairs in front of
them, those not yet visible who were approaching around a
bend in the staircase, and those who were arguing in the corridor in front of a door and throwing one another into the
room. Drunks wandered through the building singing in muffled
tones, and the mother and Therese fortunately managed to slip
through groups that were slowly closing ranks. Of course, late
that night, when people were no longer so alert and no one
would have insisted on everything being handled correctly, they
could certainly have pushed their way into one of those dormi-
tories rented out by entrepreneurs, but Therese did not understand this and her mother no longer wanted to take a rest. On
a beautiful winter morning the two of them leaned against the
wall of a house and may even have slept, or perhaps simply
gazed about them through wide-open eyes. It became evident
that Therese had lost her bundle, and her mother went through
the motions of slapping her for her inattentiveness, but Therese
could neither hear nor feel the slightest blow. They continued
on through the increasingly busy streets; her mother kept close
to the wall, they crossed a bridge where her mother brushed

the top of the balustrade with one hand and finally reached the construction site—Therese had simply accepted this at the time, but she could not understand it now—at which her mother had been asked to show up that morning. She did not tell Therese whether she should wait there or leave, and Therese took this as a command to wait, since it corresponded most closely to what she herself wished to do. So she sat down on a pile of bricks and watched as her mother undid her bundle, took out a colorful rag, and used it to tie up the scarf she had worn all night. So great was Therese's weariness that it never even crossed her mind that she might be able to help her mother. Without reporting at the construction hut, as was customary, and without asking anyone, her mother climbed up a ladder as if she already knew which tasks she had been assigned. Therese found this surprising, for the female laborers were generally only put to work down below, slaking lime, passing bricks, and carrying out other such simple tasks. She therefore thought that her mother intended to do better-paying work that day and smiled up at her drowsily. The building was not yet that high, scarcely extending beyond the ground floor, even though one could already see the tall scaffolding rods, which had not yet been tied to the boards, rise up into the blue sky. On reaching the top, her mother nimbly bypassed the bricklayers, who were laying one brick on top of the other and inexplicably failed to challenge her, stretched out her delicate hand carefully so as to be able to hold on to a wooden partition that served as a kind of railing, while in her drowsiness below Therese was astonished by her mother's nimbleness and believed that her mother had cast another friendly glance at her. But just then her mother reached a pile of bricks where the railing and probably even the gangway itself came to an end, but she ignored this and headed toward the pile of bricks, whereupon her nimbleness seemed to desert her; she knocked over the pile of bricks, fell over it and down into the depths. A large number of bricks came rolling down after her, and finally after quite a while a heavy board somewhere worked itself loose and crashed down upon her. Therese's last memory of her mother was of her lying there in her checkered skirt, still from Pomerania, of the board lying upon her and almost covering her, of people running over from every direction, and of some man or other up on the building shouting down in anger.

It had grown late by the time Therese finished her story. She had spoken at great length, which was not generally her habit, and it was precisely when she came to the insignificant parts, such as the description of the scaffolding rods rising into the sky one by one, that she had to stop, tears welling up in her eyes. Now, ten years later, she knew every little thing that had happened back then, and since the last memory that she had of her mother alive was of her lying on the half-finished ground floor above and since it was never possible for her to convey that sight clearly enough to her friend once she had finished telling her story, she wanted to go back to that incident, but instead she faltered, laid her face in her hands, and fell silent.

However, there were also merrier occasions in Therese's room. On his first visit Karl had seen a manual for business correspondence lying about and had requested and borrowed it. At the same time they agreed that Karl should complete the exercises in the book and hand them to Therese; she had already studied the book as much as was required for her minor duties. Karl then spent entire nights lying awake in his dormitory bed, his ears stuffed with cotton wool, trying out every conceivable position for the sake of diversion as he read the book and with a fountain pen jotted down the exercises in a little notebook—a present from the head cook to thank him for having devised and neatly carried out a large inventory that had turned out to be very practical. Whenever he was disturbed by the other youths, he usually managed to turn the situation around by asking them continually for tips about the English language until they grew tired and left him in peace. Often he marveled at how the other youths were completely reconciled to their present situation; they could not even sense how temporary it was—no lift boys older than twenty years of age were permitted—failed to recognize the necessity of making a decision about their future profession, and in spite of the example set by Karl, read only detective stories that got passed around from bed to bed in dirty tatters.

During their meetings Therese corrected Karl's work in an excessively meticulous fashion; contentious opinions were exchanged. Karl invoked his great New York professor as a witness, but she was as little impressed with him as with the lift boys' notions of grammar. She would take the fountain pen from his hand and cross out the passage that she considered erroneous, but though no authority greater than Therese would usually ever lay eyes on such questionable passages, for the sake of accuracy Karl would insist on crossing out Therese's crossouts. The head cook would occasionally join them, though she always sided with Therese, which of course proved nothing, since Therese was after all her secretary. Still, she brought about a general reconciliation, for tea was made, pastries fetched, and Karl was asked to talk about Europe, though his observations were frequently interrupted by the head cook, who often asked questions and expressed astonishment, making Karl realize how many changes from the bottom up had occurred within a relatively short period and how much else had completely changed in his absence and was still changing continually.

Karl must have been in Ramses about a month when Renell said in passing one evening that a man called Delamarche had approached him and asked about Karl. Having no reason to conceal anything from the man, he had truthfully told him that Karl was a lift boy but that owing to the head cook's patronage, he had good prospects of obtaining positions of a very different sort. Karl noticed the careful treatment Renell had received at the hands of Delamarche, who had even invited him to share a meal that evening. "I no longer have any dealings with Delamarche," said Karl. "You too should be wary of him!" "I should?" said Renell, straightening up, and then he rushed off. He was the most delicate youth in the hotel, and according to a rumor circulating among the other waiters, the source of which was impossible to track down, he had been showered with kisses in his lift by an elegant lady, a long-time hotel resident. Anyone familiar with that rumor would have been amused to see that self-assured lady, whose outward appearance give no indication whatsoever of the possibility of such conduct, walk by with her light gait, delicate veils, and tightly corseted waist. She lived on the first floor, for which a lift other than Renell's was designated, but when the other youths happened to be busy, one could not prevent such guests from entering a different lift. And so every now and then this lady rode in Karl and Renell's lift and indeed always exclusively when Renell was on duty. This may have simply been a coincidence, but no one believed it, and the departure of the lift ferrying them upstairs always gave rise to such barely suppressed unrest along the entire row of lift boys that there were even times when one of the head waiters had been obliged to intervene. In any case a change had come over Renell, whether due to the lady or to the rumors that had begun to circulate; he had become vastly more self-assured and now left all of the cleaning to Karl, who awaited a chance to raise the issue with him; he no longer came to the dormitory. No one else had so completely abandoned the community of lift boys, for generally they stuck together, at least with regard to service-related issues, and had an organization of their own, which was recognized by the hotel management.

Karl considered all of this, thought about Delamarche too, and otherwise performed his duties as usual. Toward midnight he had a little diversion, for Therese, who often surprised him with little presents, brought him a large apple and a chocolate bar. They talked for a while, scarcely disturbed by the interruptions caused by his trips up and down in the elevator. The conversation turned to Delamarche, and Karl noticed that for some time now he had let himself be influenced by Therese and had begun to regard Delamarche as a dangerous person, for that was certainly how he seemed to Therese from Karl's stories. But on the whole Karl considered him a mere wretch who had let himself be spoiled by misfortune and with whom one could nonetheless get along. Therese disputed this vigorously, though, insisting in lengthy speeches that Karl should promise her that he would never say a word to Delamarche again. Instead of making such a promise, he urged her repeatedly to go to sleep, and when she refused to do so, he threatened to leave his post and escort her back to her room. When she was at last ready to leave, he said: "Therese, why burden yourself with such unnecessary worries? In the hope of helping you sleep better, I'll gladly promise you that I shall speak to Delamarche, but only if there's no other way." He then had to make numerous trips, since the youth in the adjacent lift was engaged in some other errand and Karl had to attend to both lifts. There were some guests who spoke of a great mess, and one gentleman, accompanied by a lady, gave Karl a little tap with his walking stick, prompting him to hurry up, but this admonition was quite uncalled for. If, after noticing that one of the lifts was unattended, the guest had only gone over to Karl's lift right away—but no, instead of doing so, they went to the adjacent lift and stood there, holding the door handle or even stepping into the elevator, even though this was something that—according to the most severe paragraph in the service regulations—the lift boys were supposed to prevent at all cost. Karl therefore had to run back and forth wearily without even having the satisfaction of knowing that he was carrying out his duties exactly as intended. And then on top of it all, toward three in the morning a porter, an old man with whom he was on fairly friendly terms, wanted some help from him, but Karl certainly could not help him now, for there were guests standing before both of his lifts, and it took considerable presence of mind to select one group and stride toward it. So he was glad when the other lift boy resumed his duties, and he shouted a few words of reproach at him over his lengthy absence, even though he was probably not to blame. After about four in the morning things quieted down a little, but by then Karl urgently needed some rest. Leaning heavily on the balustrade by his elevator, he slowly ate the apple, which even after the first bite gave off a strong fragrance, and gazed down into one of the light shafts, which was surrounded by the great windows of the pantries, behind which hung masses of bananas that still shimmered in the dark.

VI

THE ROBINSON AFFAIR

Just then someone tapped him on the shoulder. Thinking that it must of course be a guest, Karl quickly put the apple in his pocket and, after scarcely looking at the man, rushed over to the elevator. "Good evening, Mr. Rossmann," said the man, "it's me, Robinson." "But you've changed," said Karl, shaking his head. "Yes, I'm doing well," said Robinson, glancing down at his clothing, which, although perhaps comprised of fairly elegant items, was so jumbled that it looked downright shabby. Most striking was a white waistcoat obviously worn for the first time, with four little pockets bordered in black, which Robinson sought to accentuate by sticking out his chest. "You certainly have expensive clothes," said Karl, and he had a fleeting memory of the beautiful simple suit in which he could have held his own even alongside Renell but that had been sold by his two bad friends. "Yes," said Robinson, "I buy something almost every day. How do you like my waistcoat?" "Quite nice," said Karl. "The pockets aren't real, though, they're just made for show," said Robinson, and he took Karl's hand so that the latter could convince himself of this. Karl, however, shrank back, since Robinson's mouth smelled unbearably of brandy. "You've begun to drink heavily again," said Karl, who had returned to the balustrade. "Not heavily," said Robinson, and, contradicting his previous remark about being so satisfied, he went on: "What else has a man got in this world." A trip interrupted this conversation, and no sooner had Karl reached the ground floor than the telephone rang, and he was informed that he should fetch the hotel doctor since a lady up on the seventh floor had fainted. As he went about this task, Karl hoped secretly that Robinson would already be gone, for he had no desire to be seen in his company and, remembering Therese's warning, did not wish to hear anything from Delamarche either. Robinson, however, was still waiting in the stiff posture of a completely intoxicated person, and just then a high-ranking hotel official in a black frock coat and cylinder hat passed by, fortunately without seeming to pay special attention to Robinson. "Rossmann, wouldn't you like to come and visit us sometime; we're living in style now," said Robinson, directing an enticing glance at Karl. "Are you inviting me or is Delamarche?" asked Karl. "Delamarche and I. Both of us see eye to eye on this," said Robinson. "Then there's something I wish you to know and would ask that you pass it on to Delamarche: just in case this wasn't already sufficiently clear, when we said goodbye it was for the last time. The two of you have given me more grief than anyone else. Do you really want to go on pestering me like this?" "But we are your comrades," said Robinson, his eyes filling with vile tears of intoxication. "Delamarche would like you to know he wants to make amends for everything that happened earlier. We're living with Brunelda, she's such a marvelous singer." And he would have sung a song in a high-pitched voice had Karl not managed to hiss at him just in time: "Be quiet this instant, don't you realize where you are?" "Rossmann," said Robinson, who was intimidated only concerning his singing, "after all, no matter what you say, I'm still your comrade. And since you've now got such a fine position here, could you let me have some money?" "But you'll just drink it all away again," said Karl. "I can even see some kind of brandy bottle sticking from your pocket; you must have drunk

from it while I was away, for at first you were still fairly coherent." "It's just to fortify me on the road," Robinson said apolo-
getically. "I don't want to reform you anymore, that's for
sure," said Karl. "But what about the money!" said Robinson,
with wide-open eyes. "Delamarche must have told you to bring
back some money. Fine, I'll give you some money, but only on
condition that you leave at once and never visit me here again.
If there's something you want to let me know, you can write
to me. Karl Rossmann, elevator boy, Occidental Hotel, that
should suffice as an address. But I'll say it again, you may not
come to see me anymore. I'm on duty and don't have time for
visitors. So are you going to accept the money on that condition?" Karl asked, reaching into his waistcoat pocket, for he
had decided to part with that night's tips. In response, Robinson merely nodded and breathed deeply. Karl interpreted this
incorrectly and asked again: "Yes or no?"

Just then Robinson waved him over and whispered amid
gagging motions that were already quite unmistakable: "Rossmann, I feel very sick." "What the devil," Karl exclaimed
involuntarily, and then with both hands he seized Robinson
and dragged him over to the balustrade.

And now it flowed out of Robinson's mouth, down into the
depths. Between bouts of sickness, he groped at Karl, helplessly
and blindly. "You're really a good boy," he said continually, or
"It's about to stop," which was far from true, or "What sort of
stuff did those dogs pour down my throat!" Out of unease and
disgust Karl could not tolerate being so close to him and began
to walk up and down. Here in the corner beside the elevator
Robinson was of course somewhat hidden, but what if someone were to notice him, one of those rich nervous guests who
simply cannot wait to complain to a rapidly approaching
hotel official, who then wreaks furious vengeance on the entire
household staff, or if one of those constantly changing hotel

detectives—whom nobody, aside from the management, knows and whom one sees of course in every passerby—gives probing looks, perhaps only because he happens to be shortsighted. And of course, since the restaurant was open at night, all it would take would be for someone to go into the pantries in the dining rooms below, notice that abominable mess in the light shaft, and telephone Karl, demanding to know what in heaven's name was going on up there. And could Karl truthfully deny all knowledge of Robinson? And if he did, wouldn't Robinson decide not to apologize and in his idiocy and despair simply mention Karl's name? And wouldn't Karl have to be dismissed on the spot, for something truly outrageous had happened, a lift boy, the lowest and most dispensable employee in the huge hierarchy of hotel servants, had through his friend's behavior led to the hotel being fouled up, the guests startled and perhaps even driven away? Could one continue to tolerate a lift boy who had such friends and who, moreover, let his friends visit him while he was on duty? Mustn't such a lift boy be a drinker or possibly even worse, and didn't it look as if he had so overfed his friends with the hotel's provisions that they had finally perpetrated a certain deed, like Robinson's only a moment ago, in some corner of that same, always meticulously maintained hotel? And why should such a youth confine himself to stealing food when there were actually countless opportunities to steal, thanks to the notorious carelessness of the guests who leave closets open everywhere, valuables lying about on the tables, boxes torn open, and keys strewn about so thoughtlessly?

Just then from afar Karl saw guests emerge from a cellar bar, in which a variety performance had just ended. Karl took up his post at his elevator, without even daring to turn toward Robinson for fear of what he might see. It was scarcely reassuring that there was not a sound, let alone a sigh, coming from that direction. Although he attended to his guests and rode up and down with them, he could not altogether conceal his distraction, and on each downward trip he was prepared to encounter an embarrassing surprise below.

At last he found time to check up on Robinson, who was crouched in his corner, head pressed against his knees. He had pushed his hard round hat up off his forehead. "Away you go," said Karl, softly and decisively, "here's the money. If you hurry up, I can show you the shortest way." "I can't go," said Robinson, wiping his forehead with a tiny handkerchief, "I'll die here. You can't possibly imagine how ill I feel. Delamarche takes me to all of the fine restaurants, but I cannot stand such dainty fare; I say this to Delamarche every day." "Well, you certainly can't stay here," said Karl, "do remember where you are. If you're found here, you'll be punished and I'll lose my position. Is that what you want?" "I can't go," said Robinson, "I'd rather jump down there," and he pointed between the bars of the balustrade and down into the light shaft. "I can manage to sit here like this but can't stand up; I did give it a try while you were away." "Then I'll get a cab and you will go to the hospital," said Karl, giving Robinson's leg a little shake, for there were alarming indications that he could at any moment lapse into utter apathy. But no sooner had Robinson heard the word *hospital*, which seemed to awaken dreadful fears in him, than he began to weep loudly and to hold out his hands toward Karl, beseeching mercy.

"Be quiet," said Karl, and after slapping Robinson's hands aside, he ran to the lift boy for whom he had substituted that night, asked him to return the favor, hurried back, and pulling the still-sobbing Robinson to his feet with all his might, whispered to him: "Robinson, if you want me to look after you, make an effort and walk just a little bit of the way. You see, I'll take you to my bed and you may stay there until you're better.

You'll be amazed how soon you'll recover. But do behave sensibly, since the corridors are crowded, and my bed is in a dormitory. If anyone notices you, even if only barely, I won't be able to do anything more for you. And you must keep your eyes open; I can't carry you around like some deathly ill person." "I certainly want to do everything you think is right," said Robinson, "but you can't carry me all by yourself. Couldn't you get Renell to help?" "Renell isn't here," said Karl. "Oh, of course," said Robinson, "Renell is with Delamarche. It was, of course, those two who sent me to fetch you. I'm getting everything mixed up." Taking advantage of this rambling statement and several other incomprehensible monologues, Karl pushed him forward, and in this way they arrived unscathed in a rather poorly lit corridor that led to the lift boys' dormitory. Just then a lift boy came running toward them, only to pass them at top speed. All such previous encounters had been quite harmless; between four and five o'clock was the quietest time, and Karl surely knew that unless he succeeded now in getting rid of Robinson, there could be no question of doing so at dawn amid the early rush.

A great fight, or some such event, was under way at the other end of the dormitory; one could hear rhythmical clapping, agitated foot tapping, and sporting cheers. In the beds on the side closest to the door one could see only a few resolute sleepers; most lay on their backs staring into space while every now and then one would jump out of bed, dressed or unclothed as he was, so as to gauge the situation at the other end of the dormitory. Almost unobserved, Karl led Robinson, who could now walk a little better, to Renell's bed, since it was near the door and fortunately unoccupied, whereas even from a distance he could see that his own bed was occupied by a strange boy, whom he didn't know at all and who was still sound asleep. Robinson no sooner felt a bed under him than he fell asleep at once, one leg still dangling from the bed. Karl pulled the blanket up over his face in the belief that he would not have to worry about Robinson, at least not for now, since he would certainly not wake up before six in the morning, and by then he himself would have returned and, possibly with the help of Renell, found a way to take Robinson away. It was only in exceptional cases that inspections of the dormitory were carried out by some of the higher authorities; some years ago the lift boys had managed to get rid of the once-customary general inspection, and so from that side too there was nothing to be feared.

When Karl reached his elevator again, he saw that both his elevator and that of his neighbor were ascending. Uneasily, he awaited an explanation. His own elevator came down first, and he could see emerging from the other the youth who had just run down the corridor. "Well, where have you been, Rossmann," he asked. "Why did you go off? Why didn't you notify the authorities about your absence?" "But I told him he should fill in for me briefly," Karl answered, and he pointed at the youth who was approaching from the neighboring lift. "I was his substitute for two hours at the busiest time of day." "That's all very well," said his interlocutor, "but it's really not good enough. Don't you realize that even such brief absences must be reported to the head waiter's office? After all, that's what you have a telephone for. I'd have been happy to fill in for you, but as you know, it isn't so easy. Just then there were new guests from the four-thirty express standing in front of both lifts. I couldn't run to your lift first and keep my own guests waiting, so I went up first in my own lift." "Well?" Karl asked expectantly, since both youths had fallen silent. "Well," said the youth from the neighboring lift, "the head waiter, who was passing by, sees people waiting at your lift who aren't being helped, and this makes his blood boil, and he asks me, who has just run over, where you are; I haven't a clue since you didn't say a word about where you were going, so he telephones the dormitory at once to tell them that another boy should come over right away." "I ran into you in the corridor," said the youth who had filled in for Karl. Karl nodded. "Of course," insisted the other youth, "I said at once that you had asked me to fill in for you, but does he ever listen to such excuses? You probably don't know him yet. And we're supposed to tell you that you should go to his office at once. So don't stand around here, just run over to him. He may forgive you, you were actually only gone for two minutes. Feel free to use my name and to mention that you asked me to fill in for you. It'd be best not to mention your having filled in for me, and do take my advice on this, though there's no way I can get into trouble since I had permission to leave; all the same, it's not a good idea to talk about that sort of thing and confuse it with this entirely unrelated affair." "It's the first time I ever left my post," said Karl. "That's always the way, except nobody believes that is so," said the youth, and ran to his lift, since there were people approaching. Karl's substitute was a boy of about fourteen who, evidently feeling pity for Karl, said: "We've had many cases in which people were forgiven such things. They usually get transferred to other jobs. So far as I know, only one person has been dismissed for anything of that sort. You must simply come up with a good excuse. Under no circumstances should you say that you were suddenly taken ill, since he would just laugh at you. It would be better if you said that one of the guests gave you an urgent message to take to another and that you no longer know who the first was and weren't able to find the second." "Well," said Karl, "it won't be that bad"; however, after everything he had heard, he no longer believed in a favorable outcome. And even if he were forgiven this dereliction of duty, Robinson, the very embodiment of his guilt, still lay in the dormitory, and it was only too probable, given the head waiter's choleric temperament, that they would not be content with a superficial investigation and would eventually succeed in tracking down Robinson. There was probably no express prohibition against taking strangers into the dormitory, but that was only because that which is inconceivable is never prohibited.

As Karl entered the office, the head waiter was sitting over his morning coffee; he took a sip and looked at a ledger presented for inspection by the chief hotel porter, who was also present. The latter was a large man whose sumptuous, richly decorated uniform—there were various gold chains and bands snaking all the way across his shoulders and arms—made him seem even more broad-shouldered than he was in reality. A glistening black mustache, pointed in the manner favored by Hungarians, did not stir when he turned his head around quickly. Moreover, owing to the weight of his clothes, the man could move only with difficulty and always positioned himself with his legs spread sideways so as to distribute his weight properly.

Karl had entered freely and in haste, as he was accustomed to do at the hotel, for the slowness and caution that is considered polite in private individuals is taken for laziness in lift boys. Besides, they mustn't notice his sense of guilt the moment he entered. Though the head waiter glanced up briefly when the door opened, he returned to his coffee and reading, without paying any further heed to Karl. But the porter, perhaps feeling disturbed by Karl's presence or perhaps having some kind of confidential news or request to report, gazed angrily at Karl the entire time, head stiffly inclined, and then, after having met Karl's gaze—evidently on purpose—turned his head toward the head waiter. Karl, however, thought it would not look at all good if, after having come to the office, he were to leave now without receiving explicit orders from the head waiter to do so. The latter continued studying the ledger; now and then he took a piece of cake, shook off some sugar, and ate it without interrupting his reading. When a page from the ledger fell to the floor, the porter did not even attempt to pick it up; he realized that he was incapable of doing so; besides, it was also unnecessary since Karl had already reached the spot and passed the page to the head waiter, who merely reached out his hand and took it, as though it had flown up from the floor somehow all by itself. But that small good deed was of little avail, for the porter did not cease casting angry glances at him.

Nevertheless Karl was more composed than before. Even the fact that the head waiter evidently attached so little importance to his affair could be taken as a good sign. This was after all only understandable. A lift boy is a nobody, so he cannot allow himself liberties, but then again precisely because he's a nobody, he cannot get up to exceptional mischief either. Besides, in his youth the head waiter himself had been a lift boy—which was still the great pride of this generation of lift boys—it was he who had first organized the lift boys, and there must certainly have been an occasion when he left his post without permission, even if no one could force him to recall that and though it was undeniably true that, precisely because he was a former lift boy, he saw it as his duty to keep that profession in order by occasionally exercising relentless severity. Karl now pinned his hopes on the advancing hour. According to the office clock, it was already shortly after a quarter past six, and Renell could come back at any moment; perhaps he was even there already, for he must surely have noticed that Robinson had not returned; besides, Karl now realized that Delamarche and Renell could not have been that far from the Occidental Hotel, for in his miserable condition Robinson could not have found his way there alone. If Renell encountered Robinson in his bed, as was bound to happen, everything would be fine. For given Renell's practical bent, especially when his own interests were concerned, he would somehow find a way to remove Robinson from the hotel, which could be brought about more easily now that Robinson had meanwhile gained a little strength, and besides, Delamarche was probably already waiting outside the hotel, ready to take delivery. Once Robinson had at last been removed, Karl could approach the head waiter much more calmly, and this time maybe he would get off with a reprimand, although it might be a fairly severe one. Then he would speak with Therese about whether to tell the head cook the truth—he himself could see no obstacle—and if it were possible, the matter could be disposed of without causing any real damage.

No sooner had Karl succeeded in calming himself down a little with the help of such reflections and discreetly begun to count the night's tips, for he sensed that they were especially abundant, than the head waiter uttered the words "Wait a little longer please, Feodor," put the ledger on the table, sprang up, and shouted at Karl so loudly that all he could do was stare into the great black cavern of his mouth.

"You left your post without permission. Do you know what this means? It means that you're dismissed. I don't want to hear any excuses, you may keep your deceitful excuses to yourself; for me the fact that you were absent is entirely sufficient. If I tolerate and excuse this even once, it won't be long before all forty lift boys abandon their duties, and I'll end up having to carry my five thousand guests up the stairs all by myself."

Karl remained silent. The porter approached and tugged Karl's jacket, which was rather creased, no doubt so as to draw the attention of the head waiter to this slight dishevelment in Karl's suit.

"Perhaps you became ill all of a sudden?" the head waiter

asked craftily. Karl gave him a searching look and answered: "No." "Then you weren't even ill?" the head waiter shouted, even louder than before. "Then you must have fabricated some big lie. Out with it. So what's your excuse?" "I didn't know one had to request permission by telephone," said Karl. "Well, that's quite priceless," said the head waiter, and seizing Karl by the collar of his coat, carried him, almost floating in the air, to the official regulations for the lifts, which were nailed to the wall. The porter followed them to the wall. "There. Read that," said the head waiter, pointing to a paragraph. Karl thought that he was supposed to read it silently. "Out loud!" the head waiter commanded. Rather than read it aloud, Karl said in hopes of calming the head waiter: "I'm familiar with that paragraph; I did of course receive the official regulations and read them carefully. But that is precisely the kind of stipulation one forgets since one never has any need of it. I've been serving here for two months and never once left my post." "You will now, though," said the head waiter, and walking over to the table, he picked up the ledger again, as though he wished to go on reading, but slapped it down on the table instead, as if it were a useless rag, and began to walk up and down the room, forehead and cheeks aflame. "And all for such a rascal! Such excitement on the night shift!" he exclaimed several times. "Do you know who was about to go up when this fellow ran away from his lift?" he said, turning to the porter. He named a name, and the porter, who certainly knew all of the guests and could tell their worth, was so horrified that he glanced at Karl, as if only the sheer existence of the latter could confirm that the owner of such an illustrious name had had to wait in vain for some time at a lift whose operator had run away. "That's dreadful!" the porter said, shaking his head slowly in boundless unease at Karl, who gazed sadly at him, thinking that now he would have to pay for this fellow's obtuseness in addition to

everything else. "Besides, I know you," said the porter, extending his large fat index finger and pointing it stiffly at Karl.
"You're the only boy who consistently refuses to greet me.
What on earth do you think you're doing? Everyone who passes
the porter's lodge must greet me. While you may do as you
wish with the rest of the porters, I expect to be greeted. Sometimes I act as though I were not watching, but even if you are
absolutely quiet, I know precisely who greets me and who does
not, you lout." He turned away from Karl and, rising to his
full height, strode toward the head waiter, who, instead of
commenting on the porter's affair, finished his breakfast and
glanced at a morning newspaper, which a servant had just
handed in to the room.

"Mr. Head Porter," said Karl, who at least wished to sort
out the issue with the porter while the head waiter was not
paying attention, for he realized that although the porter's
reproach would do him no harm, his hostility surely would. "I
most certainly do greet you. You see, I've not been in America
long and come from Europe, where, as everyone knows, people
greet one another much more than is necessary. I haven't been
able to give up that habit yet, and only two months ago in New
York, where I happened to move in upper social circles, people
tried to convince me continually to cease being so exaggeratedly polite. And yet you accuse me of not greeting you. I did
greet you, several times every day. But of course not every time
I saw you, since I pass you a hundred times a day." "You must
greet me every time, every time without exception, and whenever you speak to me, you must hold your cap in your hand
and always call me Head Porter, not Sir. And all of this you
must do every time, every time." "Every time?" Karl repeated
softly, remembering how many severe and reproachful glances
the porter had directed at him while he was at the hotel, beginning with that very first morning, when, still not quite adjusted

to his subservient position, he had questioned this very porter insistently and in great detail, and thus perhaps too boldly, as to whether two men had asked after him and possibly left a photograph for him. "Now you'll see where that sort of behavior lands you," said the porter, who had returned and now stood rather close to Karl, and he pointed to the head waiter, who was still reading, as if he were the representative of his revenge. "You'll certainly know how to greet the porter at your next job however wretched a dive it may be."

Karl realized that he had in fact already lost his position, for the head waiter had just made the announcement, the head porter had repeated it as an established fact, and in the case of a lift boy, they surely did not need confirmation of the dismissal from the hotel management. But everything had gone more quickly than he had expected, for he had, after all, served for two months as best he could and certainly better than some of the other boys. At the critical moment, though, such things obviously aren't taken into account, neither in Europe nor in America, and the decision that is reached simply follows the verdict someone utters in an initial outburst of fury. Perhaps it would have been best if he had said goodbye at once and gone away, for the head cook and Therese might have been asleep still, and so as to spare them at least the disappointment and grief over his conduct, at least during a personal leave-taking, he could have said goodbye by letter, packed his bags quickly, and slipped away quietly. But if he were to stay even one day longer—and he certainly could have used some sleep—all he could expect was the escalation of his affair into a scandal, reproaches from all sides, the unbearable sight of Therese's tears and possibly even those of the head cook, and ultimately perhaps punishment too. On the other hand, he was held back by the thought that he faced two enemies, and that one or the other would always criticize everything he said and put a negative construction on it. So he remained silent, taking pleasure for now in the silence that had descended in the room, for the head waiter was still reading the newspaper and the head porter was rearranging the pages of the ledger, which were scattered over the table, a task that, evidently due to shortsightedness, he accomplished only with great difficulty.

At last the head waiter put down the newspaper with a yawn, assured himself through a glance that Karl was still present, and switched on the bell on the table telephone. He shouted hello several times, but there was no answer. "There's no answer," he said to the head porter. The latter, who was, Karl thought, following the telephone conversation with particular interest, said: "Well, it's a quarter to six. She must be awake by now. Try to make it ring louder." At that moment, without further prompting, an answering call came through. "Hello, this is Head Waiter Isbary," said the head waiter. "Good morning, Madame Head Cook. But I hope I haven't awakened you. I'm very sorry. Yes, yes, it's already a quarter to six. All the same, I'm truly sorry I gave you a fright. You should turn off the telephone when you go to sleep. No, no, I don't really have any excuse, especially given the trivial nature of the affair I wish to discuss with you. But of course I have time, please go on, and if you don't mind, I shall remain on the line. She must have run to the telephone in her nightdress," the head waiter smilingly informed the head porter, who throughout this exchange had been bent over the telephone apparatus with a tense expression on his face. "I did wake her. She's usually awakened by the little girl who does her typewriting and who, quite exceptionally, must have neglected to do so today. I'm sorry I startled her; she's already nervous enough." "Why has she stopped talking?" "She's gone to find out what happened to the girl," replied the head waiter, who had already put the receiver to his ear, since the telephone was ringing again. "She'll turn up all right," he continued, speaking into the telephone. "You shouldn't let everything scare you so. You really need a complete rest. Well, here's my little question. There's a lift boy, called"—he turned around and glanced inquiringly at Karl, who was paying close attention and could therefore help by giving his name—"well, called Karl Rossmann; if my memory serves me right, you took a certain interest in him; unfortunately, he did little to repay your kindness, left his post without permission, causing me great difficulties of still unknown dimensions, so I've just dismissed him. I hope you're not taking this to heart. What do you mean? Dismissed, yes, dismissed. But I told you that he left his post. No, dear Madame Head Cook, I really cannot yield to you in this instance. It's a question of my authority, there's a great deal at stake here; it takes only one such boy for the entire gang to go bad. One has to be devilishly alert, especially with those lift boys. No, no, in this case I cannot do you a favor, although I always very much endeavor to defer to your wishes. And if despite all this I did leave him here, it would serve no other purpose than to keep my blood boiling; and indeed it is for your sake, yes, for your sake, Head Cook, that he cannot stay. He certainly doesn't deserve the interest you take in him, and since I not only know him but you too, I realize that this would inevitably create the most grievous disappointments for you, and I wish to spare you those at all costs. I'm being very frank with you, even though the obstinate boy we're talking about is standing only a few steps away. He's dismissed, no, no, Head Cook, entirely dismissed. No, no, he's not being transferred to some other work, he's completely unusable. Besides, I keep on hearing additional complaints. For instance, the head porter, what was that again, Feodor; well, the head porter has been complaining about the boy's cheekiness and impoliteness. Beg your pardon, you're saying this won't suffice? Listen, Madame Head Cook, you're going against your own nature merely for the sake of this boy. And you mustn't pester me like this."

Just then the porter bent down to the head waiter and whispered a few words in his ear. At first the head waiter looked at him in astonishment, and then he spoke so rapidly into the telephone that Karl could not quite understand him at first and advanced two paces on tiptoes.

"Dear Madame Head Cook," he said, "to be honest, I would never have thought that you could be such a bad judge of character. I just discovered something about your angelic youth that will thoroughly change your opinion of him and almost regret that it is I who must tell you. Well, this ever-so-fine youth, whom you call a model of decency, does not let a single night he has off-duty go by without running into the city, from which he doesn't return until the following morning. Yes, yes, Madame Head Cook, this has been proven by completely unimpeachable witnesses. And maybe you could tell me how he comes up with the money for such diversions? How can he remain sufficiently alert to carry out his duties? And do you really want a detailed description of what he actually gets up to in the city? I want to get rid of that boy as quickly as possible. Please take this as a warning about how careful one must be with youths who just show up at the door."

"But Mr. Head Waiter," cried Karl, who was truly relieved by the great mistake that seemed to have occurred, which could conceivably lead to an unexpected turn for the better on all sides. "There has certainly been some confusion here. I believe the head porter has told you that I go off every night. That's absolutely untrue, I'm actually in the dormitory all night, and all of the boys can vouch for this. When I'm not sleeping, I'm learning how to write business letters and don't ever set foot outside the dormitory at night. That can be easily proven. The head porter is obviously confusing me with somebody else, and I can understand now why he thinks I don't greet him."

"Will you be quiet at once," shouted the head porter, shaking his fist where others would merely have wagged a finger, "you say I'm confusing you with somebody else. Well, then I can no longer be a head porter if I keep confusing people like that. Listen, Mr. Isbary, if I get people confused, I can no longer be head porter. But in my thirty years of service I've never confused a single person, and the hundreds of head waiters we have had in the meantime would certainly confirm this, yet the first person whom I supposedly got confused was you, you wretched boy. You of all people, with your strikingly smooth mug. But how could there have been any such confusion, for even if you had run off every night into the city behind my back, one need take only one look at your face to see that you are an utter scoundrel."

"Stop, Feodor!" said the head waiter, whose telephone conversation with the head cook seemed to have been suddenly interrupted. "This is a very simple matter. How he entertained himself at night is absolutely irrelevant. Of course, before he leaves, he may indeed want us to carry out a large-scale investigation of his nighttime activities. I can easily imagine that would please him. Then we'd have to summon all forty lift boys and interview them as witnesses, and of course all of them would confuse him with someone else, so we would gradually have to call the entire staff as witnesses, and then of course the hotel would have to be shut down for a while, and so by the time he was finally thrown out, he would at least have had some fun. But let's not do him any such favor. He's already fooled the head cook, who is such a decent woman, and that is enough already. I don't want to hear one more word from you; you're dismissed from the service this instant for neglect of duty. I'm writing out a note for the bursar's office requesting payment for the wages you are owed, up to today. Besides, between the two of us, given how you have conducted yourself, I am simply giving this to you as a present, solely out of consideration for the head cook."

A telephone call prevented the head waiter from signing the instructions right away. "But those lift boys, they're giving me such trouble today!" he cried, on hearing the first few words from the other end of the line. "That's really outrageous!" he cried, after a brief pause. And turning away from the telephone to look at the head porter, he said: "Feodor, please hold that fellow for now. There are still a few matters we need to discuss with him." And he gave an order into the receiver: "Come up at once!"

Now the head porter could at least let off steam, which he had not managed to do as he spoke. He seized Karl by his upper arm, not with a steady grip, which would have been bearable, but rather by loosening his grip and then gradually tightening it, which on account of his great physical strength felt as if it would never cease and caused a darkening of Karl's vision. Yet he not only held Karl but pulled him up in the air and shook him, as though he had also been given orders to stretch out his body, while telling the head waiter repeatedly, almost as a question: "So I'm confusing him now, so I'm confusing him now."

Karl was saved by the entrance of the top lift boy, a forever-panting fat youth named Bess, who drew some of the head waiter's attention. Karl was so exhausted that he scarcely greeted him, and to his astonishment, he saw Therese slip in behind the boy, pale as a corpse, dressed untidily, her hair bound loosely. A moment later she stood beside him and whispered: "Does the head cook already know?" "The head waiter telephoned her," Karl responded. "Well then, everything will be fine, just fine," she said quickly, her eyes animated. "No, it won't," said Karl. "After all, you don't know what they have against me. I'll have to go away; even the head cook has already been persuaded of this. Please don't stay here, go upstairs, and I shall come to say goodbye." "What's got into you, Rossmann? You can stay here as long as you want. You see, the head waiter does everything the head cook wants; he does love her; I just found this out recently by accident. So calm down." "Please, Therese, go away now. I cannot defend myself so well in your presence. And I have to defend myself accurately since they're bringing up lies against me. The more I pay attention and the better I defend myself, the greater my hopes of staying. So, Therese"—unfortunately, due to a sudden attack of pain he could not refrain from adding quietly—"if the head porter would only let me go! I really had no idea he was an enemy of mine. But the way he keeps on grabbing and pulling me." "Only why am I saying this!" he thought at the same time. "No woman can listen to this calmly." And indeed, before Karl could use his free hand to restrain her, Therese turned to the head porter and said: "Mr. Head Porter, please let go of Rossmann at once. You're hurting him. The head cook will soon be here in person, and then it'll become quite clear how unjustly he's being treated in every respect. Let him go, what pleasure can you get from tormenting him?" And she even reached for the head porter's hand. "It was an order, young miss, an order," said the head porter, drawing Therese amiably toward himself with his free hand while squeezing Karl even more strenuously with the other, as though he not only wanted to cause him pain but also had special designs on the arm currently in his possession that were by no means realized yet.

It took some time for Therese to extricate herself from the head porter's embrace, and then, just as she was about to intercede for Karl with the head waiter, who was still listening to the rather long-winded Bess, the head cook strode into the room. "Thank God," cried Therese, and for a moment all one could hear in the room were those two loud words. The head waiter immediately jumped up, pushing aside Bess: "So you've come in person, Madame Head Cook. On account of such a trifling matter? After our conversation on the telephone it dawned on me that this might be so, but I couldn't quite believe it. And this matter with your protégé is becoming ever more serious. I fear I won't be able to dismiss him and shall have to have him locked up instead. Come here and listen for yourself!" And he beckoned Bess to approach him. "First, I should like to say a few words to Rossmann," said the head cook, and she sat down on a chair since the head waiter forced her to do so. "Karl, please come closer," she said. Karl complied, or rather was dragged over by the head porter. "Do let him go," said the head cook angrily, "after all, he's not a thief and murderer." The head porter let him go but only after giving Karl such a tight last squeeze that the strain brought tears to his eyes.

"Karl," said the head cook, and then she calmly put her hands in her lap and looked at Karl with her head bent down toward him—this really didn't seem like an interrogation— "what I especially want to tell you is that I still have complete confidence in you. The head waiter too is a just man, I can vouch for that. All in all, both of us want to keep you on." She gave the head waiter a fleeting glance, as though requesting that she not be interrupted. The head waiter remained silent. "So forget what these people here may have told you. You don't have to take all that so seriously, especially what the porter may have said. Though he is quite wound up, which isn't surprising given his duties, he does have a wife and children and realizes that there's no need to subject a boy who is entirely thrown back on his own resources to unnecessary torment, since the world at large will certainly see to that."

The room fell silent. The head porter looked at the head waiter, demanding an explanation; the latter looked at the head cook and shook his head. Behind the head porter's back, Bess, the lift boy, grinned absurdly. Therese sobbed in joy and sorrow and had to make a great effort to prevent others from overhearing her sobs.

Even though Karl realized that such conduct would necessarily be taken as a bad sign, rather than looking at the head cook, who was certainly trying to catch his eye, he chose to gaze at the floor. The pain in his arm was throbbing all over, his shirt had stuck to the weal, and he really ought to have removed his jacket and taken a look at it. What the head cook said was, of course, very kindly meant, but it seemed to him that this behavior on the part of the head cook would unfortunately make it quite clear that he deserved no such kindness and that he had quite undeservedly enjoyed the head cook's favor for two months and indeed that all he simply deserved was to fall into the head waiter's hands.

"I'm telling this to you," the head cook continued, "so that you can answer forthrightly, as you would have done anyhow, from what I know of you."

"Please, may I go and get the doctor, the man could be bleeding to death," said the lift boy, interrupting the conversation in a polite but most disruptive manner.

"Yes, go," said the head waiter to Bess, who ran off at once. Then he said to the head cook: "This is how things stand: the head porter has not detained that boy merely for the fun of it. Downstairs in the lift boys' dormitory a complete stranger was found lying in one of the beds, heavily intoxicated, with the covers pulled up carefully over him. They woke him, of course, and wanted to get rid of him. But the man made quite a racket and kept shouting out that the dormitory belonged to Karl Rossmann, that he was a guest of Karl Rossmann, who had brought him there and would punish anyone who dared to lay hands on him. Besides, he would have to wait for that fellow Karl Rossmann, he said, for he had promised him money and had just gone to get it. Please take careful note of this, Madame Head Cook: he promised him money and went to get it. Rossmann, you too should take note of this," the head waiter said to Karl, who had just turned toward Therese; she in turn stared at the head porter, as if spellbound, and pulled her hair back from her forehead, perhaps simply as an automatic gesture. "But perhaps I ought to remind you of certain appointments you've made. You see, the man downstairs went on to say that when you return, you two will pay a nighttime visit to a certain female singer, whose name no one could understand since the man could pronounce it only when he was singing."

Just then the head waiter interrupted what he was saying, since the head cook, who had grown visibly pale, rose from his chair, which she pushed back a little. "I shall spare you the rest," said the head waiter. "No, please, no," said the head cook, seizing his hand. "Go on, I want to hear everything, that's why I've come." The head porter stepped forward and, so as to signal that he had seen through everything from the outset, beat himself loudly on the breast, whereupon the head waiter addressed him with the words: "Yes, you were quite right, Feodor!" calming him down while upbraiding him also.

"There's not much left to say," said the head waiter. "Boys are boys; first they laughed at the man, then got into a fight with him, and since there were always a few good boxers standing around, he was simply boxed to the floor, and I dared not even ask where, and in how many spots, he was bleeding, for these boys are formidable boxers, and of course they have an easy time with a drunk."

"Well," said the head cook, holding her chair by the armrest and staring at the place she had just vacated. "So please do speak, Rossmann!" she said. Therese had already run across to the head cook from her position, and taken the head cook's arm, which Karl had never seen her do before. The head waiter stood right behind the head cook, slowly smoothing out the head cook's small plain lace collar, which was turned up a little. The head porter, who still stood next to Karl, said: "So out with it now," merely so as to conceal a punch in the back that he was giving Karl.

"It's true," said Karl, sounding less confident than he would have wished on account of the punch, "I did take the man into the dormitory."

"That's all we wish to know," said the porter, speaking on behalf of everybody else. The head cook turned silently to the head porter and then to Therese.

"I had no other choice," Karl continued. "That man is my former comrade, and after not seeing each other for two months, he came to visit me, but was so drunk he could not leave on his own."

The head waiter, who now stood next to the head cook, mumbled to himself in a low voice: "So he came to visit and was so drunk afterward that he couldn't leave on his own." The head cook whispered a few words over her shoulder to the head waiter, who appeared to raise objections, smiling in a manner evidently unrelated to this affair. Out of helplessness Therese—Karl had eyes only for her—pressed her face up to the head cook, seeking to block out everything else. The only person whom Karl had completely satisfied with his explanation was the head porter, who said repeatedly: "That's absolutely right, a man has got to help his drinking buddy," and sought to impress this explanation on all present by means of gazes and gestures.

"So I'm to blame," said Karl, and he paused, as if awaiting from his judges a kind word that might give him the courage to go on defending himself, but the word never came, "I'm to blame only for taking that man, whose name is Robinson—he's an Irishman—into the dormitory. As for everything else he said, he said so only because he was drunk and it's not true."

"So you didn't promise him any money?" asked the head waiter.

"Yes," said Karl, and he regretted that he had forgotten this altogether; whether out of rashness or distraction, he had all too definitely called himself blameless. "Rather than go fetch it, I wanted to give him the tips I had earned last night." And to prove this was so, he pulled the money from his pocket and showed a couple of small coins in the palm of his hand.

"You keep getting lost," said the head waiter. "To be able to believe what you say, one would continually need to forget what you just said. So first you took that man—I can't even believe you when you say his name is Robinson; ever since Ireland has existed, there's never been an Irishman of that name—first you say that you merely took him into the dormitory, which is, by the way, already sufficient to get you thrown out at once—and that you didn't initially promise him any money, but then when one surprises you with the question, you admit that you did promise him some money. But this isn't a question-and-answer game; we want to hear your justification for your actions. At first you didn't want to fetch the money and instead give him tips for today, but then it turns out that you do still have that money on you, so you obviously did intend to fetch more money, and your lengthy absence supports this interpretation. Finally, there would really be nothing odd about your wanting to fetch more money from your trunk for him, but it's certainly odd that you're trying to deny this so emphatically. Just as you seek the whole time to conceal the fact that you made the man drunk at the hotel, and there can be no doubt whatsoever about this since you yourself admitted that he came on his own but was unable to leave on his own, and of course, in the dormitory he himself shouted out that he was your guest. So there are only two questions that must still be clarified, which, if you wish to simplify the affair, you can answer yourself; besides, we can establish this without your help. First, how did you succeed in gaining access to the pantries, and second, how did you amass enough money to be able to give some away?"

"It's impossible to defend oneself in the absence of good-will," Karl said to himself, and he ceased to answer the head waiter, however painful for Therese this might be. He knew that whatever he could say would end up seeming very different from the way it had been intended and that the way they assessed the matter was critical, since it alone would determine the final judgment of good or evil.

"He isn't answering," said the head cook.

"It's the most sensible thing he can do," said the head waiter.

"He's sure to come up with something," said the head porter, taking the hand that had just engaged in cruel acts and stroking his beard delicately with it.

"Be quiet," the head cook said to Therese, who was beginning to sob. "Look, he's not answering, so how can I do anything for him? After all, I'm the one the head waiter is going to fault. But tell me, Therese, was there something I could have done and neglected to do?" How could Therese know how to answer this, and what could be gained by asking and entreating the little girl so publicly, which might cause the head cook to lose face with the two gentlemen?

"Madame Head Cook," said Karl, pulling himself together once again for the sole purpose of sparing Therese the obligation of answering, "I don't think I disgraced you at all, and after examining the matter carefully, everybody else would have to come to the same conclusion."

"Everybody else," said the head porter, pointing a finger at the head waiter, "that's a barb directed at you, Mr. Isbary."

"Well, Madame Head Cook," said the latter, "it's half past six, and now it's time, high time. I think it would be best if you gave me the last word in this affair, which has been dealt with far too leniently."

Little Giacomo had entered and sought to approach Karl, but startled by the silence in the room, he gave up and waited.

Ever since Karl had last spoken, the head cook kept her eyes trained on him and nothing suggested that she had heard the head waiter's remark. Her eyes looked squarely at Karl; they were large and blue but slightly clouded by age and constant strain. On seeing her stand thus, feebly shaking the chair in front of her, one might easily have expected her to say: "Well, Karl, when I think about it, I realize that this affair has not yet been properly settled, and as you rightly pointed out, a more careful investigation is called for. And we will conduct it right away, for whether one approves of this course of action or not, justice must be done."

Instead, however, after a brief pause that nobody had dared interrupt—except for the clock, which, confirming what the head waiter had said, struck half past six, accompanied, as everybody realized, by all the other clocks in the hotel; so that in one's ear and in one's imagination the sound seemed like the twofold twitching of one great disembodied impatience—the head cook said: "No, Karl, no, no! We're not going to allow ourselves to accept that. Just causes have a quite distinctive appearance, whereas yours, I must admit, does not. I can say this and am indeed obliged to say so since I'm the one who was most favorably inclined toward you when I came in. Look, even Therese has fallen silent." (But she had not fallen silent; she was weeping.)

Overcome by a new resolve, the head cook faltered and said, "Karl, come here," and when he approached her—the head waiter and the head porter gathered at once behind his back and struck up a lively conversation—she put her left hand around him and led him and the impassive, docile Therese far into the room, then back and forth a few times, before saying: "It is possible Karl—and indeed, you seem to be confident of this, for I simply could not understand you otherwise—that such an inquiry will corroborate that you are right, at least in certain details. Well, why not? Perhaps you actually did greet the head porter. I'm even quite sure of that; besides, I know quite well what I ought to think of the head porter; as you can see, I'm still very frank with you. But minor justifications of that sort won't be of any help to you. Over the course of many years I've come to respect the head waiter as a good judge of character; of all the people I know, he is the most reliable, and he has after all stated clearly that you are guilty, which I too find incontrovertible. You may simply have acted rashly, or then again you may not be the person I initially assumed you were. And yet"—she stopped for a moment, looked back at the two gentlemen, and then went on—"yet I still cannot give up on the idea that you're a fundamentally decent boy."

"Madame Head Cook! Madame Head Cook!" admonished the head waiter, who had caught her eye.

"We're just about finished," said the head cook, who now began to address Karl more rapidly and insistently: "Listen, Karl, the way I see things, I'm even glad the head waiter doesn't want to open an investigation, for if he tried to do so, I should have to put a stop to it for your sake. There's no need for anyone to find out how—and with what provisions—you fed the man, who can hardly be one of your former comrades, as you made out, for you had a big fight with them as you were saying goodbye and therefore you could not be hosting one of them now. So it can only be some acquaintance or other you met in some city bar at night and quite rashly accepted as a buddy. Karl, how could you have concealed all this from me? Perhaps you found life in the dormitory unbearable and this was the innocent reason for your nighttime ambles, but if so, why did you never say a word about it? You know I wanted to get you a room of your own and gave up on the idea only after you repeatedly asked me not to do so. It now seems as if you chose the dormitory because you felt less restricted there. And you kept your money in my safe and brought me your tips every week, so for God's sake, boy, where did you get the money for your diversions, and where did you intend to find the money for your friend? Naturally, I cannot even drop a hint to the head waiter about any of this just now, for that might make an investigation unavoidable. So you must definitely leave the hotel, and in fact as quickly as possible. Go straight to the Brenner Pension—you were there with Therese several times— and on the strength of this recommendation they will take you in without asking for payment"—the head cook drew a gold pencil from her blouse and wrote a few lines on a visiting card without even interrupting what she was saying—"I shall send on your trunk right away; Therese, run to the lift boys' wardrobe and pack his trunk" (but Therese did not stir, for just as she had endured all the sorrow, she now wanted to witness fully the improvement in Karl's affair thanks to the kindness of the head cook).

Somebody opened the door a crack without letting himself be seen and shut it again at once. This was evidently intended for Giacomo, for he stepped forward and said: "Rossmann, I have a message for you." "Just a moment," said the head cook, and put her business card into Karl's pocket as he listened, head inclined, "I shall keep your money for now. You know you can entrust me with it. Stay at home today and think over the affair, and then tomorrow—I don't have time today and have already been here far too long—I shall come to the Bren-ner, and then we'll see what else we can do for you. I shall not abandon you; I can already assure you of that. It's not the future you should be concerned about, but rather the recent past." Whereupon she tapped him lightly on the shoulder and approached the head waiter; Karl lifted his head and looked at this large, imposing woman, who set off at a calm pace and with sovereign bearing.

"Well," said Therese, who had stayed behind with him, "aren't you pleased everything has turned out so well?" "Oh yes," said Karl, and he smiled at her, although he had no idea why he should be pleased about being dismissed as a thief. Therese's eyes glittered with joy, as if she could not care less whether Karl had done something wrong and been justly condemned, if only they let him go, either honorably or in disgrace. And it was Therese who was behaving thus, the very Therese who handled her own affairs so meticulously that whenever the head cook used some not entirely unambiguous expression, she would turn it over in her mind and analyze it for weeks at a time. He asked her quite deliberately: "Will you pack my case right away and send it off?" Involuntarily, he had to shake his head in astonishment over the speed with which Therese took in the question; she was so convinced that certain items in the trunk needed to be hidden from everyone that she failed to glance at Karl or give him her hand and simply whispered: "Yes, of course, Karl, right away, I'll pack your trunk right away." And she was already gone.

Now, however, Giacomo, could no longer contain himself, and upset over the long wait, he called out in a loud voice: "Rossmann, that man is rolling about in the corridor downstairs and won't let us cart him off. We wanted to send him to the hospital, but he's putting up a fight and insists you would never stand for his being taken to the hospital. He told us we should hire a car and send him home, and you'd pay for the car. Is that what you want?"

"The man does seem to trust you," said the head waiter. Karl simply shrugged his shoulders and counted his money into Giacomo's hand: "That's all I have," he said.

"I was also told to ask if you want to accompany him in the car," added Giacomo, jingling the money.

"He's not leaving," said the head cook.

"So, Rossmann," said the head waiter quickly, without even waiting until Giacomo had left, "you're dismissed this instant."

The head porter nodded several times, as if those were his very words and the head waiter were merely repeating them.

"I cannot state the reasons for your dismissal out loud, for in that case I'd have to have you locked up."

The head porter gave the head cook a remarkably severe glance, for he must have realized that she was instrumental in bringing about this excessively lenient treatment.

"And now go to Bess, get dressed, hand over your livery, and leave the building at once, and I do mean at once."

The head cook closed her eyes so as to soothe Karl. As he took his bow, he caught a glimpse of the head waiter clasping the head cook's hand, as if furtively, and playing with it. With heavy steps, the head porter accompanied Karl to the door, which he did not let him shut but held open so as to call out after him: "I want to see you pass me at the main gate in fifteen seconds sharp, don't forget."

Karl hurried along as fast as he could, simply in order to avoid being pestered at the main gate, but everything took a great deal longer than he had wished. First Bess could not be found, there were of course people everywhere since it was breakfast time, then it turned out that a boy had borrowed Karl's old trousers, and Karl was therefore obliged to search through the clothes stands at the foot of virtually every bed until he found his trousers, so that five minutes had probably elapsed before Karl reached the main gate. Walking just ahead of him was a lady flanked by four gentlemen. They approached a large waiting automobile, the door to which was held open by a footman who held his free left arm stretched out stiffly to the side, which looked most formal. Karl had in vain hoped to slip out behind those elegant people without being observed. The head porter now seized him by the hand, drawing him in between two gentlemen, to whom he apologized. "You call that a quarter of a minute," said the head porter, looking sideways at Karl, as though at a malfunctioning clock. "So come here," he said, and led him into the large porter's lodge, which Karl had always wanted to explore, but now that he was being pushed in by the porter, he entered it most mistrustfully. He had already reached the doorway when he turned around and tried to push aside the head porter and get away. "No, no, it's this way," said the head porter, and spun Karl around. "But I've been dismissed," said Karl, meaning that he no longer had to take orders from anybody at the hotel. "Well, you've not been dismissed as long as I'm still holding you," said the head porter, which was certainly true too.

In the end Karl could find no reason why he should put up a fight against the porter. After all, what more could happen to him? Besides, the walls of the porter's lodge consisted entirely of gigantic glass panes through which one could clearly see masses of people streaming past one another in the lobby, as though one stood in their midst. There did not even seem to be a corner anywhere in the porter's lodge where one could hide from the eyes of those people. For all their rushing about—they sought to advance, arms extended, heads lowered, eyes peering, luggage raised in the air—hardly any of them failed to glance into the porter's lodge, where important announcements and news for the guests and staff hung behind the window-panes. Besides, there was a direct connection between the porter's lodge and the lobby, for two underporters, seated at two sliding windows, were continually busy dispensing information about the most disparate concerns. Those people were truly overburdened, and from what he knew of the head porter Karl could have sworn that in the course of his career he had somehow managed to sidestep such posts. These two information-givers—and one couldn't picture this properly from outside in the lobby—always had at least ten inquiring faces standing at the window before them. There was often a confusion of tongues among the ten questioners, who changed continually, as if each had been dispatched from a different country. There were always several inquiring at the same time and others constantly talking among themselves. Most either wanted to fetch something from the porter's lodge or drop something off, so there were always hands to be seen, rising out of the throng and gesticulating impatiently. On one occasion one of them expressed a desire to see a certain newspaper, which suddenly unfolded from above and briefly blocked out all the faces. The two underporters had to bear the brunt of everything. Simply talking would not have sufficed for the task; they chattered, especially one, a gloomy man with a beard enveloping his entire face, who gave out information without ever pausing. He neither looked at the tabletop, where he had to fiddle about constantly with his hands, nor at the face of one or the other questioners, but always stared stiffly straight before him, evidently so as to preserve his energy and gather strength. Besides, his beard made his speech a little hard to understand, and in the few moments Karl stood next to him he could understand very little of what the man said, and though there were English overtones, he must have been speaking in the foreign languages he was obliged to employ. Besides, it was confusing how quickly the answers came and how easily they merged into one another, so that a questioner would often remain there, listening with a tense face, in the belief that the underporters were still talking about his affair, only to notice after some time that he was finished. One also had to get used to the fact that the underporter never asked for a question to be repeated, even if it was mostly comprehensible and had simply not been phrased clearly enough, and in such cases a barely perceptible head shake would indicate that he had no intention of answering the question and that the questioner ought to discover his own mistake and come up with a better phrasing. As a result, some people spent a great deal of time in front of the window. To support the work, each underporter was assigned an errand boy who had to run back and forth hastily between a bookshelf and various closets, gathering whatever the underporter happened to need. Those were the best, if also the most strenuous, hotel posts that were available for the very young at the hotel, and in a way those youths had an even harder time of it than the underporters, since the latter merely had to think and talk, whereas those young people had to think and run. Whenever they happened to bring him the wrong item, the underporter could of course not tarry to give them lengthy instructions and so instead he simply threw whatever they had put on the table down on the floor in one great sweep. It was worth watching the underporters change shift, which happened shortly after Karl entered. Of course, such shift changes must have occurred often, at least during the day, for there was surely no one who could have tolerated standing behind that window for more than an hour. To signal a change of shift, a bell would ring out, and the two underporters about to go on duty would emerge from a side door, each with his own errand boy. They would position themselves at the counter and for a moment merely observe the people waiting outside so as to determine what stage the information dispensing had reached. If they thought it was the right moment to intervene, they tapped on the shoulder of the underporter whom they were about to replace, and even though he had completely ignored everything that took place behind his back, he understood at once and vacated his position. All this happened so quickly that the guests standing outside were often startled and almost recoiled in fright at the new face suddenly rising before them. The two men who had been replaced first stretched out and then poured water onto their stifling heads as they leaned over two washbasins, which were always kept at hand for that purpose, yet the errand boys who had been replaced could not stretch out yet and spent some time picking up and putting away the objects that had been thrown onto the floor during their shift.

All this Karl had absorbed with strained attentiveness within a few moments, and then quietly, with a slight headache, he followed the head porter, who led him forward. The head porter had evidently noticed how greatly impressed Karl was with this way of dispensing information, for he suddenly seized his hand and said: "Look, this is how the work gets done here." Well, Karl had certainly not lazed about at the hotel, but he had been completely unaware of any such work, and having forgotten for now that the head porter was his great enemy, he looked up at him and nodded in assent. But the head porter evidently took this not only as an indication that Karl overestimated the underporters but also perhaps as a personal slight, for, as if he assumed Karl were a fool, without showing the slightest concern that he might be overheard, he shouted out: "Of course, that's the most stupid work in the entire hotel; one need only listen for an hour to hear nearly every question that people ask, and the rest one can leave unanswered. If you hadn't been rude and ill mannered, if you hadn't lied, loafed about, got drunk, and stolen, then perhaps I could have given you a job at one of these windows, for it's a post I always reserve for blockheads." Karl completely failed to hear the insults aimed at him, so angry was he on discovering that the head porter not only failed to appreciate all of the honest hard work put in by the underporters but even subjected it to mockery, the mockery of a man who, had he dared sit down even just once at such a counter, would surely have had to clear off after a few minutes amid the laughter of all those making inquiries. "Leave me alone," said Karl, whose curiosity about the porter's lodge had been more than sated, "I don't want to have anything more to do with you." "You're not getting away that lightly," said the head porter, who squeezed Karl's arms so that he could not move them and even carried him to the far end of the porter's lodge. Did those people in the lobby not see the head porter's assault? Or if they saw it, what did they make of it, given that nobody stopped, no one even tapped on the pane to let the head porter know that he was being watched and could not treat Karl as he saw fit.

But Karl soon lost all hope of obtaining help from the lobby, for the head porter pulled a cord, and in half of the porter's lodge black curtains were drawn over the glass panes right up to the very top. Of course there were some people in this section of the porter's lodge too, but all were fully absorbed in their work, keeping their eyes and ears sealed against everything unrelated to the work at hand. Besides, they were completely dependent on the head porter and, instead of helping Karl, would have chosen to help cover up whatever the head porter might think of doing. There were, for instance, six underporters positioned by six telephones. As one immediately noticed, things were set up in such a way that one of them focused exclusively on taking down the conversations, while his neighbor, drawing on the notes he had received from his colleague, passed on the messages by telephone. These were the latest telephones and did not require telephone booths, since the ringing sound they produced was scarcely louder than a chirp; one could speak into the telephone in a mere whisper and yet, owing to a special form of electrical amplification, the words could nevertheless reach their destination at a thunderous pitch.

Consequently, one could barely hear the speakers on their telephones and might easily have imagined that they were muttering while observing some incident taking place in the telephone
receiver as the three others let their heads sink onto the paper
they were supposed to fill with writing, as if dazed by the noise
that penetrated through to them but was inaudible to all those
around. Here too there was a boy standing beside each of the
three speakers in order to assist them: these three boys merely
listened with their heads craned toward their particular gentlemen and then very hastily, as if they had been stung, leafed
through enormous yellow books—the massive rustling was
much louder than all the noise coming from the telephones—so
as to find the telephone numbers.

Karl could not resist the temptation to follow all this closely,
even though the head porter, who had sat down, held him in
some kind of hold. "I am duty bound," said the head porter,
and he shook Karl as if he simply wanted to get him to turn his
face toward him, "to make up at least partially on behalf of
the hotel management for what the head waiter himself has
somehow, for whatever reasons, repeatedly failed to do. Here
everybody covers for everyone else. Otherwise an operation
of this size would be inconceivable. You may object that I'm
not your immediate supervisor, but that only makes it all the
more remarkable that I should take on this derelict affair.
Besides, as head porter I am, as it were, placed above everybody else since I'm responsible for all of the hotel gates, in
other words, the main gate, the three middle ones, and the ten
side ones, not to mention the countless little doors and the exits
that have no doors. Naturally, all of the relevant service personnel have to obey me unconditionally. Having been entrusted
with such honors, I too naturally have obligations toward the
hotel management and must therefore refuse to let even slightly
suspicious-looking people leave the premises. And as it so hap-

pens, I find you especially suspect." And in sheer delight he raised his hands, then dropped them so fast that there was a great smack, which hurt. "It's possible," he added, sounding royally pleased, "that you could have left through another gate without being seen, for I didn't want to bother issuing special instructions just for you. But now that you're here, I'm going to get some pleasure out of you. Besides, I never doubted that you'd turn up at the main gate for our little rendezvous, since a person who is cheeky and disobedient will usually give up his vices just when it's harmful for him to do so. You'll certainly be getting frequent opportunities to experience this in person."

"Don't imagine," said Karl, inhaling the musty odor wafting over from the head porter, which he had only just noticed, even though he had been standing so close to him, "don't imagine," he said, "that I'm entirely at your mercy, for I can scream." "And I can stuff your mouth," said the head porter, just as calmly and as quickly as he might well intend to carry out that threat if necessary. "And do you really believe that if any of those people came in here on account of you, even one of them would side with you, as opposed to me, the head porter. So you can surely see that your hopes are futile. You know, when you were still wearing your uniform, you looked reasonably presentable, but the same cannot be said for you now in that suit, which would be presentable only in Europe." And he tugged at various parts of the suit, which, though it had been almost new five months ago, was now worn, creased, and above all stained, mostly owing to the carelessness of the lift boys, who in their laziness had responded to the general order that the dormitory floor be kept smooth and free of dust, not by undertaking any real cleaning, but simply by sprinkling some kind of oil on the floor every day, managing to leave dreadful splashes on all of the clothes on the clothes stands. Well, wherever one put one's clothes, there was always someone around who did not have his own clothes at hand and easily found a few concealed clothes belonging to someone else and borrowed them. And one of the boys entrusted with the task of cleaning the dormitory might not simply sprinkle oil on his clothes but smear them from top to bottom. Renell alone had managed to find for his expensive clothes a secret hiding place, where they had been left virtually undisturbed; the lift boys simply took clothes wherever they found them, for no one borrowed anyone else's clothes out of, say, malice or greed but merely in haste and out of carelessness. But even on Renell's outfit there was a circular reddish oil stain, right in the middle of the back, and thanks to that stain any knowledgeable city dweller could still have recognized traces of the lift boy.

Recalling those incidents, Karl said to himself that he had already suffered quite enough as a lift boy and that all this suffering was futile, for contrary to the hopes he had entertained, the job as a lift boy was not a stepping-stone to a better position; rather he had been pushed down even further and was even close to prison. What's more, he now found himself held by the head porter, who was probably thinking of ways to inflict further shame on him. Completely forgetting that the head porter was certainly not the kind of man who could be persuaded to change his mind, Karl slapped his forehead repeatedly with his free hand and cried: "And if in fact I did not greet you, how can a grown man become so vindictive merely on account of a single failure to greet him?"

"I'm not vindictive," said the head porter. "I simply want to search through your pockets. But I'm convinced that I shall not find anything, for you were no doubt sufficiently cautious as to ask your friend to cart things off bit by bit, a little every day. But you must be searched." Whereupon he dug into one of Karl's coat pockets with such force that the seams on the side burst. "So there's nothing left," he said, combing through the contents of Karl's pockets, which he had spread out in his palm: a hotel advertising calendar, a page with an exercise from a business correspondence manual, several coat and trouser buttons, the head cook's visiting card, a nail-polishing stick, which a guest had thrown to him while his trunks were being packed, an old pocket mirror Renell had given him as thanks for covering for him about ten times, and several other small items. "So it's all gone," repeated the head porter, and he threw everything under the bench as though Karl's possessions, insofar as they had not been stolen, belonged under the bench. "That's enough," Karl said to himself—his face must have been bright red—and when, rendered incautious through sheer greed, the head porter began to dig about in a second pocket of Karl's, Karl jumped out of his coat sleeves in one great bound, pushed an underporter up against his telephone, ran through the humid air to the door, although somewhat more slowly than he had intended, and yet was fortunately outside by the time the head porter in his heavy coat had even managed to get to his feet. The security service must not have been that exemplary; true, there were bells ringing in some parts of the hotel, but God only knew to what end, and indeed there were so many hotel employees walking back and forth at the main gateway that one could almost imagine they were making a discreet attempt to block the exit, for otherwise all that movement to and fro would have seemed quite senseless—in any case Karl soon found himself outdoors; but he was obliged to walk on the pavement in front of the hotel for it was impossible to reach the street because of the continuous line of cars passing the main gate in fits and starts. In their endeavor to get to their masters as fast as possible, these automobiles had almost collided, each propelled by the one behind. Here and there pedestrians in a particular hurry to reach the street climbed between the individual automobiles, as though there were a designated crossing, regardless of whether the occupants consisted solely of a chauffeur and servants or also included the most distinguished individuals. Yet such behavior struck Karl as excessive, for you probably had to know the situation very well before you took such a risk; he could so easily chance upon an automobile whose occupants would take offense and throw him off, causing a scandal, which he, a suspicious-looking hotel employee in shirtsleeves who had run away from his workplace, had most to fear. Finally, the line of automobiles could hardly go on forever like this, and besides, the closer he stayed to the hotel, the less suspect he would seem. At last Karl reached a spot where the line of automobiles, though not at an end, turned into the street and loosened up. He was just about to slip into the traffic in the street, where there must surely have been others far more suspicious-looking than he, when he heard somebody call out his name. He turned around and saw two very familiar lift boys dragging a stretcher laboriously out of a small low doorway, which looked like the entrance to a vault, and upon that stretcher, as Karl now saw, lay Robinson, whose head, face, and arms were covered with numerous bandages. It was revolting to watch him raise his arms to his eyes and use the bandage to wipe off his tears of pain or sorrow or even of joy upon seeing Karl again. "Rossmann," he cried reproachfully, "why have you kept me waiting so long? I spent an hour struggling to avoid being carted off before you got here. Those fellows"—and he butted one of the lift boys, as though the bandages offered sufficient protection against any possible blows—"they're true devils. Oh yes, Rossmann, I've certainly paid a high price for having visited you." "But what have they done to you?" said Karl, approaching the stretcher, which the lift boys set down, laughing, so as to take a rest. "You insist on asking," sighed Robinson, "though you can see how I look. Just imagine! That beating has most likely crippled me for the rest of my life. I've terrible pains from here to here"—and he pointed first to his head, then to his toes. "I wish you could have seen the way my nose was bleeding. My waistcoat is completely ruined, I simply left it there, my trousers too were torn to shreds, I'm just in my underpants"—and raising the blanket a little, he bade Karl look underneath. "What'll become of me! I'll have to spend a few months lying in bed, and I want to tell you right away that you're the only one I can rely on to take care of me, Delamarche is really much too impatient for that. Oh Rossmann, my dear little Rossmann!" And Robinson stretched out his hand to Karl, who had stepped back a little, so as to win him over with caresses. "Oh, why did I have to visit you!" he repeated several times so as to ensure that Karl would not forget that he was partly to blame for the misfortune. Karl immediately realized that Robinson's complaints stemmed not from his wounds but rather from the massive hangover afflicting him, for no sooner had he fallen asleep in a severely intoxicated state than he had been awakened and, much to his surprise, boxed around and bloodied and could no longer find his way about in the wide-awake world. That his wounds were minor was clear from the misshapen bandages, consisting of old rags, in which the lift boys had, obviously in jest, completely enveloped him. And now and then the two lift boys holding the ends of the stretcher burst out laughing. Well, this was not the place to bring Robinson back to his senses, for pedestrians continued to storm past, paying no heed to the group by the stretcher; when, with truly athletic leaps, several jumped over Robinson, the latter together with the chauffeur, who had been paid with Karl's money, cried, "Come on now, come on," and drawing on their last strength, the lift boys raised the stretcher. Robinson grabbed Karl's hand and said cajolingly, "Come along, do come along," after all, in the suit he wore, wouldn't Karl be better off in the dark automobile? And so he sat down beside Robinson, who leaned his head on him: the lift boys stayed behind and, reaching through the coupe window, shook hands amicably with him, their former colleague, and then with a sharp turn, the automobile veered toward the street; it looked as if there would inevitably be an accident, but it was not long before the all-embracing traffic calmly accepted even the arrowlike momentum of this automobile into its midst.

The suburban street in which the automobile halted must have been quite remote, for there was not a sound to be heard anywhere; on the curb children sat playing; a man with a large bundle of old clothes strung over his shoulders had his eyes fixed on the windows of the buildings as he shouted up; in his weariness Karl felt uncomfortable stepping from the automobile onto the asphalt, which seemed bright and warm in the morning sun. "You really live here?" he shouted into the automobile. Robinson, who had slept peacefully throughout the trip, muttered a few affirmative words and then seemed to wait for Karl to lift him out. "So there's no need for me here anymore. Goodbye," said Karl, intending to set off down the slightly sloping street. "But what do you think you're doing, Karl?" cried Robinson, who was so worried that he had already risen and now stood in the car, fully upright, save for his quivering knee. "But I must go," said Karl, who had noticed how quickly Robinson was recovering. "In your shirt-sleeves?" asked Robinson. "Well, I'll soon earn enough to buy myself another jacket," Karl answered, and giving Robinson a confident nod, he raised a hand in farewell and would have left had the chauffeur not called out: "Just a moment, sir." Disagreeably enough, the chauffeur claimed that he was owed an additional sum for waiting outside the hotel. "Yes indeed," Robinson cried out from the automobile, confirming that the chauffeur's demand was justified, "I had to wait such a long time for you. You do have to give him a little something." "Well, if only I had something left," said Karl, reaching into the pockets of his trousers, although he knew that it would be futile. "You're the only one I can turn to," said the chauffeur, rising with his legs spread wide apart, "I can't ask anything of that sick man there." Approaching from the gate was a young fellow with a wasted nose who halted a few paces away and began to listen to what was being said. Just then a policeman on his rounds through the street looked down at the man in shirtsleeves, sized him up, and halted. Robinson, who had also noticed the policeman, cried out stupidly from the other window, "It's really nothing, nothing at all," as if one could shoo away a policeman the way one shoos away a fly. The children, who had been observing the policeman, were alerted by his coming to a standstill to the presence of Karl and the chauffeur, and they scampered toward them. In the doorway opposite stood an old lady, staring intently.

"Rossmann," cried a voice from above. It was Delamarche shouting down from the top balcony. Only indistinctly visible against the whitish blue sky and evidently still in his dressing gown, he was observing the street through opera glasses. Spread out beside him was a red parasol, with a woman evidently sitting underneath. "Hello," he shouted strenuously in an effort to be heard, "is Robinson there too?" "Yes," answered Karl, powerfully boosted by another louder yes from Robinson in the car. "Hallo," the voice shouted back, "I'm coming." Robinson leaned out of the car. "What a man," he said, and this praise of Delamarche was addressed to Karl, the chauffeur, the policeman, and anybody else who chose to listen. Above on the balcony, which everyone was still absently watching although Delamarche was already gone, a strapping woman in a red dress rose, took the opera glasses from the balustrade, and looked down at the crowd, who only gradually averted their gaze. While waiting for Delamarche, Karl looked in the main gate and farther along into the courtyard, which was being crossed by an almost unbroken line of office workers, each carrying on his shoulders a small though clearly very heavy box. The chauffeur had walked over to his car and, so as not to waste time, set about polishing its headlights with a rag. Robinson patted all his limbs, seemed astonished by how little pain he sensed no matter how intently he observed himself, and therefore lowered his face and began to loosen carefully one of the thick bandages on his leg. The policeman held his little black truncheon in front of his chest and waited quietly, with the great patience that policemen must always demonstrate, whether they are carrying out their regular duties or lying in wait. The fellow with the wasted nose sat down on a gatepost and stretched out his legs. The children gradually approached Karl, taking little steps, for although he took no notice of them, they considered him to be the most important of them all on account of his blue shirtsleeves.

One could gauge the great height of the building from the time it took Delamarche to reach them. And Delamarche came rushing down, his dressing gown still only loosely tied. "So you're here!" he cried, sounding pleased yet stern. Each big step he took briefly exposed his colorful underwear. Karl could not quite understand why Delamarche walked about in the city, in that enormous tenement and out here in the middle of the street, dressed in such casual clothes, as if he were in his private villa. Like Robinson, Delamarche had greatly changed. His dark, smooth-shaven, scrupulously clean face, with its coarsely bulging muscles, looked proud and imposing. The bright sheen of his eyes, which were always half closed, came as a surprise. His violet dressing gown was certainly old, stained, and too large for him, but from this ugly article of clothing billowed a

powerful dark cravat of heavy silk. "Well?" he said, addressing
the question to everybody present. The policeman moved a
little closer and leaned against the hood. Karl offered a brief
explanation. "Robinson is worn out, but if he makes an effort,
he can manage to get up the stairs; this chauffeur here wants an
additional sum on top of the fare I've already paid. I'm leaving.
Good day." "You're not leaving," said Delamarche. "That's
exactly what I told him," Robinson announced from inside the
car. "I am leaving," said Karl, and he moved a few paces. Delamarche was already standing behind him, however, and now
pushed him back forcibly. "I'm telling you, you're staying," he
shouted. "Let me go," said Karl, preparing to fight for his freedom with his fists, however slight the prospect of success with
a man such as Delamarche. After all, the policeman was still
standing there, the chauffeur too, and now and then groups of
workers came down this street, which to be sure was usually
quiet; would they just stand by if Delamarche did him an injustice? Certainly he would not have wanted to be left alone in
a room with him, but out here on the street? Quietly, Delamarche paid the chauffeur, who pocketed the undeservedly
large sum amid much bowing and approached Robinson out of
gratitude, evidently in order to discuss how best to lift him out.
Karl noticed that there was nobody watching; maybe Delamarche would more easily tolerate his leaving if he did so
silently; it would be best if a fight could be avoided, so Karl
stepped onto the street in an attempt to escape as quickly as
possible. The children flocked toward Delamarche so as to
make him aware of Karl's flight, but he himself did not have to
intervene since the policeman held out his truncheon and said,
"Stop!"

   "What's your name," he asked, sticking his truncheon under
his arm and slowly pulling out a book. Whereupon Karl looked
at him closely for the first time; he was a powerfully built man,

but his hair had already gone completely white. "Karl Rossmann," he said. "Rossmann," said the policeman, who was doubtlessly repeating the name merely because he was a calm and methodical individual, but Karl, who was encountering American authorities for the first time, saw in this repetition a sign that he was considered somewhat suspect. And things certainly did not look good for him, since even Robinson, who was so preoccupied with his own worries, waved his hands vigorously from inside the car, beseeching Delamarche to help Karl. However, Delamarche fended him off with a quick headshake and looked on impassively, with his hands stuck in his huge pockets. The fellow sitting on the gatepost explained everything that had occurred from the very start to a woman who had just come out through the main door. The children stood in a half circle behind Karl, gazing silently up at the policeman.

"Show me your papers," said the policeman. This was surely only a formality, for if you don't have a jacket, you probably don't have identification papers either. So Karl did not answer, preferring to respond in detail to the next question, thereby concealing insofar as possible the fact that he had no papers. But then came the next question: "So you don't have any papers?" and Karl had to answer: "Not on me." "Well, that's no good," said the policeman, and he surveyed the circle of people pensively, tapping with two fingers on the cover of his book. "Do you have an income of any sort?" the policeman finally asked. "I was an elevator boy," said Karl. "You were an elevator boy, in other words you aren't anymore, and so what are you living off now?" "I'll be looking for new work." "So you were let go?" "Yes, an hour ago." "Suddenly?" "Yes," said Karl, raising his hand as if to excuse himself. He could not tell the whole story here, and even had this been possible, it seemed hopeless to ward off a threatened injustice by talking about an injustice he had suffered. And if he had not obtained his rights through the kindness of the head cook and the insight of the head waiter, he could certainly not expect it from this crowd on the street.

"And you were let go without a jacket?" asked the policeman. "Well yes," said Karl; so in America too the authorities made a point of asking questions even when they could see perfectly well for themselves. How annoyed his father had become over the useless questions the authorities had asked when they were applying for his passport. Karl had a great desire to run away and hide somewhere instead of having to listen to more such questions. And the policeman even asked the question that Karl had most feared, and probably because of the unease with which he had anticipated the question, he responded more carelessly than he might otherwise have done. "Which hotel did you work at?" He lowered his head and did not answer; that was a question he absolutely did not want to answer. What had to be avoided at all costs was the following: that he would be escorted back by the police to the Occidental Hotel, that hearings would be held to which his friends and enemies would be summoned, and that the head cook would completely abandon her favorable, if already weakening, opinion of Karl; she had thought he was at the Pension Brenner and would now find that he had come back in his shirtsleeves, did not have her visiting card, and had been picked up by a policeman; whereas the head waiter would perhaps give a knowing nod, and the head porter would talk of the hand of God that had finally caught the rascal.

"He was employed at the Occidental Hotel," said Delamarche, and moved close to the policeman. "No," cried Karl, stamping his foot, "that isn't true." Delamarche looked at him, narrowing his mouth mockingly as though there were matters of a very different nature that he could still disclose.

Karl's unexpected outburst set the children in motion, and they approached Delamarche in order to examine Karl closely from that position. Robinson had leaned his head completely out of the car and was so intent on what was happening that he remained absolutely quiet; he blinked from time to time but otherwise remained motionless. The fellow at the gate clapped his hands in delight; the woman beside him gave him a dig in the side to silence him. Just then the porters were on their breakfast break; all emerged, holding great pots of black coffee, which they stirred with little bread sticks. Several sat down on the pavement, all slurped their coffee.

"Surely you know the boy," the policeman asked Delamarche. "Better than I'd like," said Delamarche. "I did a lot for him at one time, but he showed little gratitude, as you can easily understand even after only asking him a few questions." "Yes," said the policeman, "he does seem a stubborn youth." "He certainly is," said Delamarche, "but that isn't even his worst trait." "Really?" said the policeman. "Oh yes," said Delamarche, and sticking his hands in his pockets, he launched into a speech that caused his whole gown to sway, "he's a fine fellow all right. My friend over there in the car and myself, we happened to come across him when he was living in misery; he had no idea then about conditions in America, having just come from Europe, where they couldn't find any use for him either; so we took him along, let him live with us, explained everything to him, tried to get him a job, believing despite all the signs to the contrary that we could still manage to turn him into a useful person; and then one night he disappeared, was simply gone, under circumstances I'd rather not disclose. Isn't that so?" Delamarche asked at last, tugging Karl by his shirtsleeve. "Step back, children," cried the policeman, for they had pressed so far forward that Delamarche almost tripped over one of them. Meanwhile the porters, who had initially underestimated the potential interest of this questioning by the policeman, began to pay attention and gathered in a tight circle behind Karl, who could no longer have retreated a single step and whose ears were continually engulfed by the babbling voices of the porters, who did not so much speak as thunder in an English that was absolutely incomprehensible and may have included a smattering of Slavic words.

"Thanks for the information," said the policeman, saluting Delamarche. "In any case I shall take him and make sure he's brought back to the Occidental Hotel." But Delamarche said: "May I ask that you leave the boy in my care for now, I've got a few things to sort out with him. I promise to take him back to the hotel myself." "That I cannot do," said the policeman. Delamarche said, "Here's my visiting card," and handed him a small card. The policeman looked at it appreciatively but said with an engaging smile: "No, it's pointless."

However wary of Delamarche Karl had been, he now saw him as his sole means of salvation. Though there was admittedly something rather suspect about the way in which he appealed to the policeman to let him take Karl, it would be easier to persuade Delamarche rather than the policeman not to escort him back to the hotel. And even if he had to go back to the hotel with Delamarche holding his arm, it would not be quite so bad as being taken there under police escort. But of course, Karl could not divulge that he did want to go to Delamarche's, for in that case everything would be lost. And he gazed apprehensively at the policeman's hand, which could at any moment jump up and seize him.

"But at least I would need to find out why he was suddenly dismissed," said the policeman at last, as Delamarche looked aside sullenly, crushing the visiting card between his fingertips. "But he certainly was not dismissed," cried Robinson, to everyone's surprise, and while leaning on the chauffeur, he reached

as far as he could out of the car. "On the contrary, he actually
has a good position there. He's the top person in the dormitory
and can bring in anyone he wants. But he's exceedingly busy,
and if you want to obtain anything from him, you must wait a
long time. He's always consulting with the head waiter and the
head cook, and is considered trustworthy. He certainly hasn't
been dismissed. I've no idea why he said that. How can he have
been dismissed? I injured myself badly at the hotel, he was
given the task of bringing me home, and since he wasn't wearing a jacket, he simply left without a jacket. I couldn't keep
waiting until he got his jacket." "Well then," said Delamarche,
with his arms outstretched and speaking as if he were chiding
the policeman for his inadequate grasp of human nature; those
two words lent the vagueness of Robinson's remark the sem-
blance of incontrovertible clarity.

"But is that really true?" asked the policeman in a wavering
voice. "And if it's true, why does the boy pretend he was dismissed?" "You should say something," said Delamarche. Karl
gazed at the policeman, who was meant to keep order among
these strangers who could think only of themselves, and some
of his general worries passed over to Karl. He did not want to
lie and held his hands tightly clasped behind his back.

At the gate a supervisor appeared and clapped his hands to
indicate that the porters should return to work. They poured
out the grounds from their coffeepots and headed into the
house with faltering steps. "If we go on like this, we'll never get
finished," said the policeman, and he attempted to seize Karl
by the arm. At first Karl shrank back a little involuntarily, but
sensing the free space that had opened up for him now that the
porters had marched off, he turned around and, after jumping
up in the air several times, burst into a run. The children broke
out in one great scream and for a couple of paces ran alongside
him, arms outstretched. "Stop him!" the policeman shouted

down the long and nearly empty street, and continuing to emit the same cry at regular intervals, he ran in a powerful silent stride, which showed that he was no novice. It was lucky for Karl that he was being chased through a workers' district. Workers have no use for the authorities. Karl ran down the center of the road, for he met with fewer obstacles there, and occasionally saw workers halting here and there on the side of the road to observe him quietly as the policeman shouted, "Stop him!" and, sensibly remaining on the smooth road and keeping his truncheon pointed at Karl, charged ahead. Karl now had little hope and almost lost the remainder when the policeman began to let out nearly deafening whistles, for they were approaching side streets where there must also have been police on patrol. The only advantage Karl possessed was his light clothing; he flew or rather flung himself down the continuously sloping street, even though in his sleepy state he often leaped too high, which was useless and time consuming. Besides, the policeman always had his goal before him and never had to think, whereas for Karl the running itself was of secondary importance, for he had to consider everything, choose among various options, and then choose all over again. His rather desperate plan was to avoid the side streets for now, for it was impossible to know what might lurk there, and he could easily have run right into a police station; he wanted to stick as long as possible to this street, which had a clear view and much farther down led to a bridge that no sooner began than it vanished amid a haze of water and sun. Karl had scarcely taken that decision and was collecting himself so that he could run faster and cross the first intersecting street in one great dash when he saw lying in wait, not far off, pressed up in the shade against the dark wall of a house, a policeman all set to jump out at Karl at the first opportunity. The side street was now his only hope, so when someone in that street called out his name—though this seemed an illusion at first, for his ears were ringing the entire time—he no longer hesitated and, so as to catch the police by surprise, if possible, he swung about on one foot and turned into that street.

He had scarcely advanced two bounds—having once again forgotten that someone had called out his name; the second policeman had started whistling and one could sense his still untapped vigor; some distant passersby on this side street seemed to quicken their pace—when someone reached out from a little doorway to Karl and pulled him into a dark corridor with the words "Be careful." It was Delamarche, quite out of breath, cheeks flushed, hair plastered down all over his head. Carrying his dressing gown under his arm, he was dressed only in shirt and underpants. Turning to the door, which happened not to be the main door but merely an inconspicuous side entrance, he shut and locked it. "Just a moment," he said, and then straightening up his head, he leaned against the wall and took deep breaths. Now Karl nearly lay in his arms, pressing his face half-unconsciously up against Delamarche's chest. "That's the gentlemen running past," said Delamarche, listening attentively and pointing toward the door. And the two policemen did run past; on the empty street their steps sounded like steel striking stone. "You're really beat," said Delamarche to Karl, who was still gasping for breath and could not speak. Delamarche set him down carefully on the ground, knelt beside him, patted his forehead several times, and observed him. "I'm fine now," said Karl at last, and with effort got to his feet. "Then hurry up," said Delamarche, who had put on his dressing gown and now seized Karl, whose head was still bowed out of weakness, and pushed him forward. Now and then he shook Karl to revive him. "You say you're tired?" he said. "But you were able to run like a horse out in the open, whereas I had to crawl along those damned corridors and courtyards. But, fortunately, I'm a runner too." In his pride he gave Karl an energetic slap on the back. "Having races with the police like that is such good exercise!" "I was already tired when I started running," said Karl. "There's no excuse for a bad run," said Delamarche. "If it hadn't been for me, they'd have caught you long ago." "I can believe that," said Karl. "And I'm very obliged to you." "There's no doubt about that," said Delamarche.

They walked down a long narrow corridor paved with smooth dark stones. Now and then a flight of stairs opened off to the right or left, or one could suddenly see down another longer corridor. There were almost no adults visible, only a few children playing on the empty stairs. Standing on a balcony was a little girl, weeping so copiously that her entire face glistened with tears. No sooner had she noticed Delamarche than she ran up the stairs with her mouth wide open, gasping for breath, and composed herself only after she had climbed up higher, after turning around several times to assure herself that no one was following her or was about to do so. "That's the one I just ran over," said Delamarche, laughing, and threatened her with his fist, causing her to run up higher, screaming.

Even the courtyards that they crossed were almost completely deserted. Here and there an office boy pushed along a two-wheeled cart, a woman filled a can with water at the pump, a postman crossed the entire courtyard with a steady gait, and an old man with a large white mustache sat cross-legged before a glass door, smoking a pipe; boxes were unloaded in front of a shipping agency; the idle horses turned their heads indifferently; a man in a smock was supervising all this work, paper in hand; there was a window open in one office, and an employee seated at his desk had turned aside and was looking pensively out toward the spot where Karl and Delamarche were passing.

"One certainly couldn't ask for a quieter neighborhood,"

said Delamarche. "For a couple of hours in the evening there's a great deal of noise, but by day it's ideal." Karl nodded; it was too quiet, he thought to himself. "I certainly couldn't live anywhere else," said Delamarche, "since Brunelda can't tolerate the slightest noise. You know Brunelda? Well, you'll be seeing her. But I would urge you to be as quiet as possible."

By the time they reached the steps that led to Delamarche's apartment, the automobile had already left, and without showing the least surprise, the fellow with the wasted nose announced that he had carried Robinson upstairs. Delamarche simply nodded at him as though he were merely a servant who had carried out a routine task, and seizing Karl, who hesitated a little and gazed out at the sunny street, he dragged him up the stairs. "We'll be there any moment," Delamarche announced several times as he climbed the stairs, but his prediction refused to come true, for each flight of stairs was always followed by another leading off in an almost imperceptibly different direction. On one occasion Karl halted, not so much from weariness as from helplessness over the number of stairs. "The apartment is very high up all right," said Delamarche as they went on, "but that has its advantages too. One seldom goes out and can stay in one's dressing gown all day; it's very cozy. Of course, being this high up we don't get many visitors." But where could the visitors possibly come from? Karl thought to himself.

At last Robinson could be seen on a landing before a closed apartment door, and now they had arrived; the staircase did not even end but went on in the dusk, and there was no sign of its ending. "Just as I thought," said Robinson in a low voice, as if still racked by pain. "Delamarche is bringing him! Rossmann, what would you do without Delamarche!" Dressed only in his underwear, Robinson tried to wrap himself as best he could in the small blanket given to him at the Occidental Hotel; it was not at all clear why he did not go into the apartment instead of making a spectacle of himself in front of possible passersby. "Is she asleep?" asked Delamarche. "I don't think so," said Robinson, "but I wanted to wait until you came." "First we must look and see whether she's asleep," said Delamarche, bending down to the keyhole. After gazing through it for a while, turning his head frequently every which way, he rose and said: "I can't see her properly, the blind's been let down. She's sitting on the settee, maybe she's sleeping." "Is she sick, then?" asked Karl, since Delamarche was standing there, as if looking for advice. But he responded sharply: "Sick?" "Well, he doesn't know her," said Robinson by way of excuse.

A few doors down two women had entered the corridor; they cleaned their hands on their aprons, looked at Delamarche and Robinson, and seemed to be talking to them. Then a very young girl with glistening blond hair jumped out from a doorway and snuggled up between the two women, linking arms with them.

"They're such repulsive women," said Delamarche softly, though evidently simply out of consideration for the sleeping Brunelda. "It won't be long before I report them to the police, and then I'll have a few years' peace. Stop looking," he hissed at Karl, who could see nothing wrong with gazing at those women, since they did have to wait in the corridor for Brunelda to wake up. And he shook his head crossly as though he did not have to accept any admonitions from Delamarche, and just as he was about to show this more clearly by approaching the women, Robinson restrained him by seizing his arm and saying, "Be careful, Rossmann," and Delamarche, who was already annoyed at Karl, became so furious over a short burst of laughter from the girl that he rushed toward the women, flailing about with his arms and legs until they disappeared into their own doorways one by one, as if they had been blown away. "I often have to clean out these corridors like this," said Delamarche, returning more slowly; then, recalling Karl's resistance, he said: "But I expect a very different sort of behavior from you; otherwise you could have some bad encounters with me."

Just then an inquiring voice asked gently if wearily: "Delamarche?" "Yes," answered Delamarche, looking at the door with a friendly mien, "may we come in?" "Oh yes," came the answer, and then, after pausing to glance at the two others waiting behind him, Delamarche slowly opened the door.

One stepped into complete darkness. The curtain on the balcony door—there was no window—had been let down all the way to the floor and was only barely translucent; besides, the clutter in the room with all the furniture hanging about also made the room darker. The air was musty, and one could almost smell the dust that had gathered in nooks that no one could evidently reach by hand. The first thing Karl noticed on entering were three cupboards lined up tightly, one behind another.

Lying on the settee was the woman who had looked down upon them from the balcony. The bottom of her red dress had been pulled out of place and hung to the ground in one great swath; her legs were visible almost to the knees; she wore thick white woolen socks but no shoes. "It's so hot, Delamarche," she said, and then, averting her face from the wall, let her hand hang out limply toward Delamarche, who took it and kissed it. Meanwhile Karl gazed only at her double chin, which also rolled about as she turned her head. "Perhaps I should get them to raise the curtain?" asked Delamarche. "Anything but that," she said, closing her eyes, and as if in desperation: "That will only be even worse." Karl had approached the foot end of the settee to take a closer look at the woman; he was surprised by her complaints, for the heat was by no means extreme. "Wait, I'll make things a bit more comfortable for you," said Delamarche anxiously, opening a few buttons on her neck and parting the fabric, which freed her neck and the top of her breast, exposing the delicate yellowish lace fringe of her camisole. "Who's that?" the woman suddenly asked, pointing at Karl, "why is he staring at me like that?" "It won't be long before you can make yourself useful," said Delamarche, pushing aside Karl and soothing the woman with the words: "It's just the boy I've brought along as your servant." "But I don't want any-body," she cried, "why are you bringing strangers into my apartment." "But you've always said you wanted a servant," said Delamarche, and knelt down; despite its great width the settee could not accommodate anyone next to Brunelda. "Oh Delamarche," she said, "you don't understand me, you don't understand me." "Then I really don't understand you," said Delamarche, taking her face into his hands. "But nothing has actually happened; if you like, he shall leave this instant." "Well, now that he's here, he should stay," she said, and on hearing those words, which were perhaps not kindly meant, Karl in his weariness was so grateful that—lost as he was in vague reflections about the endless staircase, which he should perhaps have immediately descended again, and stepping over Robinson, who was sleeping peacefully on a blanket—ignoring the angry gesticulation from Delamarche, he said: "In any case I should like to thank you for letting me stay a little longer. I've probably not slept for twenty-four hours or so, but I've cer-tainly worked hard enough and had to deal with a number of unsettling matters. I'm dreadfully tired. I don't really know where I am. But once I've had a few hours' sleep, you may send me off without needing to feel in the least bit concerned, and I shall be happy to go." "You can definitely stay," said the woman, and then she added ironically: "As you can see, we have more than enough space." "So you must leave," said Delamarche to Karl. "We have no use for you here." "No, he should stay," said the woman, sounding serious again. Delamarche said to Karl, as if he were carrying out Brunelda's request: "Then just lie down somewhere." "He can lie on the curtains but must take off his boots so he doesn't tear anything." Delamarche showed Karl to the place that she meant. A large heap of the most oddly assorted window curtains had been thrown on the floor between the door and the three cupboards. Had they been properly folded, the heaviest at the very bottom, the lighter ones more toward the top, and finally the boards and wooden rings that were also part of the heap taken out, it would have made a fairly tolerable bed, but now it was only a swaying, sliding mass on which Karl immediately lay down, for he was too tired to make special preparations before bed, and besides, out of consideration for his hosts he had to refrain from causing any trouble.

He was almost asleep when he heard a loud scream, rose to his feet, and saw Brunelda, who was sitting on the sofa, fling her arms wide apart and lock the kneeling Delamarche in an embrace by twining herself around him. Embarrassed by the sight, Karl lay back down and sank into the curtains so as to go back to sleep. It seemed quite clear to him that he would not last even two days here, and it was therefore all the more necessary to get some sound sleep so that he could have all his wits about him and quickly make the right decision.

But Brunelda had already noticed Karl's weary wide-open eyes, which had startled her once before, and shouted: "Delamarche, I can't stand this heat anymore, I'm boiling, I must get undressed and have a bath, so send those two out of the room, wherever you like, into the corridor, out onto the balcony, only make sure I cannot see them. I'm in my own apartment yet I keep on being disturbed. Delamarche, if only I could be with you alone here. Oh my God, they're still here! Look how shamelessly that Robinson is stretching out in his underwear in the presence of a lady. And see how that young stranger, who gave me such a wild look only a moment ago, has lain down so as to deceive me. Off with them, Delamarche, they're a burden to me, they lie heavily upon my breast, and if I should die now, it would be on account of them."

"They'll be gone in a second, so you can start getting undressed," said Delamarche, and he went over to Robinson and shook him with his foot, which he had placed on his chest. At the same time he shouted to Karl: "Rossmann, get up! Both of you have to go out on the balcony! And woe betide you if you come back before you're called! And be quick about it, Robinson." He shook Robinson more vigorously—"And you, Rossmann, watch out, or I'll have a go at you too"—and he made two loud clapping sounds with his hands. "It's taking so long!" cried Brunelda from the settee; while seating herself, she had spread her legs far apart to create more room for her immoderately fat body, and only with the greatest effort, amid a great deal of panting and frequent pauses for rest, did she manage to bend down far enough to grab the tops of her stockings and pull them down a little, for she could not remove them entirely—that was a job for Delamarche, whom she awaited impatiently.

Completely numb from weariness, Karl crept down off the heap and slowly approached the door to the balcony; a piece of curtain material wound itself around his foot, and he dragged it along nonchalantly. As he passed by Brunelda, in his absentmindedness he even said, "I wish you good night," and then ambled past Delamarche, who pulled the curtain on the door aside a little, and out onto the balcony. Right behind Karl came Robinson, who was probably no less drowsy than Karl, for he was humming to himself: "And to be mistreated like this always! If Brunelda doesn't come, I won't go out on the balcony." But in spite of this assertion, he went out without any resistance and, since Karl had already sunk into the armchair, lay down at once on the stone floor.

When Karl awoke, it was evening, there were already stars in the sky, and the moonlight rose behind the tall houses on the other side of the street. It was only after he had looked about a little in this unfamiliar neighborhood and taken in some of the cool refreshing air that he realized where he was. How careless it had been of him to ignore all the head cook's suggestions, all Therese's warnings, all his own fears, and now here he was, seated quietly on Delamarche's balcony, having even slept here for half a day as if his great enemy, Delamarche, were not there behind the curtain. That lazy fellow Robinson lay on the floor, writhing and tugging at Karl's foot, which was obviously how he had awakened Karl, for he said: "You're such a sound sleeper, Rossmann! Oh, the carefree ways of youth. But how much longer do you want to sleep. I could have let you sleep, but first, it's too boring lying on the ground, and second, I'm very hungry. Please stand up, only for a moment; I've saved myself something to eat under that armchair and want to pull it out. And then you'll get some too." Karl, who stood up, watched as Robinson rolled over on his stomach without getting up and, with his hands stretched flat, pulled out a silver dish of the kind used, say, for keeping visiting cards. But the bowl contained only one half of a very black sausage, a few thin cigarettes, an opened and still very full can of sardines, and numerous mostly crushed sweets that had turned into one great lump. There then appeared a large slice of bread and a sort of perfume bottle, which however seemed to contain something other than perfume, since Robinson took special pleasure in pointing it out to Karl as he smacked his lips. "You see, Rossmann," said Robinson, devouring one sardine after another and wiping his hands on a woolen cloth that Brunelda had evidently left on the balcony. "See, Rossmann, that's the way you must keep your food, unless you want to starve. Listen here, though, I've been pushed aside entirely. And if you keep on being treated like a dog, you start thinking this is in fact what

you are. It's good you're here, Rossmann, for at least there's
somebody here now that I can talk to. No one in this building
ever talks to me. Everyone hates us here. And all because of
Brunelda. She certainly is a magnificent woman, of course.
Listen"—and he motioned to Karl to bend down so that he
could whisper in his ear—"I once saw her naked. Ah!" And
recalling the joy, he started squeezing and slapping Karl's legs
until Karl shouted, "Robinson, you're absolutely crazy,"
grabbed his hands, and pushed them away.

"You're really still only a child, Rossmann," said Robinson,
then drew from his shirt a dagger that hung from a piece of
string tied around his neck, took it from its scabbard, and cut
the hard sausage into little pieces. "You still have a lot to learn.
But you've come to the right place for that. Do sit down. You
don't want to eat? Well, you can develop an appetite as you
watch me eat. You don't want to drink either? You don't want
anything? And you're not especially talkative either. But it
really doesn't matter who's out here on the balcony, so long as
there's somebody else here. You see, I'm often out on the balcony. It's a great sport for Brunelda. She's always thinking of
something new, first she's cold, then she's hot, then she wants to
sleep, then she wants to comb her hair, then she'd like to open
her corset, then she wants to put it on, so I'm always being sent
out on the balcony. At times she actually does what she says,
but for the most part she stays on the settee and doesn't stir.
Often I would part the curtains a little and look in, but ever
since one such occasion when Delamarche—I know for certain
that it wasn't his idea and that he did so only at Brunelda's
request—hit me on the face with a whip—can you see the weals
it left?—I don't dare look anymore. So I lie out here on the balcony, and the only pleasure left is eating. The day before yesterday, as I lay here all alone in the evening, still wearing my
elegant clothes, which, alas, I then lost at your hotel—those

dogs! the way they tore those expensive clothes from my body—as I lay here all alone, gazing down between the columns of the balustrade, everything somehow seemed so sad that I started to bawl. Though I didn't notice right away, at that moment Brunelda came out wearing her red dress—it's the one that suits her best—and, after watching me for a while, she finally said: 'Dear little Robinson, why are you crying?' Then she lifted her dress and wiped my eyes with the hem. Who knows what else she might have done if Delamarche hadn't called for her just then and she hadn't had to go back into the room right away. Of course, I thought it was going to be my turn, so I asked through the curtain whether I could go back into the room. And what do you think Brunelda said? 'No,' she said, and then she said, 'How dare you?' "

"But why do you stay if that's how you're treated?" Karl asked.

"I'm sorry, Rossmann, but that's not a very clever question," Robinson answered. "You'll stay too even if you get worse treatment. Besides, I'm not being treated so badly."

"No," said Karl, "I'm leaving, possibly even this evening. I'm not staying with you."

"But how, for instance, do you want to go about leaving this evening," asked Robinson, who had cut out the soft part of the bread and was dipping it carefully into the oil in the sardine tin. "How can you leave if you're not allowed into the room?"

"Why can't we go in?"

"We're not allowed in until the bell rings," said Robinson, and he devoured the greasy bread with his mouth, which he had opened as wide as possible, using one hand to catch the oil dripping from the bread so that now and then he could dip the rest of the bread into the palm of his hand, which served as a reservoir. "Everything has become stricter. At first there was only a thin curtain, you couldn't see through it, but at night you could make out their silhouettes. Brunelda found that unpleasant, and I had to make a curtain out of one of her theatrical gowns and hang it up here instead of the old curtain. And now it's impossible to see anything at all. I used to be allowed to ask whether I could go in, and depending on what was happening, they would answer yes or no, but I probably abused this by asking too often. Brunelda couldn't stand that, for in spite of her girth, she has a weak constitution; she has headaches often and gout in her legs almost always—so they decided I would no longer be allowed to ask but could go in whenever they pressed the bell on the table. It rings so loud that it rouses even me from my sleep—I used to have a cat here to amuse myself a bit, but it ran off, frightened by that ringing, and never came back. Well, that bell still hasn't rung today—and if it does it'll mean I may, or rather must, go in—and if it doesn't ring for such a long time, it can take a lot longer."

"Yes," said Karl, "but what's true for you isn't necessarily true for me. Besides, that is true only for those who are prepared to put up with that kind of thing."

"Why not," cried Robinson, "why shouldn't it be true for you too? Of course it applies to you. Just wait quietly until the bell rings. And then you can try to get away."

"But why don't you move away? Is it only because Delamarche is, or rather was, your friend? But is this a life? Wouldn't you be better off in Butterford, where you wanted to go first? Or even in California, where you have friends."

"Yes," said Robinson, "nobody could have predicted this." And before continuing with his story, he added, "Here's to your health, my dear Rossmann," and took a long sip from his perfume bottle. "Well, when you were so nasty as to leave us in the lurch, things were going badly for us. We couldn't find any work for the first few days; besides, Delamarche didn't want to find any work; he would have found some if he'd made an effort, but he always sent me out on my own instead, and I never have any luck. All day he simply knocked about, then it was almost nighttime, and all he brought back was a lady's purse; though it was very beautiful, made of pearls, he's since given it to Brunelda as a present—there was next to nothing in it. Then he said we should go begging in the apartments, one can come up with some useful items on such occasions, so we went begging, and I sang at the apartment doors so as to make a favorable impression. And since Delamarche is always so lucky, we had gone no farther than the door of the second apartment, where we sang some little ditty for the cook and the servant, when the lady who owns this apartment, in other words, Brunelda, comes up the stairs. Maybe she was a little too tightly laced, in any case she couldn't climb up the last few steps. But she looked so beautiful, Rossmann! She wore an absolutely white dress, with a red parasol. She was so lickable! So drinkable! Oh God, oh God, how beautiful she was. What a woman! But tell me, how can such a woman even exist? Of course, the girl and the servant ran over and almost carried her upstairs. We stood right and left by the door and saluted, that's how we do it here. She stopped for a moment, for she was still out of breath, and I don't really know how this happened, but I was so hungry I wasn't in my right mind, and well, she was even more beautiful up close, enormously broad, and thanks to her special corset, which I can show you in the drawer inside, so firm all over—in any case, to cut a long story short, I did touch her a little from behind, but, well, only very lightly, I barely even touched her. And of course having a beggar touch a rich lady is something that simply cannot be tolerated. There was really almost no touching, but in the end there was a little contact. Who knows how badly all of this would have turned out if Delamarche hadn't given me such a hard slap in the face that I needed both hands for my cheeks."

"You're always up to something," said Karl, and spellbound by the story, he sat down on the floor. "So it was Brunelda?"

"Well, yes," said Robinson, "it was Brunelda."

"Didn't you at one point say she's a singer?" Karl asked.

"Of course she's a singer, a great singer," answered Robinson, rolling a mass of candy on his tongue and now and then using his fingers to push in a piece that his mouth had ejected. "Of course at the time we didn't know yet; we could only see she was a rich lady and a very elegant one too. She acted as if nothing had happened and may indeed not have felt a thing, since I had really only touched her with my fingertips. But she kept on looking at Delamarche, who in turn gazed straight into her eyes—as only he is capable of doing. Then she said, 'Come in for a bit,' motioning to Delamarche with her parasol that he should lead the way into the apartment. The two went in, and the servants closed the door behind them. They forgot me outside, and at first I thought it wouldn't take so long and sat there on the steps waiting for Delamarche. But it was not Delamarche but the servant who came out, bringing me a dish of soup filled to the brim; 'Courtesy of Delamarche!' I said to myself. The servant stayed with me for a moment as I ate and told me a few things about Brunelda and then I could see what this visit to Brunelda's might mean for us. For Brunelda was a divorced woman, had a large fortune and was completely independent. Though her former husband, a cocoa manufacturer, still loved her, she didn't want to have anything to do with him anymore. He often came to the apartment, always very elegantly dressed, as if for a wedding—this is all absolutely true, I know him personally—but despite the biggest bribes, the servant wouldn't dare ask Brunelda whether she would receive him, for he had already asked several times, and Brunelda had always taken whatever she had at hand and thrown it in his face. Once she happened to grab her large filled hot-water bottle and knocked out one of his front teeth with it. Yes, Rossmann, imagine that!"

"How do you know the man?" Karl asked.

"Sometimes he comes up here," said Robinson.

"Up here?" and in his amazement Karl tapped the floor lightly with one hand.

"You've good reason to be amazed," Robinson continued, "I, too, was amazed when the servant told me. Just imagine: if Brunelda wasn't at home, the man would ask the servant to take him to her rooms, and he always took some little trifle as a keepsake, always leaving something very expensive and elegant for Brunelda, and the servant was strictly forbidden to say who it was from. But once, after he had brought some priceless porcelain object—so the servant said, and I can certainly believe him—Brunelda must somehow have recognized it; she threw it on the floor, stepped on it, spat on it, and did certain other things to it; the servant was so nauseated, he could hardly carry it out."

"So what had the man done to her?" asked Karl.

"I don't actually know," said Robinson. "But I don't believe it was anything out of the ordinary, or at least he himself knows of no such thing. I've often spoken with him about this. Every day he waits for me at the street corner, and whenever I go, I must always give him some news, and whenever I can't, he waits half an hour and then goes off. It's been a good sideline for me, since he pays for such news quite handsomely, but ever since Delamarche found out, I've had to hand everything over to him, and so I go less often."

"But what does the man want?" asked Karl, "What does he really want? After all, he can hear that she doesn't want him."

"Yes," sighed Robinson; he lit a cigarette and, swinging his arms about, blew the smoke in the air. Then, apparently changing his mind, he said: "Why should I care? All I know is he'd happily pay a great deal of money just to be able to lie on the balcony like this."

Karl rose, leaned over the balcony, and gazed down at the street. The moon was already visible, but its beams had not yet pierced through to the depth of the street. The street, so empty during the day, was now packed, especially by the front gates, the mass of people moving slowly and cumbersomely; the shirt-sleeves of the men, the bright dresses of the women stood out feebly in the dark; none of them wore a hat. All of the numerous balconies in the vicinity were now occupied: depending on the size of the balcony, the families either sat around a little table in the light cast by an electric lightbulb, or on chairs set up in a row, or at least stuck their heads out from the room. The men sat, legs wide apart and feet stretched out between the bars of the railing, reading newspapers that almost reached the floor, or playing cards without seeming to make any noise, though they slapped the tables with great force; the women had their laps full of knitting and only rarely spared a quick glance for the surroundings or the street; a weak blond woman on the neighboring balcony yawned continually, crossed her eyes as she did so, and kept raising to her mouth the piece of laundry that she was mending; even on the smallest balconies the children managed to chase one another about, much to their parents' irritation. In numerous rooms people had set up gramophones that blasted out songs or orchestral music; they scarcely heeded the music, aside from the occasional father of a family, who would give a signal, and then someone would hurry into the room to put on a record. At some of the windows one could see utterly motionless couples. One such pair stood upright at a window facing Karl; the young man had his arm around the girl and was squeezing her breast.

"Do you know any of those people next door?" Karl asked

Robinson, who had risen too and, since he was shivering, wrapped himself not only in the bedspread but also in Brunelda's blanket.

"Almost nobody. Well, that's the bad thing about my job," said Robinson, drawing Karl closer so that he could whisper in his ear, "aside from that, though, I can hardly complain at the moment. Brunelda, you see, sold everything she had on account of Delamarche and moved into this suburban apartment with all of her riches so she could devote herself completely to him and so they wouldn't be disturbed, and by the way, that was what Delamarche wanted too."

"And she dismissed her domestic staff?" asked Karl.

"You're quite right," said Robinson. "For where could they house the servants? As for those servants, they're certainly a demanding lot. Once at Brunelda's, Delamarche drove one such servant from the room by slapping him repeatedly until he was outside. The other servants naturally took his side and began to make a racket outside the door, then Delamarche came out (though I wasn't a servant then but rather a friend of the house, they put me in with the servants) and asked: 'What do you want?' The oldest servant, a certain Isidor, said: 'You cannot say anything to us since it's Madame who's our mistress.' As you've probably noticed, they greatly admired Brunelda. But ignoring them, Brunelda ran over to Delamarche—she was not so heavy yet—hugged him in front of everyone, kissed him, and called him 'dearest Delamarche.' 'And do send these apes away at once,' she said at last. Apes—that was what she called the servants; you can imagine their faces when they heard that. Then Brunelda steered Delamarche's hand to the purse she had on her belt, Delamarche reached inside and began to pay off the servants; Brunelda merely stood there with her purse open. Delamarche had to reach inside quite often, for he handed out the money without counting it or checking the servants' claims. At last he said: 'Well, since you don't want to talk to me, I'll

simply say this on behalf of Brunelda: "Clear off at once." '
That's how the servants were dismissed; there were a few court
cases, Delmarche even had to appear in court once, but I don't
have any specific information about that. After the servants
had left, though, Delamarche said to Brunelda: 'But now you
don't have any servants?' She said: 'Well, there's always Robinson.' At that Delamarche slapped me on the shoulder and said:
'So you'll be our servant.' And Brunelda gave me a little tap on
the cheek; if you ever have the opportunity, Rossmann, ask her
to give you a little tap on the cheek, you'll be amazed how
lovely it is."

"So you became Delamarche's servant?" said Karl, summa-
rizing what Robinson had said.

Overhearing a sympathetic note in the question, Robinson
answered: "I'm a servant, but few people notice this. You yourself didn't know, even though you've been with us for a while.
You saw how I was dressed at the hotel that night. I wore the
finest of the fine—do servants go about dressed like that? I cannot go away often, you see, for I always have to be at hand in
this household, there's always something that needs to be done.
One person isn't enough for all the work. As you may have
noticed, there are still quite a few of our belongings lying about
in that room, everything we couldn't sell during the big move
we had to take along. Of course, they could have been given
away, but Brunelda never gives anything away. Just think how
much work it took to carry all those things up the stairs."

"Robinson, you carried all that upstairs?" cried Karl.

"Who else?" said Robinson. "There was a laborer too, but
he was a lazy bum, and I had to do most of the work on my own.
Brunelda was below by the car, Delamarche upstairs explaining
where everything had to be put, and I was running up and
down the entire time. It took two days—that's a long time, isn't
it? But you've no idea how many things there are in that room,

all the closets are full, and the rest is piled up to the ceiling behind the closets. If they'd hired a couple of people to transport all of that, it would all have been done quickly, but Brunelda wouldn't entrust the task to anyone but me. Well, that was very nice, but now I've ruined my health for the rest of my life, and what did I have other than my health? If I exert myself ever so slightly, I get a pain there and here. If I were healthy, do you think those boys in the hotel, those grass toads—what else would one call them?—could possibly have defeated me. But no matter what's wrong with me, I won't breathe a word to Delamarche and Brunelda; I'll work as long as possible, and until it's not possible anymore, then I'll lie down and die, and only then, when it's too late, will they see that, though I was sick, I was still working, always working, and that I actually worked myself to death in their service. Oh Rossmann," he concluded, drying his eyes on Karl's shirtsleeves. After a short pause he said: "But don't you feel cold, standing there in your shirt."

"Come, Robinson," said Karl, "you're continually crying. I don't believe you're so ill. You look completely healthy, but since you're always lying out here on the balcony, you've just imagined all sorts of things. You may occasionally get a pain in your chest, but then so do I, so does everybody. If everybody cried over every little trifle as you do, then all those people up on all the balconies would be crying too."

"Well, I certainly know more about that than you do," said Robinson, wiping his eyes with the tip of his blanket. "The student in the apartment next door, which belongs to the landlady, who also cooks for us, told me last time as I was returning the dishes: 'Listen here, Robinson, aren't you ill?' I'm not allowed to talk to anybody, so I put down the dishes and wanted to leave. At that moment he came up to me and said: 'Listen, man, don't run yourself into the ground, you're ill.' 'So, tell me please, what should I do,' I asked. 'That's your business,' he said, turning aside. The people sitting at his table laughed, we have enemies everywhere here, so I chose to leave."

"So you believe those who make a fool of you, but don't believe those who mean well by you."

"But I must know how I feel," said Robinson, flaring up only to resume his weeping.

"That's just it, you don't know what's wrong with you; you should find yourself some decent job instead of acting as Delamarche's servant. So far as I can tell from the stories you've told and from what I've seen, this isn't service, it's slavery. No human being could endure this, I believe you. But you think you shouldn't leave Delamarche simply because you're his friend. That's wrong; if he cannot see what a miserable life you're leading, you don't have any further obligation toward him."

"So, Rossmann, you really think I'll recover if I stop serving here?"

"Yes, certainly," said Karl.

"Certainly?" asked Robinson.

"Most certainly," said Karl smiling.

"Then I could certainly start recovering right away," said Robinson, glancing at Karl.

"What do you mean?" asked Karl.

"Well, since you're meant to take over my work," answered Robinson.

"But who told you so?" asked Karl.

"It's actually an old plan. They've been talking about it for a number of days. It all began when Brunelda scolded me for not keeping the apartment sufficiently clean. Of course, I promised to tidy everything up at once. But it's very difficult. In my condition I cannot, for instance, crawl in everywhere to wipe away the dust; it's already impossible to move around in the middle of the room, so how can one get in between the furniture and the supplies. And for a thorough cleaning, the furniture has to be pushed aside, and how am I supposed to do that on my own? Besides, it would have to be done very quietly, since Brunelda hardly ever leaves the room and may not be disturbed. So even though I promised to clean everything, I did not actually do any cleaning. When Brunelda noticed, she told Delamarche that this simply couldn't go on and that they'd need to take on another helper. 'Delamarche,' she said, 'I don't ever want you to reproach me for not taking good care of the household. I can't overdo it, as you well know, and Robinson is simply inadequate; he was so fresh and at first kept looking about, but now he's always tired and just sits around, most often in a corner. But a room filled with as many objects as ours can't stay tidy on its own.' And so Delamarche began to think about what could be done, for in such a household you cannot simply take on just any person, even on a trial basis, since there are people watching on all sides. Since I'm your good friend, and since Renell told me how you had to slave away at the hotel, I did mention your name. Delamarche agreed right away, in spite of your having been so cheeky toward him back then, and of course I was very pleased I could help you in this way. You see, this position is made for you, you're young, strong, and handy, whereas I'm simply worthless now. But I do want to add that you haven't been taken on yet; if Brunelda doesn't like you, we cannot use you. So do try to be nice to her, and I'll take care of everything else."

"And what'll you do if I become the servant here?" Karl asked; he felt so free, the initial fright on hearing the news from Robinson had dissipated. So the worst Delamarche had in mind was to make him a servant—if his intentions had been any worse, that blabbermouth Robinson would certainly have divulged them—but if this was indeed actually so, then Karl could risk leaving that night. Nobody can be forced to accept a position. And after being dismissed from the hotel, Karl had

worried about whether he would obtain a position that would
not only be suitable but, if at all possible, no less unprepossess-
ing than his previous one, and would manage to find one soon
enough that he wouldn't go hungry; now, however, when compared with the position assigned to him here, which he found
repugnant, every other position was, he now believed, quite
tolerable, and he would rather have opted for the misery of
unemployment than for this present position. He did not even
try to make this clear to Robinson, particularly since the latter's hope that Karl would ease his burden had undoubtedly
affected every judgment he made.

"Well then," said Robinson, accompanying his remarks
with complacent gestures—he had propped up his elbows on
the balustrade—"first I'll explain everything to you, and then
I'll show you the supplies. You're an educated man and must
have beautiful handwriting, so you could make a list of everything we have. Brunelda has wanted this done for a long time.
If the weather tomorrow is good, we'll ask Brunelda to sit out
on the balcony, and then we can work away in the room, quietly and without disturbing her. And that, Rossmann, must be
your top priority. Not to disturb Brunelda, above all else. She
can hear everything—as a singer she probably has especially
sensitive ears. Say you're rolling out the schnapps barrel from
behind the closets; since it's heavy, it makes a lot of noise, and
because of all those objects lying about everywhere you can't
just roll it along. Brunelda is, say, lying quietly on the settee
catching flies—she's especially bothered by them. So you think
she's paying no notice to you and go on rolling your barrel. But
in the blink of an eye, just when you don't expect it and are
making the least amount of noise, she suddenly sits up and hits
the settee with both hands, with the result that one cannot even
see her because of all the dust swirling about—during the entire
time we've been here, I've never beaten the settee; there's no

way I can, for she's always lying there—and she starts to shout horribly, like a man, and goes on shouting for hours. Her neighbors forbade her to sing, but no one can forbid her to shout; she has to shout, and, by the way, this happens only rarely now—Delamarche and I have become very careful. Besides, that shouting harmed her too. Once she even lost consciousness and—Delamarche happened to be away—I had to send for the student next door; he sprayed her with some liquid from a large bottle, which helped but gave off an unbearable stench, which you can still smell if you put your nose up to the settee. That student is certainly our enemy, like everyone else here; you must be wary of everyone and keep your distance."

"Heh, Robinson," said Karl, "it's really an onerous service. You've recommended me for such a splendid post!"

"Don't worry," said Robinson, and, closing his eyes, he shook his head to fend off any possible worries Karl might have, "the post also has advantages that no other post could possibly offer. You're always in the presence of a great lady, Brunelda, and sometimes even get to sleep in the same room, which, as you can imagine, can be quite agreeable. You'll receive lavish pay, there's plenty of money; as a friend of Delamarche's I received nothing, aside from the money Brunelda chose to give me whenever I went out, but you'll naturally get paid, like any other servant. And of course that is indeed what you are. But most important for you, I'll make the post easy for you. Of course, at first I won't do a thing so that I can recover, but then once I've recovered even just a little, you can rely on me. Now the task of caring for Brunelda—in other words, cutting her hair and dressing her—I'll generally reserve for myself insofar as Delamarche hasn't already seen to that. You'll be responsible for tidying up the room, shopping, and the heavier domestic chores."

"No, Robinson," said Karl, "I find all of that most unappealing."

"Don't be stupid, Rossmann," said Robinson, who was now very close to Karl's face, "don't throw away this wonderful opportunity. Where would you get another post right away? Who knows you? Whom do you know? Take us two, men who've been through a great deal and have a considerable amount of experience; we ran around for weeks without finding work. It is not easy, it's even desperately difficult."

Karl nodded, marveling at how sensibly Robinson could speak. But this advice didn't apply to him for he oughtn't to stay; somewhere in the big city he could find a lowly position somewhere for—and he knew this for certain—every single tavern was full all night, they needed servants to take care of the guests, and of course he had some experience at that and would surely have no difficulty fitting quickly and inconspicuously into some outfit or other. In fact, down below in the building opposite was a small tavern from which one could hear the fleeting sound of music. The main entrance was covered only by a big yellow curtain that was occasionally lifted up by a gust of wind and fluttered about on the street. Otherwise, the street had become much quieter. Most of the balconies were dark; one could see only a solitary light here and there in the darkness, but no sooner had one fixed one's gaze upon it than the people who sat there rose, and as they pressed back into the apartment, a man who had remained behind on the balcony reached for the lightbulb and, after glancing down at the street, turned off the light.

"It's almost nighttime," Karl said to himself, "if I stay any longer, I'll become one of them." He turned around to pull aside the curtain on the door into the apartment. "What do you want?" said Robinson, positioning himself between Karl and the curtain. "I'm trying to get away," said Karl, "leave me alone, leave me alone!" "But you hardly want to disturb them," cried Robinson, "what do you think you're doing?" And he put his arms around Karl's neck, hung on to him with his entire weight, and locking his legs around Karl's, pulled him quickly to the ground. However, during his time among the elevator boys, Karl had picked up a few fighting skills, so he was able to shove his fist under Robinson's chin, though not too hard and with great restraint. Showing no consideration whatsoever, the latter kneed Karl quickly and sharply in the stomach, then put both hands on his chin and began to howl so loudly that a man on the neighboring balcony clapped his hands wildly, demanding, "Silence." Karl lay there quietly for a moment so as to recover from the pain caused by Robinson's blow. He simply turned his face toward the curtain, which hung calmly and heavily in front of the evidently dark room. The room now seemed empty; perhaps Delamarche had gone out with Brunelda and Karl was therefore completely free now. So he must indeed have shaken off Robinson, who was really acting like a watchdog.

Then from afar, by way of the street, came the sounds of drums and trumpets as if in bursts. The scattered cries of numerous people soon merged into one general shout. Karl turned his head and saw that all of the balconies were becoming animated again. Slowly he rose, for he could not lift himself up completely and had to lean heavily against the balustrade. Upon the pavements below young fellows strode along, arms stretched out, caps in upraised hands, faces looking back. The thoroughfare was still empty. A few figures waved tall poles with lamps shrouded in a yellowish smoke. Just then deep rows of drummers and trumpeters stepped into the light, and Karl was astonished these were so numerous; then he heard voices behind him, turned around, and first saw Delamarche raise the heavy curtain, then Brunelda step out from the darkness of the room wearing her red dress, a lace wrap around her shoulders, and a small dark cap over her hair, which was probably not yet coiffed and had merely been gathered up with the ends peeking out here and there. In her hand she held a small open fan, but did not move it, pressing it against her body instead.

Karl pushed his way through along the side of the balcony so as to make room for them both. Nobody would force him to stay, that's for sure, and even if Delamarche should try, Brunelda would upon Karl's request dismiss him at once. She certainly couldn't stand him; his eyes frightened her. But no sooner had he taken a step toward the door than she noticed him and said: "Wait, little one, where are you off to?" Karl faltered under Delamarche's severe gaze, and Brunelda drew him toward herself. "But don't you want to look at the parade down below?" she said, pushing him in front of her toward the balustrade. "Do you know what's going on?" Karl could hear her say behind his back, and he moved aside involuntarily in an unsuccessful attempt to free himself from the pressure she was exerting. Sadly he gazed down at the road, as if the reason for his sadness lay there.

At first Delamarche stood behind Brunelda with his arms crossed, and then he ran into the room and brought out opera glasses for Brunelda. Below, behind the musicians, the main section of the parade had appeared. Seated on the shoulders of an enormous man was a gentleman of whom all one could see from this height was a faintly glistening bald spot and a top hat perpetually raised in greeting. All around him people carried wooden signs that seemed completely white—at least as seen from the balcony; the signs were set up in such a way that they were literally leaning on the gentleman, who towered up in their midst. Since everything was moving, the wall of signs was continually loosening up and continually arranging itself anew. The gentleman's supporters surrounded him, filling the entire width of the street—but only for a relatively short distance, at least insofar as one could make out in the dark—all of them clapped their hands and probably proclaimed his name in a rhythmic chant, which, however, was short and quite incomprehensible. Cleverly scattered about in the crowd, several of them carried car lamps with extremely strong lights, which they slowly trained up and down the houses along both sides of the street. At Karl's height the light was no longer bothersome, but one could see the people on the lower balconies that it had briefly illuminated putting their hands over their eyes.

At Brunelda's request Delamarche asked the people on the neighboring balcony to explain the significance of the event. Karl was a little curious to find out if those people would answer and what they would say. And Delamarche had to ask three times, without once receiving an answer. He leaned over the balustrade quite perilously as Brunelda stamped her foot lightly in irritation at her neighbors; Karl could feel the pressure of her knee. At last they gave an answer of sorts, but just then everybody on the packed balcony began to laugh out loud. Whereupon Delamarche shouted out something so loudly that if there hadn't been so much noise coming from the street, everybody would have stopped and listened in astonishment. At any rate it caused the laughter to subside unnaturally fast.

"There's an election for a judge in our district tomorrow, and that fellow being carried about down there is a candidate," said Delamarche, and having completely regained his composure, he went back over to Brunelda. "No!" he cried, clapping Brunelda affectionately on the back. "We have no idea anymore about what's happening in the world."

"Delamarche," said Brunelda, returning to the conduct of their neighbors, "I'd be so happy to move if it weren't so exhausting. But unfortunately, I don't think I could handle it." Clearly agitated and distracted, and sighing heavily, Brunelda nestled up against Karl's shirt while Karl tried as inconspicuously as possible to push aside those fat little hands, which he managed to do quite easily since Brunelda was not thinking about him; her thoughts were elsewhere.

However, before long Karl too forgot about Brunelda and endured the weight of her arms on his shoulders, for he was captivated by the events taking place on the street. Upon a command from a small group of gesticulating men—who marched just ahead of the candidate and whose conversations must have been particularly important, for one could see rapt faces craning toward them from all sides—the procession halted unexpectedly in front of the tavern. Raising his hand, one of the pacesetters signaled to the crowd as well as to the candidate. The crowd fell silent, and the candidate, who repeatedly tried to stand on the shoulders of his carrier, only to fall back several times onto his chair, gave a brief speech, in the course of which he waved about his top hat at lightning speed. This was quite visible since all of the car lamps were directed at him, and he was therefore at the center of a brightly illumined star.

One could see, however, that the entire street was now beginning to take an interest in this affair. On the balconies occupied by members of the candidate's party, everybody began to shout out his name, and their hands, which hung far out over the balustrades, began to clap like machines. On the other balconies, which were in fact in the majority, there arose a powerful countersong that, however, failed to produce a coherent effect, since the people singing were supporters of different candidates. Still, all the enemies of the present candidate came together in a general round of whistling, and one could even hear numerous gramophones being switched on again. Between the balconies political arguments erupted that were all the more intense given the lateness of the hour. Most people were still in their nightclothes and had simply thrown robes about them, the women having covered themselves with great dark cloths; the unsupervised children climbed up alarmingly on the frames of the balconies and emerged in ever greater numbers from the dark rooms in which they had already been asleep. Now and then unrecognizable objects were flung by a few especially overheated individuals at their opponents, sometimes they reached their target, but mostly they fell on the street, where they often triggered howls of anger. Whenever the clamor became too much for the leading personages below, they instructed the drummers and trumpeters to intervene, and the interminable crushing sound that they produced with all their might suppressed all the human voices up to the roofs of the buildings. And then always quite suddenly—this was hard to believe—they would stop, and the crowd, which had obviously been well trained precisely with this purpose in mind, would bawl out the party anthem in the momentary hush—one could see each person's mouth opening wide in the light from the car lamps—at which point their opponents, who had meanwhile regained their composure, would shout out ten times louder from all of the balconies and windows, thereby—at least insofar as one could tell from this height—reducing the party below, after its short-lived victory, to silence.

"How do you like it, little fellow?" asked Brunelda, who moved back and forth, squeezing up against Karl so that she could get the best possible view with the opera glasses. Karl responded merely with a nod. He noticed too that Robinson was zealously communicating several matters to Delamarche, obviously concerning Karl's behavior, but Delamarche seemed to consider them insignificant, for he kept trying to push Robinson aside with his left hand, while embracing Brunelda with his right. "Don't you want to look through the glasses?" asked Brunelda, tapping Karl on the chest to indicate that she was addressing him.

"I can see well enough," said Karl.

"Do try them," she said, "you'll see better."

"I've good eyes," Karl answered, "I can see everything." When she brought the glasses close to his eyes, he felt that this was not so much kindness as an intrusion on her part, and indeed she said only one word, "Here!" in a melodious but also rather threatening manner. Karl already held the glasses to his eyes and could not in fact see anything.

"I can't see anything," he said, and tried to get rid of the glasses, but she held them tight, and in any case he could not push his head, which was embedded on her breast, back or even to the side.

"But you can see now," she said, twisting the knob on the glasses.

"No, I still can't see anything," said Karl, and he thought of how he had quite inadvertently relieved Robinson of a burden, for he himself had now become the target of Brunelda's insufferable moods.

"When will you finally be able to see," she said—Karl now found his entire face suffused with her heavy breath—and continued to twist the knob. "Now?" she asked.

"No, no, no!" cried Karl, even though he could in fact make out everything, if only indistinctly. But at that moment Brunelda was preoccupied with Delamarche; she held the glasses loosely in front of Karl's face, and so, without her noticing, Karl could look down under the glasses at the street below. After that she no longer insisted on having her way and used the glasses herself.

From the tavern below a waiter had appeared and now rushed back and forth across the threshold, taking orders from the leaders. One could see how he leaned over to obtain a view of the interior of the inn and summon as many servants as possible. Throughout these preparations for a great round of free drinks, the candidate evidently did not cease speaking. After every few sentences his carrier, the huge man whose sole task was to serve only him, always turned around slightly so that the candidate's speech could reach each section of the crowd. The candidate generally stayed hunched up and sought, by means of jerky movements of his free hand and top hat, to lend the greatest possible urgency to his statements. But every now and then, and indeed at regular intervals, he became captivated by an idea and rose, arms outstretched; at such moments he addressed not one particular group but rather the entire gathering; he spoke to the residents of the houses all the way up to the top floors, although it was quite clear that nobody, even on the lowest floors, could hear him, and that nobody would have wanted to listen to him had this been possible, for there was at least one speaker at each window and on each balcony, shouting at the top of his voice. Meanwhile some waiters from the tavern brought out a board, roughly the size of a billiard table, with sparkling glasses filled to the brim. The leaders organized the distribution, which took the form of a procession past the tavern door. Yet although the glasses on the board were repeatedly refilled, this did not suffice for the crowd, and two lines of bar boys slipped out continuously along each side of the board in order to keep the crowd supplied. By now of course the candidate had already finished speaking and took advantage of the break to fortify himself anew. Away from the crowd and the harsh light, his carrier bore him slowly back and forth, and only a few of his closest supporters accompanied him and spoke to him from below.

"Just look at the little fellow," said Brunelda, "he's staring so hard, he's forgotten where he is." And taking Karl by surprise, she used both hands to turn his face toward her so that she could look into his eyes. This lasted only a moment, though, since Karl shook off her hands right away; annoyed at not being left in peace for a few moments, and at the same time very eager to go down to the street and see everything from close up, he sought with all his strength to free himself from Brunelda's grip and said:

"Please let me go."

"You're staying with us," said Delamarche, and without even taking his eyes off the street, he reached out his hand to prevent Karl from leaving.

"Stop that," said Brunelda, warding off Delamarche's hand. "He'll stay, all right." And she pressed Karl even more firmly against the balustrade; he would have had to put up a fight to extricate himself. And even if he succeeded, what would he accomplish. Delamarche still stood on the left; Robinson had just lined up on the right; he was truly imprisoned.

"You can be happy you're not being thrown out," said Robinson, clapping Karl on the back with the hand that he had pulled out from under Brunelda's arm.

"Thrown out?" said Delamarche. "You don't throw out a thief who's run away—you hand him over to the police. And that's precisely what may happen to him tomorrow morning if he is not absolutely quiet."

From that moment on Karl took no pleasure in the spectacle unfolding below. Unable to stand up on account of Brunelda, he was compelled to lean over the balustrade for a while. Filled with his own worries, he gazed distractedly at the people below: approaching the tavern door, twenty men or so at a time, they seized the glasses, turned around, waved their glasses at the candidate who was now lost in his thoughts, shouted out a party slogan, emptied their glasses, and, finally, set them down on the board with a thud, which at this height was of course inaudible, in order to make way for a new group that was impatiently stirring up a din. On instructions from the leaders the band that had been playing in the tavern stepped out onto the street; their great wind instruments glistened in the dark among the crowd, but the sounds that they made were almost lost in the general din. At least on the tavern side the street was now thronged with people coming from every direction. From above, the way Karl had come that morning by automobile, they poured down and also ran up from the bridge below, and even the people in the houses had been unable to resist the temptation to get directly involved; only women and children mostly were left behind on the balconies and at the windows, the men surged out from the gates of the houses. The music and the food had now accomplished their purpose; the crowd was now large enough; flanked by two car lamps, one of the leaders signaled that the music should cease and gave a shrill whistle; and one could now see the carrier and the candidate, who had wandered slightly off course, approach rapidly along a path that his supporters had cleared for him.

No sooner had the candidate reached the door of the tavern than he began to give another speech amid the tight circle of the car lamps held up all around him. But now everything was much more difficult than it had been before; the carrier could no longer move about freely, the crush was simply too great. The candidate's closest supporters, who had tried in every way possible to reinforce the effect of his speeches, now had difficulty staying close to him; straining to the hilt, some twenty supporters now clung to the carrier. Yet even that strong man could not advance a single step of his own volition; there was no longer any hope of affecting the crowd by moving in a certain way and advancing or retreating as seemed appropriate. The crowd flowed aimlessly, everybody was packed cheek to jowl, no one could stand upright; the candidate's opponents seemed to have multiplied with the new arrivals; for a long time the carrier had remained close to the glass door of the tavern, but now, apparently without any resistance, he let himself be driven up and down the road; the candidate was still speaking, but one could no longer tell whether he was laying out his program or calling for help, for if one was not completely mistaken, an opposition candidate had appeared, or perhaps several of them; for when one of the lights suddenly began to flicker here and there, it was possible to catch a glimpse of a man with a pale face and clenched fists who had been lifted up by the crowd and now gave a speech that was hailed with numerous shouts.

"So what's happening?" Karl asked, turning in breathless confusion to his keepers.

"It's getting the little fellow so excited," said Brunelda to Delamarche, and she caught Karl by the chin in order to draw his head toward her. But Karl had no such desire, and since the events on the street had made him positively reckless, he shook himself so vigorously that Brunelda not only let go but drew back and released him altogether. "But now you've seen enough," she said, obviously irritated by Karl's conduct, "go into the room, make the bed, and get everything ready for the night." She held out her hand, pointing to the room. This was actually the direction in which Karl had wanted to go for several hours now; he was not about to object. Just then one could hear the crash of splintering glass from the street. Unable to restrain himself, Karl jumped over to the balustrade to take another quick look. A possibly decisive attack by the opponents had succeeded; all the supporters' car lamps, which at least enabled the entire public to follow the main events and also ensured that everything stayed within certain limits, had been smashed to bits; the candidate and his carrier were now swathed only in the fickle general lighting, which had spread out so suddenly that the effect resembled that of complete darkness. One could not have hazarded even a rough guess as to the location of the candidate, and the illusory quality of the darkness was further enhanced by the broad, uniform sounds of singing approaching from the bridge below.

"Haven't I told you what you must do now," said Brunelda, "hurry up. I'm tired," she added, stretching her arms up in such a way that her breasts bulged out even more than usual. Delamarche, who was still clasping her, pulled her off into a corner of the room. Robinson followed them in order to push aside the leftovers from his meal, which were still strewn on the floor.

Karl had to seize this favorable opportunity—this wasn't the time to take another look down; once below he would get to see enough of what was happening on the street and indeed more so than from above. In two bounds he rushed through the room with its reddish glow, but the door was locked, the key having been removed. He needed to find it, but who could find a key in this mess, especially given the precious little time left. By now he should really have been out on the stairs, running as fast as he could. But here he was, still looking for the key! And after looking in all of the drawers he could reach, he rummaged about on the table, where he found an assortment of dishes and napkins and a piece of embroidery that someone had only just begun; lured by an armchair laden with a completely entangled pile of old clothes, he realized that though the key could be there, it would be impossible to find, and in the end threw himself down onto the foul-smelling settee so that he could grope for the key in all its corners and folds. He then gave up searching and halted in the middle of the room. Brunelda must have fastened the key to her belt, he said to himself, for there certainly were quite a few things suspended from it; there was no point in searching any further.

And Karl seized two knives blindly and drove them in between the two wings of the door, one above, the other below, so as to create two pressure points at some distance from each other. But no sooner had he pulled on the knives than the blades broke in two, as was only to be expected. Still, he could not have hoped for a better outcome since the two stumps, which he could now push more forcefully, would hold. And now he pulled on them with all his strength, spreading his arms, pressing his legs apart, groaning, and keeping an eye on the door. It could not long withstand this pressure, as he noticed with delight from the clearly audible loosening of the bolts, but the slower it went, the better; the lock should by no means burst open, for the people up on the balcony would notice that, instead it should come apart very slowly, and so that was what Karl sought to accomplish with great care, moving his eyes ever closer to the lock.

"Look," he heard Delamarche's voice saying. All three now stood in the room, having drawn the curtain behind them; Karl must not have heard them enter; at the sight his hands fell from the knives. But he had no time to say a word in explanation or apology, for in an outburst of rage far exceeding the present occasion, Delamarche—whose loose dressing-gown cord described a great figure in the air—jumped on Karl. At the last moment Karl evaded the attack; he could have pulled the knives from the door and used them to defend himself but did not do so; however, bending down a little and jumping up in the air, he reached out for the wide collar of Delamarche's dressing gown, pulled it up, then dragged it even higher—Delamarche's dressing gown was really much too big for him—and then fortunately Delamarche, taken by surprise, caught his head in his dressing gown, merely waved his hands blindly at first, and then, little by little, began to strike Karl on the back with his fist, and though this had little effect, it did force Karl to throw himself against Delamarche's chest in order to protect his own face. However much he writhed with pain and however hard Delamarche's fists bore down on him, Karl endured the blows, and how could he possibly have acted any differently, for he could already see victory ahead. Keeping his hands on Delamarche's head and his thumbs probably just above his eyes, he pressed him up against the worst pile of furniture and at the same time tried to wind the cord of the dressing gown around Delamarche's feet and thus trip him up.

Being so completely preoccupied with Delamarche, particularly since he could feel his resistance grow and the hostile body press every more wirily against him, he truly forgot that he and Delamarche were not alone. However, he was soon reminded of this fact, for all of a sudden his feet gave way, pressed apart by Robinson, who had thrown himself on the ground behind him and was now shouting too. Panting, Karl released Delamarche, who withdrew another step. Brunelda stood in the middle of the room, legs wide apart, knees bent, in her full expanse; she followed the incident with shining eyes. As if she were an actual participant in the fight, she inhaled deeply, took aim with her eyes, and slowly raised her fists. Delamarche turned down his collar, he could now see clearly again, so this could no longer be considered a fight, it was simply punishment. He grasped Karl by the front of his shirt, almost lifting him off the ground, and refusing to look at him out of contempt, he threw him with such force against a cabinet a few paces away that Karl initially thought that the stabbing pain in his back and head, caused by his striking the closet, had been dealt directly by Delamarche's hand. "You scoundrel," he could hear Delamarche exclaim in the darkness that rose before his trembling eyes. And in the first few moments of complete exhaustion after he had collapsed beside the chest, the sound of the words "Just wait" still reverberated weakly in his ears.

When he regained consciousness, it was completely dark all around him; it must have been late at night; from the balcony a sliver of moonshine penetrated under the curtain into the room. One could hear the calm breathing of the three sleepers;

Brunelda's was by far the loudest, for she panted as she slept, just as she occasionally did as she spoke; still, it was not so easy to determine exactly where each of the sleepers lay, since the entire room was filled with the noise of her breathing. Only after taking a little look about could Karl think about himself, and he became very frightened, for even though he was completely crooked and stiff from the pain, he had never even considered the possibility that he might have suffered a severe, bloody injury. But now he had a load weighing down on his head; his entire face, his neck, and—underneath the shirt—his chest felt damp, as if there was some blood. He would have to move into the light so that he could determine his precise condition. Perhaps they had even crippled him, in which case Delamarche would surely be glad to let him go, but what should he do then, for he would be without prospects. He recalled the fellow with the wasted nose whom he had seen in the gateway, and for a moment buried his face in his hands.

Quite involuntarily he turned to the door and groped toward it on all fours. Probing with his fingers, he soon felt a boot and then a leg. It was Robinson, who else slept in his boots? He had been given an order to lie down across the doorway so as to prevent Karl from fleeing. But didn't they know about Karl's condition? He did not want to flee just now, he simply wished to get into the light. And so if he could not go through the door, he would have to go to the balcony.

The dining room table was evidently in a different position than the night before, and the settee, which Karl naturally approached with great caution, was surprisingly empty; but in the middle of the room he came across piled-up but tightly compressed clothes, blankets, curtains, cushions, and carpets. At first he thought that it was only a little heap, like the one he had come across at night on the settee, which must have toppled onto the floor, but as he crawled along he noticed to his astonishment that there was an entire cartload of such objects, which were probably removed at night from the chests in which they were stored by day. He crawled around the heap and soon saw that the whole thing was actually a kind of bed, at the summit of which, as he assured himself through careful groping, Delamarche and Brunelda were resting.

So now he knew where everybody slept, and he hurried out onto the balcony. Beyond the curtain was an entirely different world; quickly he rose to his full height. In the fresh night air and the light from the full moon, he walked up and down the balcony several times. He glanced at the street, which was rather quiet; from the tavern music still rang out, but only in a muted fashion; by the front door a man was sweeping the pavement, and on this very street where only that evening it had been impossible amid the chaotic general din to distinguish the shouting of an election candidate from thousands of other voices, one could clearly hear a broom scratching the pavement.

The sound of a table being pulled up on the adjacent balcony made Karl realize that somebody sat there, studying. It was a young man with a little pointed beard that he kept on twisting, moving his lips rapidly all the while. Seated at a small table covered with books, his face turned toward Karl, he had taken the electric lamp from the wall and clamped it between two large books and was now bathed in its harsh light.

"Good evening," said Karl, who thought he had noticed the young man glance over at him.

But he must have been mistaken, since the young man did not seem to have noticed him and put his hand over his eyes so as to ward off the glare and find out who had greeted him all of a sudden, and then since he could not see a thing, he raised the lamp to cast some light on the adjacent balcony. "Good evening," he said, and for a moment he looked over sharply, then added: "Now, what can I do for you?"

"I'm disturbing you?" asked Karl.

"Yes, yes," said the man, putting the lamp back.

By responding in that fashion, the man had rejected all attempts to establish contact, yet Karl did not leave the corner of the balcony where he was closest to him. He watched silently as the man read in his book, turned the pages, and occasionally checked something in another book that he always picked up at lightning speed, often making entries in a notebook, his face always bent surprisingly low over it.

Could this man be a student? He did seem to be studying. At home it hadn't been so different—it was so long ago now—when Karl sat at his parents' table writing his homework as Father read the newspaper, wrote ledger entries and correspondence for a club, and Mother occupied herself with a piece of sewing, continually pulling the thread high up over the fabric. So as to avoid disturbing Father, Karl had put only his copybook and writing materials on the table and arranged the other books he required on some chairs right and left. How quiet it had been! How seldom strangers had entered that room! Even as a little child Karl had always watched with pleasure as Mother locked the front door with the key. She had no inkling that Karl had now sunk so low that he even sought to break down strangers' doors with knives.

And what had he achieved through all that studying! He had certainly forgotten everything; if he had had to continue his studies here, it would have been very difficult. He remembered how he had been out sick for a month once at home—what an effort it had taken to resume his interrupted studies. And now, with the exception of that manual for English business correspondence, he had not read a book in such a long time.

"You there, young man," Karl heard a voice addressing him all of a sudden, "couldn't you stand somewhere else? It's terribly disturbing, how you keep staring over at me. At two o'clock at night one can surely expect to be able to work on the balcony without being disturbed. Do you want anything from me?"

"You're studying?" asked Karl.

"Yes, yes," said the man, using the few moments lost to his studies to rearrange his books.

"Then I don't want to disturb you," said Karl, "and in any case I'm going back into the room. Good night."

The man did not even answer; once this disturbance had been removed, he suddenly resolved to resume his studies and sat with his forehead resting heavily on his right hand.

Just before he reached the curtain, Karl remembered why he had come out here—he still had no idea about his condition. What was that weight on his head? He reached up and was astonished, there was no bloody injury, as he had feared in the darkness of that room; it was only a turbanlike bandage, which was still damp. To judge from the remnants of leftover lace still clinging to the bandage, it had been torn from an old piece of Brunelda's underwear, which Robinson had most likely wrapped quickly around Karl's head. Only he had forgotten to wring it out, and consequently, while Karl was unconscious, a great deal of water had run over his face and down under his shirt, giving him such a fright.

"So you're still there?" the man asked, blinking over at Karl.

"But now I'm really going," said Karl. "I simply wanted to take a look at something out here; it's completely dark in the room."

"Well, who are you?" said the man, and after putting his fountain pen on his book, which lay open before him, he stepped over to the balustrade. "What's your name? How do you come to be with those people? Have you been here long? Well, what do you want to look at? And do turn up your electric lamp so that I can see you."

Karl did so, but drew the curtain on the door so that nobody inside would be able to see anything. "Please," he said in a whisper, "excuse me for speaking so softly. If the people inside hear me, there'll be another row."

"Another row?" asked the man.

"Yes," said Karl, "just this evening I had a big fight with them. I probably still have a dreadful bruise." And he felt the back of his head.

"Well, what was the fight about?" asked the man, and since Karl did not answer at once, he added: "You can confide all your heartfelt grievances against those people. You see, I hate all three of them, especially their Madam. Besides, I'd be surprised if they haven't already spoken maliciously of me. My name is Josef Mandel, and I'm a student."

"Yes," said Karl, "they did tell me about you, nothing bad, though. They say you once treated Mrs. Brunelda, isn't that so?"

"Yes, it's true," said the student, laughing, "does the settee still reek of it?"

"Oh yes," said Karl. "Well, I'm glad about that," said the student, running his hand through his hair, "and why do they give you such bruises?"

"There was a fight," said Karl, wondering how he should explain this to the student. However, he then broke off and said: "But am I not disturbing you?"

"Well, first of all," said the student, "you've already disturbed me, and unfortunately I'm so nervous, I need a long time to get started again. I haven't accomplished anything since you started walking about on the balcony. And secondly, I always take a break at three o'clock. So take your time and tell me. I'm really very interested."

"It's quite simple," said Karl. "Delamarche wants me to become a servant at his place. But I don't want to. I would rather have left yesterday evening right away. He wouldn't let me and locked the door; I tried to break it down, and that's when the scuffle broke out. I'm less than pleased to be still here."

"Do you have another job?" asked the student.

"No," said Karl, "but I don't care, if only I could get away."

"Wait a minute, though," said the student, "you don't care?" And both were silent for a moment.

"But why don't you want to stay with those people," asked the student.

"Delamarche is a bad person," said Karl, "I know him from before. I once spent an entire day on a long march with him and was glad not to be around him anymore. And I'm supposed to be a servant at his place?"

"If every servant were as finicky in choosing his master as you are!" said the student, and he seemed to smile. "Look, I'm a salesman by day, the lowest-ranking salesman, actually an errand boy, in Montly's department store. Montly is undoubtedly a scoundrel, but that doesn't really bother me, what infuriates me is the miserable pay. So do take me as an example."

"What?" said Karl. "You're a salesman by day and study at night?"

"Yes," said the student, "there's no other way. I've explored many possibilities, but I've never found a better way of life. You see, some years ago I was exclusively a student, day and night, but I almost starved, had to sleep in a dirty old hole, and didn't dare go into the classrooms wearing the suit I had back then. But that's all over now."

"When do you sleep, though?" asked Karl, looking at the student in amazement.

"Oh, as for sleeping!" said the student, "I shall sleep once I'm finished with my studies. As for now, I just drink black coffee." And he turned around, pulled a large flask from under his desk, poured black coffee into a little cup, and downed it, the way one swallows medicines quickly so as to avoid noticing the taste.

"It's such a great thing, black coffee," said the student, "it's a pity you're so far away and I can't hand you some."

"I don't like black coffee," said Karl.

"Nor do I," said the student, laughing. "But where would I be without it. If it weren't for black coffee, Montly wouldn't keep me a moment longer. I always say Montly, but of course he doesn't even have the slightest notion I exist. I really have no idea how I would keep going at work if I didn't always keep a flask this big in my desk, for I've never yet dared to give up drinking coffee, but believe me, it wouldn't be long before I'd be lying behind the desk fast asleep. Unfortunately, people can sense this, at work they call me Black Coffee; it's a stupid joke that has certainly harmed my chances of getting ahead."

"And when will you be finished with your studies?" asked Karl.

"It's slow going," said the student, lowering his head. He left the balustrade and sat down at the table again; after propping his elbows on the open book and running his hands through his hair, he said: "It can take between one and two more years."

"I too wanted to study," Karl said, as though this particular circumstance gave him the right to expect even more confidences than the student, who was beginning to fall silent, had already revealed.

"Well," said the student, and it was not altogether clear whether he had begun to read his book again or was simply gazing at it absently, "you can be happy about having given up your studies. I myself have been studying for years, out of pure single-mindedness. It has given me little satisfaction and even less chance of a decent future. And in any case, what sort of prospects did I really want! America is full of bogus doctors."

"I wanted to become an engineer," Karl said hastily to the student, who appeared to have lapsed into complete indifference.

"And now you'll be a servant for these people," said the student, looking up for a moment, "of course, that must be painful."

The conclusion drawn by the student stemmed from a misunderstanding, but perhaps it could help Karl make some headway with him. Karl therefore asked: "Maybe I too could get a job in the department store?"

This question tore the student away from his book; but it never even crossed his mind that he could help Karl look for a position. "Try," he said, "or better still, don't try. Obtaining that post at Montly's has been the greatest success in my life. If I had to choose between my studies and that post, I would naturally choose the post. All my efforts are geared toward avoiding the necessity of having to make such a choice."

"So it's that difficult to get a post there," said Karl, more to himself than to the student.

"Well, what do you think," said the student, "here, of course, it is easier to become a district judge than a door-opener at Montly's."

Karl remained silent. After all, this student, who was much more experienced than he and who, for reasons unknown to Karl, hated Delamarche and certainly bore Karl no ill will, could not come up with a single reason for encouraging Karl to leave Delamarche. And yet he knew nothing about the threat from the police that Karl faced and from which he was somewhat shielded only at Delamarche's.

"You saw the demonstration below yesterday evening, didn't you? If you didn't know anything about the circumstances, you could easily imagine that this candidate, Lobter is his name, might actually have some chance, or at least be in the running."
"I know nothing about politics," said Karl.

"That's a mistake," said the student. "But leaving that aside, you do have eyes and ears. As you can hardly have failed to notice, that man undoubtedly had friends and enemies. And keep in mind that, at least in my opinion, the man doesn't have the slightest chance of being elected. I happen to know all about him, just by accident; someone living here knows him. He doesn't lack ability, and so far as his views and political past are concerned, he would be an eminently suitable judge for this district. But no one thinks he can be elected, he will fail as splendidly as one can fail; he'll have wasted a few dollars on his election campaign, that's all."

For a moment Karl and the student regarded each other in silence. The student nodded, smiling, and pressed his hand to his weary eyes.

"Well, aren't you going to bed?" he asked, "I must really get on with my studies. See how much work I've still got to wade through." And he flicked quickly through half the pages in a book so as to give Karl an idea of the work still awaiting him.

"Well, good night then," said Karl, bowing.

"But do come over to see us sometime," said the student, who was already seated at the table again, "of course, only if you'd like. You'll always find quite a few people here. I've also time for you, from nine to ten in the evening."

"So you advise me to stay with Delamarche?" Karl asked.

"Absolutely," said the student, bending his head over his books. It seemed as if he had not uttered that word but rather as if it had come from a voice deeper than the student's; it continued to resound in Karl's ears. Slowly he approached the curtain, cast another glance at the student, who now sat quite still within his circle of light, with darkness on all sides, and slipped into the room. He was greeted by the unified breathing of the three sleepers. Then he groped his way along the wall, looked for the settee, and upon finding it stretched out quietly, as though it were his usual bed. Since the student, who knew Delamarche well and had a precise understanding of the situation here and who, moreover, was an educated man, had advised him to stay, he had no qualms at all for now. He did not have such lofty aspirations as the student, for even at home who knew where he would have managed to finish his studies, and if this seemed scarcely possible at home, no one could expect him to do so here in this foreign country. But he would have greater hope of finding a post in which he could achieve something and be recognized for his achievements if he accepted the servant position at Delamarche's, and then once he had that secure position, he could wait for a favorable opportunity to arise. On this very street there appeared to be many offices of middling or low stature, and if they were short of staff, they might not be all that particular about choosing new employees. If necessary, he would gladly become a messenger boy, but it was certainly not altogether inconceivable that he would be hired solely for office work and would someday become an office employee and sit at his own desk, where he could spend some time looking out the window without a care in the world, like the official he had seen that morning as they marched through the courtyard. When he closed his eyes, he was struck by the soothing thought that he was after all still young, and that Delamarche would eventually have to let him go; this household certainly didn't look as if it would last forever. But if Karl should ever obtain such an office position, he would occupy himself exclusively with his office work and not dissipate his energy like the student. Besides, he would, if necessary, dedicate some nighttime hours to the office and indeed would even be required to do so because of his limited business training. He would think only of the interests of the business he served and gladly take on every task, even those that other clerical workers would reject as being unworthy of them. These good intentions jostled one another in his head as if his future boss stood before the settee reading them from his face.

Immersed in such thoughts, Karl fell asleep, and his initially light sleep was disturbed only by the mighty sighing of Brunelda, who, evidently tormented by heavy dreams, tossed and turned on her bed.

"Get up! Up!" cried Robinson the moment Karl opened his eyes. The curtain on the door had not yet been opened, but one could tell from the steady sunlight falling through the chinks how late in the morning it already was. Robinson ran zealously back and forth, looking very preoccupied; first he carried a towel, then a bucket of water, then a few pieces of underwear and some clothing, and whenever he passed Karl, he tried to persuade him to get up by nodding his head and holding up in the air whatever he happened to be carrying, so as to show how hard he was toiling one last time on behalf of Karl, who could naturally not be expected on his first morning there to understand the specific requirements of the service.

But Karl soon realized whom Robinson was actually serving. In a space Karl had not yet seen, partitioned from the rest of the room by two closets, a great washing was under way. One could see Brunelda's head, bare neck—her hair had just been flung into her face—and the nape of her neck rise above the closet, and every now and then Delamarche's hand held up the dripping bath sponge with which he was washing and scrubbing Brunelda. One could hear the curt commands that Delamarche now gave Robinson, who, unable to hand the objects through the regular entrance to the alcove because it had been blocked off, had to make do with a little gap between a closet and a folding screen, holding out his arm and averting his face every time he handed in an item. "The towel! The towel!" cried Delamarche. No sooner had Robinson, who was still searching for some other object under the table and now withdrew his head, been startled by this demand than there came another cry: "What the devil happened to the water," and Delamarche's enraged face peered over the closet. There were repeated demands in every conceivable sequence for all sorts of things that would, to Karl's mind, only be needed once while washing and dressing. There was always a bucket with water heating up on a small electric stove, and Robinson repeatedly carried the heavy burden between his parted legs to the wash-room. Given the amount of work to be done, it was under-standable that he did not always stick to his orders and once, when a towel was requested, simply took a camisole from the great bedstead in the middle of the room and threw it in over the closets in one great ball.

Delamarche, however, was also hard at work and was per-haps annoyed at Robinson—so annoyed that he had forgotten all about Karl—only because he could not satisfy Brunelda himself. "Oh," she shouted in such a way that even Karl, who felt largely indifferent, shuddered, "you're hurting me! Go away! I would rather wash myself than suffer like this! I can't even lift my arm again. I'm getting very sick from the way you're squeezing me. My back must be covered in bruises. But of course you're not about to tell me. Wait a moment, I shall get Robinson to have a look at me, or our little fellow there. No, I won't really do so, but be a little more gentle. And show me some consideration, Delamarche, but I can say this every morning as often as I like, and yet you will never, ever show me the slightest consideration; Robinson," she called out suddenly, waving little lace underpants above her head: "Come and help me, see how I'm suffering, that Delamarche likes to call this torment a scrubbing. Robinson, Robinson, where are you, are you heartless too?" Karl silently motioned to Robinson with his finger that he should approach her, but Robinson lowered his eyes and shook his head disdainfully; he knew better. "What's come over you?" said Robinson, bending down to whisper in Karl's ear, "that's not what she means. I only went in once, and never again. Both of them grabbed me and dunked me in the tub till I almost drowned. For days afterward Brunelda accused me of being shameless and kept on saying, 'It's been ages since you've been in the bath with me' or 'Tell me, when are you coming to have another look at me in the bath?' Only when I went down on my knees to implore her did she stop. I'll never forget it." And as Robinson spoke, Brunelda cried out repeatedly: "Robinson! Robinson! What's keeping that Robinson!"

Although no one came to her aid and her cry went unanswered—Robinson had sat down beside Karl and both gazed silently at the dresser, above which one could now see the heads of Brunelda and Delamarche—Brunelda nevertheless did not cease complaining loudly about Delamarche. "But Delamarche," she cried, "I can't even feel your scrubbing. What have you done with the sponge? Well, get a move on! If only I could bend, if only I could move! Then I would show you how to scrub. Where now are those days on my parents' estate when, as a young girl, I used to go swimming every morning in the Colorado, and to think I was the most agile of all my girlfriends! And now! But when will you learn how to give me a good scrubbing, Delamarche, you keep on waving the sponge about, making a great effort, and I can feel nothing. When I said you shouldn't rub me till I'm sore, I certainly didn't mean I'd like to stand around and catch a cold. So now I must jump out of the tub and run off as I am."

But she did not carry out this threat—which she would have been completely incapable of doing—and Delamarche, anxious lest she catch a cold, evidently caught her and pushed her into the tub, for there was a great splash.

"You're good at it, Delamarche," said Brunelda, a little more softly, "flattering me over and over again whenever you've made a mess of something." Then for a moment there was silence. "He's kissing her," said Robinson, raising his eyebrows.

"What do we do next?" asked Karl. Since he had after all finally decided to stay, he wanted to assume his duties right away. Leaving behind Robinson, who did not answer, on the settee, he began to pull apart the great encampment, which was still compressed from the heavy weight of the sleepers in the course of that long night, so as to take each item from this massive heap and fold it neatly, which had probably not happened for weeks.

"Take a look next door, Delamarche," said Brunelda, "I think they're pulling our bed apart. I always have to think of everything and never have a moment's peace. You must be stricter with those two, for if not they'll simply do as they please." "That must be the little fellow who's so damned eager," cried Delamarche, evidently intending to rush out from the washroom; Karl immediately threw away everything he had in his hands; fortunately, Brunelda then said: "Don't go, Delamarche, don't go. Oh, the water is hot, it makes one so weary. Stay with me, Delamarche." Only then did Karl notice the steam continually rising from behind the closets. Robinson, who looked shocked, put his hand on his cheek as if Karl had done something wrong. "Just leave everything as it was," Delamarche's voice rang out, "how come you didn't even realize that Brunelda always rests for an hour after her bath? What a wretched household! Just wait until I get to you. Robinson, you must be daydreaming again. You, and you alone, are responsible for everything that happens here. You've simply got to restrain that boy—this

place isn't run according to his lights. When one wants something, one cannot get it from you, and then when there's no
need to do anything, you are diligent. Just crawl away into
some corner now and wait until you're needed."

But all this was immediately forgotten, for Brunelda whispered very wearily, as if she were being deluged by the hot
water: "The perfume! Bring the perfume!" "The perfume,"
shouted Delamarche. "Get a move on." Yes, but where was the
perfume? Karl glanced at Robinson, Robinson in turn at Karl.
Karl realized that he would have to take charge of everything
himself; Robinson had no idea where the perfume was but
merely lay down on the floor and waved both arms under the
settee, which yielded only balls of dust and women's hair. First
Karl rushed to the washstand next to the door, but all he could
find were various old novels in English and some magazines
and sheet music, since the drawers were so overstuffed that
when one finally managed to open them, it was impossible to
get them to close again. "The perfume," sighed Brunelda. "It's
taking you so long! Will I even get my perfume today!" Karl
could not conduct a proper search since Brunelda was so impatient that he had to rely on a cursory first glance. The bottle
was not in the washstand; it merely contained some old medi-
cine and ointment bottles, for everything else had been taken in
to the washroom. Perhaps the bottle lay in a drawer of the dining room table. But on his way to the table—Karl thought only
of the perfume and of nothing else—he collided with Robinson, who had finally given up searching under the settee and
who, overcome by a sudden intuition about the whereabouts of
the perfume, ran toward Karl, as though he were blind. One
could clearly hear their heads collide; Karl remained silent, and
though Robinson did not cease running, he sought to ease
his pain by continually shouting out in an exaggeratedly loud
voice.

"Instead of looking for the perfume, they're fighting," said Brunelda. "Delamarche, this whole mess is making me ill, and I'll certainly die in your arms. I must have that perfume," she cried, rousing herself. "I must absolutely have it. I'm not getting out of this tub until they bring it in to me, even if I have to stay here till this evening." And with her fist she hit the water—one could hear it splashing.

However, the perfume was not in the dining table drawer either, for the contents consisted exclusively of Brunelda's toiletries, such as old powder puffs, small makeup jars, hairbrushes, locks of hair, and many other small items, all matted and stuck together. There was no sign of the perfume. And Robinson too, who was still shouting and now stood in a corner made up of a hundred or so piled-up boxes and small crates, opened them one by one, rifled through them, causing half the contents—mostly sewing items and letters—to fall on the floor, and left them lying there without managing to find anything, as he occasionally indicated to Karl by shaking his head and shrugging his shoulders.

Just then Delamarche jumped out of the washroom in his underwear, while Brunelda could be heard weeping convulsively. Karl and Robinson ceased to look and glanced at Delamarche, who was completely drenched, the water was even running down his face and hair, and who cried: "Kindly start searching right away!" First he ordered Karl to look by saying, "Here!" then told Robinson, "There!" Karl did look, inspecting even the places where Robinson had been ordered to search, but he had no more luck finding the perfume than did Robinson, who was less intent on searching than on glancing sideways at Delamarche, who stomped up and down in the room, insofar as he could in the tight space, and would certainly have preferred to give both Karl and Robinson a beating.

"Delamarche, come here," cried Brunelda, "and at least

make an effort to dry me off. Those two certainly won't find the perfume and are making a complete mess of everything. They should stop looking right away. This instant! And they must drop everything. And not touch anything else! They sure seem to want to turn this apartment into a barn. Delamarche, grab them by the collar if they don't stop! But they're still at it—a box has just fallen down out there. They shouldn't pick it up but simply leave everything as it is and get out of the room! Then latch the door after them and come to me. I've lain in this water too long, my legs are chilly." "I'm coming, Brunelda, I'm coming," cried Delamarche, rushing to the door with Karl and Robinson. Before releasing them, however, he asked them to fetch breakfast and, if possible, to borrow a good perfume somewhere for Brunelda.

"Your place is so messy and dirty," said Karl, once they were out in the corridor, "after we get back with the breakfast, we'll have to tidy up."

"If only I weren't so ill," said Robinson. "And then all this mistreatment!"

Robinson was surely offended that Brunelda had not distinguished in any way between himself, who had already been serving for months, and Karl, who had only appeared the day before. But he deserved no better, and Karl said: "You've got to pull yourself together a little." But then, so as not to abandon him entirely to his despair, Karl went on: "It's a task that only needs to be done once. I'll set up a sleeping place for you behind the closets, and once the room is pretty much tidied up, you can lie there all day without having to take care of anything and will soon recover."

"So you do understand the state I'm in," said Robinson, averting his face from Karl so that he could be alone with his sorrows. "But will they ever let me lie there quietly?"

"If you like, I shall bring this up with Delamarche and Brunelda."

"Does Brunelda ever show the slightest consideration?" cried Robinson, and without giving Karl any advance warning, he held out his fist and pushed open a door that they had just reached.

They entered a kitchen with a faulty oven that emitted little black clouds. Before the oven doors knelt one of the women whom Karl had seen in the corridor the day before and who was using her bare hands to put large pieces of coal into the fire, which she inspected from every angle. She sighed, kneeling in a position that was no doubt uncomfortable for such an old woman.

"Of course, that pest would have to come too," she said on catching sight of Robinson, and she rose laboriously, keeping one hand on the coal bucket, then shut the oven door after first covering the handle with her apron. "It's now four o'clock in the afternoon"—Karl gazed at the kitchen clock in astonishment—"and you still need breakfast? What riffraff!

"Sit down," she said, "and wait till I've time for you."

Robinson drew Karl onto a little bench by the door and whispered to him: "We must do as she says. You see, we're dependent on her. We rent our room from her, and at any moment she can give us notice. After all, we cannot move to another apartment—how could we possibly get all those things out again, especially since Brunelda isn't transportable."

"And there's no other room to be had on this corridor?" Karl asked.

"Well, no one will take us in," Robinson answered, "no one in this entire building will take us in."

And thus they sat on their little bench, waiting quietly. The woman ran incessantly back and forth between two tables, a tub, and the oven. From her frequent exclamations one could gather that her daughter was not well, so she had to take care of all the work alone, in other words, the serving and feeding of thirty tenants. Besides, the oven was defective, the food took forever: there was a thick soup simmering in two giant pots, and however often the woman checked it, using ladles and letting it drip down into the pots, it simply would not turn out right, and since this was probably due to the poor fire, she sat down in front of the oven door, almost on the floor, and stirred the glowing coals with a rake. The smoke filling the kitchen made her cough, sometimes so severely that she reached for a chair and for a while could do nothing but cough. She stated repeatedly that she was not going to provide them with breakfast that late in the day, having neither the time nor the inclination to do so. Since Karl and Robinson had been ordered to fetch the breakfast but could not possibly force her to provide it, they did not respond to such remarks and simply remained there, sitting quietly on their chairs.

The tenants' unwashed breakfast dishes still lay strewn about on chairs and footstools, on top of and underneath the tables, and even, crammed into a corner, on the floor. There were small coffeepots still containing some coffee or milk and also bits of leftover butter on a number of the little plates; a large tin box had fallen down, and a few biscuits had spilled out. In fact, if one used all of this, one could put together a breakfast that even Brunelda could not fault, so long as she did not discover its origins. Just as Karl was considering this possibility and glancing at the clock, which made him realize that they had already spent half an hour waiting and that Brunelda had perhaps grown furious and was inciting Delamarche against the servants, the woman, who was still coughing, shouted—while staring at Karl: "You can sit there, but you're not getting any breakfast. But in two hours you'll be getting your supper."

"Come, Robinson," said Karl, "we'll put the breakfast together." "What," cried the woman, lowering her head. "Please be reasonable," said Karl, "why don't you want to give us our breakfast. We've been waiting for half an hour, which is certainly long enough. After all, you get reimbursed for all of this, and we certainly pay you better than everybody else. It's surely a nuisance for you that we're having breakfast at this late hour, but then we are your tenants and are accustomed to having a late breakfast, and you should also accommodate us a little too. Of course that will be especially difficult today owing to your daughter's illness, but then again we're prepared to put together a breakfast using those leftovers if there's no other way and you aren't prepared to give us any fresh food."

But the woman had no desire to engage in a friendly conversation with anybody; to her mind, even the remnants of the communal breakfast were evidently too good for such tenants; still, she was fed up with the persistence of the two servants and so she seized a tray and thrust it up against Robinson's body; it took him a while to realize that he was meant to hold out the tray and accept the food that the woman would choose herself. In a great hurry she loaded the tray with a huge number of items, but the resulting heap looked more like a pile of dirty dishes than a breakfast that could actually be served. As the woman pushed them out and they hurried toward the door, bent over, as if fearful of being scolded or beaten, Karl took the tray out of Robinson's hands, for it did not seem sufficiently safe in Robinson's keeping.

In the corridor, once they were far enough from the landlady's door, Karl sat down on the floor with the tray, primarily to clean it, to gather items that belonged together by pouring the milk into a single container and scraping the various leftover pieces of butter onto a plate, and then to remove all traces of prior use, in other words, to clean the knives and spoons, and to cut off the half-eaten portions of the rolls, thereby improving the overall appearance. Robinson insisted that this was unnecessary work, claiming that their breakfast had often looked far worse, but Karl would not let Robinson deter him and was happy that the dirty-fingered Robinson would not be helping with this chore. In order to keep him quiet, Karl had immediately doled him out a few cakes, pouring the thick residue of hot chocolate into a little pot.

When they arrived at their apartment and Robinson reached without hesitation for the door handle, Karl restrained him, for it was not clear whether they were permitted to enter. "Why, of course," said Robinson, "he's still doing her hair." And Brunelda was indeed sitting in the armchair, legs spread wide apart, in the room, which had not yet been aired and in which the shutters were still closed; Delamarche, who stood behind her with his face inclined, was combing her hair, which was short and probably all tangled. Brunelda again wore a very loose-fitting dress, only this time it was light pink and perhaps a little shorter than the one she wore the day before, for one could see her coarsely woven white stockings almost as far as the knee. Having become impatient over the time it took to comb her hair, Brunelda flicked her thick red tongue between her lips; from time to time she cried, "But Delamarche!" and tore herself away from Delamarche, who waited quietly, comb raised in the air, for her to lower her head again.

"It's taken so long," Brunelda said to no one in particular, and then to Karl: "If you want to satisfy us, you'll have to be a little more nimble. You shouldn't regard that lazy glutton Robinson as a model. You've probably already had your breakfast somewhere, but listen: Next time I won't stand for this."

This was very unjust, to be sure, and Robinson too shook his head and moved his lips, though without making a sound; however, Karl realized that the only way to win over these masters was by showing them work of unquestionable quality. So he drew a low Japanese table from a nook, covered it with a cloth, and set up the items they had brought. Anybody who

had seen this breakfast come about could not help but be satisfied with how everything had turned out, but as Karl had to
admit, there were still a few shortcomings.

Fortunately, Brunelda was hungry. Though nodding agree-
ably at Karl as he prepared everything, she frequently hindered
him by picking out little mouthfuls prematurely with her soft
fat hand, possibly squashing everything. "He did a good job,"
she said, smacking her lips, and drew Delamarche, who had
left the comb in her hair for possible later use, onto a chair
beside her. At the sight of the food even Delamarche became
friendly; both were very hungry, and their hands rushed to and
fro over the little table. Karl realized that if one wished to satisfy these people, one always had to bring back all one could
and, remembering that he had left various usable food items
lying about on the floor, said: "This first time I didn't know
how everything should be set up, but I'll do a better job next
time." Yet even as he spoke he remembered whom he was
addressing; he had become much too caught up in the details of
this affair. Brunelda nodded contentedly at Delamarche and
rewarded Karl by passing him a handful of biscuits.

FRAGMENTS

(I)

BRUNELDA'S DEPARTURE

One morning Karl pushed the invalid cart in which Brunelda was seated through the front gate. It was not as early as he had hoped. They had agreed to undertake the exodus while it was still night so as not to cause a stir in the streets, which would have been unavoidable by day, no matter how modestly Brunelda tried to cover herself in a great gray cloth. Yet carrying her downstairs had taken too long despite the most helpful assistance from the student, who as became evident on this occasion was much weaker than Karl. Brunelda behaved decently, hardly sighed, and sought to ease the work of her carriers any way she could. Nevertheless, they were obliged to set her down on every fifth step so that she and they could take the most necessary breaks. It was a cool morning; in the corridor gusts of cold air blew about as in a cellar, but Karl and the student were covered in perspiration, and during the breaks each had to dry his face with a corner of Brunelda's shawl, which she graciously handed them. Two hours elapsed before they reached the ground floor, where the little cart had stood since the previous evening. At first it would take a little work to lift Brunelda into the cart, but then the whole thing could be considered a success, since the cart could be pushed along quite easily, thanks to the large wheels, and the only remaining concern was that the little cart might fall apart under Brunelda's weight. Still, one had to take that risk, for it would not really be possible to take along a replacement cart such as the one the student had half-jokingly offered to provide for them and even to push himself. Then they took leave of the student and very warmly at that; all of the previous disagreements between Brunelda and the student appeared to have been forgotten; the student even apologized for the insult he had given when Brunelda was ill; however, Brunelda declared that all was long forgotten and that he had more than made amends. Finally, she asked the student to be so kind as to accept as a memento of herself, a dollar, which she laboriously extricated from one of her many skirts. That gift was significant, especially considering Brunelda's notorious stinginess, and the student was indeed very pleased, so much so that he threw the coin high in the air. But then he had to go looking for it on the ground, and Karl was obliged to assist him; Karl found it at last under Brunelda's cart. Of course, Karl and the student found it easier to say goodbye; they simply shook hands, expressing the conviction that each would see the other again and that at least one of them—the student claimed this of Karl, and Karl in turn of the student—would by then have accomplished something worthy of fame, though that had unfortunately not come about yet. Then in good spirits Karl seized the handle and pushed the cart through the gate. The student watched, waving with a handkerchief, until they vanished from sight. Karl often nodded back; Brunelda would also have liked to turn around, but such movements were too strenuous for her. So as to make it possible for her to say one last goodbye, once they had reached the bottom of the street Karl pushed the cart around in a full circle so that Brunelda too could see the student, who seized the opportunity and began to wave his handkerchief with special zeal.

Karl, however, then said that they should not make any further stops since they had a long journey ahead and had left much later than anticipated. And indeed one could already see carriages here and there, and even a few isolated figures heading to work. By that remark Karl had meant only what he had in fact said, but in her tactful way Brunelda had understood it differently and now covered herself entirely in her gray shawl. Karl did not object to this; true, having the handcart covered with a gray shawl was quite conspicuous, but incomparably less so than if one were to carry Brunelda in there without any covering. He pushed the cart very carefully; before turning a corner, he always looked into the next street first and only then left the cart, if necessary, and went forward alone; whenever he anticipated a possibly unpleasant encounter, he waited until it could be avoided or even decided to go down an entirely different street. And since he had studied every possible route, there was never any danger of having to make a big detour. Of course, there were still some obstacles to be feared, yet one couldn't really have foreseen the particulars. For instance, all of a sudden, in a street that sloped gently uphill, could be easily surveyed, and, pleasantly enough, was quite empty— Karl turned this to his advantage by hurrying up—a policeman stepped from a dark corner at one of the front gates and asked Karl what he was carrying in his carefully covered cart. Yet despite the severe looks he directed at Karl, the policeman had to laugh when he lifted the cover and saw Brunelda's overheated and frightened face. "What?" he said. "I thought you had ten bags of potatoes and now it's only one woman? Where are you going? Who are you?" Brunelda did not dare to look at the policeman and simply gazed at Karl, clearly doubting that even he could save her anymore. Karl had enough experience with policemen, though; none of this seemed dangerous. "But Miss," he said, "show the officer the document you've got." "Oh yes," said Brunelda, and she searched for it in such a hopeless manner that she now began to seem truly suspect.

"The young miss," said the policeman with obvious irony, "won't be able to find the document." "Oh, but she will," said Karl calmly. "She certainly has it and has simply misplaced it." He now searched for it himself and soon pulled it out from behind Brunelda's back. The policeman merely gave it a cursory glance. "So that's it," the policeman said, laughing. "She's that sort of young miss. And your job, little fellow, is to make arrangements and transport her? Is that really the best job you can find?" Karl simply shrugged his shoulders; once again the police were meddling. "Well, pleasant trip," said the policeman when he did not receive an answer. There was probably a certain contempt in the policeman's tone, which caused Karl to leave without saying goodbye; after all, it was better to arouse the contempt of the police than to attract their attention.

Shortly afterward he experienced what was possibly an even more unpleasant encounter. For approaching him was a man, pushing a cart laden with large milk cans, who was extremely eager to learn what lay beneath the gray cloth on Karl's cart. Although it was unlikely that he was heading in the same direction as Karl, he stayed beside him in spite of the unpredictable turns Karl would suddenly take. At first he settled for remarks such as "You must be carrying a heavy load" or "You didn't load the cart properly; something up on top is bound to fall off." Then he asked bluntly: "What are you carrying under that cloth?" Karl said: "What concern is it of yours?" But since this only made the man all the more curious, Karl finally said: "Apples." "You have so many apples," the man said in astonishment, repeating the remark over and over again. "That's an entire harvest," he said. "Well, yes," said Karl. But whether he did not believe Karl or whether he wanted to annoy him, he carried this even further, and—all without breaking his stride—began to reach out his hand toward the cloth, as if in jest, and finally he even had the audacity to tug at the cloth. The things

Brunelda had to endure! Out of consideration for her, Karl did not want to get into a fight with the man and therefore entered through the next open gate, as though that were his destination. "This is where I live," he said. "Thanks for the company." The man remained at the gate, looking in astonishment at Karl, who was prepared to walk all the way across the first courtyard. The man could no longer be in any doubt as to Karl's intentions, but in order to satisfy his malice one last time, he left his cart, pursued Karl on tiptoes, and gave the cloth such a sharp tug that he almost exposed Brunelda's face. "Just to give your apples a little air," he said, and ran off. Karl swallowed even that insult, for it would free him from that man at last. Then he guided the cart into a corner of the yard where several boxes afforded some privacy and where he could say a few soothing words to Brunelda. But he had to spend a great deal of time cajoling her, since she wept a great deal and implored him in all seriousness that they should stay behind the boxes all day and not set off again until nightfall. Perhaps he alone could not have convinced her how misguided that would have been, but when someone at the far end of the pile threw an empty box to the ground, making a resounding noise in the empty courtyard, she was so startled that, without even daring to say another word, she pulled the cloth up over herself and was probably more than happy when Karl resolved to set off right away.

Though the streets were becoming increasingly animated, the cart did not attract as much attention as Karl had feared. It might even have been wiser to pick another time for this move. Should another such journey become necessary, Karl would risk setting off at noon. Without encountering any worse annoyance, he turned into the dark narrow street where Enterprise No. 25 was located. The manager stood by the door, holding his watch, and squinting. "Are you always so unpunc-

tual?" he asked. "There were obstacles of various kinds," said
Karl. "Naturally, there always are," said the manager. "But
here in this building we make no allowance for them. Mark my
words!" Karl barely heeded such speeches; everyone took
advantage of his power and yelled at his underlings. But once
you became used to that, it sounded no different than the regular ticking of a clock. But what *did* startle him as he pushed his
cart along the corridor was the dirt lying everywhere, though
he had admittedly expected something of the sort. However, on
closer scrutiny, the dirt was inexplicable. The stone floor in the
corridor had been swept almost clean, the paint on the walls
was relatively new, not much dust had collected on the artificial
palms, but everything was greasy and repulsive; it was as if
everything had been subjected to such abuse that no amount of
cleaning could remedy it. Whenever Karl arrived somewhere,
he liked to think about the improvements that could be made
and how pleasant it would be to get started right away, however endless the work required. But in this case he did not
know what could be done. Slowly he removed the cloth from
Brunelda. "Welcome, miss," the manager said in an affected
manner; there could be no doubt that Brunelda made a favorable impression on him. Brunelda had no sooner noticed this
than she turned it to her advantage, as Karl noticed with satisfaction. All the fear of those last hours disappeared. She

(2)

At a street corner Karl saw a poster with the following announcement: "Today on the racetrack in Clayton the theater in Oklahama is taking on staff, from six o'clock in the morning until midnight! The great Theater of Oklahama is calling you! It is calling only today, only this once! Anyone who misses this opportunity shall miss it forever! Anyone who is thinking of his future belongs in our midst! All are welcome! Anyone who wants to become an artist should contact us! We are a theater that can make use of everyone, each in his place! And we congratulate here and now those who have decided in our favor. At twelve o'clock everything shall close and won't open again! Accursed be those who don't believe us! And now, off to Clayton!"

Many people stood in front of the poster, yet it appeared to meet with scant approval. There were so many posters, no one believed in posters anymore. And this poster was even more implausible than such posters tend to be. Above all, it had one great flaw; there was nothing about wages. If the pay had been worthwhile, the poster would have mentioned it; it wouldn't have omitted what was most enticing. No one wants to be an artist, but everyone wants to be paid for his work.

The poster offered Karl one great enticement. "Everyone is welcome," it said. Everyone—in other words, Karl too. Everything he had ever done was forgotten, no one would reproach him anymore. And he could sign up for work that was not shameful and could be advertised openly! And they promised just as openly that he too would be taken on. He certainly could ask for no better; he just wanted to start off at last in some respectable career, and perhaps this was it. For even if all of that boasting on the poster was a lie, and even if the great Theater of Oklahoma was merely a little strolling circus, it wanted to hire people, and that was good enough. Karl did not read the poster a second time, but glanced through it to find the sentence: "Everyone is welcome."

At first he thought of going to Clayton on foot, but that would have taken three hours of vigorous marching, and he would have arrived there only to discover that all available positions were filled. According to the poster, there was no limit on the numbers to be taken on, but that was how such job offers were always phrased. Karl realized that he would either have to give up on the prospect of this job or else take the train. He counted out his money; were it not for this trip, it would have lasted eight days; he pushed the small coins to and fro in the palm of his hand. A gentleman who had been watching him patted him on the shoulder and said: "Good luck for your trip to Clayton." Karl nodded silently and went on counting. But before long he made up his mind, separated out the money for the trip, and ran to the subway.

After getting out in Clayton, he heard the clamor of a great many trumpets. It was a confused clamor, the trumpets were not in tune; they were being played quite heedlessly. Still, this did not bother Karl since it merely confirmed in his mind that the Theater of Oklahoma was a large enterprise. But on stepping out of the station, where he could survey the entire complex spread out before him, he saw that it was far bigger than he could possibly have imagined, and he could not understand how an enterprise of this kind was able to go to such expense merely for the purpose of adding staff. In front of the entrance to the racetrack was a long, low platform on which hundreds of women, dressed as angels in white robes with large wings on their backs, blew long trumpets that shone like gold. But they were not directly on the platform; each stood on her own pedestal, which however was not visible, for it was completely covered by the angels' long billowing robes. Since the pedestals were very high, a good two meters tall, the figures of these women looked gigantic, though this impression of great size was somewhat marred by their small heads; even their loose hair was too short and looked almost ridiculous, as it hung down between their large wings and down along their sides. To avoid seeming monotonous, pedestals of greatly differing sizes had been used; some women were not much larger than life size, while others alongside them soared so high that one imagined that the lightest gust of wind could imperil them. And now all of these women blew their trumpets.

There wasn't much of an audience. Looking quite small compared to these large figures, some ten youths walked back and forth in front of the platform, gazing up at the women. They pointed at one or the other; however, they seemed to have no intention of walking in and seeking admission. One could see only one older man, who stood somewhat aside from the others. He had already brought along his wife and a child in a baby carriage. With one hand his wife held on to the carriage and with the other leaned on her husband's shoulder. Though they marveled at the spectacle, one could see that they were disappointed. They too must have expected that there would be an opportunity for them to find employment, but this trumpet-blowing merely left them confused.

Karl's situation was no different. He approached the man, listened for a moment to the trumpets, and said: "Is this the admissions office for the Theater of Oklahama?" "I thought so too," said the man, "but we've been waiting for an hour and have only heard those trumpets. There's no poster, no announcer, no one who can give us any information." Karl said: "Perhaps they're waiting until some more people come. There are still very few people." "That's possible," said the man, and they fell silent. With the noise from the trumpets it was difficult to hear anything. But just then the wife whispered something to her husband; he nodded, and she called out to Karl at once: "Couldn't you go over to the racetrack and ask where people are admitted?" "Yes," said Karl, "but I'd have to walk across the platform, straight through the angels." "Why would that be so difficult?" the woman asked. She believed that Karl could easily make his way there but was unwilling to send her own husband. "Well, all right," said Karl, "I shall go." "You're most obliging," said the woman, and both she and her husband shook Karl by the hand. The youths ran over to get a closer look at Karl as he climbed onto the platform. It sounded as if the women were blowing their trumpets more loudly to greet the first job applicant. But those whose pedestals Karl passed actually lowered the trumpets from their lips and leaned over to observe his progress. At the other end of the platform Karl saw a man walk up and down quite restlessly, obviously awaiting new arrivals so as to give them all the information they could possibly desire. Karl wanted to approach him but then heard someone above call out his name. "Karl," an angel cried. Karl looked up and began to laugh in delighted surprise; it was Fanny. "Fanny," he cried, greeting her with a wave. "Do come up," cried Fanny, "surely you're not going to walk right past me." And she flung aside her robe, exposing the pedestal and the narrow steps leading to the top. "Is one allowed to go up?" Karl asked. "Who would forbid us to shake hands," cried Fanny, casting an angry glance around to see whether anyone was coming to forbid them from doing

so. Karl was already running up the steps. "Slow down," cried
Fanny, "or the pedestal will fall over, with the two of us." But
nothing of the sort occurred; Karl reached the last step safely.
"See," said Fanny, after they had exchanged greetings, "see
what a great job I have here." "It's certainly beautiful," said
Karl, looking about him. All of the women close by had
already noticed Karl and were giggling. "You're nearly the
tallest," said Karl, stretching out his hand to gauge the height
of the other angels. "I saw you at once," said Fanny, "as you
came out of the station, but unfortunately I'm in the last row,
it's impossible to see me here, and I couldn't call out to you. I
blew especially loudly, but you didn't recognize me." "All of
you play the trumpet so poorly," said Karl. "Give me a chance
to play." "Why, of course," said Fanny, handing him the trumpet, "but don't spoil the chorus, or I'll be dismissed." Karl
began to play; he had imagined it was a crudely made instrument, only for making noise, but it was in fact an instrument
capable of producing almost every refinement. If all the other
instruments were of this quality, they were being greatly mis-
used. Ignoring the noise from the others, Karl inhaled deeply
and played with all his breath a tune he had once heard in a bar
somewhere. He was happy to have met an old friend, to be let
play the trumpet, which at least gave him a chance of obtaining
a good position here. Many of the women stopped playing and
listened to him; when he broke off all of a sudden, scarcely half
of the trumpets were being played, and it took a while for the
noise to build up to its full strength again. "You're an artist,"
said Fanny, as Karl returned her trumpet. "Try to get taken on
as a trumpeter." "They take on men too," asked Karl. "Yes,"
said Fanny, "we play the trumpets for two hours. And then our
places are taken by men dressed as devils. Half blow the trumpet, the others beat on the drums. It's very beautiful, all very
elaborate, as is the whole staging. Aren't our dresses very beau-

tiful too? And what about the wings?" She glanced down at herself. "Well," Karl asked, "do you think even I could get a job here?" "Why, of course," said Fanny. "After all, it's the largest theater in the world. It's so wonderful we'll be together again. But that depends on what kind of job you get. You see, even if both of us are employed here, we might not manage to see each other." "Is the entire outfit really that big?" Karl asked. "It's the largest theater in the world," Fanny repeated. "Though I've never seen it myself, some of my co-workers who've already been to Oklahoma say it's almost limitless." "But there aren't many joining," said Karl, pointing down at the youths and the little family. "That's true," said Fanny. "But remember that we're taking on people in every city, that our recruiting troupe is always out traveling, and that there are many more such troupes." "Has the theater not opened yet?" Karl asked. "Oh yes," said Fanny, "it's an old theater, but it's being expanded all the time." "It is surprising," said Karl, "that there isn't more of a crush." "Yes," said Fanny, "that is very odd." "Well," said Karl, "this extravagant use of angels and devils may frighten off more people than it attracts." "How can you tell," said Fanny. "But that is possible. Do tell our leader, maybe you can help him this way." "Where is he?" Karl asked. "On the racetrack," said Fanny, "up on the judges' stand." "That's also surprising," said Karl, "why do people get admitted on the racetrack?" "Well," said Fanny, "wherever we go, we prepare everything for the largest possible crowds. And of course, there's a great deal of space on the racetrack. And the admissions offices are set up in all of the stands where the bets are usually placed. There must be two hundred different offices." "But," cried Karl, "does the Theater of Oklahoma take in so much money that it can afford to support recruiting troupes like this?" "Why should we have to worry about that," said Fanny, "but do get going, Karl, so you don't miss anything; besides, I have to start playing again. Do your best to get a position with this troupe, and come back at once to let me know. Remember I'll be anxiously waiting to hear from you." She squeezed his hand, warned him to be careful climbing down, and put the trumpet to her lips again, but did not begin to play until she could see that Karl had reached the ground safely. Karl drew her robes back over the steps, just as he had found them; Fanny thanked him with a nod, and then, reflecting from various points of view on what he had just heard, Karl went toward the man, who had already seen Karl up beside Fanny and had walked over to the pedestal to wait for him.

"You want to join us?" the man asked. "I'm the personnel manager for this troupe, and I'd like to welcome you." He leaned forward slightly, as if out of politeness, and minced about, yet without moving from the spot and toying all the while with his watch chain. "Thank you," said Karl, "I've read your company's poster and am getting in touch as requested." "You've done the right thing," the man said appreciatively, "unfortunately, there are some people here who don't always do the right thing." Karl considered telling the man that if the recruiting methods were not particularly successful, it was because of their very splendor. But he did not say so, for this man wasn't the troupe leader, and since he himself still hadn't actually been taken on, he would hardly make a good impression if he started suggesting improvements right away. So he merely said: "There's someone else waiting outside who wants to sign up and has sent me ahead to ask. May I go and get him?" "Of course," said the man, "the more the better." "He's got a woman with him too, and a little child in a carriage. Should they come too?" "Of course," the man said, appearing to smile at the doubt that Karl had expressed. "We can make use of everyone." "I'll be right back," said Karl, and ran to the edge of the platform. He waved to the couple and cried that they could all come. He helped to lift the baby carriage onto the platform and they went on together. Seeing this, the youths conferred with one another, then slowly, hesitating until the last moment, they climbed onto the platform, hands still stuck in their pockets, and only then followed Karl and the family. At that moment new passengers emerged from the subway station who, on seeing the platform with the angels, raised their arms in astonishment. It did seem as if the application process was about to liven up. Karl was very pleased to have arrived so early, maybe even first; the married couple was anxious and asked several times how demanding the work was. Karl said that though he knew nothing for sure, he had really received the impression that every single person would be taken on. They could, he thought, be very confident.

The personnel manager was already approaching; very satisfied to see that so many were coming, he rubbed his hands, greeted each one with a little bow, then made them line up. Karl came first, then the married couple, and finally, the others. Once everyone had lined up—the youths milled about confusedly at first, and it took a while for them to calm down—the personnel manager said, as the trumpets fell silent: "I'm greeting you on behalf of the Theater of Oklahama. You've come early (though it was almost noon) and since there are no crowds here yet, the formalities of your admission can be taken care of right away. You do, of course, have all of your identification papers with you." The youths quickly took some papers from their pockets and waved them at the personnel manager; the husband nudged his wife, who drew a bundle of papers from the feather bed in the baby carriage; Karl, however, had none. Might this hinder his admission? It wasn't inconceivable. From experience, however, Karl knew that one could with a little determination easily get around such regulations. The personnel manager inspected the line, making sure everyone had papers, and since Karl too raised his hand, empty though it was, the manager assumed that he too had his papers in order. "That's fine," the personnel manager said, waving aside the youths who wanted to have their papers examined at once, "your papers will be inspected at the admission offices. As you'll have noticed from our poster, we can make use of everyone. But we have to know the prior occupation of each individual so that he can be assigned to the right position, where he can make use of his expertise." Of course, this is a theater, Karl thought skeptically, and listened very attentively. "We've set up admissions offices in the betting booths," the personnel manager continued, "one office for each occupational category. So each of you should let me know his occupation; as a general rule, families should report to the husband's admission office, and afterward I shall take you to the offices where your papers will be vetted by experts, who will then ascertain what you know—it'll only be a very short exam, there's no need for anyone to be afraid. You'll be admitted at once and will then receive further instructions. So let's get started. As the sign indicates, this first office is meant for engineers. Perhaps there's an engineer among you?" Karl raised his hand. He thought that precisely since he had no papers he should try to complete all the formalities as quickly as possible; besides, he did have a certain justification for raising his hand, for he had in fact once wanted to become an engineer. However, on seeing Karl raise his hand, the youths grew jealous and each raised his hand. The personnel manager rose to his full height and said to the youths: "You are engineers?" Whereupon all lowered their hands slowly; Karl, however, stood by his initial statement. The personnel manager looked at him skeptically, for he considered Karl too miserably dressed and too young to be an engineer, but he said nothing further, perhaps out of gratitude, since Karl had, at least in his opinion, brought in the other applicants. He merely beckoned enticingly toward the office, and Karl went toward it as the personnel manager turned around to the others.

In the office for engineers two gentlemen sat on either side of a rectangular desk, comparing two large ledgers that lay before them. One read aloud as the other marked the names called out by his colleague. When Karl appeared before them and greeted them, they put away the ledgers quickly and picked up some other large books, which they opened. One of them, evidently only a clerk, said: "I should like to see your identity papers." "Unfortunately, I don't have them with me," said Karl. "He doesn't have them with him," the clerk said to the other gentleman, who promptly entered Karl's response in his book. "You're an engineer?" asked the other man, who seemed to be the chief office manager. "Not yet," Karl said quickly, "but—" "That's quite enough," said the gentleman, speaking even more quickly, "then you don't belong here. I would ask that you heed the signs." Karl clenched his teeth; the gentleman must have noticed, for he said: "There's no need to worry. We can make use of everyone." And he waved to a servant who was wandering idly between the barriers: "Take this gentleman to the office for people with technical skills." Interpreting the order literally, the servant took Karl by the hand. They walked between numerous booths, in one of which Karl saw one of the youths, who had already been admitted and now shook hands gratefully with the gentlemen. In the office into which Karl was now taken, the procedure was, as Karl had foreseen, similar to that in the first office. However, on hearing that he had attended middle school, they sent him to the office for former middle school students. But once in that office, when Karl said that he had attended a European middle school, they declared that they were not responsible for such cases and requested that he be taken to the office for former European middle school students. It was a booth at the outermost edge, only smaller and even lower than all of the others. The servant who had taken him there was furious about the lengthy detour and the numerous rejections, which he blamed entirely on Karl. This time he did not even wait for the questioning and ran off at once. This office might indeed be his last refuge. When Karl saw the office manager, he was almost startled by the resemblance between this man and a teacher who was probably still teaching at his vocational school at home. Although, as instantly became clear, the resemblance was limited to a few specific traits, Karl was nonetheless bewildered by the glasses resting on the broad nose, the full blond beard immaculately kempt as if it were a showpiece, the gently stooped back, and the loud voice, which always burst out unexpectedly. Fortunately, he did not even have to be particularly attentive, for the procedure here was simpler than in the other offices. But here too they wrote down that his identification papers were missing, which the office manager called an instance of incomprehensible negligence, and which the clerk, who had the upper hand here, quickly disregarded; just after the manager asked a few short questions and was preparing to ask a more elaborate one, the clerk announced that Karl had been admitted. With his mouth wide open, the manager turned toward the clerk; however, the latter waved his hand conclusively, said, "Admitted," and entered the decision quickly in the ledger. The clerk evidently thought that merely being a European middle school student was something so shameful that anyone making such a claim could be taken at his word. Karl in turn raised no objection and approached the man to thank him. But there was yet another little delay while they requested his name. He did not answer at once; he had qualms about giving his real name and letting them write it down. Once he had obtained even the most minor position here and carried out the work in a satisfactory manner, they could find out about his name, but not now, for he had kept it secret so long that he could not disclose it yet. And so, unable to come up with a name on the spot, he simply gave them the nickname from his last few positions: "Negro." "Negro?" the manager asked, turning his head and grimacing, as if Karl had attained the height of implausibility. The clerk too scrutinized Karl for a moment, but then repeated, "Negro," and wrote down the name. "But you didn't write down Negro," the manager snapped. "Yes, Negro," the clerk said calmly, waving his hand as though the manager should see to the rest. Overcoming his reluctance, the manager rose and said: "So the Theater of Oklahama has—" But he got no further, for unable to quell his scruples, he sat down and said: "His name isn't Negro." The clerk raised his eyebrows, then rose and said: "In that case I'll announce that you've been admitted by the theater in Oklahama and are about to be introduced to our leader." Again a servant was summoned, who led Karl to the judges' stand.

Karl noticed the baby carriage on the steps below; just then the married couple came down, the woman holding the child in her arms. "Have you been admitted," asked the man, who was much more animated now, as was the woman, who looked at him over her shoulder, laughing. When Karl answered that he had just been admitted and was heading toward the presentation, the man said, "Then I'd like to congratulate you. We've been admitted too; it seems a good outfit; of course, one can't get the hang of everything right away, but it's like that everywhere." They said goodbye, and Karl climbed up on the stand. He walked slowly, since the rather small space on top seemed crowded and he did not wish to intrude. He even stopped for a moment and looked out over the large racetrack, which extended on all sides up to the distant woods. All of a sudden he was overcome by a desire to see a horse race; he hadn't yet had a chance to do so here in America. As a small child in Europe he had once been taken to a race, but all he could recall was his mother pulling him along through a crowd that would not step aside. So he had never actually seen a race. Behind him a mechanism began to whir; he turned around and saw the following banner being hoisted on a device employed to announce the winners of the races: "Merchant Kalla with his wife and child." So it was from here that the names of those who'd been taken on were relayed to the offices.

Just then several gentlemen ran down the steps, talking animatedly, pencils and notebooks in hand; Karl squeezed up against the balcony in order to let them pass, and since there was some free space on top now he went up the steps. In a corner of the platform, which was enclosed by wooden railings—the whole thing looked like the flat roof of a narrow tower—sat a gentleman whose arms were stretched along the railings and who wore, slung across his chest, a white silk sash with the words: "Leader of the Theater of Oklahoma's Tenth Recruiting Troupe." On a little table beside him stood a telephone, which certainly was used at the races and now was employed to apprize the leader of all necessary details about the individual applicants even before they were introduced; for at first he did not ask Karl any questions, and merely said to a gentleman who was reclining beside him, legs crossed, hand on his chin: "Negro, a European middle school student." As if he had thereby disposed of Karl, who gave a deep bow, he looked down the steps to see if there was anyone else coming. Since no one came, he listened from time to time to the other gentleman's conversation with Karl, but for the most part he gazed out over the racetrack, tapping his fingers on the railing. Those delicate but strong, powerful, and rapidly moving fingers sometimes drew Karl's attention, even though the other gentleman had already become sufficiently demanding.

"You were unemployed?" the gentleman asked first. Like almost all of the other questions that he asked, this one was very simple, completely straightforward, and he made no attempt to verify Karl's answers through further questioning; yet by opening his eyes wide, leaning forward, and observing the effect of his questions, which he occasionally repeated with his head sunk into his chest, he was able to lend them a special significance that eluded one's understanding but the mere intimation of which was enough to make one cautious and diffident. Frequently Karl felt an urge to withdraw the answer he had just given and to substitute another that might meet with greater approval, but he always held back, for he knew what a bad impression that sort of dithering would inevitably make and, moreover, what an unpredictable effect his answers would have. Besides, it certainly did seem as if the decision to admit him had already been taken; this awareness buoyed him up.

To the question whether he had been unemployed he simply responded, "Yes." "Where were you employed last?" the gentleman insisted. Karl was about to answer when the gentleman raised his index finger and repeated: "Employed last!" Karl had understood the question correctly the first time; brushing off that last remark with an involuntary movement of his head, he answered: "In an office." This was certainly true, but if the gentleman had gone on to ask what kind of office it was, he would have had to lie. But rather than doing so, the gentleman asked a question that could easily be answered truthfully: "Were you satisfied there?" "No," Karl cried, almost cutting him off. Karl noticed through a side glance that the leader was smiling slightly; Karl regretted having answered so heedlessly, but it had simply been too tempting to shout "No," for throughout his last period in service his sole wish had been that some unknown employer would walk in and ask that very question. Besides, that answer could also put him at a disadvantage

since the gentleman could now ask why he hadn't been satisfied. But instead the gentleman merely asked: "For what kind
of job do you think you are suited?" This question could be a
trap, for why did he ask, since Karl had already been taken on
as an actor; he could not bring himself to explain that he did
not feel especially suited to the theatrical profession, though he
realized full well he was not. He therefore evaded the question and, at the risk of appearing defiant, said: "I saw the
poster in the city and signed up because it stated that you could
make use of everybody." "That we already know," the gentleman said, falling silent and thereby underscoring his insistence
on obtaining an answer to his previous question. "I've been
taken on as an actor," said Karl, in a hesitant voice so that
the gentleman might understand the difficult situation the last
question had created for him. "Well," said Karl—and all his
hopes of having found a position began to fade—"I don't
know if I'm suited to acting. But I'll certainly try very hard to
carry out each and every assignment." The gentleman turned
to the manager, and both nodded; Karl appeared to have given
the right answer; summoning his courage again, he straightened up and waited for the next question: "What did you want
to study first?" In an effort to come up with a more precise
formulation—this gentleman was always adamant about for-
mulating everything precisely—he added: "In Europe, I mean."
As he spoke, he removed his hand from his chin and waved it
about feebly as if wishing to signal the remoteness of Europe
and the insignificance of any plans that might have been made
there. Karl said: "I wanted to become an engineer." It wasn't
easy to say so, for he was acutely aware of his track record in
America and realized how ridiculous it was to dredge up that
old memory of having once wanted to become an engineer—
would he have ever really become one, even in Europe?—but
since that was the only answer he could come up with, it was

the one he gave. But the gentleman took this seriously, as seriously as he took everything else. "Well," he said, "you probably can't become an engineer right away, but the most appropriate course for you right now would be to take on some simple work as a technician." "Certainly," said Karl, who was quite satisfied; if he accepted this offer, it would of course mean that he'd be taken out of the actors' group and put in with the technicians, but he believed that being in such a position would really allow him to prove his worth. Besides, he kept repeating to himself, what mattered was not so much the kind of work he did as finding a lasting foothold somewhere. "But are you strong enough for the more strenuous kind of work?" the gentleman asked. "Oh yes," said Karl. Whereupon the gentleman asked Karl to come closer and felt his arm. "He's a strong lad," he said, taking Karl's arm and drawing him toward the leader. Smiling, the leader nodded, held out his hand to Karl, and without standing up, said: "Then we're all set. Everything will be checked again in Oklahama. Bring honor to our recruiting troupe!" Karl bowed in farewell; he wanted to say goodbye to the other gentleman, but as if his work were already completed, the latter was already walking up and down the platform with his head raised. As Karl descended the stairs, a sign was hoisted on the signboard near the steps: "Negro, technician." Since everything was falling into place so easily, Karl would have had few regrets if his real name had appeared on the signboard. Everything had been so carefully arranged, for already awaiting him at the foot of the steps was a servant who fastened a band around his arm. And when Karl lifted his arm to see the words written on the band, he saw that the inscription was completely accurate: "technician."

No matter where they might take him, Karl first wanted to tell Fanny how well everything had gone. But much to his regret, he heard from the servant that the angels, and the devils too, were already heading toward the recruiting troupe's next destination in order to announce the arrival of the troupe for the following day. "That's a pity," said Karl—this was his first disappointment in this outfit—"I knew one of the angels." "You'll get to see her in Oklahoma," the servant said, "but come on, you are the last." He led Karl along the rear of the platform where the angels had stood and now there were only empty pedestals. Karl's assumption that more job-seekers would come once the music from the angels had ceased turned out to be mistaken, for there were no longer any adults lined up before the stand, only a few children fighting over a long white feather, which had probably fallen from an angel's wing. A boy held it up in the air while the other children tried to pull down his head with one hand while stretching out the other so as to seize the feather.

Karl pointed to the children, but the servant, who did not even glance at them, said: "Hurry up; it took them quite a while to decide to admit you. They must have had some doubts?" "I don't know," said Karl, taken aback; but he did not believe it was true. Even in the most clear-cut of situations, there is always someone who insists on causing grief for his fellow man. But at the pleasant sight of the large spectators' stand that they had just reached, Karl soon forgot the servant's remark. On this stand there was even a very long bench covered with a white cloth; all those who had been admitted sat on the next bench, with their backs to the racetrack, and were now being served a meal. Everyone was cheerful and excited, and just as Karl, the last to arrive, sat down on the bench without being noticed, a number of them stood up and raised their glasses, while one gave a little speech toasting the leader of the Tenth Recruiting Troupe, whom he called "the father of all job-seekers." Somebody pointed out that one could actually see the leader from where they sat, and the judges' stand with its two platforms was indeed not that far off. All now raised their glasses in that direction; Karl too took the glass in front of him, but however loudly they shouted and however much they tried to draw attention to themselves, there was no sign that anyone on the judges' platform had noticed their round of applause or might soon do so. The leader was still leaning against the corner, and beside him stood the other gentleman, stroking his chin.

A little disappointed, everyone sat down again; now and then one of them would turn around to glance at the judges' platform, but before long everyone was completely absorbed by the lavish meal; large fowl such as Karl had never seen before, with numerous forks stuck into the crisply roasted meat, were carried around; the servants kept on pouring wine—hunched over one's place, one scarcely noticed the stream of red wine dropping into one's glass—and anyone who did not wish to take part in the general conversation could look at the pictures of the Theater of Oklahoma, which were stacked at one end of the table and were supposed to be passed around. But the others showed little interest in the pictures, and consequently only a single picture reached Karl, who was last. If this one was any indication, all of the others must have been worth seeing too. It showed the box reserved for the President of the United States. At first glance one might easily have believed that it was not simply a box but the actual stage, so forcefully did the balustrade sweep out into open space. The entire balustrade was gilded. Hanging side by side between its small pillars, which looked as though they had been cut out with the finest scissors, were medallions of former presidents, one of whom had a remarkably straight nose, thick curved lips, and eyes that looked straight down from beneath his arched brows. Rays of light streamed around the box, from all sides and also from above; the section of the box in the foreground was bathed in a

white yet soft light, whereas its deeper recesses, behind red vel-
vet draped in folds of varying shades all along the perimeter of
the box and held in check by cords, seemed like a dark red-
shimmering void. So grandiose did everything look that one
could scarcely imagine people in this box. Though Karl did not
neglect his food, he gazed often at the reproduction, which he
had placed beside his plate.

Moreover, he certainly would have dearly liked to see at
least one of the other pictures, but he did not wish to fetch it
himself since a servant had placed his hand on the pictures—
which no doubt had to be kept in order—and therefore merely
sought to look out over the table to ascertain whether another
picture might not be heading his way. Whereupon to his astonishment he noticed that among the faces bent lowest over the
food—at first he could not believe it—was a familiar one: Giacomo. He ran up to him at once. "Giacomo," he cried. Shy as
always whenever anything took him by surprise, Giacomo first
rose from his meal, turned around in the narrow space between
the benches, wiped his mouth with his hand, and only then
revealed how pleased he was to see Karl; he said Karl should
sit down beside him, or he would come over to Karl's seat,
and then they would tell each other everything and always
stay together. Karl did not want to disturb the others and said
that they should keep their own seats for now; the meal would
be over soon and then they would, of course, stick together
always. Nevertheless Karl remained beside Giacomo, simply
to gaze at him. What memories of bygone days! Where was
the head cook? What was Therese doing? As for Giacomo, he
looked virtually unchanged; the head cook's prediction that he
would have become a big-boned American within six months
had not come to pass; he was still delicate as ever, his cheeks
were still just as sunken, except that now they were bulging, for
he had placed an excessively large piece of meat in his mouth

and was slowly sucking out the superfluous bones and throwing them onto his plate. As Karl saw from Giacomo's armband, he had been admitted not as an actor but as an elevator boy; the Theater of Oklahoma did seem able to find a use for everyone.

Lost in contemplation of Giacomo, Karl remained away from his seat too long, and just as he was about to go back, the personnel manager came, climbed onto one of the higher benches, clapped his hands, and gave a brief speech; most people rose, prompting those who were still seated and could not tear themselves away from their food to do likewise. "Well," he said—Karl had already tiptoed quickly back to his seat— "I do hope you were satisfied with our welcome dinner. People generally do praise the food served by our recruiting troupe. Unfortunately I must break up this gathering, though, since the train meant to take you to Oklahoma will be leaving in five minutes. It's a long trip, but as you'll see, you'll be well taken care of. And now I should like to introduce you to the gentleman who will be in charge of your transportation and whose orders you should follow." A small, thin gentleman climbed onto the bench beside the personnel manager, barely took the time to give a hasty bow, and stretching out his trembling hands, quickly began to show everyone how to assemble, get into line and start moving. But they did not comply right away, since the person in their group who had earlier on given the speech slammed his hand on the table and began to deliver a rather lengthy thank-you speech despite the recent announcement that the train was about to leave—and Karl became very uneasy. Completely ignoring the fact that he no longer had the ear of the personnel manager, who was giving various instructions to the transportation manager, the speaker embarked on a lengthy speech listing all of the courses that had been served, pronouncing judgment on each, and concluding with the cry: "Honorable gentlemen, this is certainly the way to win us over." Everyone—except those he was addressing—laughed, although there was more truth than jest in what he said.

The price they paid for this speech was that they now had to run to reach the station. Still, this wasn't terribly difficult, for as Karl only now noticed, no one was carrying any luggage and indeed the only piece of luggage was the baby carriage that the father pushed along at the head of the troupe and that bounced up and down as if careening along of its own accord. What suspect types, without possessions, had found their way here, and yet they were being so well received and cared for! And they must have made quite an impression on the transportation manager. For he seized the handlebars of the baby carriage with one hand, raising the other up in the air so as to persuade the group to move forward; now he appeared behind the last line, driving them on; now he ran along the sides, keeping an eye on some of the slower ones in the middle, and tried to show them how to run by swinging his arms.

When they arrived at the station, the train was ready. The people at the station pointed out the troupe to one another; one could hear cries such as, "They all belong to the Theater of Oklahama"; the theater seemed to be much better known than Karl had assumed, but then he had never taken much interest in the theater business. An entire carriage had been set aside for their troupe, and the transportation manager outdid the conductor in pressing everyone to get on. First he looked into every compartment, straightened out something here and there, and only then climbed on himself. By chance Karl obtained a window seat and drew Giacomo over beside him. They sat pressed together; each looked forward to the journey; never before had they been so carefree on a journey in America. When the train began to move, they waved out the window, and the fellows opposite, finding their behavior ridiculous, gave one another nudges.

They traveled for two days and two nights. Only then did Karl come to understand the vastness of America. Tirelessly he gazed out the window, and Giacomo kept edging over until the fellows opposite, who often occupied themselves with card games, grew weary and voluntarily gave up their window seat. Karl thanked them—it wasn't always easy to make sense of Giacomo's English—and as inevitably happens among compartment mates, they became much friendlier, yet their friendliness too was a nuisance, for whenever a card, say, fell down on the floor and they went looking for it, they would pinch Karl's or Giacomo's leg as hard as they could. Giacomo, always surprised anew, would cry out and lift his leg in the air; at times Karl tried to respond with a kick, but for the most part he bore everything in silence. Everything taking place in that little compartment, which filled up with smoke even when the windows were open, paled in comparison with the sights unfolding outside.

On the first day they passed through a tall mountain range. The sharp angles of the bluish-black masses of rock went right up to the train; they leaned out the window and searched in vain for the peaks; dark narrow jagged valleys opened up, and with their fingers they traced the direction in which the valleys disappeared; broad mountain rivers swept forward in great waves over the craggy base, pushing along thousands of small foamy waves, plunging under the bridges over which the train passed, and coming so close that the breath of their chill made one's face quiver.

ACKNOWLEDGMENTS

I should like to thank: a cohort of students at Elizabethtown College, who patiently transcribed my scrawled corrections, especially Jamie Hudzick, Valerie Reed, Greg Rohde, and Stephen Marks; Adrian Daub, at the University of Pennsylvania, who offered useful suggestions about the translation; and the following centers, which provided congenial settings for translating—and reflecting on—*The Missing Person:* the Mac-Dowell Colony in Peterborough, New Hampshire; the Ledig House International Writers Residency at Omi, in the Hudson Valley; the Djerassi Resident Artists Program, Woodside, California; the European Translators Colloquium in Straelen, Germany; and the Tyrone Guthrie Center in Annaghmakerrig, Ireland. I should also like to thank the Office of the Federal Chancellor of Austria for financial support, Elizabethtown College for a sabbatical leave, and last but not least, my wife, Nina Menke, and daughters, Eva and Ciara, for bearing with me at times when I must have seemed like a missing person.

CHRONOLOGY

1883   3 July: Franz Kafka is born in Prague, son of Hermann Kafka and Julie, née Löwy.

1889   Enters a German primary school. Birth of his sister Elli Kafka, his first surviving sibling.

1892   Birth of his sister Ottla Kafka.

1893   Enters the Old City German Secondary School in Prague.

1896   13 June: Bar mitzvah, described in family invitation as "Confirmation."

1897   Anti-Semitic riots in Prague; Hermann Kafka's dry goods store is spared.

1899–1903   Early writings (destroyed).

1901   Graduates from secondary school. Enters German University in Prague. Studies chemistry for two weeks, then law.

1902   Spring: Attends lectures on German literature and the humanities. Travels to Munich, planning to continue German studies there. Returns to Prague. October: First meeting with Max Brod.

1904   Begins writing "Description of a Struggle."

1905   Vacation in Zuckmantel, Silesia. First love affair.

1906   Clerk in uncle's law office. June: Doctor of Law degree.

1906–07   Legal practice in the *Landesgericht* (provincial high court) and *Strafgericht* (criminal court).

1907–08   Temporary position in the Prague branch of the private insurance company Assicurazioni Generali.

1908   March: Kafka's first publication: eight prose pieces appear in the review *Hyperion*. 30 July: Enters the semi-state-owned Workers Accident Insurance Company for the Kingdom of Bohemia in Prague; works initially in the statistical and claims departments. Spends time in coffeehouses and cabarets.

1909   Begins keeping diaries. April: Kafka's department head lauds his "exceptional faculty for conceptualization." September: Travels with Max and Otto Brod to northern Italy, where they see airplanes for the first time. Writes article "The Aeroplanes in Brescia," which subsequently appears in the daily paper *Bohemia*. Frequent trips to inspect factory conditions in the provinces.

1910   May: Promoted to *Concipist* (junior legal adviser); sees Yiddish acting troupe. October: Vacations in Paris with Brod brothers.

1911   Travels with Max Brod to northern Italy and Paris; spends a week in a Swiss natural-health sanatorium. Becomes a silent partner in the asbestos factory owned by his brother-in-law. 4 October: Sees Yiddish play *Der Meshumed* (The Apostate) at Café Savoy. Friendship with the Yiddish actor Yitzhak Löwy. Pursues interest in Judaism.

1912   18 February: Gives "little introductory lecture" on Yiddish language. August: Assembles his first book, *Meditation;* meets Felice Bauer. Writes the stories "The Judgment" and "The Transformation" (frequently entitled "The Metamorphosis" in English). Begins the novel *The Missing Person* (first published in 1927 as *Amerika,* the title chosen by Brod). October: Distressed over having to take charge of the family's asbestos factory, considers suicide. December: Gives first public reading ("The Judgment").

1913   Extensive correspondence with Felice Bauer, whom he visits three times in Berlin. Promoted to company vice secretary. "The Stoker" published by Kurt Wolff. Takes up gardening. In Vienna attends international conference on accident prevention and observes Eleventh Zionist Congress; travels by way of Trieste, Venice, and Verona to Riva.

1914   June: Official engagement to Felice Bauer. July: Engagement is broken. Travels through Lübeck to the Danish resort of Marielyst. Diary entry, 2 August: "Germany has declared war on Russia—swimming club in the afternoon." Works on *The Trial;* writes "In the Penal Colony" and the Theater of Oklahoma chapter in *The Missing Person.*

1915 January: First meeting with Felice Bauer after breaking engagement. March: At the age of thirty-one moves for the first time into own quarters. September: In diary entry compares fate of Karl Rossmann with that of Josef K. November: "The Transformation" ("The Metamorphosis") appears; Kafka asks a friend: "What do you say about the terrible things that are happening in our house?"

1916 July: Ten days with Felice Bauer at Marienbad. November: In a small house on Alchemists' Lane in the Castle district of Prague, begins to write the stories later collected in *A Country Doctor.*

1917 Second engagement to Felice Bauer. September: Diagnosis of tuberculosis. Moves back into his parents' apartment. Goes to stay with his favorite sister, Ottla, on a farm in the northern Bohemian town of Zürau. December: Second engagement to Felice Bauer is broken.

1918 In Zürau writes numerous aphorisms about "the last things." Reads Kierkegaard. May: Resumes work at insurance institute.

1919 Summer: To the chagrin of his father, announces engagement to Julie Wohryzek, daughter of a synagogue custodian. Takes Hebrew lessons from Friedrich Thieberger. November: Wedding to Julie Wohryzek is postponed. Writes "Letter to His Father."

1920 Promotion to institute secretary. April: Convalescence vacation in Merano, Italy; beginning of correspondence with Milena Jesenská. Comments on Milena's Czech translation of "The Stoker." May: Publication of *A Country Doctor,* with a dedication to Hermann Kafka. July: Engagement to Julie Wohryzek is broken. November: Anti-Semitic riots in Prague; Kafka writes to Milena: "Isn't the obvious course to leave a place where one is so hated?"

1921 Stays at sanatorium at Matliary in the Tatra Mountains (Slovakia). August: Returns to Prague. Hands all his diaries to Milena Jesenská.

1922 Diary entry, 16 January: Writes about nervous breakdown. 27 January: Travels to Spindlermühle, a resort on the Polish border, where he begins to write *The Castle*. 15 March: Reads beginning section of novel to Max Brod. November: After another breakdown, informs Brod that he can no longer "pick up the thread."

1923   Resumes Hebrew studies. Sees Hugo Bergmann, who invites him to Palestine. July: Meets nineteen-year-old Dora Diamant in Müritz on the Baltic Sea. They dream of opening a restaurant in Tel Aviv, with Dora as cook and Franz as waiter. September: Moves to inflation-ridden Berlin to live with Dora. Writes "The Burrow."

1924   Health deteriorates. March: Brod takes Kafka back to Prague. Kafka writes "Josephine the Singer." 19 April: Accompanied by Dora Diamant, enters Dr. Hoffman's sanatorium at Kierling, near Vienna. Corrects the galleys for the collection of stories *A Hunger Artist*. 3 June: Kafka dies at age forty. 11 June: Burial in the Jewish Cemetery in Prague-Strašnice.

BIBLIOGRAPHY

PRIMARY

While all of Kafka's works are interrelated, the following titles have a direct bearing on *The Missing Person*.

Kafka, Franz. *The Complete Stories.* Ed. Nahum N. Glatzer. New York, 1983.
———.*The Diaries, 1910–1923.* Ed. Max Brod. New York, 1988.
———. *Letters to Felice.* New York, 1973.
———. *Letter to His Father.* Bilingual edition. New York, 1966.

SECONDARY

BIOGRAPHICAL

Begley, Louis. *The Tremendous World I Have Inside My Head: Franz Kafka: A Biographical Essay.* New York, 2008.
Brod, Max. *Franz Kafka: A Biography.* Trans. G. Humphreys Roberts and Richard Winston. New York, 1960.
Citati, Pietro. *Kafka.* Trans. Raymond Rosenthal. New York, 1990.
Harman, Mark. "Biography and Autobiography: Necessary Antagonists?" *Journal of the Kafka Society* 10 (1986): 56–62.
———. "Missing Persons: Two Little Riddles about Kafka and Berlin." In *New England Review* 25 (2004): 225–32.
Murray, Nicholas. *Kafka: A Biography.* New Haven, 2004.
Pawel, Ernst. *The Nightmare of Reason: A Life of Franz Kafka.* New York, 1985.

Stach, Reiner. *Kafka: The Decisive Years*. Trans. Shelley Frisch. New York, 2005.

Wagenbach, Klaus. *Franz Kafka: Pictures of a Life*. Trans. Arthur S. Wensinger. New York, 1984.

———. *Kafka*. Boston, 2003.

THE MISSING PERSON

Alter, Robert. "Franz Kafka: Wrenching Scripture." *New England Review* 21, no. 3 (2000): 7–19.

Anderson, Mark. "Kafka in America: Notes on a Travelling Narrative." In *Kafka's Clothes: Ornament and Aestheticism in the Habsburg "Fin de Siècle,"* pp. 98–122. Oxford, U.K., 1992.

Bamforth, Iain. "Self-Made Man: Kafka and America." *PN Review* 30, no. 3 (2004): 43–47.

Bergel, Lienhard. "Amerika: Its Meaning." In *Franz Kafka Today,* ed. Angel Flores and Homer Swander, pp. 117–125. Madison, Wisconsin, 1958.

Boa, Elizabeth. "Karl Rossmann, or the Boy who Wouldn't Grow Up." In *From Goethe to Gide,* ed. Mary Orr, pp. 168–83. Exeter, U.K., 2005.

Doctorow, E. L. "Franz Kafka's *Amerika*." In *Creationists: Selected Essays, 1993–2006,* pp. 129–41. New York, 2006.

Duttlinger, Carolin. "Visions of the New World: Photography in Kafka's *Der Verschollene*." *German Life and Letters* 59, no. 3 (2006): 423–45.

Emrich, Wilhelm. "The Modern Industrial World: The Novel *The Man Who Was Lost Sight Of*." In *Franz Kafka,* trans. S. Z. Buehne, pp. 276–315. New York, 1968.

Fuchs, Anne. "A Psychoanalytic Reading of *The Man Who Disappeared*." In *The Cambridge Companion to Kafka,* ed. Julian Preece, pp. 25–41. Cambridge, U.K., 2002.

Harman, Mark. "Kafka Imagining America: A Preface." *New England Review* 29, no. 1 (2008): 10–22.

Hermsdorf, Klaus. "Kafka's *America*." In *Franz Kafka: An Anthology of Marxist Criticism,* ed. and trans. Kenneth Hughes, pp. 22–37. Hanover, N.H., 1981.

Northey, Anthony. "The Discovery of the New World: Kafka's Cousins and *Amerika*." In *Kafka's Relatives: Their Lives and His Writing,* pp. 51–68. New Haven, Conn., 1991.

Payne, Kenneth. "Franz Kafka's *America*." *Symposium* 51, no. 1 (1997): 30–42.

Politzer, Heinz. "*Der Verschollene*: The Innocence of Karl Rossmann." In *Franz Kafka: Parable and Paradox*, pp. 116–62. Ithaca, N.Y., 1966.

Ruland, Richard E. "A View from Back Home: Kafka's *Amerika*." *American Quarterly* 13 (1961): 33–42.

Spilka, Mark. *Kafka and Dickens: A Mutual Interpretation*. London, 1963.

Shaked, Gershon. "The Sisyphean Syndrome: On the Structure of Kafka's *Amerika*." In *The Dove and the Mole: Kafka's Journey into Darkness and Creativity*, ed. Moshe Lazar and Ronald Gottesman, pp. 135–49. Malibu, Calif., 1987.

Steiner, Carl. "How American Is *Amerika?*" *Journal of Modern Literature* 6, no. 3 (1977): 455–65.

Tambling, Jeremy. "The States and the Statue: Kafka on America." In *Lost in the American City: Dickens, James and Kafka*, pp. 181–229. Basingstoke, U.K., 2001.

Tedlock, E. W., Jr. "Kafka's Imitation of *David Copperfield*." *Comparative Literature* 7, no. 1 (1955): 52–62.

Zilcosky, John. "The 'America' Novel: Learning How to Get Lost." In *Kafka's Travels: Exoticism, Colonialism, and the Traffic of Writing*, pp. 41–70. New York, 2003.

GENERAL

Adorno, Theodor. "Franz Kafka." In *Prisms*, trans. Samuel and Shierry Weber, pp. 243–71. Boston, 1997.

Alter, Robert. *Necessary Angels: Kafka, Benjamin, Scholem*. Cambridge, Mass., 1990.

Anderson, Mark, ed. *Reading Kafka: Prague, Politics, and the Fin de Siècle*. New York, 1989.

Arendt, Hannah. "Franz Kafka: A Reevaluation." In *Essays in Understanding, 1930–1945*, ed. Jerome Kohn, pp. 69–80. New York, 1994.

Beck, Evelyn Torton. *Kafka and the Yiddish Theater: Its Impact on His Work*. Madison, Wis., 1971.

Benjamin, Walter. "Franz Kafka on the Tenth Anniversary of his Death." In *Illuminations*, ed. Hannah Arendt, trans. Harry Zohn, pp. 111–45. New York, 1969.

Borges, Jorge Luis. "Franz Kafka: The Vulture." In *Selected Non-Fictions,* ed. Eliot Weinberger, pp. 501–3. New York, 1999.

———. "Kafka and His Precursors." In *Selected Non-Ficitons,* ed. Eliot Weinberger, pp. 363–65. New York, 1999.

Bruce, Iris. *Kafka and Cultural Zionism.* Madison, Wis., 2007.

Corngold, Stanley. *Franz Kafka: The Necessity of Form.* Ithaca, N.Y., 1988.

Calasso, Roberto. *K.* Trans. Geoffrey Brock. New York, 2005.

Gilman, Sander. *Franz Kafka: The Jewish Patient.* New York, 1995.

Harman, Mark. "Making everything a 'little uncanny': Kafka's deletions in the manuscript of *Das Schloss.*" In *Companion to the Works of Franz Kafka,* ed. James Rolleston, pp. 325–46. Rochester, N.Y., 2002.

———. "Life into Art: Kafka's Self-Stylization in the Diaries." In *Franz Kafka (1883–1983): His Craft and Thought,* ed. Roman Struc and J. C. Yardley, pp. 101–116. Waterloo, Ontario, 1986.

Robert, Marthe. *As Lonely as Franz Kafka.* Trans. Ralph Manheim. New York, 1982.

Robertson, Ritchie. *Kafka: Judaism, Politics and Literature.* Oxford, 1985.

Rolleston, James. *Kafka's Narrative Theater.* University Park, Pa., 1974.

Sokel, Walter H. *The Myth of Power and the Self: Essays on Franz Kafka.* Detroit, Mich., 2002.

Spector, Scott. *Prague Territories: National Conflict and Cultural Innovation in Franz Kafka's Fin de Siècle.* Berkeley, Ca., 2000.

Weinberg, Helen. *The New Novel in America: The Kafkan Mode in Contemporary Fiction.* Ithaca, N.Y., 1970.

Zischler, Hanns. *Kafka Goes to the Movies.* trans. Susan H. Gillespie. Chicago, 2002.

TRANSLATING KAFKA

Coetzee, J. M. "Translating Kafka." In *Stranger Shores: Literary Essays: 1986–1999,* pp. 74–87. New York and London, 2001.

Corngold, Stanley. "On Translation Mistakes, with Special Attention to Kafka in *Amerika.*" In *Lambent Traces: Franz Kafka,* pp. 176–93. Princeton, N.J., 2004.

Crick, Joyce. "Kafka and the Muirs." In *The World of Franz Kafka,* ed. J. P. Stern, pp. 159–75. New York, 1980.

Damrosch, David. "Kafka Comes Home." In *What Is World Literature?*, pp. 187–205. Princeton, N.J., 2003.

Durrani, Osman. "Editions, Translations, Adaptations." In *Cambridge Companion to Kafka*, ed. Julian Preece, pp. 206–25. Cambridge, U.K., 2002.

Gray, Ronald. "But Kafka wrote in German." In *The Kafka Debate*, ed. Angel Flores, pp. 242–52. New York, 1977.

Harman, Mark. " 'Digging the Pit of Babel': Retranslating Franz Kafka's *Castle*." *New Literary History* 27, no. 2 (1996): 291–311.

Kundera, Milan. "A Sentence." In *Testaments Betrayed: An Essay in Nine Parts*. Trans. Linda Asher. New York, 1995, pp. 97–118.

VISUAL ARTS AND ILLUSTRATION

Kippenberger, Martin. "The Happy Ending of Franz Kafka's *Amerika*." Installation. Hamburg, Germany, 1999.

Mairowitz, David Zane, and Robert Crumb. *Introducing Kafka*. Cambridge, Mass., 1993.

FILM

Class Relations. Film based on *The Missing Person*. Directed by Danièlle Huillet and Jean-Marie Straub. France/Germany, 1984.

Intervista. Directed by Federico Fellini. Italy, 1987.

THEATER

Amerika, or The Disappearance. Adapted and directed by Gideon Lester. Boston, 2005.

Amerika. Adapted by Ip Wischin and directed by Tino Geirun. Vienna, Austria, and Washington, D.C., 2004.

Amerika. Adapted and directed by Osamu Matsumoto. Tokyo, 2001.

A NOTE ON THE TYPE

The text of this book was set in Sabon, a typeface designed by Jan Tschichold (1902–1974), the well-known German typographer. Designed in 1966 and based on the original designs by Claude Garamond (ca. 1480–1561), Sabon was named for the punch cutter Jacques Sabon, who brought Garamond's matrices to Frankfurt.

Composed by Creative Graphics
Allentown, Pennsylvania

Printed and bound by R. R. Donnelley,
Harrisonburg, Virginia

Designed by Kristen Bearse